PERFECT DARK
INITIAL VECTOR

TOR BOOKS BY GREG RUCKA

Perfect Dark: Initial Vector
Perfect Dark: Second Front

PERFECT DARK
INITIAL VECTOR

GREG RUCKA

TOR®
A TOM DOHERTY ASSOCIATES BOOK
NEW YORK

PERFECT DARK: INITIAL VECTOR

www.perfectdarkzero.com

A Tor Book
Published by Tom Doherty Associates, LLC
175 Fifth Avenue
New York, NY 10010

www.tor.com

ISBN 0-765-35473-X
EAN 978-0-765-35473-0

First edition: October 2005
First mass market edition: June 2006

Printed in the United States of America

0 9 8 7 6 5 4 3 2 1

This book is dedicated to
the shareholders.

ACKNOWLEDGMENTS

The effort, time, and goodwill of several people went into making this novel possible. Of the many, here are a handful deserving of special mention.

Eric Trautmann, who had the big idea in the first place and who persevered to see it come to pass.

Eric Raab, at Tor, for having the stomach for the big idea and the nerves to stay at the wheel.

David Hale Smith, who thought it wasn't such a big idea in the first place, but that it might be worth doing anyway, and what would it hurt? If he had only known.

At Microsoft, most especially Nancy Figatner of the Franchise Development Group for helping to bring it all together; thanks also to Edward Ventura, Sandy Ting, and Steve Schreck; Peter Moore; Shane Kim; Ken Lobb; Jim Veevaert; John Dongelmans; Justin Kirk and, singled out for conspicuous gallantry, Chris Kimmell.

In Olympia, thanks to Gabi, and if she doesn't know why, nobody should tell her until she figures it out.

In Portland, Jennifer, Dashiell, and Elliot.

And finally, at Rare, who gave us not only Jo, but her world, special thanks to the following: Duncan Botwood, Dale Murchie, Richard Cousins, Lee Schuneman, Tim Stamper, and Chris Stamper.

PROLOGUE

Stony Mountain
Medium Security Institution—
Manitoba, Canada
February 8th, 2016

The outbreak started three days into the new year. A family of four was admitted to the Royal Victoria Hospital in Montreal, all diagnosed as suffering from acute bouts of influenza. The only thing remarkable about this was that the bug had hit the whole family at once with equal severity, from the adults down to the youngest child, a little girl named Penelope, age three.

Even that fact failed to raise any substantial interest, and truly, it shouldn't have. To all appearances, this was nothing more sinister than the latest iteration of the venerable influenza A virus. Here it was, the dead of winter, the heart of flu season, and the Center for Disease Control and Prevention down south in the United States had already issued a warning for the prevalent 2015-16 strain, identified as influenza A subtype H7N10.

Another year, another shift in the virus, but nothing to raise alarms about.

The fourth of January saw another eleven cases admitted, bringing the total to fifteen.

The fifth saw the number quadruple, to sixty, and with it came the first round of fatalities. All four of the patients admitted on the third had died, as had five of the eleven admitted on the fourth.

On the morning of the sixth, the Canadian government broadcast an emergency health warning about the growing epidemic. Later studies revealed that their warnings went largely unheeded; the public preferred to get their news from more trusted corporate sources.

By noon, the number of diagnosed cases in Montreal alone had mushroomed to seven hundred and seventeen. By midnight, the death toll had reached one hundred and fifty-two. These were official numbers, and certainly wildly inaccurate, as no attempt had yet been made to tally the undocumented cases. Hospitals as far as Vancouver to the west and Halifax to the east began reporting bed shortages. Emergency relief personnel were activated, and the Canadian Red Cross opened triage centers in almost all of Canada's major urban zones. Rumors of a declaration of martial law began to circulate.

At which point, nobody who was paying any sort of attention at all thought they were dealing with influenza A subtype H7N10 any longer.

This was something different, something much more virulent, and something far more resistant to treatment.

On the seventh of January, 2016, the virus exploded, with over twenty-three thousand, four hundred and forty-two cases of what the media was now calling "the Canadian superflu" diagnosed all across the country. Scientists at the CDC and elsewhere were calling it influenza A subtype H17N22, but that was at best unbridled optimism, because the government scientists who examined the virus didn't have the first idea what they were looking at.

Everyone else had taken to calling it "The Flu."

The death toll broke one thousand, and was picking up speed.

International travel to and from Canada was cancelled as the country went into massive quarantine. Rioting broke out in Edmonton, Calgary, Winnipeg, and St. John's as false rumors of a vaccine spread in each respective community. The RCMP and Canadian Army were turned out onto the streets to keep order. The United States closed all northern crossings, and issued orders that border patrol agents were to shoot to kill anyone attempting to enter the country.

Beck-Yama InterNational, dataDyne, and Core-Mantis OmniGlobal all took the unprecedented step of closing their Canadian offices, ordering their employees to remain at home—or more precisely, ordering them to stay away from their offices—unless they could provide notarized proof that they were virus-free. Global markets responded immediately to the action of the three largest hypercorporations, promptly plummeting an average of twenty-three percentage points. Trading was closed on the New York, Tokyo, Sydney, and London exchanges.

Pundits were now comparing the Canadian outbreak to the Spanish flu epidemic of 1918–19, which had left twenty-five million dead before it had run its course. In Las Vegas and Atlantic City, bookies were giving three-to-one odds that the death toll would break fifty million before the virus burnt itself out.

By the tenth of January, 2016, Canada had come to a spasmodic, wheezing, and fever-wracked halt.

The world waited, afraid to breathe.

It was a matter of priorities, and prisons didn't rate, not in a crisis.

Hospitals had to be staffed, emergency medical teams

dispatched, and like all things in the age of the so-called "hypercorporations," the best care went to those with the most money. First it went to the executives at data-Dyne and Core-Mantis OmniGlobal and Beck-Yama InterNational and the like. Next, to their resources, namely, their employees. From there it moved to essential services, government offices, police, fire, military, and medical.

Then, and only then, did it trickle down to the general public.

For those people in societal limbo, the homeless, institutionalized, or imprisoned, there was nothing left.

And this was why, when Laurent Hayes was discovered at Stony Mountain Medium Security Institution, it wasn't just a miracle that he was alive.

It was a gift from God.

He was found locked in his cell in solitary confinement, secured behind his door, just as every other inmate had been discovered. He was dressed in a powder-blue prison jumpsuit, the same as every other inmate had worn. And like every other inmate, the hair at the back of his head had been seared off, to allow for easy reading of the barcode tattooed there.

It was only when the disposal team member, dressed in his hazmat gear and sucking wet and stale oxygen through his rebreather, reached down to scan the barcode on the back of Laurent Hayes's neck that it was discovered he wasn't like every other inmate. It had nothing to do with the actual inmate data that filled the palm-sized reader, not the fact that his name was Laurent N. Hayes, or that he was only sixteen years old, or that he was serving life for a string of three murders he'd committed at the age of fourteen.

It was that when the reader touched the base of Laurent Hayes's skull, Laurent Hayes *spoke.*

"Piss off," Laurent Hayes croaked.

He was rushed to St. Boniface Hospital in Winnipeg, where he was initially treated for starvation and dehydration. Blood was drawn, tested, and then, three hours later, drawn and tested a second time. Four separate teams of physicians examined him over the next eighteen hours, culminating, finally, in a visit from a team of specialists, some from as far away as Geneva.

It was at this point, being poked and prodded by yet another set of unfamiliar and unwelcome hands, that Laurent Hayes began to wonder what all the fuss was about. So he reached out and grabbed the nearest invading hand by the wrist, discovering that it was attached to a middle-aged woman intent on giving his lungs yet another listen.

"They just didn't feed me, all right?" Hayes said. His voice, when he spoke, came out softly, his throat still raw from dehydration. "Screws stopped feeding me, the whole damn place went quiet."

"Screws?"

"Guards, the guards."

She nodded slowly, then tried to free her hand from his grip. Laurent held her wrist a fraction longer, to make his point, before releasing it.

"The guards stopped coming to work when the inmates began getting sick," she told him. "That was almost two weeks ago."

"Sick?"

"When did you go into solitary?"

He couldn't remember. It was one of the things he hated about prison, the loss of time. He shrugged.

"We thought that might be why, you understand," she said. "You'd been in solitary and hadn't been exposed."

"What the hell are you talking about?" Hayes asked.

"Canada is in the grip of a massive influenza pandemic, Mister Hayes. Millions have died."

He stared at her, blankly, trying to imagine something that could kill millions and get away with it.

"We thought you had avoided exposure," she continued. "That locked in solitary, you had avoided contracting the superflu. But the blood tests keep coming back the same, and that's why we're here, Mister Hayes."

"I've got it, I've got this bug?"

"Yes and no, Mister Hayes. Viruses don't die off in the bloodstream. They either continue to replicate and take over, or they're rendered ineffective. So, technically, yes, you have the superflu."

Hayes swore, thinking that it was just another example of how the universe hated him, how every good thing he ever managed to get, it would take away. Here he was, out of prison, and this white coat was smiling down at him while she delivered his death sentence.

He was swearing so much, in fact, that he entirely missed the rest of what she was telling him.

"What?" Laurent Hayes demanded.

"I said, you appear to be immune," the woman repeated, and she gave him a big smile. "You're one of a kind, Mister Hayes. In your blood, right now, is a cure that can save millions, perhaps hundreds of millions of people."

He stared at her, suspicious. "My blood?"

"Yes, Mister Hayes."

He considered that, thinking that for once, perhaps, the universe was finally doing right by him. His blood could save millions, maybe hundreds of millions.

"All right," Laurent Hayes said, after a moment. "How much are you going to pay me for it?"

As it turned out, they wanted his blood for free, and when he objected, they put him in restraints and posted a guard on his room. He shouted and cursed until he'd used what little of his voice had returned, and then began thrashing against his restraints until two orderlies and the smiling woman had to return to sedate him.

The world was just beginning to slip away from him when the screaming started somewhere down the hall.

He heard gunshots.

Then he heard nothing.

dataDyne
Your life, our hands

For Immediate Release to approved news outlets:

dataDyne Subsidiary CEO Awarded Nobel Prize

Los Angeles, California—10 December 2016

dataDyne is pleased to congratulate Dr. Friedrich Murray, Director of Research and New Product Development for pharmaDyne Corporation, for receiving the Nobel Prize in Physiology or Medicine from the Nobel Assembly at Karolinska Institutet. Dr. Murray, who will shortly move to the CEO position of pharmaDyne, was instrumental for his discovery of a vaccine for influenza A subtype H22N17.

The influenza A subtype H22N17 outbreak earlier this year visited a medical horror on the people of Canada the likes of which has never before been seen in the history of mankind. Over the course of three months, this "superflu" pandemic ravaged Canada, tragically claiming over thirty-seven million lives before its spread was arrested by the distribution of Dr. Murray's vaccine. Without question, it was Dr. Murray's work, and the work of his pharmaDyne team, that not only led to the containment of the virus, but to its ultimate eradication.

dataDyne is proud of Dr. Murray's accomplishments, and how his discovery reflects our core company values: innovation, dedication, and a commitment to improving the quality of life for our customers, and for people around the globe.

---

dataDyne Corporation was founded as a technology company (dataDyne Industries) in 1985 by industrialist/philanthropist Zhang Li. Today, dataDyne is a diversified, global company, with subsidiaries in the media/entertainment, technology, personal electronics, defense and aerospace, and pharmaceutical industries.

pharmaDyne is a Toronto-based subsidiary of dataDyne, with research and development facilities in Vancouver, Montréal, and Ottawa.

This release is © 2016, dataDyne Corporation/Media Relations Division, and is authorized for personal use and for distribution through dataDyne approved news sources and dataDyne lifeCard PDA newsfeed subscribers only. Unauthorized distribution is prohibited and punishable under the 2012 International Corporate Information Security Act, Section 30, Subsection 19, Paragraph 10.2.1.A.

CHAPTER 1

pharmaDyne Corporate Headquarters—
Comox Street, Vancouver,
British Columbia
September 4th, 2020

The primary goal was always to preserve his cover, to keep himself safe in the enemy's camp, and for that reason Benjamin Able was ordered to make contact with the Institute solely at his discretion, and never, ever directly after leaving work. It was a directive straight from Carrington himself: Institute assets within dataDyne or any of its subsidiaries were to be preserved at all costs.

Ben knew the edict, and it gave him no small amount of comfort. He knew what he did was dangerous, he knew that, potentially, it could cost him his life. He knew, as well, that it would have been so much easier to simply buy the package, to believe the lie, exactly as it seemed the way the rest of the world had. To submit to the benevolent care of the hypercorporations, to Core-Mantis and Beck-Yama and Zentek.

To submit to the will of dataDyne, whose slogan, ever-present beneath the double-D diamond logo, was the closest thing to truth the corporation ever offered the world: *Your life, our hands.* For the longest time, Benjamin Able had believed he was the only person who understood the irony in that, and the implicit threat.

Until the man from the Carrington Institute had tracked him down over five years earlier, knocking on the door of his dorm room at the University of British Columbia in the middle of a bitterly cold winter's night. Ben was majoring in political science, burning midnight oil to complete a term paper. A certain brunette in his Lit class had finally agreed, after weeks of persistence on Ben's part, to go out for pizza and a movie, but he was far enough behind in his work that he worried he'd have to cancel. When he'd answered the door, he'd expected to have friends from down the hall and the offer of a diner run, and he was already readying his excuses for staying behind.

What he got instead was a man he had never seen before, and an offer of an entirely different sort.

"I'm Jonathan," the man had said. "I want to talk to you about the blog."

Ben tried to close the door then, all of his worst fears flooding into him at once. Until that moment, he'd allowed himself to believe that what he'd written, what he'd posted, was beneath the notice of the hypercorps. In the seas of propaganda and controlled media, the islands of truth were few and far between. Ben had considered his own island to be minuscule, certainly nothing like the other sites that had inspired him, sites with names like CorpTruth and CorruptionNet. Those were the sites that had awoken him, where he'd first read about the dataDyne takeovers of Zimbabwe and Brazil, the Core-Mantis purchase of the Solomon Islands. Where he'd seen the photos of troops—honest-to-God troops—wearing corporate uniforms and fighting side by side with UN peacekeepers, or, worse, directing their activities.

Where he'd read the first-person accounts of the atrocities, and the cover-ups, and the purges, and the labor camps. All the things the media spun or obfuscated or outright ignored.

Which made it so very easy for everyone else to ignore it all, too. After all, ignorance wasn't a crime; in fact, it was openly encouraged.

So Benjamin Able had tried to close the door on the man who called himself Jonathan, suddenly and acutely afraid for his life. But Jonathan stepped forward before he could act, blocking the exit and putting a hand out to catch the door. Ben stepped back, almost stumbling.

"It's all right, Ben," Jonathan said. "I'm on your side."

Given the time and the place and the entrance, it was a hard statement to believe. When Jonathan stepped fully into the room, closing the door after him and giving Ben a looking-over, it became even harder. Jonathan didn't look much past his mid-twenties, putting him perhaps five years ahead of Ben, but it was five years that seemed to carry a world of difference. He had four or five inches on Ben, and probably another thirty pounds or so, almost all of that in muscle. Already, Ben had a sense of purpose and focus from the man, down to the smallest gestures, everything done with precision and economy.

"Look," Ben said. "Look, I'll take it down, I'll delete it, all of it."

Jonathan nodded slightly, taking in the room. Not by moving his head, Ben noticed, but with his eyes alone. "Yes, you'll have to do that. They've probably found you already. After all, we did."

"I'll take it down," Ben assured him.

Jonathan settled his gaze on him again, and then his expression softened, a cockeyed, honest smile appearing. "You were sloppy. The other sites, the big ones, they know how to move around, how to stay hidden."

The statement confused Ben. "I didn't . . . I'm not a tech guy."

"Yeah, neither am I, to be honest." Jonathan tilted his head, as if listening for something, then straightened. "Look, Ben, I'm going to make this quick. Do you believe what you've been posting?"

The question confused Ben further, unleashing another wave of suspicion. "I—"

"Yes or no."

"Yes," Ben said. "Yes, I do. I know how it sounds, all right? I know people think I'm crazy, that I'm worked up about stuff that nobody else cares about, stuff that they don't even think is real. But I *do* believe it."

"You're a junior," Jonathan said. "Declared poli sci major. What're you going to do with that? You thinking of teaching?"

Again, the question threw him off balance. If there was logic to the course of the conversation, Ben couldn't see it. "I hadn't . . . I don't know."

"Almost every school has been bought and paid for, you know that, right? From the primaries on up to this place, it's how they keep recruitment up. They dump money in, they get to dictate the curriculum. They think of it as preparing the workforce."

"I know, I—"

"What I'm saying is that you're not going to be able to teach what you believe, Ben. You'll be teaching the lie. Can you live with that?"

"No, I don't—"

"So maybe you should consider a different line of work. Something where you can make a difference, a real difference. Something where you can fight these bastards."

Jonathan fell silent, fixing him with an intent stare. Ben shook his head, bewildered. "Who the hell are you?"

"I told you, my name's Jonathan."

"But who do you work for? Who sent you? Are you government?"

Jonathan laughed. "No, not government."

"Then who?"

"Who says I work for anybody?"

"Everyone works for someone," Ben said.

"True enough. I work for a man in London, Ben."

"There are a lot of men in London."

"Not like this one there aren't." Jonathan shook his head. "I'd like to tell you more, but I can't. Not yet."

"You're trying to recruit me for a fight, I don't even know who I'll be fighting for!"

"But you know it's a war. And you know who the enemy is."

"All right, how?" Ben asked. "How am I supposed to make a difference? How am I supposed to fight them?"

"There we go," Jonathan said, softly. "That's it. You want the fight? You're willing to take them on, all of them?"

"Yes," Ben said, quickly. "Hell yes, I—"

"No, don't answer yet. These are organizations that destroy not just lives but whole countries, Ben. You hurt them badly enough, they won't come after just you. They'll come after everyone and everything around you, as well. Family, friends—even that little brunette you've been making eyes at in Lit class—they'll all be targets."

Ben started to answer, then stopped himself, taking in what Jonathan had just said.

"You need to think about it," Jonathan said. "That's good, we'd have been wrong about you if you'd just say yes blindly. You'd be a fool, and we don't need fools. So that's good, take some time." He moved closer, lowering his head slightly to meet Ben's eyes. "You decide you want to do this, change your major. Pre-law or pre-med, but pre-law would be better. We'll be watching, we'll see the sign."

"Pre-law?" Ben asked.

"They always need lawyers, Ben." Jonathan turned for the door, reached out to open it. "And take down the blog. Even if you don't want in, take it down. For your own sake."

And then he was gone, leaving Ben to stand at a crossroads in his tiny dormitory room, leaving him to decide his future.

Before he went to sleep that night, he killed his blog, and deleted all of the associated files.

Two days later, he went to the registrar's office and changed his major to pre-law.

That was how it started, with Jonathan Steinberg recruiting him to the Carrington Institute's nascent Operations Division, and together with the man himself, Daniel Carrington, they built Benjamin Able a legacy that would resist any but the most determined assault. He graduated fourth from the top of his law school class, interviewed with the dataDyne recruiter, had his background checked. He was offered a job with pharmaDyne in Vancouver, in the Rights and Properties division. He took it eagerly, underwent a second, more thorough check, and then joined the team of attorneys who spent their days in zealous defense of pharmaDyne's intellectual property.

It was a stepping-stone position, and Ben worked among almost two dozen other young legal eagles, all of them trying to prove themselves. Distinction in the department would lead to upper-level promotion, perhaps even away from pharmaDyne to its parent company, a position with dataDyne in its Los Angeles, Chicago, or even Beijing offices.

If his cover had remained intact, that was where Benjamin Able might well have ended up, a mole planted at dataDyne's highest levels, steadily feeding the Carrington Institute a stream of priceless information. He'd passed every check, he had placed himself beyond suspicion. He was young, and hungry, and viciously good at his job—everything pharmaDyne could have wanted from him. He was the perfect double agent.

And if it hadn't been for Kimiko Wu in Accounting, he would have stayed that way.

He struck up the relationship with her simply as a matter of asset acquisition, as Carrington termed it.

Like every other hypercorp, pharmaDyne was heavily compartmentalized. The beauty of his position in Legal was that it gave Ben wide access to all of the corporation's departments, since he could almost always claim an interest in one division's work or another on legal grounds. At the same time, however, his access was rarely very deep, and so Ben took steps to address the problem. To know what pharmaDyne was truly up to at any given moment, he had to know what it was doing with its money.

So targeting someone in accounting made sense, and when Ben first met Kimiko, the idea became all the more appealing. She was in her early twenties, new to the company, and graced with the kind of beauty that had men from four floors above and below her office taking regular detours just to catch sight of her. Ben met her in the course of his work, authorizing the payment on one of the few negligence settlements ever made against the company.

They became friends, and then the friendship turned into a couple of dates, and the dates became something more.

Whether he truly fell in love with her, Ben couldn't

say. Certainly, he enjoyed her company, and he enjoyed the sex, but to his mind, it was always toward a singular goal. He wanted access to her office, to her computers and her files and the endless spreadsheets that crossed her desk. If there was a problem in how he achieved these things, he didn't acknowledge it. He was a spy in the enemy's camp, he was a soldier in a cold war, and as far as he was concerned, that made everything fair game.

On alternate Fridays of each month, Accounting held a general staff meeting in the afternoons, and that was when Ben made a point of stopping by her office to drop off a bouquet of flowers. The first time she came back from a meeting to find the half-dozen roses sitting in a narrow glass vase beside her terminal, Kimiko had been surprised and touched. When he'd done it again, she'd been amused.

When he did it a third time, Ben turned the act into a ritual, and the flowers into an expectation. The flowers died, of course, normally after a couple of days, but once in a while they'd survive the duration, and he would have the pleasure of replacing them himself. On those few occasions, Ben would also surreptitiously remove the remote access transmitter he'd hidden amongst the petals. The transmitter was minuscule, developed by the Carrington Institute's technicians, astronomically expensive to produce, and more often than not, ended up in the trash along with the dead flowers. It was a minor triumph whenever Ben could recover one of them intact.

It was, however, also worth the expense, because with the transmitter's help, Ben could return to his office, boot up his own laptop, and safely behind his closed doors, reach into Kimiko's computer and download everything he could get his cursor on. The intrusion—assisted in part by a heavily modified electronic device called a "data thief"—was almost entirely invisible, both on the inside and the outside. dataDyne's CORPSEC, internal security division, regularly monitored employees, both visually and electronically. In the halls, even in the offices, employees were on camera at almost all times. When at their computers, the in-house network constantly scanned for aberrant and unauthorized access. Since the actual access to Kimiko's terminal was coming *from* her terminal, the access was not only authorized, it was expected. Since Ben was on camera the entire time he was in the building, up to and including when he was delivering flowers to her office, nothing he was doing even began to raise suspicion.

That was how Benjamin Able acquired the data.

Getting it out of the building and into the Carrington Institute's hands was another matter entirely, and one solved, ironically, by turning pharmaDyne's own paranoia against itself. To gain access to the building, each and every employee—from the CEO on down to the custodial staff—had to pass through one of the five security stations in the lobby. The checks were comprised of three stages: an ID card login, a biometric match to confirm employee identity, and finally a physical search of any containers entering or leaving the building. The security surrounding the visitors to the building was even tighter.

Once through the lobby, though, the biometric matches and physical searches were abandoned, and CORPSEC relied on their surveillance cameras and the ID cards alone. The cards, in particular, were keys, used to open the magnetic locks on the stairwells between the floors and all of the senior offices and labs. They were even tied to the computers, with readers affixed to every terminal, requiring the user to swipe their card before being able to access the in-house network. Each card carried a microchip imprinted with the user's employee data, and a magnetic strip replicating the same information. That information took, perhaps, less than 1 percent of the data storage available on the card.

Again using Carrington technology, Ben would download data from Kimiko's terminal to his laptop, and then, using the reader, upload the data again to the magnetic strip on his own ID card. At the end of each day, he would again pass through lobby security, repeating the entry process—ID card, biometric, physical search—and the guards focused almost exclusively on the physical search, checking briefcases and purses and backpacks, scanning each for smartdrives or other forms of data storage. And while they searched Benjamin Able's briefcase, he would slip his ID card back into his wallet, and wait patiently until they were finished, whereupon he would make his way home.

Back in his apartment, he would use his own reader to upload the stolen data to a burst transmitter that sent the information back to the Institute headquarters in London. He would then delete the spent information from his card, careful not to alter his own ID signature, and the next day return to repeat the procedure.

The system was elegant, efficient, and suffered from only one drawback. Every three months or so, Ben had to requisition a new ID card. He kept burning out the magnetic strips.

That was how they caught him.

CHAPTER 2

Carrington Institute—
London, England
September 13th, 2020

Joanna Dark was tired of killing.

Her lungs burned for air, the muscles in her thighs, back, and arms ached, and her mouth felt filled with hot sand. Sweat stung her eyes, blurring her vision, perspiration running freely down her face and neck, soaking her shirt until it felt five pounds heavier in water weight alone. Blood and smoke burns peppered her skin. The stench of cordite and feces and rotting trash assailed her in concert, and she was half-deaf from the repeated sound of gunfire, both hers and that of her enemies. For the first time since her father had taught her to shoot, her hands felt clumsy and thick when she wrapped them around the butts of her pistols.

She crouched on her aching haunches in the alleyway, her back to the wet brick of the nightclub wall, trying to catch her breath. Neon flashed off puddles formed in the uneven asphalt, and overhead, barely audible beyond the ringing in her ears, she could discern the whine of the city traffic as it flew past, cars riding on their self-made pockets of anti-grav. She licked her lips, tasted salt, and hoped it was sweat and not blood, and that, if it was blood, it wasn't her own.

Jo tried to tally her kills and realized she'd lost count, but she wasn't certain when. Somewhere in the mid-sixties, she suspected, when the dataDyne recovery team had ambushed her outside the hotel. That had been a good fight—there'd been eight of them, all in body armor and armed to the teeth, laying down a spray of automatic-weapons fire that had drawn sparks like a string of fire-crackers along the walls. She'd taken cover behind a Bowman Constellation, one of the new null-grav luxury models, just as it had landed, then rolled out and dropped three of them in quick order, all with single shots: two to the neck, one straight through his faceplate.

Then she'd used a grenade, blowing up the rest of them along with the car and half of the windows on the first floor of the hotel.

Despite her fatigue, the memory made her grin. That had been a while ago, quite a while ago. Maybe in Rio.

She wasn't certain where she was now. What she could see of the signage on the buildings around her looked Korean. Maybe Pyongyang? Maybe Los Angeles?

It didn't matter.

Jo checked her pistols, the two Falcons she'd been working with almost exclusively, feeling the heat radiating from their barrels. Good guns, the Falcons. Her father had taught her to shoot on them. Eighteen-round semi-autos that could fire as fast she could squeeze their triggers, and sweetly accurate. When she worked with the Falcons, Jo could make the bullets go exactly where she wanted.

She pulled a last deep breath, filling her muscles with oxygen, then launched herself forward, at the rusted metal door planted in the wall opposite her. She took the impact on her left shoulder and the door gave way, and Jo pitched through, turning the move into a roll, tumbling through an instant of darkness, coming up again into a low crouch.

It was a Japanese restaurant, all tatami mats and rice-paper walls and soft white lighting, and Jo turned slowly in place, swinging each of the Falcons with her, covering her arcs. Silhouettes glided past, hidden by the walls around her, clad in kimonos and robes, and Jo held her fire, not wanting to kill anyone who didn't have it coming to them.

Ahead of her, the hallway reached a T-junction, and just as she started to move, a black canister bounced into view, clattering to a halt on the floor fifteen feet away.

Jo launched herself left, up and through the wall, tearing paper and wood and flying into a private dining room. She sprawled onto a low table, sending California rolls and teacups flying. Patrons screamed, recoiling. It wasn't until she'd made the move that Jo understood why she'd done it, why she'd gone left, instinctively moving in the direction the grenade had come.

The explosion came, tearing flame and shrapnel through the insubstantial walls, and she saw the first target then, a Caucasian male in gang colors, shotgun in hand. Jo fired once, still in motion, and the left Falcon put a bullet into the man's ear. The screaming around her got louder.

Jo finished her slide, rolling off the edge of the table, turning as she came up, and now she could see three more of them, all in the same colors, all men, two of them with shotguns and the third packing a Liberator submachine gun. She hit the Liberator first, a double tap with the right Falcon, both shots to the high sternum, and the man dropped without firing a round. She took the first shotgun with the left Falcon, again double-tapping, this time both bullets hitting the target's groin.

The second shotgun fired and Jo spun out of the blast just short of in time, felt the slap of buckshot as it peppered her right cheek, felt the sting and her own blood starting to spill. She came around fully to her feet, and the last one was tracking her as fast as he could, trying to get the shotgun around for a second blast, but he wasn't anywhere near quick enough, and it felt like Jo had all the time in the world. She put both pistols on him, pulled the triggers, then pulled them again, and again, until the body hit the ground and didn't move again.

Jo stopped, catching her breath, feeling all of her aches return, the slick heat of blood running from her cheek down the side of her neck. Behind her, she heard whimpering, the sounds of the frightened patrons.

Then she felt her head snap forward, the impact of something small and hard and sharp against the back of her skull, and the world flared white, then began to fill with red.

Oh shit, Joanna Dark thought. *I'm dead.*

The red-tinged world vibrated, shimmered, and vanished, abruptly replaced by a view of Daniel Carrington looking down at her with disapproval, holding on to the power cord he had just yanked from the wall.

"I think that's enough of that," he told her.

"I wasn't finished." Her voice was thin, hoarse from disuse, and she coughed to clear it.

"Yes, you are, Joanna." Carrington frowned, the creases around his watery brown eyes etching deeper. She was unsure of his exact age, but guessed him to be in his early sixties. It was hard to tell; Carrington had the kind of weathered face that made gauging age difficult. Silver hair and a salt-and-pepper beard didn't help the estimate much.

Jo pulled the visor from her face and tossed it aside harder than she'd meant to, immediately regretting it. The headset sailed across her room, hit the wall with an audible crack, then dropped to the carpet. She hoped it wasn't broken. The DeathMatch virtual reality set was delicate equipment, despite the violence it faked, and not cheap to replace.

She got out of her chair, feeling her wet shirt peel free from the leather backrest. Her sweat soaked her clothes, as it had in the simulation, and the air-conditioned room turned the perspiration cold, making her shiver. She rubbed her arms, glaring at Carrington.

"I wasn't finished," she repeated.

"Admittedly, I don't know as much about these things as you do," Carrington said. "But my understanding is that a bullet to the back of the head leads to death, which, in almost every instance, translates to game over. You're finished."

He looked at the cable still held in his thick hand, as if offended by what it represented, then dropped it.

"It's a dataDyne product, as well." He looked back at her, scowling. "You don't know what it's doing to your mind."

"Fine, I'll go back to using HoloMan."

"And is there a reason that you're so eager to disappear into virtual realities, Joanna? A particular bloodlust you're hoping to satisfy?"

She didn't answer, glaring at him.

"I may be mistaken about this, as well," Carrington said mildly. "But I would hazard a guess that there are more productive ways of dealing with grief."

"I'm not grieving."

Carrington opened his mouth to challenge her obvious lie, then seemed to think better of it, closing it again and, instead, shaking his head slightly.

"It's midnight, Joanna. You're exhausted, you haven't

taken food or drink or sleep in over a day and a half, and right now you're looking for a fight anywhere you can find one. Denied an imaginary enemy, you're making me one."

"You're not my friend."

"I've told you that I am. I've told you that I'll take care of you."

Jo snorted, brushed her limp hair from where it clung to her forehead. "My father told me about you, Mister Carrington, you know that."

"I do."

"He told me not to trust you."

"It's probably good advice, Joanna. Your father was a very smart man." Carrington smoothed his beard, then added, "But he wasn't a terribly good judge of character."

"Don't insult—"

"It's not an insult, Joanna. Your father was a police officer and then he was a bail enforcement agent, a bounty hunter. Neither profession encourages a very optimistic view of humanity, both focusing, as they do, on society's dregs. I think it's safe to say he had a small bias, don't you?"

"I don't know," Jo said. "Do you think of yourself as one of society's dregs?"

It was a good shot, and Jo thought for certain it would get a rise out of him—for a fraction of a second, she believed she was right. People didn't talk this way to Daniel Carrington, she knew that, especially not a guest in his own home. Not to one of the richest men in the world, not to an acknowledged scientific genius, the man responsible for implementing portable anti-gravity and revolutionizing the way the world worked. Not to the founder of the Carrington Institute.

Something flashed across Carrington's eyes, appearing for an instant from behind the grandfatherly façade, but then, to Jo's disappointment, it vanished as quickly as it had appeared. Carrington shook his head again, smiling. To her annoyance, he began to chuckle softly.

"Teenagers," Carrington said. "I'd forgotten what they're like."

"I'm twenty," Jo retorted, annoyed.

"Ah, a perfect lady, then. I stand corrected." Carrington hefted the walking stick in his left hand, demonstrating the irony before switching it to his right and then planting it once more. He turned to the door. "If you'd like to join me for breakfast tomorrow in my office, you can even have an opportunity to prove it. Goodnight, Joanna."

She watched him leave the room, then moved to shut and lock the door behind him, more as a declaration of privacy than anything else. She'd lived on the Institute grounds for six months already, she understood how the security here worked, even if she didn't understand all the reasons for it.

She picked up the DeathMatch headset, running her thumb over the double-D diamond logo embossed on its side absently, examining the unit. Both of the projection lenses had cracks in them, and the basal sensor had snapped in two. Jo tossed it in the trash can beside the desk, then went into the bathroom and ran water at the sink. She drank several mouthfuls from her hands, splashed more of it on her face, and then found she was staring at herself in the mirror and not really recognizing who she was seeing at all.

Blue eyes that her father said she'd inherited from her mother, eyes like sapphires, he called them, granted by a woman Jo had never known. Roughly cut hair that burned like copper and that fell to her shoulders, currently limp and matted with dried sweat, with a blond forelock, some genetic quirk that no one could ever explain. Her father's nose, straight and small, and again what he'd called her mother's mouth. The only thing all her own that she could see was her tattoo, a purple five-pointed star at the left side of her neck she'd had done in Hong Kong on her seventeenth birthday.

Her father had hated the tattoo. "It makes you look cheap," he'd said when he'd first seen it. "You're not cheap, Jo, you're priceless."

Joanna looked at herself, and saw water coming to her eyes.

She was going to be his partner, Dark & Dark Bail Retrieval, that was how it was supposed to have been. Hours and days and weeks and months and even years training on HoloMan VR, learning Jack Dark's trade, waiting for the day and the chance when he would finally look at her and say, yes, all right, you're ready, this time we do the job together.

And dataDyne had killed him, and Jo had found revenge, but no measure of peace. Then Daniel Carrington had come offering her a place to stay, to rest, to figure out what to do next. Six months along and it might as well have been six days for all that had changed, because she was now exactly where she was then.

Alone.

Miss you, Da, she thought. *I miss you so much and I don't know who I am without you, I don't know why I'm here, I don't know what I'm supposed to do.*

Thoughts that wouldn't give her peace.

And worst of all was her growing suspicion that, while she didn't know the answers, Daniel Carrington did.

CHAPTER 3

Pacific Centre—
Vancouver, British Columbia
September 26th, 2020

Vancouver had fared better than most cities during the superflu, losing only a third of its population to the outbreak, and now, four years later, it appeared to most eyes to be well into its recovery. The streets downtown were no longer barren, the shops were once again open, people no longer barricaded themselves indoors. Even the economy was coming back, in part due to the efforts of the hypercorps, but even more to the efforts of the neighbor to the south. The United States had poured unprecedented billions into Canada in an attempt to stabilize its neighbor, a move seen in the US as alternatively charitable or foolish, depending on who you spoke to.

But the signs remained, with more shops and restaurants out of business than in it, and for that reason, when Benjamin Able took Kimiko Wu for a night on the town, they invariably started the evening at the Pacific Centre, though more often than not they ended it at either her apartment or, less frequently, his. Before the outbreak, the

Centre had been downtown's grand underground mall, a multi-level structure built for high-end shopping and entertainment. Post outbreak, the Centre had come back with a vengeance, as most of the survivors had been those with money, and now it was a shopping venue as fine as any to be found in Beverly Hills, Milan, or Hong Kong.

They moved through the Centre holding hands, window-shopping, with Ben waiting patiently as Kimiko first tried on shoes at Pegabo, then bought a new jacket at Danier Leather. At La Belle Femme, she found a white silk robe and matching lingerie, showing them to him with a twinkle in her eye.

"What do you think?" Kimiko asked.

"I think you'd make them look even better," Ben told her.

Her smile in response was radiant, and she pecked his cheek gently with her lips, moving off to make her purchases and leaving him for the moment alone, surrounded by women's underwear. He watched her at the register, chatting with the salesclerk, sharing a laugh, and tried to relax, but his nerves were taut and he couldn't manage it, not really.

He ran a hand inside his coat, to the pocket beneath his left arm, felt the shape of his ID card, still resting where he'd placed it upon leaving work. The card that carried gold, solid gold intelligence that had been too good to pass up. After months of stealing into Kimiko's computer, and through it into the pharmaDyne mainframe, he'd finally cracked the Director's account, gaining access to Doctor Friedrich Murray's personal files. To Ben—and more, to Carrington—it was the pharmaDyne holy grail.

And hidden, encrypted, in Doctor Murray's computer, he had found a folder labeled, simply, *Rose*. It was that combination, the innocuous name coupled with the extreme security, that had made Ben certain it was important, that it was something worth stealing. It had been too good to be true.

It was only after he'd transferred the files to his ID card that he began to think he'd made a mistake. Steinberg had warned him often enough during training lectures: If something looks too good to be true, it probably is.

The logical thing to do, then, would have been to dump the data as quickly as possible, to send it off to the Institute as soon as he could. But it was Friday, and he and Kimiko had made plans for after work, and Ben didn't want to risk drawing attention to himself —or, for that matter, to her— by canceling. If he was being set up by CORPSEC, if one of Anita Velez's ghosts was onto him and the access to Murray's files had been the bait to a trap, then the only thing Benjamin Able could do for the time being was to play it cool, to play it as if everything was normal. He'd heard dozens of water-cooler fables about the dataDyne security chief, enough dark talk to convince him he never wanted to meet Anita Velez, under any circumstances.

Kimiko finished making her purchases, returning to him amidst the silk and lace, offering Ben her arm. He shifted his briefcase to his left hand to accommodate her, and they stepped out of the store and onto the second-floor walkway. A handful of well-dressed and heavily tattooed teens flooded past them as they took the escalator up to the third-story restaurants. An indoor waterfall cascaded noisily down from above, multi-colored lights shining on the streams as they plummeted to the pool below.

"You made reservations?" Kimiko asked, resting her head against his shoulder, as they arrived at the restaurant. Ahead of them in line, a young couple dressed in retro-punk were making out as they waited for their table. Ben thought the dye job on the woman's Mohawk looked hurried, her hair hot pink, but still a bit brown at the tips.

"Of course," he told Kimiko, and then kissed her forehead lightly to reassure her.

All of the restaurants on the third floor shared the same space, open plan, in what had once been a food court. Now the area was broken into separate venues, décor designed to match the offered cuisines: Japanese, nouveau Thai, French, and Italian. Restaurants brushed against one another in a kind of visual culture shock, red-checkered tablecloths and wine-bottle candlesticks surrounding wood-topped sushi bars. Waitresses in kimonos threaded their way past waiters in black tie. A glass ceiling arched above, revealing the lights of the surrounding high rises shining in the night.

They took a table in France, and Ben ordered a Californian Shiraz to start, and it was while their waiter was explaining the day's specials that he made the surveillance. Four tables to his left, just on the border with Thailand, a man and a woman working on their entrées. They had been conversing, and had abruptly stopped, but that wasn't the tell, just a part of it. It was the fact that, when they'd stopped speaking, each of them had almost imperceptibly, and almost at the exact same instant, inclined their heads. The whole thing was so subtle, in fact, that Ben wasn't certain he'd seen it at all. They were good enough that they never moved their hands from their meals, never reached reflexively for the subcutaneous microphones in their ears.

They didn't need to. Ben knew it for what it was, and it made his stomach suddenly cramp with apprehension.

"Monsieur?" the waiter asked.

He brought his attention back to his own table, saw Kimiko opposite him, her lovely brow furrowing with concern. He looked to the waiter, who was either trying to affect French disdain or was simply failing to hide his annoyance with Ben's lack of attention.

"Are you ready to order?" the waiter repeated.

Ben ordered the duck, knowing that he wouldn't touch a bite of it.

The waiter departed, and Kimiko moved her purse from where it rested at her elbow to hang by its strap over the back of the chair. Ben shifted his gaze past her, looking for more, the second team, his mind beginning to spin with questions. It was possible that the two sitting on the edge of Thailand weren't even here for him, part of the surveillance of another mark entirely. It was possible that they *were* here for him, but that they *weren't* dataDyne; the word on the office grapevine lately was that Beck-Yama had grown increasingly aggressive in their recruitment practices. If that was the case, maybe they weren't here for him: Ben was a low-value target, as was Kimiko.

Kimiko was asking him some question, leaning forward slightly, two of her long fingers toying with the stem of her wineglass, her other hand resting properly in her lap, out of sight. She wanted to know if they were still planning on heading up to Whistler in the morning, to try to catch some of the early-season skiing. Ben told her that it sounded like a great idea.

Over in Italy, a table of three men, all in business suits, all apparently straight from the office, were hunched over plates of pasta, briefcases and laptop cases resting beside their chairs near their feet. At first, Ben didn't mind them, and the affected French waiter returned with salads, and he and Kimiko tucked into the food. He had a forkful of wilted spinach halfway to his mouth before he realized why they seemed off.

Three businessmen, Friday evening, out to dinner—and on the table, three glasses of water. Not wine, not scotch and soda, not martinis, but water.

Ben glanced back to the border with Thailand, saw that the couple he'd spotted earlier had paid and were now headed back to the escalators, past the line of people still waiting for a table. The two retro-punks were still waiting for a table, no longer wrestling tongues, no longer touching. Ben was certain that the woman with the hot-pink

Mohawk said something to the other couple as they passed.

That clinched it for him. Seven of them that he could spot—it had to be a capture team, and his stomach clenched further, making him regret the two bites of salad he'd already managed. Seven of them, which meant at least two more on the ground, and then a third one, the operation controller, monitoring from someplace off site, probably from the extraction vehicle.

Ben drained the rest of his wineglass, then reached across the table for Kimiko's hand, leaning forward and giving her his best mischievous smile. "You know what? Let's go back to your place, order in."

She raised her eyebrows, bewildered. "Ben! We just ordered."

"What can I say, Kim?" He picked up his briefcase, moving it into his lap. "I want to see you in that new nightie."

"Ben—"

He started to get up. "Seriously, let's go."

"Ben, sit down," Kimiko said.

He'd been half out of the chair, already turning to see that the retro-punks had spotted his movement, were now moving to cover the elevators beyond Japan, when she spoke. It was her tone that did it, the command, and he froze for a moment as the realization cascaded down upon him.

Ben sat back down, resting his briefcase again on his lap, and looked levelly at Kimiko. Her smile was gone, as was the mirth in her eyes, and as he watched she brought the hand she'd kept in her lap up, onto the table, covered with her white linen napkin. Beneath the fabric, Ben could see the tiny muzzle—not much bigger than a .22—of a Tranq-7, a short range dermal injection device, non-lethal, if he remembered from Steinberg's lectures, but at this range it was enough to put him down for the count with one shot.

"Put the briefcase back on the floor, Benjamin," Kimiko said. "Then put your hands flat on the table."

For a second, Ben thought about trying to feign innocence, incredulity, but realized as quickly that the moment for denials had passed. Kimiko knew, obviously she knew, she was probably a CORPSEC agent and had been all along. How long she had known, and exactly *what* she knew, those were other questions, and he didn't think he'd be getting any answers from her, at least not here.

"Son of a bitch," he said softly.

"Put it down." She moved the Tranq-7 slightly, as if to remind him of its presence. "I don't want to have to dope you here, Ben, but I will."

"So you're going to dope me later?"

"Not if you're forthcoming."

Past her, the three businessmen seated in Italy had stopped pretending they liked their pasta, were now looking their way. Two of them had their laptop cases in their laps, open just enough to allow them to reach inside for the weapons Ben was certain they'd stored there. He glanced around behind him, saw the retro-punks now fully in position, covering any attempt to escape via the escalator. The first couple he'd spotted, the man and the woman, were nowhere to be seen.

He looked back to Kimiko, sighed, and set his briefcase down beside the chair, sliding it forward beneath the table. "CORPSEC?" he asked her, struggling without much success to keep the bitterness out of his voice. "You're one of Velez's pet spooks, right?"

"pharmaDyne local, actually. Doctor Murray prefers us to handle breaches in-house, rather than bringing in Director Velez. We don't want to appear unable to handle our own problems. Is it in the briefcase, Ben? What you've stolen, is it on your laptop?"

"Would you believe me if I said no?"

For a moment, the smile that he adored reappeared on her face, but only for a moment. "No."

"So what now?"

Behind her, two of the three businessmen quickly transferred hands from their laptop cases to beneath their coats. Ben saw the glint of metal—MagSec gun barrels. In unison, all three got to their feet and began approaching the table.

"Now we're going back to the office," Kimiko said, sliding her own chair back from the table. "Don't try to run, Ben, you'll never make it."

He nodded, slightly, agreeing with her assessment, and Kimiko freed her purse from the back of the chair, slung it over her shoulder, slipping the Tranq-7 back inside it. The retro-punks had reached them, now, and without taking her eyes off Ben, she told hot-pink Mohawk to take his briefcase, the other one to take her bag from La Belle Femme.

"And here I thought you'd bought them just for me," Ben said.

"Don't flatter yourself," Kimiko Wu told him.

He made his move when they reached the bottom of the escalator and the second floor.

The punks led the way down, followed by one of the businessmen, the other two walking just behind Ben at either flank, Kimiko taking up the rear. The only one who spoke was Kimiko, and Ben couldn't make out her words as she whispered softly to the controller over her mike. Presumably she was arranging their pickup.

It wasn't that Ben liked the location, or his chances; in

fact, he liked neither. But once they had him out of the Centre and into their transport, he knew where and how it would all end. "Back to the office" meant back to pharmaDyne, yes, but not to any of the floors above ground. He'd end up in one of the sub-basements, locked away in an interrogation room where they'd go to work on him. He had no illusions about how that would go, either. At best, he might be able to hold out the better part of a day before they started in with the drugs. Once they used the drugs, though, he knew he'd tell them everything.

It wasn't his best chance, then; it was his only one.

He waited until the businessman ahead of him had come off the escalator, close on the heels of the two punks who had taken point. As the step turned flat beneath him, Ben lurched backward, bracing himself and reaching into his coat pocket at the same time. He heard the businessmen cursing behind him, each of them backpedaling as well, trying to avoid the collision. He slammed back into them hard, and heard them fall as Kimiko shouted a warning, a moment too late. Ben lunged forward, hand still in his pocket, feeling for the strip of Velcro, feeling it tear free beneath his fingers.

The punks and the remaining businessman had already begun turning, all of them moving to block him and index their weapons at the same time. The one with the Mohawk dropped Able's captured briefcase just as he'd hoped she would, sending it clattering down in front of her, and Ben brought his left arm up and across his eyes as he dove, squeezing the Velcro, pressing down hard on the thin button trapped beneath the fabric. There was an instant crack, and even with his eyes squeezed shut and shielded behind his forearm, he could swear he saw the magnesium flare as the briefcase exploded, the flash-bang sequence detonating.

The concussion was enormous, a thunderclap in a closet, and it rang throughout his skull. Even knowing it was coming, Ben found it disorienting, and for a miserable instant of darkness and noise he didn't know where he was, what he was trying to do. Then he came back to himself, opening his eyes and discovering he was flat on the ground, and he scrabbled to his feet, the echo of the explosion still singing in his ears. He spun, saw that the businessmen and the punks were alternately on their knees or their backs, hands to their eyes or ears, and he saw their mouths working, but he couldn't hear what they were saying. Kimiko was the only one on her feet, stumbling blindly.

Ben ran, his loafers sliding on the slick floors of the Pacific Centre, trying to formulate a new plan, a way to escape. Shoppers scattered around him, pointing, shouting things he couldn't hear. He took the corner beside the Prada outlet too fast, lost his footing entirely, and came down hard on his side. A raindrop of yellow and green exploded on the floor beside his hand—the payload from the Tranq round—as he scrambled back to his feet, and he saw Kimiko with the Tranq-7 extended, lurching drunkenly in his direction. Two of the businessmen were following close on her heels, their MagSecs now brandished for all to see.

They weren't firing, though, and Ben realized they wanted him alive, and thought that might give him a little more time.

He reached the railing to the stairs, half vaulted, half tumbled over it, and then dropped almost three meters into the pool at the base of the waterfall. A rusty spike of pain lanced from his right ankle to his hip, and Ben was certain he'd cried out, but he still couldn't hear anything. He spun in place, soaked with water, then lunged for the edge of the pool. The two punks came around the corner ahead of him, perhaps twenty meters away, each of them brandishing weapons of their own. Ben reversed, splashing back in the opposite direction. Above him, he caught sight of Kimiko and her three businessmen running along the upper walkway, moving to cut him off.

Ben realized he wasn't going to make it. Kimiko must have called for reinforcements by now, which meant that all of the exits to the mall would be covered. Blowing the briefcase had expended his only weapon, and while Steinberg had trained him in both defensive pistolcraft and hand-to-hand combat, Ben had never been much of a fighter. He wasn't going to be able to run, and he wasn't going to make a stand.

They were going to catch him, it was just a matter of when.

It took him less than a second to realize all these things, and just as quickly, he made his decision and began moving again, this time cutting left, making toward the base of the waterfall. He skirted the edge, feeling the spray being thrown up, stinging his face, then pulled himself over the raised ledge and broke into a sprint. He didn't look back, searching the mall ahead of him, weaving his way through stunned and gaping shoppers and feeling his contempt of them burn suddenly hot in his chest. These were the people he was fighting for, and here they stood, slack-jawed cattle, seeing and not understanding.

No one offered to help him.

Twenty meters away, wedged between a Banana Republic and a "We Care" Clinic, he spotted what he was looking for, a bank of ATM/Com terminals, and course-corrected toward them. There were five of them, two surcharge machines, one a Core-Mantis OmniGlobal, and the remaining two belonging to dataDyne. He had the ID card out of his pocket and in his hand before he reached the machine, and in almost one move, he slammed the ID into the slot.

Through the ringing in his ears, he heard Kimiko's voice, almost shrieking. "Stop him!"

The terminal sucked the card in greedily, and Ben allowed himself a moment of satisfaction at the irony. Just as he'd used pharmaDyne's own network against itself when he accessed Kimiko's terminal, he was about to do the same thing here.

The surcharge machines were for the general public and for general use—anyone with a credit card could use them to withdraw cash or to access the Net for a "modest" service charge. The sponsored machines were another beast entirely, dedicated to serving the employees of their corporate owners. To access them, one needed the appropriate corporate ID, but once that was inserted, employees could network with their offices, check email, video conference, essentially anything and everything they could do from their personal workstation. If one was so inclined, the user could even withdraw cash.

The terminal lit immediately, accepting Ben's ID, and he was halfway through his twelve-digit PIN when he saw another yellow and green raindrop spatter on the screen. He heard Kimiko's voice again, this time clearer, and he ignored it, ignored all the noises that were suddenly reaching him, as if some universal volume control was being steadily cranked higher and higher. He finished inputting his PIN, punched the CONNECT button, began scrolling down his list of options.

He managed to select *home network* before the sting came, the impact high in his back, a sliver of glass that buried itself between his shoulder blades. Almost immediately his vision went, blurring and fogging, and Ben felt his mouth fill with dry grass, his tongue swelling like a balloon. His fingers fumbled on the miniature keypad, and he prayed to God that he wasn't misspelling the command, that he would get it right the first time. Five little letters, that was all he needed.

He'd managed the *p* and the *a* and the *n* when Mohawk reached him with her partner, and through his fading vision, he saw their reflections in the terminal, distorted and grotesque. One of them—he didn't know which—grabbed at his arm, and he brought his elbow back, felt it connecting with something soft, and the grip was gone. He managed to punch the *i* and then was torn away from the terminal.

Two more sets of hands reached him, pulling his arms, and he ignored them, his whole world contracting to contain only the illuminated miniature keyboard and nothing else. The keys pulsed in his vision, and he strained desperately to reach them, heard himself screaming in outrage and fury. Something bit at his neck, another shot from the Tranq-7 finding its target, and Ben felt his legs melting like wax.

He screamed a final time, surged forward, and his index finger hit the *c* on the keyboard.

He managed a momentary howl of triumph, and then the velvet cloak of the tranquilizer crushed him to the ground.

CHAPTER 4

Luxe Life Resort—
Kauai, Hawaii
September 26th, 2020

Cassandra DeVries hadn't had a vacation in sixteen years, ever since starting at DataFlow as an entry-level code monkey.

She'd come to the company straight out of Cambridge, and begun pursuing her graduate education via telecommunications admission, earning a masters, then the first of two doctorates. She was never late for work. She never took a sick day. She never asked for vacation time but once a year, and then it was only a day, and always the same day. June 16th, and if anyone had ever asked the significance of that—and they didn't—she would have explained that June 16th was the day her seven-year-old brother had been killed by a drunk driver. Cassandra had been nine at the time.

She did all these things and more for DataFlow. She was driven, professional, committed, all the things that theoretically earned promotion. Yet promotion—at least, promotion that mattered—never came.

For the better part of ten years, Cassandra DeVries was shuffled laterally within the company, posted to one department or another, asked to work on this system or that design. Wherever she went within DataFlow, her work was consistently outstanding. Whenever she was shuffled to the next office, she left the last better than when she'd found it.

Which was precisely the problem, because in those days, DataFlow had been about as rigid and uncreative an organization as one could imagine. In the eyes of her supervisors, Cassandra DeVries was a threat. It wasn't just that she always had a new idea, a better way, and that she was always willing to argue the point. It wasn't just that she could spot the flaws in a programmer's code in less time than it took most people to tie their own shoes. It wasn't just that she was considered a maverick in a corporate culture that frowned on individualism and creativity.

It was that each and every time she submitted a proposal, or, worse, took it upon herself to fix a perceived error, she was *right.*

Thus Cassandra created a Catch-22 for herself. On no account could her supervisors acknowledge her brilliance, for fear of revealing their own shortcomings; at the same time, they couldn't dare get rid of her, for precisely the same reason.

Then Daniel Carrington taught the cars of the world how to fly, and Cassandra DeVries wrote a program that made it safe for them to do it. AirFlow.Net, she called it, and suddenly not only did the corporate execs at DataFlow know who Cassandra DeVries was, but her name was being spoken throughout their parent company of dataDyne, as well.

A genius, they called her, not so much because AirFlow.Net all but eliminated anti-grav vehicular accidents practically overnight, but because it made dataDyne roughly thirty-seven billion dollars in the first quarter of its release alone.

Suddenly, the code monkey was an executive vice president overnight, and never mind that the night had lasted over ten years.

Two years after her promotion to Executive Vice President of Software Design, dataDyne's CEO and founder, Zhang Li, appointed Cassandra DeVries to the position of Chief Executive Officer of DataFlow, a dataDyne subsidiary. Now the code monkey was called *Director* DeVries.

Still, she never took a vacation, not a real one, at least. In point of fact, Cassandra didn't understand the other CEOs and Directors who did, the ones who had regular golf games on Wednesdays or took a month off to hike, or swim, or ski, or "recharge." There was always too much that needed doing, always another program that needed tweaking, another idea that needed exploring. While Cassandra DeVries had hungered for recognition, that had never been the motivation behind the creation of AirFlow.Net. She had written the program for one reason alone: to make the world a better place. More precisely, to make the world a place where little brothers didn't have their lives stolen from them by drunk drivers.

While Cassandra enjoyed the perks and pleasures of her new position, unlike her fellow Directors in countless other dataDyne subsidiaries, she never viewed them as entitlements.

She was at Luxe Life because she didn't have a choice in the matter. The dataDyne Board of Directors had "invited" all of the subsidiary heads to a "mandatory retreat," to discuss the future of the parent corporation. The invitation made no mention of CEO Li's disappearance, nor that of his daughter, Mai-Hem. The invitation most specifically did *not* say that the Board was convening to discuss the possibility of electing a new dataDyne CEO. Most important of all, it nowhere said that, in all likelihood, the new CEO would be named from one of the subsidiary Directors.

It said none of those things, and Cassandra DeVries knew it meant all of them. She had to go.

But it didn't mean she had to enjoy it, and upon first arriving at the resort, she busied herself with work, confining herself to the presidential suite that Anita Velez, the Director of dataDyne Security Operations, had assigned her. Velez had arranged for all of the Directors' accommodations personally, in keeping with the extraordinariness of the situation. The full Board of Directors and all of the key CEOs were gathered in one place, something that, to Cassandra's knowledge, had never happened before in the history of dataDyne. If a competing hypercorp got wind of that, it was a no-brainer that they'd move for a hostile takeover. Cassandra could just imagine the executives at Core-Mantis OmniGlobal salivating at the chance, and the less said about the bastards at Beck-Yama, the better.

To say the security at the resort was tight, then, would be to say the Pacific Ocean was wet. A true enough statement, but one that lacked an appropriate sense of scale.

The situation surely was giving Velez nightmares, Cassandra imagined, and there was security enough to prove the point. The whole of the resort, built to accommodate 2,179 guests at capacity, currently accommodated 106, and over half that number were Velez's own guards—or "agents," as Velez herself termed them. The Board, the Directors, and their skeleton support staff comprised the rest of the number. As for those Luxe Life employees actually working the resort for the duration of the dataDyne retreat, all had undergone comprehensive background checks, and all were subjected to screenings and searches both coming and going to work.

To Cassandra DeVries, it was like living in an opulent, tropical ghost town.

She enjoyed the solitude at the start, and used the time to work on those projects that had suffered from lack of attention. She was drafting code for what she hoped would become AirFlow.Net version 2.0, and had been shepherding a team of her favorite programmers on a new project, exploring the viability of true artificial intelligence. The AI project was at least another three years from completion, but it excited her, and now that she had the free time, she eagerly reviewed their progress.

When those things were done, she caught up on her reading. She watched some of the many movies that friends and colleagues had told her she shouldn't miss. She discovered, for the most part, that she hadn't been missing much of anything at all.

And she waited for the Board to summon her and the other CEOs, whose company she had quite intentionally been avoiding.

It was on her sixth day at the resort, when she discovered herself no longer staring at her laptop screen but instead staring past it, that Cassandra actually saw the ocean shining outside her window. Her suite was on the ground floor, with French doors that opened directly onto the pristine beach, and the Hawaiian sun glimmered off water that shone a brilliant blue-green, and quite abruptly she reached for the phone on her desk and called the gift shop.

"I need someone to bring me a bathing suit, please," Cassandra DeVries said.

It was mid-afternoon on the ninth day of the retreat that Cassandra DeVries emerged from the Pacific to see Anita Velez standing on the beach, waiting for her beside the small pile of her things, her towel and sandals and sarong. She felt a pang of apprehension.

"They've reached a decision?" Cassandra called from the water.

Instead of replying, Velez bent and picked up Cassandra's beach towel, holding it out for her. From this distance, Cassandra couldn't make out her expression.

The apprehension grew into a more tangible fear. If it wasn't the Board finally summoning them, then Cassandra could think of only one other reason Velez would want to speak with her. If Velez knew about *that,* Cassandra could not only forget about becoming the next CEO of dataDyne; she could forget about remaining Director of DataFlow, as well. Of the five Directors gathered at the resort, Cassandra knew for a fact that two of the three married ones had lovers, and that Takahata Sato, who like herself was single, didn't only because he was more interested in the games that could be played with LoveMatch VR.

Cassandra DeVries had few things she kept from dataDyne. The fact that she had a lover of her own was one of those things.

She drew a breath, wiped the seawater from her face. Velez hadn't moved; the towel was still extended. With a sigh, Cassandra waded her way out of the gentle surf, up the hot sand of the beach.

"Have they made a decision?" she asked again.

"They want to see the Directors." Velez handed over the towel, then turned her head to look down the length of the beach. "I've been told to double the protection details on yourself, Doctor Murray, Mister Sexton, Mister Sato, and Ms. Waterberg. Draw your own conclusions, Doctor DeVries."

"They're hedging their bets." Cassandra ran the towel

over her face, using the fabric to hide the relief she was feeling for a moment before continuing to dry herself off. "They don't want to make a decision."

"Would you?" Velez asked, turning her scan now to check up the beach. Her accent, a mixture of German and American, made almost everything she said sound at once curt and vaguely antagonistic.

"It's been almost six months. I should think someone would have heard something from Master Li by now, don't you?" she said, feeling somewhat silly for using the "Master" honorific, but it was how Zhang Li had insisted his underlings address him. "If not from him, then from his daughter, at least. At this point, their silence speaks volumes."

"Unfortunately, no one knows what it's saying." Velez turned her head to scan the length of the beach in the opposite direction. She stood over six feet, which put her nearly half a foot taller than Cassandra, and easily fifty pounds heavier, all of it from bone and muscle. Today's suit—and Cassandra had noted that Anita Velez *always* wore suits, and always trousers with them, never skirts—was of linen, off-white and perfectly tailored. It was the kind of outfit that, if Cassandra had tried to wear it, would've gotten her accused of looking "too masculine." Velez could make it work, however, somehow managing to convey both authority and professionalism without utterly abandoning femininity.

Cassandra stopped toweling off long enough to follow Velez's gaze. Perhaps thirty meters down the beach, one of Velez's uniformed agents stood on post, an assault rifle slung across his back. The security uniforms were black, and Cassandra could only imagine the guard's discomfort, standing on the beach in the heat. When she checked the opposite direction, it was like looking in a mirror, only the second guard was female.

Cassandra put her attention back on Velez. "You don't know what's happened to them."

"Is that a question?"

"You *are* the Director of Security, Anita—"

"Not for him, nor for his daughter." Velez looked at her sharply. "I am responsible for the protection of the Board, the Directors, and their holdings. Personal security and counterespionage, Doctor DeVries, that's all."

"Personal security would imply—"

Velez's brown eyes seemed to flare darker for a moment. "Not to Master Li. Not to Mai-Hem. They handled their own arrangements."

"I'm not attacking you, Anita."

"That's probably wise of you, Doctor."

"I'm asking if you have any idea as to their whereabouts."

Velez cocked her head slightly, frowning. "Don't you think I would have said as much already if I did?"

Not bloody likely, Cassandra thought. That was the problem with CORPSEC in general, and Anita Velez in particular; Cassandra never had any idea as to what the older woman thought at any given time, and reading her was next to impossible.

Everyone at the resort had secrets, Cassandra knew, including herself. Whether or not Anita Velez knew those secrets was always a question.

"I suppose so," Cassandra said.

Velez maintained the frown for a moment longer, then stepped back, again scanning the beach. Cassandra moved forward, slipping her feet into her sandals as she ran the towel over her blond hair. She was still unused to its length. Before coming to Kauai for the retreat, her hair had been long enough to reach the small of her back. Then she'd dropped five thousand euros on a makeover at a Paris salon, and maybe because it was the most Cassandra DeVries had ever spent on her appearance in single sitting, she'd allowed the stylist to persuade her that a "trim" was in order.

In Cassandra's view, what she'd ended up with was less a "trim" than a "shear," and now her hair barely reached the nape of her neck in the back. When she'd first seen the results in a mirror, she'd thought it made her look too severe, but the stylist had assured her it made her look "professional" instead.

Velez cleared her throat. "When I said they wanted to see the Directors, I meant to say they wanted to see all of the Directors, and that they wanted to see them right now."

"I'll need to head back to the suite and get changed."

"Now, Doctor DeVries."

"Anita, I can't be expected to speak to—"

"If it makes you feel better, Doctor, Mister Sato was located in the sauna, and Mister Sexton on the fourteenth hole."

She swore softly to herself, picking up her sarong and wrapping it quickly around her hips. This changed things. If the Board was growing insistent, it could only mean that they *had* made their decision. In which case, Cassandra was keeping them waiting, and that certainly wasn't a wise thing to do.

"Hello," she muttered to herself, knotting the sarong in place at her hip. "I'm Doctor DeVries of DataFlow, and I'd like to be dataDyne's next CEO."

"If that's the case," Velez said. "You'd better get a move on."

dataDyne
Your life, our hands

For Immediate Release to dataDyne shareholders:

dataDyne to Name New Chief Executive Officer

With the announcement that CEO Zhang Li is retiring from both public and professional life, the dataDyne Board of Directors has embarked on an aggressive search for a new Chief Executive to guide the corporation and its holdings to a bold new future that will at once honor and augment the legacy created by the corporation's esteemed founder. In accordance with the philosophy pioneered by CEO Zhang Li, and in the belief that dataDyne continues to employ only the best and the brightest in all of its holdings, the Board is focusing its search within, rather than without.

At this time, five candidates are in consideration for the position; all five candidates are supremely qualified in their own right, each of them a luminary in his or her respective field, and a Director of one of dataDyne's most profitable and innovative subsidiaries.

In order to allay shareholder apprehension during this exciting time in dataDyne's corporate life, brief biographical information on the five candidates follows:

Cassandra V. DeVries, Ph.D.:
Chief Executive Officer of DataFlow for the past three years, Dr. DeVries has overseen explosive growth and a 74% increase in market share during her tenure. A world-renowned expert in software design and application, Dr. DeVries is the creator of AirFlow.Net, a DataFlow proprietary software used to coordinate and manage anti-gravity air traffic in cities all around the globe, which, since its introduction to the market, has been directly responsible for a 98.7% decrease in null-grav vehicular accidents.

Dr. DeVries holds degrees from King's College at Cambridge University, MIT, and the University of Cambridge, as well as an honorary doctorate from Harvard University.

She is thirty-seven years old, single, in excellent health, and resides in Paris, near her offices at DataFlow's corporate headquarters.

Friedrich R. Murray, M.D., Ph.D.:
The Nobel Prize–winning CEO of pharmaDyne for almost four years, Dr. Murray is world-renowned for his discovery of the influenza A subtype

H22N17 vaccine that stopped the spread of the 2016 "superflu" outbreak. A pioneer in the field of elective lifestyle-enhancement surgeries and performance-enhancing medications, Dr. Murray has overseen the introduction to the market of *Cognitia, Endexcite,* and *Perpet D,* amongst others.

Dr. Murray holds degrees from Stanford University, the Johns Hopkins University, and McGill University, as well as multiple honorary degrees.

He is fifty-six years old, a widower, in excellent health, and resides in Vancouver, British Columbia, near pharmaDyne's corporate headquarters. He has one son, Laurent, age twenty.

Takahata Sato:

Mr. Sato is a public-relations and marketing specialist, who served as the Director of Media Relations for dataDyne from 2012–2016, until spearheading the creation of dataDyne's ServAuto Robotics division in 2017. Mr. Sato—who has long-standing ties to the robotics research and development community through his alma mater, Japan's Wasada University—introduced the lifeHelp 1.0 line of personal domestic automata, which continues to generate an estimated five billion dollars annually, and currently controls 41% of the global personal automation market. In addition, ServAuto Robotics has launched a program in conjunction with dataDyne R&D/Aerospace to develop unmanned robotic drone aircraft for military and law enforcement use.

Mr. Sato holds an MBA from Wasada University's Graduate School of Asia-Pacific Studies.

He is forty years old, single, in excellent health, and resides in Tokyo.

Paul H. Sexton:

Mr. Sexton is the CEO of Royce-Chamberlain/Bowman motors, dataDyne's premier automotive manufacturer. He was the Vice President of Business Development for Royce-Chamberlain, and led the initiative to merge with Bowman Motors Group in 2016. Under his leadership, R-C/Bowman has captured a staggering 79% of the personal air vehicle market, and has launched an aggressive program to develop null-grav vehicles for use by municipal emergency services.

Mr. Sexton is a graduate of the Georgia Institute of Technology, with a Masters of Science in Mechanical Engineering, as well as several honorary degrees in automotive design, and is the Director of Personal Mobility Studies at Detroit's Carson Center for Futurist Transportation and Modeling.

Mr. Sexton is forty-nine years old. He resides in Detroit with his wife, Eileen, and two sons, Christopher, seventeen, and Thomas, nineteen.

Amanda L. Waterberg:
The CEO of Patmos Casualty and Liability/Global, Ms. Waterberg has overseen dataDyne's most profitable subsidiary for the past eight and a half years. It was Ms. Waterberg who developed the first dataDyne "We Care" Clinics as an alternative to hospital treatment, and who successfully lobbied for mandatory comprehensive genetic screening of insurance applicants. Since her appointment as CEO, Patmos Casualty and Liability/Global has decreased claimant awards 64%, while continuing to dominate the life, property, and medical insurance fields.

Ms. Waterberg was educated at Basel University, Switzerland, where she earned her MBA.

She is fifty-four years old, married, in good health, and resides in Los Angeles. She has two children, a son, Aleks, twenty-seven, employed by R-C/Bowman Motors (Europe), and a daughter, Dina, twenty-four.

The Board of Directors is delighted to introduce these candidates to dataDyne's shareholders. Each of them embodies and illuminates the qualities and skills that have made us the world leader in value-added services.

CHAPTER 5

Carrington Institute—
London, England
September 27th, 2020

Jo fought herself awake, clawing free from the nightmare with force of will alone. She opened her eyes, saw the dead gray threads of another overcast dawn spreading across the ceiling. Her heart was still wild in her chest, and she heard her breathing, rapid and shallow. She tried to move her right arm, to pull herself free from her twisted sheets, but the arm didn't respond, and Jo thought then that it hadn't been the nightmare, that it was happening again, that it was all horribly real, and she fought the immediate urge to sob, to cry for help.

With effort, Jo twisted onto her side, and almost instantly she felt the pins and needles rushing into her arm, the circulation returning—and that explained it, then. She'd fallen asleep on the limb, and in turn the limb had fallen asleep. The nightmare, for the time being at least, remained just a nightmare, and as the blood ran back into her arm and the pins and needles grew more painful, she closed her eyes and relished the sensation.

After a couple of minutes she tried unwrapping herself again, and this time managed it with ease. She swung her bare legs off the bed, feeling the hardwood floor radiating its chill through the rug and up into her feet. She relished that, too, the simple fact that she could feel it, that she could feel anything. She bent forward, stretching, running her hands over her calves, to her knees, then straightened, exhaling, finally relaxing.

The problem with the nightmare was that it wasn't one, not really. It was born of memory, and while Joanna Dark's conscious mind could barely recall the trauma, it still lived deep in her subconscious, eager to come out at night. The subconscious made it vivid, confused fact with fiction, took old fears and made them fresh again.

When she tried, and she didn't often, because it wasn't a pleasant memory, she could recall bits and pieces. Not more than three years old, flat on her back and wrapped in a brace that held her immobile, the shrieking pain that made her sob as life came back into her limbs. Days and days and weeks and months when she couldn't move, when others moved her, nurses and doctors and her father, speaking to the toddler with the broken back, telling her to be patient, that she was getting better, slowly but surely.

For most, a severed spinal column was the result of an accident, some external trauma. For Joanna Dark, it had been her natural state, the way she had entered the world. There had never been any explanation for the condition, no satisfactory reason offered other than a genetic predisposition. Some babies are breach births, some come out with the umbilical wrapped around their neck. Jo had entered the world paralyzed.

It had taken years of treatments, surgeries, and therapies, some experimental, some not, before she'd completely healed. Jo could still recall the pain of it all, and the shame. Crawling while children ran past. Needing help each and every time she wanted to dress, to eat, to bathe. She'd been five before she had mastered walking on her own.

In her nightmare, her spine was again split in two, but in her nightmare, she wasn't two or four or five. She was twenty, and it was now, and she was helpless once again.

Jo reached for the clock on the nightstand, saw that it was reading seven minutes to six in the morning. She got up, stretched again, then turned back to make the bed, laying the sheets down smooth and tight, folding the top of the blanket back one hand's width, the way her father had taught her.

"Make the bed as soon as you're done with it," he'd told her more than once. "That's a habit. You don't, you'll have to do it later, and that, Jo, is a chore."

In fact, she didn't need to make it at all, as Carrington had not one, but two maids who worked in the manor house. But even if she was a guest in the old man's home, Jo didn't want anyone coming into her room, not without her knowledge or permission. So she made the bed herself.

She dressed quickly in sweats, headed out of her room and down the empty hall. The house was quiet, still asleep. Once outside and in the chill of the gray morning, she breathed deeply air that tasted of mown grass and dew. Perhaps one hundred meters away, Jo could see the perimeter wall and the main gate, make out the tiny figures of Carrington Institute Security as they went about their rounds.

She began her run toward the gymnasium, following the flower path as it curved around the manor house and down the slope to the lake. She went slowly at first, giving her body time to ease itself the rest of the way awake, enjoying the freedom to move. She let her mind wander, thinking back to her nightmare, understanding the significance of it. It wasn't just a fear of being helpless, she knew. It was the fear of being alone.

An honest fear, at least, Jo thought.

Over six months as a guest in Daniel Carrington's home, over six months with all but unrestricted access to the grounds and the Institute, and if she'd exchanged more than two dozen words with anyone other than Carrington himself, she'd have been surprised. Of the twenty or so Institute employees she'd seen, she'd spoken to almost none of them, Jonathan Steinberg being the sole exception. Even those conversations had been brief, Steinberg always appearing preoccupied with one problem or another.

She'd actually begun to wonder if the problem wasn't her, but rather all of them. The few times she'd made an effort to start conversations, to introduce herself, had been dismal failures. She'd spent three days trying to cultivate some sort of rapport with the Armorer, a crusty old former Royal Marine named Potts, to no avail. He'd been courteous and helpful and more than willing to supervise Jo's range time, but that was all.

Jo finished her second lap of the lake, found the narrow trail that led up toward the Institute buildings, running faster now. And that was another thing, the whole Carrington Institute. She wasn't entirely certain what it was Carrington instituted there.

She'd idly skimmed some of the brochures littering a side office, and seen the "company line"—which favored phrases like *global think tank, futurist technology incubation, cutting edge scientific research,* and other flowery buzzwords—but there was far more going on under Carrington's roof than met the eye. One need look no further than his security measures to see that.

She knew he maintained and trained his own private paramilitary forces, she'd seen action with them, after all. They were good, too, military-grade, special-forces good.

Most of the Institute buildings were devoted to research, it seemed. Labs and workshops and machine shops, with the odd conference room or office wedged in between them. The vast majority of the labs and workshops seemed to be empty, in fact. A whole floor of the Institute's main building, the floor below Carrington's offices, appeared devoted to communications, and was apparently staffed twenty-four hours a day. She'd seen Steinberg running to and from there on multiple occasions, along with another man she'd heard called Grimshaw. That had been an odd pairing. Steinberg, in his late twenties, tall, fit, and handsome, was as military as close-order drill. Grimshaw, on the other hand, was short, overweight, with long hair and an ill-fitting suit that spoke to dubious taste, if not outright color-blindness.

She'd reached the gymnasium. Jo put her left eye against the retinal scanner, then put her left thumb in the reader. The locks snapped back and the lights came on as she stepped inside. Sometimes, she'd find Steinberg here, finishing his own workout, or other times the motor pool supervisor, another young American like Steinberg, named Calvin Rogers. That was it. The gymnasium was equipped to train half a dozen football teams at once, and yet Jo had never seen it used by more than two people at the same time.

She set about her workout, moving metal with muscle, frowning. She was supposed to meet Carrington for breakfast in his office at nine, the fifth of such shared meals since the day he'd disconnected her from the DeathMatch VR bender Jo had undertaken. Thus far, the breakfasts had mostly been an exercise in patience, Jo listening politely as Carrington went on and on about whatever topic seemed to suit him at the moment. "Those bastards at dataDyne" seemed to top the list, and while Jo didn't trust Daniel Carrington and wasn't even sure if she much liked the man, she certainly couldn't fault him on his choice of enemies.

Well, whatever he wants to talk about this morning, Jo thought, *I'm going to get a few answers of my own.*

One way or another, things were going to have to change. She couldn't stay here for the rest of her life, hiding from the world on the Institute grounds, eating Carrington's food and sleeping in his home. Her father had been dead for six months, almost, and it was time for Jo to move on, to get back to the business of living.

Never mind that she had no idea where she would go.

Showered, dressed, and ready for breakfast, Jo made her way to the top floor of the Institute main building, and stepped into Daniel Carrington's outer office. It was seven minutes to nine, and she was early, but Jo had been early for the five previous breakfasts as well, and thought that it at least made her consistent.

Emily Partridge, Daniel's personal assistant, sat behind her desk in the outer office, working diligently at her terminal. Like the majority of Carrington's staff, she didn't seem to be much older than Jo, perhaps only twenty-two or twenty-three. But those years seemed to make all the difference, and each time Jo saw the other woman she marveled at her maturity, at her precision and politeness. Far more than anything Daniel Carrington had said to her, Emily Partridge made Jo feel like she was still trapped in her teens.

Emily looked up, smiling primly and moving a hand to her ear, tucking back a stray blond hair. "Good morning, Joanna."

Jo inclined her head toward the hallway that ran to Carrington's office. "He's expecting me."

"Go right ahead, then." Emily Partridge turned her attention back to her work.

Jo moved to the second door, and through it into the long hallway that led to Carrington's office. The corridor was long and heavily carpeted in a dusky blue, the walls painted taupe, with pieces of art hung at regular intervals. There were paintings of sailing ships and photographs of rocket launches, and it was only today that Joanna finally understood the theme of the informal gallery. Carrington had decorated the hall with images of exploration and discovery.

She was passing the glass-walled conference room at the end of the hallway and was just about to reach Carrington's door when she heard Jonathan Steinberg's voice from within. The door was almost, but not entirely, closed, and she would have simply knocked and continued through, but then she heard not just Steinberg's voice, but what he was saying.

"They're going to kill him, Daniel."

Jo stopped, listening for Carrington's response. She heard the inflection of his brogue, but couldn't make out his words. She shifted her weight, stepping forward, bending her ear to the gap between door and frame. She caught a glimpse of Steinberg, his blue jeans and black shirt, as he moved past.

"Because we owe him!" he was saying. "Because I brought him in, he was one of our first, and because he's been good to us! We can't just leave him there!"

"He knew the risks from the start, Jon." Carrington's voice was coming from the left, out of sight, but moving closer. "All of the agents do."

Jo watched Steinberg turn to face Carrington, out of sight, giving her a view of him in profile. He was scowling, looking down at the carpet, visibly upset, though Jo couldn't tell how much was anger and how much was frustration. After a moment he lifted his head, as if deciding to try a new tack.

"He found something," Steinberg said. "Something he thought important enough to send in a panic burst before they grabbed him. I've got reports saying he was pursued halfway through the Pacific Centre mall, but he wasn't trying to make a break for it. He sacrificed his escape to get us this information."

"Information that has little value, as far as I can see." Carrington came into view, leaning heavily on his walking stick. He was dressed in his traditional Harris Tweed, his suit coat off, leaving his vest buttoned tightly over his jutting middle. He put a hand on Steinberg's shoulder.

"He's never let us down before."

"Grimshaw was working on the transmission all night, Jon. Most of it's garbled beyond his ability to reconstruct, and what isn't is so heavily encrypted he thinks it'll take him at least another two days before he can decode the data."

"Which should tell you something about its value."

"I understand its *potential* value," Carrington said gently. "But you're asking me to commit Institute resources and personnel for an operation that could precipitate an all-out war with dataDyne."

"That's a risk each and every time we go against them, it's never stopped you before. We know where he is, we know what they're going to do to him, Daniel! Give me a dropship, twelve men, we hit pharmaDyne Vancouver, we'll be in and out before CORPSEC knows we were ever there."

Carrington stiffened, cursing as he spun away on his walking stick. "Where's your head, Jonathan? That's a fantasy, and you know it."

"They won't expect—"

Carrington spun back, visibly angered. "Of course

they will! Or perhaps you didn't pay attention to this morning's briefing? Perhaps you missed the little story about how the dataDyne Board of Directors has finally acknowledged Zhang Li's absence, how they've begun their hunt for a new CEO!"

Steinberg moved forward, more excited. "That's perfect, it means they're vulnerable, we can—"

"It means no such thing!" Even from her vantage point, watching through the gap, Jo could see Carrington's cheeks coloring with anger. He was all but shouting, now. "It means they're even more paranoid than ever! It means they know they're vulnerable, that they'll be expecting an assault, if not us trying to rescue our captured agent, then from a competing hypercorp looking to increase its holdings! The answer is no, Jon, I won't risk it, not for one man!"

"Six men, then, one dropship," Steinberg said, quieter. "We can grab DeVries—"

"No!"

"—all right, Sexton then, we've had surveillance on that asshole for five months, now—"

"I said no!"

"—we snatch him, button him up someplace secure, then offer to do a swap, Able for Sexton—"

This time, Carrington did shout. "I said no!"

Steinberg fell silent, defeated, Carrington still glaring at him. Jo felt an ache of sympathy for the man. She liked Steinberg, liked the way he handled himself, liked the way he had treated her when they'd first met. He'd refused to coddle her, demanded she prove her own worth, and when she had done so, he'd been gracious enough to acknowledge it.

Of course, Steinberg was being as much of a fool about the situation as Carrington was. Even if Jo didn't fully understand everything about what they were arguing about, she'd heard enough to grasp the broad strokes.

Jo pushed open the door, and both men turned sharply in her direction, surprised at her presence.

"Joanna—" Carrington started.

"You're both bloody idiots," Jo told them.

Then she told them what to do about it.

CHAPTER 6

Carrington Institute—London, England
September 27th, 2020

"Let's hear it again," Steinberg said, rubbing his eyes and wishing the headache would just pack up and leave already.

"We're wasting time."

"I want to hear it again, Jo."

Joanna Dark, sitting opposite him, fixed him with those amazing blue eyes of hers, clearly annoyed. Steinberg waited, then broke the stare, and not because he was conceding the contest of wills.

It's those eyes, he thought. *You can get lost in those eyes.*

Then he thought, *Jesus Christ, Jon, she's a kid.*

He reached for the mug of coffee resting on the briefing room's map table, tasted it, and found it cold. He drained it anyway, then said, "Let's hear it again."

"I can do it standing on one hand. Should I do it standing on one hand?"

"Jo—"

"No, really, watch," Jo said, and she tumbled out of the chair and in one move turned into a handstand. It took her half a second to adjust her balance, and then she pulled her right hand out, extending it to her side, parallel to the ground. Upside down, she grinned at him. "See?"

"Now you're wasting time."

"I'm making a point," she said mildly. "My name is Amanda Thiesen, I'm a temp at—"

Steinberg slammed his hand down on the map table. "Dammit, knock it off! This isn't a game, Jo, you could get yourself killed!"

Joanna Dark stared at him again, and again Steinberg broke the gaze.

"Please," he said.

She stayed on her left hand for a second longer, then brought her right back to the floor and folded herself out of the handstand. He tried not to watch her as she did it, found himself doing so, anyway. It was like watching ballet, watching a dancer of perfect precision and control.

There's nothing as sexy as someone who has no idea how sexy they are, he thought.

"My name is Amanda Thiesen," Jo said, returning to her seat at the map table. "I'm a temp at HiVolt Executive, and have been with the company for the past eighteen months. My last three jobs were at Holcroft & Allan, where I did light secretarial work, Ramjet Transport, where I coordinated shipping schedules, and Huntley's World, where I was hired to help take fourth-quarter inventory. I live at 3484 West 15th, on Granville Island, just north of Shaughnessy Park, with my sister, Vicki. Her name's really Victoria, but everyone calls her Vicki."

"Tell me about Holcroft & Allan."

"They're attorneys, copyright and intellectual property, they do work for local businesses. No large clients."

"What's your sister do for a living?"

"She doesn't make a living, she's attending the university."

"Why aren't you living with your parents?"

There was a pause.

"Jo."

"They're dead," she said tightly, then added, more cheerfully, "Like how I did that? The pause there, you see, makes it clear that it's a sensitive subject, that I don't want to talk about it."

"Yes, that's very clever."

"More clever than launching an all-out assault on pharmaDyne Vancouver, I think you'd agree."

Steinberg started to retort, but was cut off by the sound of clapping coming from the entrance of the briefing room. Carrington had entered, his walking stick hooked over his left forearm, and he was smiling broadly as companion to the clapping of his hands. With him was Osgood Potts, a gunmetal briefcase in each hand. As much as Carrington looked amused, Potts did not.

Steinberg was with Potts.

"By George, I think she's got it," Carrington said, lumbering over to them. Steinberg watched as Jo turned in her seat, looking up at him, and for the moment caught her smile of pleasure before she hid it away. It was one of the things Steinberg had noticed early about Joanna Dark; she craved approval.

Carrington, Steinberg knew, had noted it as well.

As if to prove the point, the big man unhooked his walking stick from his arm, planting it in front of him and then leaning on it with both hands, smiling down at Jo. Without looking away from her, he asked Steinberg, "Fully briefed?"

"We're just finishing up," Steinberg said.

"Primary objective?" Carrington asked Jo.

"Location and extraction of Agent Benjamin Able." She turned her head, looking up to meet Carrington's eyes, as if daring him to ask her one she didn't know.

"Means?"

"Covert, nonviolent if possible."

"Window?"

"Tomorrow morning, oh-nine hundred Vancouver local. Window closes eighteen hundred local."

"Egress?"

"Signal to Mister Steinberg for dropship pickup, rapid exfil."

"And if they start shooting at you, Jo, what then?"

"I shoot back."

"That you do," Carrington agreed, then straightened up and gestured to Potts with the end of his walking stick. "You've met the Armorer, I know."

"Indeed I have. Hello, Mister Potts."

Potts grunted, coming forward and laying his two cases side by side on the map table, snapping each of them open in quick succession. As he did so, Carrington turned his attention to Steinberg.

"Jonathan, a moment alone, if you please."

"I'd like to stay for the equipment briefing."

Carrington smiled slightly, in the way that Steinberg had come to recognize over the years as indicating not amusement, but impatience. He did the grandfather act with the best of them, but Steinberg had been around the man long enough to know it for exactly that, an act. He didn't like being contradicted, and he didn't like being disobeyed, no matter how slight the refusal.

"I'm sure the Armorer can handle it," Carrington told him.

"Oh do go ahead," Jo said, and Steinberg wondered if he was hearing mockery in her voice. "We'll be fine on our own. After all, we're wasting nothing but time."

"Haste gets you killed, Dark."

"Thought it made waste."

Steinberg threw up his hands, rose, and followed Carrington out of the briefing room. The last thing he heard before the door slid shut behind them was Potts explaining to Jo that the transmitter would be injected into her neck, and that it might sting a bit.

"Can she do it?"

Steinberg considered, leaning back against the hull of the VTOL dropship. They were in the hangar bay, or the "motor pool," as Carrington insisted upon calling it. Inside the ship, Calvin Rogers was busying himself with preflight checks.

"Can she do it, Jon?" Carrington asked again, more insistently.

"I don't know," he answered finally. "You saw what she did in Africa, you know what she's capable of in combat. She's remarkably skilled, her raw talent is . . . it's almost supernatural. I've seen Special Forces operators with years of training under their belts at work, and even now, fresh as she is, she could give them a run for their money."

"She has remarkable abilities, I agree."

"But she doesn't have experience, Daniel. What she did in Africa, she did it alone, she wasn't trying to protect anyone else. And we don't know what shape Able's going to be in. If he's wounded or doped, it'll slow her down. It could slow her down a lot."

"I understood the objective was to get Agent Able out without the situation turning hot."

"You can con her, don't try to con me," Steinberg said, annoyed. "Jo's a good actress and a pretty face, and if she keeps her wits about her and bats her eyelashes, the infil won't be a problem. But you know as well as I do that as soon as she pops the locks on Able's cell, every alarm in the building's going to go off. And we're sending her in unarmed."

"She'll have the drugspy," Carrington pointed out.

"Which won't do her a damn bit of good in the middle of a firefight."

Carrington scratched at his beard, staring off into the middle distance, lost in his own thoughts for a moment and giving Steinberg a chance to be with his. Steinberg had a bad feeling about the op; he'd had it from the moment Carrington had suggested it late the previous night. It was the same gut-churning doubt he used to get in his Army days, while prowling on search-and-destroy missions in the Northwest Frontier Province between Afghanistan and Pakistan, when he'd been a Ranger and not Daniel Carrington's top operative. The same instinct that said the situation was off, that it was wrong, and that someone's life would be the extracted penalty.

Of course the overt assault was a bad idea. It had never been truly considered. Carrington and Steinberg had both quickly agreed that a covert infil was the only possible means of rescuing Able, though each of them had done so for different reasons. For Steinberg, it was about their obligation to their agent, about winning Able his freedom. For Carrington, it was about information. Whatever Grimshaw had managed to decode from the panic burst had the old man energized. Whatever it was that Able had discovered, Daniel Carrington had liked the taste and wanted more.

It had been Carrington's idea to put the scenario in front of Jo, to see if she'd bite. Steinberg hadn't liked it then, and he'd liked it even less when Jo had overheard their "argument." Not because he didn't trust the plan—though God knew it was as risky as any mission he'd personally undertaken since joining the Institute—but because he disliked the manipulation.

Carrington brought his focus back from wherever he'd been staring, smiled slightly at Steinberg. "You want to call it off?"

Again, Steinberg considered. "No."

"I'm mildly surprised."

"We owe it to Able to try to get him out."

"And I believe Joanna is our best chance of accomplishing that objective."

"I don't understand why you didn't just approach her directly, I don't understand the need to manipulate her like this."

"Manipulation implies that I knew how she'd react," Carrington said. "I didn't. Think of it as my way of taking the measure of the woman."

Steinberg shook his head, annoyed. "If we were talking about Core-Mantis, I'd accept that. But you know how she reacts when she hears the word 'dataDyne.' It was a foregone conclusion."

"So who would you send instead of her?"

"Callie Kincaid," Steinberg said immediately. "She's tasked to the campus in Seattle, she could match the cover for Amanda Thiesen with only minor alterations."

"Callie Kincaid barely passed *your* agent training program, Jon." Carrington paused, his thick eyebrows knitting together for a moment as he surveyed Steinberg. "You've got a thing for our Miss Dark, don't you?"

Steinberg fought the urge to grind his molars. "I have a thing about sending kids into combat."

"She'd knock your teeth in, she heard you calling her a kid."

"She's a kid."

"She's a kid who's seen a lot of combat."

"Not like this. We shouldn't drag her into this."

"She was dragged into this long, long ago, Jon." Carrington paused, frowning at him, then leaned forward, lowering his voice. "We're at war. Never forget that. War knows no innocents."

For the third time that morning, Steinberg started a response, only to stop himself before the words had reached his lips. Past Carrington's shoulder, he could see Jo and Potts entering the hangar bay from the elevators. Jo was now in "costume," wearing a white silk blouse, its high collar concealing the small star-shaped tattoo on her neck, and a long black skirt. A black messenger bag slung across her shoulder completed the disguise. She caught his eyes, flashed him a smile. Beside her, Potts had abandoned his briefcases, carrying only his trademark dour expression firmly in place.

Carrington followed Steinberg's gaze, pivoting to watch their approach. Steinberg took a moment to pound on the hull of the dropship, and Calvin Rogers stuck his head out the portside pilot's door.

"Yes, sir?"

"Get ready for lift off," Steinberg told him.

"Roger, boss. All aboard."

He turned back just as Jo and Potts reached them.

"You're ready?" Carrington asked her.

"I am."

"When you reach Able, I want you to ask him something for me," Carrington said. "Very simple, but I want it to be the first thing you ask him."

She raised an eyebrow, and Steinberg saw the suspicion in her expression, the wariness of Carrington and all he represented to her returning.

"I'll try," Jo said.

"The year of the Rose," Carrington told her. "That's what I want to know. Ask him the year of the Rose."

"Am I supposed to know what that means?"

"No." He put a hand on her shoulder, and Steinberg was certain he saw Jo stiffen slightly. Even if Carrington didn't see it, it was clear he'd felt it as well, and let the touch slip away. "Good luck."

Jo nodded, barely, then looked at Steinberg. "Shall we?"

"Let's do it," he told her.

She climbed into the dropship and Steinberg followed,

stepping up into the main compartment and then turning to slide the door closed. Carrington began to back away, Potts mirroring his movement.

"The year of the Rose, Jo," Carrington called before the door slammed closed. "What was the year of the Rose?"

If he said anything else after that, it was lost in the rising whine of the engines.

CHAPTER 7

**dataDyne low-orbit executive transport, Dragonfly II—
46,000 feet, descending
September 27th, 2020**

Laurent Hayes started crashing just after liftoff, and it ached enough that the irony of the situation entirely escaped him. Here he was, strapped into the acceleration couch for liftoff and a forty-six minute flight from Hawaii to Vancouver, and he was coming down harder and faster than the plane itself would. Even if he had been loaded, the irony would still have escaped him. Irony had never been Hayes's strong suit.

So he spent the first eighteen minutes of the flight biting his tongue, feeling waves of prickly heat swarming his body as if he were being eaten alive by fire ants. By the time the transport approached the apex of its parabola, by the time the pilots finally released the locks on the passenger restraints, he was fiending something fierce. Then Hayes heard the click of the restraints unlocking, saw the seat-belt light flicker off, and he was out of his chair, half-floating and half-leaping across the aisle to his father. Outside the porthole, the sky was turning from blue to black, and stars were coming into view as the ship skimmed into the upper atmosphere.

Doctor Friedrich Murray glanced up from the PDA in his hand, peering over the top of his glasses at Hayes.

"Yes, son?"

Hayes wiped at his mouth with the back of his hand, and even that simple action was excruciating, made him wince. Stubble on his chin bit into his flesh, moisture from his lips seemed to slosh over his skin, each sensation exaggerated. Hayes stole an apprehensive glance past his father, down the aisle, thankful that most of the seats on the executive transport were empty. The Royce-Chamberlain/Bowman Motors CEO, Paul Sexton, was seated seven rows back, beside his secretary-slash-mistress, and there were two flight attendants working in the galley at the rear of the plane. That was all.

"Need a patch." His mouth was dry, and when he spoke, Hayes's words came out as little more than a whisper.

His father regarded him without a change in expression. "I know."

Hayes reached up and around to the nape of his neck, where the used dermal was stuck to his skin, concealed beneath his long hair. He tore it free, biting his lip to keep from crying out as the patch's adhesive pulled away from his flesh. It felt like he was flaying himself alive, like the patch was the size of a throw rug and not only a centimeter and a half square. He offered the used patch to his father.

Doctor Murray sighed, then set his PDA on the armrest to his left before gingerly taking the used dermal from his son. He folded it precisely in half, then tucked it into an outside coat pocket before reaching into an interior one to produce the thin black case that held the fresh doses. Murray snapped the case open, offering the contents to

Hayes, and Hayes pulled a fresh patch greedily, pressing it between his palms for a moment to activate the adhesive before placing it almost exactly where the previous one had been, at the back of his neck.

The sweetness of the chemical rush sank into his skin, throbbed through Hayes in time with his pulse. His senses dulled, then expanded. He could feel the minute variations in the engine thrum rumbling through the fuselage, could smell the tang of Paul Sexton's last cigar, at least six hours old. He tasted the flavor of metal in the reprocessed air. He closed his eyes and saw the blood flowing through the capillaries in his eyelids.

He pressed his forehead against his father's knee and said, "Thank you."

"You're a good boy, Laurent." He felt his father's hand rest for a moment atop his head.

Hayes nodded, eyes still closed, wrapped in the warmth and comfort of his sated addiction, and thinking that, when people talked about love, this was what they meant.

"Do we know who he was working for?" his father asked him quietly.

"Not yet."

Doctor Murray looked at him, mild surprise on his face. "What are they waiting for? Why haven't they interrogated him yet?"

"They've been questioning him for the last twenty-four hours, Father."

"Then I don't understand. Haven't they dosed him?"

"They've had to wait," Hayes explained. "It took three hits from the Tranq to bring him down."

Murray's expression smoothed into understanding. "Ah, yes, they're contraindicated, Laurent, you see? The sedative used to bring him down and the compounds used in the talking cocktail, they're at odds. They have to wait until the first is entirely out of his system before moving on to the second."

Hayes nodded, not truly understanding, and not much caring that he didn't.

"Of course, they could forgo the drugs altogether and proceed to physically encouraged interrogation."

"They're waiting for me."

"Again, wise." Murray patted Hayes's forearm with paternal pride. "You're better at it than any of them are. And they recovered all the data?"

Hayes hesitated.

"Laurent?" Doctor Murray asked.

"Wu says he managed to make a partial transmission before they brought him down."

He heard Doctor Murray inhale sharply.

"I know," Hayes murmured.

"You said he'd been into my personal files. Are you telling me he sent my personal files to whoever it is he is working for, Laurent? Is that what you are telling me?"

"Wu says it was only a partial transmission, that she shut it down before it could complete—"

"How much is 'partial'?"

"About half."

His father looked away abruptly, clearly displeased, then checked over his shoulder, glancing back to Paul Sexton, still seated beside his mistress. He put his gaze back on Hayes, and the displeasure had turned into anger. With his right hand, he took hold of Hayes by the back of the neck, digging his index finger beneath the edge of the dermal. Hayes grimaced, fought his immediate urge to whimper. He was stronger than his father—with the dermal in place *much* stronger in fact—but he didn't even consider struggling against the hold.

"You and Wu assured me that you'd stop the spy in

time. That there was no danger of anything critical being compromised," Doctor Murray hissed. "Imagine my surprise when I learned that not only had he gotten through all your security traps, but he'd also managed to get so deep into the system that he found my personal files as well. And then try and comprehend my anger, Laurent."

"I know, Father."

The grip tightened, the finger beginning to peel the patch from Hayes's skin. The freshly exposed skin felt as if it were turning to liquid, beginning to leak down his neck.

"Do you know what was in those files, Laurent?" Doctor Murray demanded. "Do you?"

"Personal information, letters, those things, please, Father—"

"Rose." The grip tightened further, and Murray forced his son to look into his eyes. "All of the payments, all of them."

Hayes didn't speak, trying to put the apology, the need for forgiveness, into his expression, all of his sorrow and shame at his failure. There was nothing in his father's look even approaching sympathy, and the grip stayed tight on Hayes's neck.

Then he let him go, falling back against his seat once more before craning his head around to check again on Sexton. Hayes put his hand quickly beneath his hair, smoothing the edge of the dermal back into place.

Without looking at him, his father said, "The first thing you will do when we get to Vancouver is begin interrogating this spy. You will find out who he works for, and you will find out who he transmitted the data to."

"Yes, Father."

"I want Zhang Li's chair, Laurent. I want his throne, and right now the biggest single obstacle I face isn't Paul Sexton and his glad-handing of the Board, and it's not Sato and his mincing little political two-step. It's not Waterberg and her profits, and it's not that whore DeVries and her arrogance.

"It's you, my boy, and your incompetence in dealing with this petty, little spy."

Hayes nodded. Pressure was rising behind his eyes, ballooning up out of the shame he could feel welling in his chest.

"I'll make it right, Father," he said. "I'll make him talk, I'll make it right."

Doctor Friedrich Murray, the man who both legally and emotionally could call himself Laurent Hayes's father, didn't bother to look at him. Instead, he simply tapped at his coat where his heart should be, and where the thin black metal case rested in its inside pocket.

"Yes," his father said. "You damn well will."

CHAPTER 8

pharmaDyne Corporate Headquarters—
Comox Street,
Vancouver, British Columbia
September 28th, 2020

Jo stood with a cluster of seven other young men and women, all of them dressed in the best professional attire they could afford, in an impersonal and undecorated conference room. Fluorescent lights flickered above, bouncing off the black table and the ivory walls. All of the temps had been through two security screenings already, once in the lobby and once outside of the Human Resources Division. This, Jo suspected, was the third, and designed to be performed without their noticing—scanners hidden in the ceiling, most likely, and fiber optic cameras peering at them from microscopic pinholes the walls.

Somewhere above—at least, if Steinberg's maps had been correct—in the central security office, members of pharmaDyne CORPSEC were watching them, taking captures of their faces in full and in profile, running them through their database. Weapon and transmission detectors were beaming into the room, through their clothes and their bodies and their backpacks and their purses, searching for telltale signs of impending treachery.

Not one of her fellow temps, at least as far as Jo could tell, even had the first idea it was happening. They all simply waited in uncomfortable silence, and she waited with them, her messenger bag on her shoulder, occasionally shifting her weight from one foot to another in what Jo hoped was an adequate display of nervous anticipation. The bag had been hand-searched twice already, and each time passed inspection without trouble, because there was no trouble within it to be found. The contents were all innocent-looking enough: a copy of the latest issue of some celebrity gossip rag, a compact, a lipstick, a travel pack of tissues, a half-emptied pack of breath mints. There was a PDA, too, and that had warranted a closer inspection during each search, but the PDA was six years old, almost obscenely bulky and under-powered by today's standards. A semi-bruised orange, to serve as a mid-morning snack, rounded out the collection.

One of the doors into the room opened, and a middle-aged black woman entered, wearing a business suit, followed by a younger man, Caucasian, holding a thick stack of papers with a box of pens balanced atop them. The woman took up a position standing at the head of the table, and the man began handing out the papers and pens.

"These are standard Work-For-Hire contracts and Nondisclosure Agreements," the woman said quickly. "You cannot work here without completing these documents. Initial each page, then sign your name—your full name, please—on the last. Include your corporate authorization workforce number. Include your temp service's tax ID number. Include your government personnel ID number. There are five openings today. They will be filled on a first-come, first-served basis, with the best positions obviously given out first."

There was an immediate flurry of activity as all of the temps raced to follow the woman's directions, more interested in signing their documents than in actually reading them, which Jo understood was precisely the point. In addition to the basic forty-two-page WFH contract and the twenty-nine-page microprinted NDA, there were liability waivers, nonunion affirmation declarations, and a standard worker's compensation abdication agreement. All in all, the stack came to 116 pages.

Jo timed it so she was the second person to deliver her completed contracts. She doubted that the temp positions were assigned first-come, first-serve; she couldn't imagine pharmaDyne putting a temp in accounting, for instance, whose referrals indicated they were weak with numbers.

The young man took her contracts, and the woman consulted the PDA in her hand—much newer and sleeker than Jo's own—then looked at her with a frown. "Thiesen?"

"Yes, ma'am."

"Holcroft & Allan."

"Yes, ma'am."

"You understand legal filing and data entry, then?"

"Yes, I do, ma'am. I'm studying to be a paralegal, you see, and—"

"Good for you, we're short-staffed in Legal, they're on thirty-four. Edmund will give you your pass. Go out the door there, turn right, go to the second bank of elevators—not the first, the second—and head on up. Do not get off at any floor other than your destination. Do you understand?"

"Yes, ma'am!" Jo said eagerly. "Thank you!"

The woman shook her head slightly, as if bewildered by anyone who would be anxious to file legal documents, tapped at her PDA, and turned her attention to the next applicant. The young man handed Jo her temporary ID card, and she headed out the door, made the right, and found the second elevator bank.

She rode up to thirty-four, and six minutes later was seated in front of a terminal in a cramped cubicle, surrounded by towering stacks of legal files that threatened to topple and trap her in bureaucratic hell forever.

At quarter past ten she was given a five-minute break, and Jo used the time to find the ladies' room. She locked herself into a stall, took the provided seat, and reached up behind her right ear to activate the dot-radio Potts had injected beneath her skin before leaving London. She didn't fully understand the technology involved, but as the Armorer had explained it, the radio was being inserted without power to keep it from being detected. Once activated, however, it would remain on, with no way for her to govern what was broadcast and what wasn't.

"Everything you say, miss, will transmit," Potts had told her. "So pick your words carefully."

Her words, he'd assured her, needn't be more than a whisper, as the radio sat neatly against her skull, and would thus pick up the vibrations as much as true audio.

"Check, check," Jo whispered. "Ahab, this is Starbuck."

"Ahoy," Jonathan Steinberg said. *"Five by five."*

"Five by five, check," Jo said.

"Where are you?"

"In the loo, if you must know. I'll be in touch, Starbuck out."

"I'll be listening. Ahab out."

pharmaDyne gave its temps forty minutes for lunch, and Jo passed on the offer, explaining to the supervising secretary that she wanted to work through the break. The secretary nodded in understanding and left her alone; Jo saw the look of mild amusement, and she knew what had brought it about. Undoubtedly, the secretary had seen hundreds of hardworking temps before her, each of them eager to make a good impression in the hopes of earning a permanent position.

She gave it almost ten minutes after the supervisor had moved off before stopping long enough to hoist her messenger bag onto the desktop beside the terminal. Throughout the morning, she'd made a concerted effort to identify and locate the surveillance cameras she was certain were watching her. She'd been able to find only two, which meant either that Legal didn't warrant close scrutiny—which she doubted—or that she'd missed several. Assuming the latter as gospel, she proceeded as if everything she was doing was being watched.

Reaching into the messenger bag, Jo quickly flicked on the PDA, then removed the package of chewing gum. She popped a piece in her mouth, dropped the package back in the bag, and left the bag leaning against the side of her monitor. If everything was working the way Potts had assured her it would, the PDA would work as a sort of bridging transmitter, allowing Grimshaw to connect with her pharmaDyne terminal here in Vancouver from the safety of his computer lab back at the Institute in London.

"Ahab," she murmured. "You're alive."

"Connecting," Steinberg said in her ear. *"It'll take a few minutes before Ishmael can bypass the firewall and crack the security logs."*

"How many minutes?"

"A few."

Jo thought Steinberg sounded unnecessarily testy, but resisted the urge to say as much. She worked through the file she'd just opened, pulled another from the stack, repeating the process, and then did it a third and then a fourth time. Finally, her rising impatience became too much to bear.

"Ahab, would you be so kind as to encourage Ishmael to move his ass, please?" Jo asked softly.

"Patience is a virtue, Starbuck—"

"So you've said," she hissed, cutting him off. "But I've seventeen minutes left on this lunch break, which means I've seventeen minutes left to move around freely before someone asks why the hell I'm not at my desk. I presume you can see the benefits of doing this now, rather than at the end of the day, when everyone and their cousin will be stampeding like mad lemmings for the lobby."

There was a pause before Steinberg responded. *"Starbuck, keep further transmissions as concise and limited as possible."*

"Ahab," Jo said, so quietly she could barely hear it herself, "go to hell."

Nothing vibrating in her ear, no retort, no response. For a frightening moment, Jo wondered if Steinberg had cut her off completely, but almost as quickly she dismissed the thought. He wouldn't hang her out to dry, not after his adamant arguments to Carrington about retrieving a lost agent.

"Ishmael's in," Steinberg murmured to her. *"Stand by."*

She took a new file off the stack and opened it, running her eyes quickly over the top sheet, preparing to enter a new sea of useless information. When she looked to her terminal, ready to resume typing, she saw that the image on the screen had altered, that a small black-framed window had opened in the lower right of the monitor.

"Can you see it?"

Jo flicked the mouse to the window, bringing it up to the front while shifting her position in her chair, moving closer to the screen in an attempt to block any surveillance. The tiny window held a diagram—a map—and it took a half second longer for her to realize it was a map of the floor she was currently on, with a tiny white dot marking her position.

"Got it," she said softly.

"Bingo," Steinberg said. *"Tracking is up and running."*

Jo felt a slight rise of relief, and realized that she'd been far more nervous than she'd thought. To cover it, she said, "Wonderful. Now, do you want to keep whispering sweet nothings in my ear, or are we going to do this?"

"Head for the elevators," Steinberg said, as if he hadn't heard her. *"Ishmael's sending you a lift."*

Jo set the open file before her to the side, then raised her hands over her head, stretching, arching back in her chair, as if muscle-sore from the morning's work.

"Very convincing," Steinberg told her.

Jo fought the urge to scowl. "You can see me?"

"Anything they can see, I can see. Get moving, Starbuck."

She got out of her chair, taking a moment to reach into the messenger bag for her orange, and then, as an afterthought, scooping up three of the files. She tucked the files beneath her arm, kept the orange in her hand.

"Nice touch."

"It's important to accessorize."

Jo left her cubicle, heading down the hall toward the elevators, with the direction and determination of a woman who knew where she was supposed to be. She passed a handful of other workers who paid her no mind, and then her supervisor, who was embroiled in a phone call at his desk. He caught her eye, mildly suspicious, and Jo held up the orange in her hand, and the supervisor nodded and immediately lost interest in her.

She caught some luck at the elevators, where she was the only person waiting, and almost immediately a car arrived, its doors sliding open.

"In," Steinberg told her.

She entered the car, whispering, "Floor?"

"Don't worry about it."

The doors slid shut, and immediately the car began to drop so quickly Jo had a moment where she was certain she could feel her stomach trying to reach her chin.

"Peel it," Steinberg said.

"Ahab, I hardly know you."

"The orange, smartass."

Jo bit into the orange, using her teeth to break the skin, tasted the sour bite of the rind. Quickly, she exposed the flesh hidden within, the whole car filling with the rich scent of overripe citrus. She let the skin fall in pieces, until finally enough of the actual fruit was exposed for her to tear it in two, revealing the acorn-sized metal sphere concealed within the hollowed-out center, the darkened lens of the drugspy visible on one side. She freed the sphere, letting the destroyed fruit fall to the floor, then used a fingernail to lift the thin sheet of plastic protecting the "eye." She slipped the drugspy into her pocket.

While she did this, Steinberg continued whispering softly to her, his voice measured and controlled.

"Ishmael estimates thirty seconds until arrival. He's bypassed the locks, you're heading straight down. You're coming out on sub-level five, the elevator opens directly on the first checkpoint, two guards posted, another six to eight making rounds. We're timing arrival so you're dealing with just the two at the checkpoint, they should have no idea you're coming. Ishmael's covering the cameras, don't worry about them. Hit the guards fast and quiet, then use the 'spy to hit the ones making rounds."

Jo murmured that she understood. She slipped out of her shoes. They were low-heeled, black and leather, exactly the kind a temp would be wearing, and absolutely wrong for someone who might have to run and jump and sneak and fight. She felt the floor of the elevator vibrating beneath her feet, felt the cold of the metal seeping into her soles.

"Six seconds," Steinberg told her. *"Five, four . . ."*

Jo positioned herself directly in front of the doors, inhaled sharply through her nose. The smell of the orange was rich and clung to the back of her throat, to the roof of her mouth. She felt her pulse beginning to slow, felt the smooth skin of the shoes in each of her hands, the slight variations in the leather beneath her thumbs.

The world began to dilate.

Steinberg's voice came as if from far away. *". . . two . . . one . . ."*

The elevator stopped and the doors cracked, pulling apart as if reluctant to do so. Jo saw pale gray cinderblock opposite her, a metal light fixture affixed to the wall, the bulb caged behind silver wire. She saw the desk and the two guards working the checkpoint, one man, one woman, and neither much older than Steinberg, she supposed. She saw their uniforms, dataDyne black but with pharmaDyne's gold and gray piping, and she saw them look up from their monitors, where they were watching the cameras, and she saw the surprise in their expressions. Whatever it was that Grimshaw-call-him-Ishmael was doing to the pharmaDyne security systems, he'd rendered them blind for the time being.

The female guard looked up from her console, and Jo stepped forward out of the elevator, smiling. The male guard began to turn in his chair, following his partner's lead. The woman started to open her mouth.

Jo threw her shoes at them.

More precisely, she threw her left shoe at the man, her right one at the woman. She did this at almost precisely the same moment, perhaps the right leading slightly. Each throw was less a sidearm than a vicious snap of the wrist, and each shoe covered the ten feet to target as if it were a dart hurtling for the bull's-eye. The heel of her left shoe struck the male guard just above his left temple, taking him utterly by surprise and sending him half falling, half sliding out of his chair, dazed. The sole of her right shoe hit the female guard in the nose, the heel smacking into the woman's mouth. The female guard brought her hands up, started to cry out, and never managed it.

Jo followed in the wake of her throws, leaping over the security console and landing neatly between the two. She hit the female guard in the face, open-palm, knocking her out of the chair and onto her back, leaving her momentarily stunned, long enough for Jo to shift attention to the man. He was still dazed, just now beginning to realize what had happened, trying to pull himself up over the seat of his chair, straining to reach the PANIC button on the console.

Jo pivoted, brought her right hand down sharply to the back of his neck, and the guard sagged, slumping once more, then toppling off the chair to the floor. Jo twisted back, saw that the female guard hadn't even begun to recover, knelt, and delivered a matching blow to her neck as she had to her partner's.

She stayed crouched, listening, catching her breath.

"Shoes?" Steinberg asked.

"Bite me," Jo told him, then freed the drugspy from her pocket and set it on the floor in front of her. "You go first."

"Follow me," Steinberg said.

Silently, the little sphere rose off the floor, tentatively at first, then higher, as if gaining confidence. Roughly the same size as a golf ball, the drugspy was a remote-controlled surveillance camera, propelled by a hyper-miniaturized version of the same null-grav technology that floated the new generation of air-cars.

During the mission load-out, Armorer Potts had not just shown her the device and how to operate it, but had then expounded at some length on the various modifications he'd made to it. Originally developed as a search-and-rescue tool—ideal for locating survivors buried in rubble from a building collapse, for example—Potts had added a close-range tranquilizer/narcotic delivery device and a sophisticated targeting system. The drugspy carried no more than a half-dozen shots, but each shot carried a sedative, "strong enough to drop a rhino," as Potts had said.

Normally, the drugspy was controlled by the agent who deployed it, something that required the agent's full attention, a risky proposition at the best of times. Since Jo had been inserted into pharmaDyne "light," Potts had not been able to fit her with the requisite control systems.

Instead, the drugspy was being controlled by Steinberg, safe in the main compartment of the dropship as Calvin Rogers hovered it in its stand-off position. The plus side of this was that Jo could stay focused on her environment. The minus was that Steinberg couldn't, and so could no longer provide the overwatch he'd previously supplied.

The little sphere bobbled, hovering for a moment before turning slowly in a full circle. When the lens focused on her for a moment, Jo stuck her tongue out at it.

"Maybe later," Steinberg said. *"Arm yourself."*

Jo hesitated, then nodded, checking the guards. Each of them carried a Global Armaments MagSec pistol in a holster on the thigh, with quickdraw packs for their spare magazines on their belts. Jo put the spares in her pockets and took the pistols in each hand. Beneath the security console, in a squat rack, sat two CMP 150 submachine guns, and a dataDyne-issue assault shotgun. She ignored them. dataDyne's weapons all pursued the same philosophy: opting for a greater volume of firepower in lieu of accuracy. The MagSecs were no exception, but she had faith in her ability to control them.

The fact was, despite hours that turned into days training on HoloMan VR or playing DeathMatch, Jo didn't relish killing, didn't even enjoy it. She had trained to do it because it was one of the skills her father had required for his work, and thus, one of the skills she had wanted to master to join him. Tools of the trade, Jack Dark had called them.

Until the last year, in fact, it had only ever been practice. Since that time, however, Jo had shed a lot of blood, and once or twice, had been happy to do it. That wasn't a feeling she had wanted to examine too closely.

So she took the MagSecs, telling herself she would use them only as a last resort.

The drugspy finished its revolution, then rose higher, above the lip of the security console, tilting slightly as it began floating forward. Jo moved to follow, soundless on her stockinged feet, one pistol in each hand. The cement floor was cold and she could smell antiseptic and bleach in the air, and it made her think of hospitals and other unpleasant places; unbidden, she found herself remembering her nightmare.

Focus, Jo, she told herself. *He's no longer watching your back. It's up to you, now.*

They made their way forward, to the ballistic glass door that marked the exit from the checkpoint. The hallway continued for another two and a half meters beyond the door, then ended at a junction, corridors running left and right. Jo pushed open the door enough to allow the drugspy to float through.

"Wait here," Steinberg told her. *"I'll clear the corridor."*

"Confirmed."

Jo watched the little metal orb glide to the intersection, then it banked left and headed out of sight. She listened, still keeping the door slightly ajar, using the side of her bare right foot to prevent it from closing, counting off seconds in her head.

She'd reached seven hippopotami when she heard the unmistakable sounds of first one body hitting the floor, then a second.

"Two down," Steinberg said. *"To the intersection, left, continue ten meters, second right."*

"Acknowledged."

Jo edged the door open another few inches, slipped through, padding silently forward. She brought the MagSecs up in each hand and crouched lower, moving forward cautiously. She paused at the intersection, checking both directions before rounding the corner to the left, and found herself in an almost identical hallway to the one she'd just left, but with the addition of doors spaced semi-regularly along each wall. The doors were metal, unmarked, the kind that would slide open rather than push out on their hinges, and each of them was framed with a heavy rubber seal. The walls were as bare as they had been in the checkpoint, and a string of caged bulbs ran along the ceiling. There had been no attempt to conceal the surveillance cameras down here, either, and she saw two of the opaque black eyes hanging above, heard the thin hum of their motorized drives as they rotated, maintaining their automated vigil on the corridor.

A couple of the doors that she passed had small windows set into them, and Jo resisted the urge to straighten up and peer through them. She didn't have time, and, frankly, she didn't want to know what kinds of work pharmaDyne pursued deep in its bowels. She had a very strong suspicion that she wouldn't like what she might discover.

At the second right she found the bodies of two more guards, one slumped against the wall, the other flat on his back. She paused, dropped to one knee, and set the

MagSec in her left hand on the floor, freeing the hand long enough to check each guard's pulse at the neck. Once she'd confirmed each was still alive, she picked up the pistol again and resumed moving forward.

The drugspy waited in front of another sliding door, this one blocking their progress, facing her. Jo caught a fragment of herself reflected in the tiny lens, and realized that Steinberg had seen her check the bodies.

If he thinks that makes me soft, screw him, she thought.

"Well?" she whispered.

"This leads to the cells," Steinberg said. *"Or, according to Ishmael, what pharmaDyne refers to as its 'Discreet Clinical Trial Sector.' It's locked and I can't bypass it. Wait here until he cracks the door, then go through. We don't know which room the White Whale's in, you'll have to check them all."*

"You're not staying with me?" She was surprised to feel a tingle of nerves spreading out in her stomach at the thought of moving on alone. She was mildly alarmed to realize it was the first true nervousness she'd experienced since they'd begun the operation.

"I'm eating the power on this thing pretty fast, Starbuck. Be a better use of the resource if I double back, try to neutralize any other security I encounter."

Jo couldn't find a flaw in the logic, and after a second of trying, nodded once, slightly.

"I'm still in your ear, I'll hear it if things go sour, don't worry."

Jo thought about asking him what, exactly, that would sound like, but thought better of it. Instead, she simply nodded again.

The drugspy bobbed in the air for a moment, then rose to her eye level and stabilized, hovering on its tiny pocket of nullified gravity. Jo expected Steinberg to add something, but he remained silent. The sphere canted forward, moved past her with a gentle whisper. As it passed her on the left, Jo felt a tingle caressing her hand and arm, the distortion of Newtonian physics. The sensation passed, and the drugspy disappeared around the corner behind her.

Jo waited, again counting hippopotami. She'd reached forty-two of the beasts when the door in front of her hissed, parting down its center and withdrawing in two halves to either side of the corridor, revealing a second security checkpoint some four meters away. Seated at the console, where he'd been monitoring the cameras, was another guard.

This one was faster than the others, and that surprised Jo, and he seemed better trained, as well. Instead of shrieking or demanding an explanation, instead of reaching for a weapon, he immediately twisted in his chair, stabbing out with his left hand for the console and the alarm.

Jo leveled the MagSec in her right, feeling the heavy barrel rising, sluggish, in her hand. The pistol had a built-in scope, thumb activated, but there had been no opportunity to zero it, and it wouldn't do her any good here and now if she had. She fired, heard the weapon's distinctive *click-hiss-bang* as it spat out a single charged round. The panel beneath the guard's left hand shattered in a shower of sparks and metal shards.

The guard tumbled from his seat, away from Jo, trying to free his own pistol from the holster on his thigh. She sprinted forward, hurdling the console. Once again the world had dilated, once again everything seemed to slow, and Jo had a moment in which she saw where her kick would land, knew it would work, and wondered if removing her shoes had, in fact, been a stupid idea.

She caught him in the face with her right heel, felt the smack of impact as she snapped his head back into the floor. She landed, spun, swinging the pistol in her left hand, preparing to use the overweighted barrel as a club, then arrested the move, seeing no need. If it hadn't been her kick that had put the man down, it had been the secondary impact, when the back of the guard's head had smashed into the concrete floor.

She didn't see any blood, but knew enough to know that meant nothing.

"Starbuck?"

"Hostile down," Jo whispered.

"Status?"

"I'm fine." She looked up from the motionless guard, running her eyes over the console. Sparks were dripping from the shattered alarm panel. Apparently, her shot had also blown out the camera reception, because the eight tiny screens arrayed across the console were alternately dark or feeding her static. "Camera's down, not sure which room he's in."

"You better get moving," Steinberg said. *"Ishmael reports the checkpoint fault has registered in the security command post. They're trying to raise the guards, and when the guards don't answer—"*

"Understood. Starbuck out."

Jo looked down the long corridor, gray and cold and silent, and again felt the chill from the floor eating into her feet. More doors were spaced irregularly along both sides of the hallway, more of the sliding variety, and she could see additional surveillance cameras mounted on the ceiling, quietly swiveling to and fro in their arcs. She turned her attention back to the sparking console, found the controls for the doors, and hit the release, praying that her shot hadn't fused the cell doors closed.

Behind her, in a diminishing echo, she heard the sound of the door seals breaking, the hiss of pneumatics. She thought for an instant that perhaps she'd just done a very stupid thing, that there was no telling what had been locked away in the cells, then thought it was too late to worry about things like that.

Jo began jogging along the cellblock, slowing only as she passed each door, looking into the cells on her left and her right. The rooms, if they could be called that, were uniformly small, a bizarre blend of prison and hospital. There were no beds, but exam tables, instead. Most were without any sort of plumbing, but two had toilets and sinks. In three of the cells, she saw streaks of black and brown along the floors, walls, and ceilings, and hoped it wasn't dried blood. The smell of urine and fecal matter was particularly strong from those rooms.

Jo heard a sound, almost plaintive, almost animal. She slowed, heard it again, located it as coming from the second to last cell. She approached cautiously, feeling her heartbeat beginning to quicken, and at last found Benjamin Able.

The cell was like many of the others, but leaned further toward the exam-room motif than away from it. A wheeled cart rested against one wall, three of its drawers open, an equipment stand beside it, a white towel covering its surface. On the towel, Jo saw a selection of surgical tools, scalpels and forceps and clamps. Puddles of dark brown stained the towel beneath each item.

Jo heard herself gasp in surprise. She didn't know what she had expected, but she knew she hadn't expected this.

Able lay flat on his back on the exam table, his arms and legs strapped to extensions that swung out from the surface, holding him almost spread-eagle. He was naked, and the bruises and swelling on his face made him almost unrecognizable from the file photo Steinberg had shown Jo during her briefing. An IV ran to his right arm, and sensor pads had been affixed to his chest and temples, apparently feeding biological data to the monitor that hung suspended over his head. Thin copper wires had been taped in a lattice across his torso and groin, and Jo could see the lines of burnt and charred skin beneath them.

"Ahab," Jo murmured. "I've found the White Whale."

Able started at the sound of her voice, then gasped in pain, falling back against the bed. He craned his neck around, and she saw the fear in his eyes, and the pain. Steinberg was saying something to her, trying to remind her of something, but she wasn't listening to him anymore.

Jo tucked the pistols into the back of her skirt, began working at the restraints holding Able's arms.

"I'm a friend," she told him gently. "I'm getting you out of here."

For a moment, Benjamin Able's expression was one of incomprehension, his mind still ruled by his fear and his pain. Then the understanding reached him, and he sagged against his restraints. Jo gave him another reassuring smile, then had to look away, as Benjamin Able started to cry.

CHAPTER 9

pharmaDyne Corporate Headquarters—
Comox Street,
Vancouver, British Columbia
September 28th, 2020

The first thing Hayes did that morning, even before he rolled out of bed, was to patch up with the dermal his father had left out for him on the nightstand the night before. It wasn't that Hayes needed it, at least not desperately, not at that moment, but the derm was there, and he wanted to start the day off right.

Once he'd fixed, though, Hayes practically sprang from his bed, leaving Kimiko still asleep in the tangle of sheets as he strode to the window that overlooked English Bay. The sensor field responded to his approach, turning the glass translucent once more until he could look out over the water and the mountains and see the sun and feel its warmth against his bare skin. He took it in, feeling powerful, certain, and pure, feeling his own eagerness for the day ahead.

Still in bed, Kimiko whimpered, rolling onto her belly and pulling one of the pillows over her head. The movement tugged the sheets away from her body, leaving her partially exposed to the sunlight, and Hayes grinned at the sight of her nakedness, the memory of her body. He could see the slight impressions his fingers had left on her upper arms.

Hayes headed into the bathroom, started the shower, and only as he stepped under the spray did he realize he was humming. Some people, he knew, didn't enjoy their work. Some people met every day with loathing and resentment, with nothing to look forward to, no sense of accomplishment or pride. But Hayes loved his work.

And on days like today, when a Carrington Institute spy would be begging Hayes to put him out of his misery before nightfall, he couldn't imagine anything better.

His father had already left for work by the time Hayes was dressed and prepared to depart himself. He'd overslept, in part due to a late night with Kimiko, whom he'd been forced to avoid while she worked counter-intelligence. With her operation closed and her target tucked safely away in a holding cell, Hayes had been finally able to indulge himself.

She was still in bed when he checked on her a last time before leaving the mansion. She'd looked sleepily at him from the pillows, kissed him hungrily in greeting, then done it again when Hayes had told her he expected to find her there when he returned.

He took the Bowman Hunter for the drive to work, disengaging the computer control and piloting the vehicle himself. It was Bowman's newest sport model, and Hayes knew the vehicle to be astronomically expensive, but then again, he hadn't had to pay for it, so it didn't bother him. Most of the new-model null-gravity vehicles were built to provide a smooth ride, in an attempt to reassure those still reluctant consumers that flight was now the only safe way to travel. Hayes liked the Hunter, however, because it let him feel the air. Behind the controls of the car, he knew he was flying.

Executive parking was on the rooftop of the pharmaDyne building, and Hayes slotted the Hunter into its bay beside his father's more stately and distinguished R-C Supremacy. When he hopped out, Hayes lay a hand against the starboard flank, feeling for engine heat, and discovered it cold. He frowned, realizing that he was running later than he'd thought, and only then checked his watch. It was twelve minutes to noon.

He checked in with his father first, striding without slowing through the outer office and past the phalanx of secretaries who attended Doctor Murray. At the mahogany doors, Hayes paused, knocked, and entered.

The office was enormous, as befitted the CEO of pharmaDyne, built in a grand circle with a wall of windows behind the desk that afforded a view of Stanley Park to the northwest, and then Black Mountain beyond. Three of the floor-to-ceiling windowpanes doubled as monitors. One displayed up-to-the-second information from the trading floors in New York, Sydney, Tokyo, and London. A second was set to regularly cycle through the major newsfeeds, talking heads spitting out nuggets of the latest news. The third was tied directly to Doctor Murray's own office computer, and currently seemed to be in the process of rendering some complex chemical equation that Hayes could never hope to understand, even if he had wanted to.

Doctor Murray himself stood behind the desk, a porcelain teacup in one hand, its companion saucer held in the other, apparently reviewing the process on the third window. Hayes saw his father shift slightly, catching sight of his son's reflection as he entered the office, and Hayes saw the smile, and knew he had worked himself back into Murray's good graces.

"Carrington, was it?" Doctor Murray said, focusing again on the chemical string that was folding and refolding itself on the window. "I suppose I shouldn't be surprised."

Hayes came closer, skirting the edge of the desk, to join his father. "He claims he hasn't spoken to that old nut in a couple of years."

"And you believe him?"

"No." Hayes grinned. "I'll get the truth before dinner, though."

His father took a final sip from his cup, then set cup and saucer down on the edge of his desk. "Did this spy, whatever his name is, did he realize what it was he'd found, my boy? Did he understand what it was he'd discovered?"

Hayes shook his head, sure of himself. "No, Father. He just knew the data was yours, and that's what made it important."

Doctor Murray met his son's eyes and gazed into them seriously, almost condescendingly. "I want to be sure about this, Laurent."

"I'll double-check, Father. I'd be happy to."

"Please do so."

"Is there anything else?"

Doctor Murray frowned, brought the manicured nails of his right hand to his throat, scratching at it lightly as he considered the question. "I've been thinking of our chances, my boy."

"You're the only logical choice to replace Master Li, Father."

"And I agree, but it wouldn't be prudent to explain that to the Board. As soon as you're finished with this Carrington agent, I want you to start looking into the other candidates. Sato doesn't concern me overmuch, he's too unpredictable, and I don't believe the Board will give him more than a cursory consideration. Waterberg has too many skeletons in her closet, as well; the Board certainly knows about that disaster in Iraq, and if they don't, they soon will.

"But Sexton and DeVries, they may prove to be more problematic. Sexton is slippery, and he's greedy, and I'd be surprised if he hasn't already put a few of the Board in his pocket. DeVries, she's an idealist, and the Board may respond to that, the idea of a sweet-faced blonde with stars in her eyes. We should take steps to ensure they do not damage our standing."

"You want me to dig deeper?"

"Quietly, yes. It would be damaging to the parent corporation if we were to lose either of them. And blackmail would give us a handle for the future, to use to keep them both in line once I've replaced Zhang Li."

"I'll get right on it."

"After you're done with the spy, Laurent."

"Of course."

"Good boy," Doctor Murray said, and turned his attention back to the windows, dismissing his son without another word.

Hayes stopped by his office long enough to check his voicemail and messages before proceeding to the security center at the heart of the fortieth floor. He ran through the watch-list with the Duty Sergeant, a former Green Beret in his early forties named Beaumont who barely hid his annoyance at Hayes's tardiness. Hayes didn't much care for the man, and felt that it was reciprocated, but Beaumont did a good job of hiding it, and if nothing else, he knew his business—and more importantly, he knew his place.

There were eleven staff absences logged that day, seven of them personnel using accrued vacation time, two on scheduled sick days. The remaining two had called in that morning with excuses. Doctor Gabriella Zimmerman, a research scientist in Cognitive Pharma, had called in claiming her son was suffering from a burst appendix, and that she was staying with him in the company hospital. The second, Jesse Ekkert, worked in Clinical Selection, responsible for acquiring and vetting test subjects for R&D. He'd called, claiming to suffer from a fever and sore throat. A quick cross-reference showed this was his fourth absence in the last seven weeks.

Hayes ordered verification surveillance on Zimmerman, and told Beaumont to continue the already active surveillance on Ekkert. After his first absence, seven weeks back, Hayes had broken into Ekkert's apartment on the day he'd returned to work, giving it a thorough search while authorizing a comprehensive review of the man's financials. What he'd discovered was that Ekkert was receiving payoffs from Core-Mantis OmniGlobal in return for passing along data about pending trials. Since then, they'd been feeding Ekkert false data to forward to their competitor. Hayes suspected that it was only a matter of time before Ekkert either lost his nerve or disappeared to take a job with Core-Mantis, and he supposed that grabbing the man now would be the smart thing to do, but he didn't, in the hopes that Ekkert would expose other Core-Mantis operatives working in the Vancouver theatre of operations.

"Today's temps," Beaumont told him after they'd finished the personnel review. "Six of them today, all of them cleared."

Hayes clicked through the pictures on the monitors, the headshots and profile angles. A young redhead caught his eye, and he brought her picture up a second time.

"Who's she?"

"Thiesen, Amanda," Beaumont said. "Assigned to Legal for the day."

"Easy on the eyes."

"If you say so, sir."

Hayes lingered over the images for a few seconds longer, then closed the set. "Let the checkpoint in Sub-Five know I'm on my way down."

Beaumont turned, relaying the order to one of the officers on the coms desk, and Hayes left the command post, heading back to his office. He removed his coat and tie, hung them from the rack just inside the door. He didn't need to bring them with him, and what he was planning on doing would only risk getting them dirtied.

He was at the elevator, waiting to ride the car down, when Beaumont radioed him on his subcutaneous.

"Sub-Five is offline," Beaumont reported. *"No response from any of the checkpoints, cameras are reading non-functional."*

"What the hell? What does that mean?"

"It means we've been breached, sir. Someone's screwing with the internals."

Hayes swore. "It's not a system fault?"

"No sir, all the other systems are still in the green."

Hayes swore again, louder. *Son of a bitch,* he thought. *Carrington, you son of a bitch, you've come to steal my prize.*

The elevator arrived, doors swishing apart to reveal a half dozen personnel on their descent from the upper floors. Hayes turned his cursing on them, reaching into the car and grabbing the nearest worker, a middle-aged man, by the necktie, yanking him out of the car.

"Out! Get out of the car!" he roared.

The car emptied.

"Dispatching Alpha and Beta response teams," Beaumont told him. *"They'll meet you there."*

Hayes swiped his ID card through the reader on the elevator panel, jabbed his thumb into the recess that slid open above the top row of buttons. "You get those cameras back!"

"Trying, sir, but—"

"No! No trying, just *get them back!* And lock down the goddamn lobby! Nobody gets in or out of the building!" The elevator lurched, confirming his ID, and began to drop. "It's a bust-out, you understand? There's a CI strike team in our goddamn building, they're trying to free their man!"

There was a momentary pause, and then Beaumont asked, *"How did we miss them?"*

"How the hell should I know? You've been sitting in front of the cameras!" Hayes kicked at the wall of the elevator, issuing a new string of curses. Somehow, a CI strike team had entered the building, had entered *his* building, and the thought of the violation enraged him. Never mind how they had done it, he was sure they had, and he could spit with the fury he was now feeling.

The elevator jerked to a sudden stop, knocking Hayes from his feet, and even with his chemically charged reflexes, he barely managed to protect his head from smacking the side of the car. There was a grinding noise from above, and all of the indicator lights on the elevator panel lit up as one.

"What the hell just happened?"

"Elevator just locked up."

"Unlock it!"

"It can't be a strike team, sir, that's at least six men, we would have—"

"Unlock the fucking elevator!" Hayes screamed.

The lights on the indicator panel began winking on and off, as if mocking him. Hayes spun in a circle, realized there was nowhere for him to go, roared his frustration a second time. There was a maintenance hatch built into the ceiling of the car, but as a matter of security, it had been welded shut. He couldn't remember if that had been his order or Beaumont's.

"Come on, come on!"

"All of the elevators are offline, sir. We're going to try to reset the system. You might want to hold on to something."

Hayes grabbed the railing along the rear of the car, just as all power to the elevators went out. He heard metal groaning, and then the floor dropped out beneath him suddenly, only to jerk to a screeching stop again. The lights flickered back on, the indicator panel coming back to life.

"Try it again," Beaumont told him.

Hayes rammed his card through the reader once more, again jabbed at the scanner with his thumb. The indicator for Sub-Five illuminated, and he felt the car once again resume its descent.

"Alpha should hit the checkpoint right behind you," Beaumont told him.

"They see anyone who isn't one of us, they shoot to kill, understood?"

"I need CEO authorization to issue that order, si—"

"Then stop talking to me and get it!"

Beaumont went mercifully silent, presumably attempting to contact his father. Hayes could only imagine what the response would be, and spared himself a second of blind, addicted panic at the thought of the punishment he would be facing if he couldn't keep the unthinkable from happening. Then he calmed himself. The building was fifty stories tall, and in complete lockdown. It didn't matter if there were six or ten or twelve of Carrington's men here on their little rescue mission.

Not one of them was getting out alive.

CHAPTER 10

pharmaDyne Corporate Headquarters—
Comox Street,
Vancouver, British Columbia
September 28th, 2020

Able tried to get to his feet but his legs wouldn't hold him, and Joanna had to catch him beneath the arms to keep him from falling. With all the care she could muster, she guided him back against the exam table, letting him use its surface for support.

"Are you going to be able to walk?" she asked him.

"I'm damn well going to try." He gave her a weak smile, revealing broken teeth behind chapped and torn lips.

"Hold still for a moment, just get your breath. I'll see if I can find you something to wear."

Able nodded weakly, and Jo was unsure if he was agreeing with her suggestion that he take a moment or with her suggestion that he clothe himself. She had removed the latticework of wires from his skin before helping him to his feet, and the burns around his body seeped interstitial fluid, glistening in the harsh fluorescent lights. She took one of the MagSecs from behind her back, pressed the pistol's handle into the man's hands.

"You know how to shoot one of these?" she asked.

"Not well," Able croaked.

"You don't have to be good, just good enough."

He made a small sound, the beginning of a hoarse laugh, which quickly transformed into an exhalation of pain.

"I'll be right back," she told him, and then, drawing the remaining MagSec, stepped back into the hall.

"You didn't ask him." Steinberg's voice was still low, still measured, but there was a new frustration in it. *"Pequod wants his answer."*

"Then Pequod can bloody well come down here and ask for himself," Jo retorted, trotting back toward the security station. There had been no "Pequod" call sign allocated during the briefing, and she could only assume that it was now Carrington's handle, and that he was actively monitoring the operation from London. "How's our status?"

"Not good. Security just made Ishmael's invasion, they're sending a response team down. He'll try to delay them, but you've got to get moving, and fast."

She reached the downed guard and began stripping off his uniform, going after his jacket first. "Fast is not in this man's vocabulary at the moment, Ahab."

"He better learn it, then—"

Jo moved to the guard's trousers, began yanking them free. When she answered Steinberg, she was speaking quickly, trying to keep the outrage from entering her voice, and failing.

"They *tortured* him, Ahab, do you understand? He's suffering multiple burns, at least two fractured ribs, and I won't hazard a guess as to the breaks in his fingers and toes. They *cut* him, he has small lacerations along the insides of each of his arms and his legs. If he can run, it'll be a miracle. It's a wonder he can stand."

Steinberg fell silent, and Jo took the moment to scoop

up the clothes she'd stripped from the guard, then sprinted back to Able's cell. The man was as she had left him, holding the MagSec in both his hands. She tossed the jacket and trousers so they landed beside him on the exam table.

"Get those on," she said. "Fast as you can."

Then she turned away, stepping back into the hallway, to watch the corridor. She'd half expected Steinberg to come back on the net, to hear his voice again rustling into her skull, but the radio silence continued. In the room behind her, she could hear Able struggling to get into the stolen clothes.

There was a whine from above her, in the corridor, and Jo snapped her head around and up, trying to locate the source as she moved back into the doorway of the cell. The surveillance cameras in the hallway had broken their pattern and were now tracking their arcs more quickly. She knew that whatever Grimshaw had done, pharmaDyne CORPSEC had just undone.

She brought her pistol up in both hands, firing twice, once at each of the cameras. Both shots hit clean, and she heard glass tinkling to the concrete floor, circuitry sizzling in protest. Behind her, Able stumbled, alarmed.

"What was that?" he asked.

"They know we're here, Mister Able," Jo said, as calmly as she could manage. "I must insist we get moving."

"Ready," he told her, and she felt his presence at her elbow, confirming the fact. "Where's the rest of the team?"

"I am the rest of the team, Mister Able." Jo peered around the edge of the doorway, down the hall. The security checkpoint at the mouth of the hall was still clear. "Follow me, please."

She moved as quickly as she dared to without losing Able, knowing that if—or rather, *when*—the shooting started, she would have to provide as much cover for him as she could manage. She still wasn't hearing anything from Steinberg, and that was beginning to worry her. At the checkpoint, she moved her pistol from her right to her left, then reached beneath the console to the weapon rack and grabbed one of the CMP-150s seated there. She thumbed off the safety, and checking once more to see that Able was still limping along behind her, started forward again.

They passed through the sliding double doors, making toward the intersection, and Jo stopped short of the junction, putting her back to the wall. She could hear noises bouncing along the hallways now, the rattle of men and movement and weapons, and then she heard a shout. A burst of automatic-weapons fire exploded, echoing so loudly off the concrete she was unsure of its origin. She heard shouting, but couldn't make out the words.

"That's it for the drugspy," Steinberg said. *"Took two of them before they blew me to bits."*

"How many left?" she asked.

"You don't want to know."

"How many, Ahab?" Jo demanded.

"I count thirteen, and that's just the two teams that they've sent down here already."

"Please tell me that's not the only elevator out from here." When Steinberg didn't immediately respond, she added, "That's *not* the only way out of here."

"We're working on it."

"Work faster," Jo urged.

The sound of the security teams had faded, and she realized they had most likely switched to hand signals, entering a search pattern. She closed her eyes for a second, listening hard, and she could hear the rustling of fabric, the rasp of leather and ballistic mesh jackets, and the harsh clatter of bootfalls. The architecture played with the noises around her, made judging distance difficult, but there was no doubt in her mind that they were coming this way.

She leaned back, turning her head to speak into Able's ear, whispering quickly. "I'm going to step out and lay down covering fire. As soon as I do that, move, quick as you can, to the right. Don't stop until you're around the corner, and don't look back for me."

Able nodded.

Jo drew a breath, steadying herself, willing her body to relax, and then shoved off the wall and out into the intersection, spinning to face the direction she had come from. There were four of them advancing cautiously on her position, all dressed in pharmaDyne colors with body armor and side arms and threat detectors and helmets, silvered shields pulled down over their faces. Each carried an assault rifle—the Dragon, manufactured by dataDyne, naturally—and something about that sang in Jo's mind in the half instant it took for her to take in the whole scene.

Then she started firing, each weapon working a different task. The CMP was about suppression, and she lay down a blanket of fire with her right hand, round after round smashing into the concrete beside the lead guard. He recoiled, panicked and flailing, trying to bring his Dragon to bear, and it was just what Jo had wanted, because it meant he was blocking the rest of his team's cone of fire.

With the MagSec, she began shooting out the lights, pitching the corridor into darkness.

Then the CMP went empty, and Jo twisted around the corner once more, back to the wall again, discarding the submachine gun and catching the MagSec in her newly freed hand. Able was disappearing around the far corner, and she hoped that, if any of the guards had actually seen his run, it would entice them to follow. She ejected the MagSec's spent clip, fished a fresh one from her pocket, and slammed it home, working quickly. Her movements felt fluid, smooth, almost effortless, and she felt questions tickling at the back of her head again, pushed them aside, telling herself there would be time for them later.

With the MagSec reloaded, she quickly shot out the rest of the lights in the corridor, plunging the immediate area into darkness. Faint illumination spilled from the direction Able had run, but that was all now. With her back still against the wall, she sank low, to her haunches, then spun out again, coming up.

The lead had been closing on the intersection cautiously, trying to catch her unawares, his Dragon locked high against his shoulder. Jo came up inside his guard, driving the heavy barrel of the MagSec upwards, beneath the face-shield and into the man's chin. She heard bone crack. Still moving, she swept her left arm over and then around his right, trapping the Dragon against her side. She drove her right knee into the guard's groin, then spun back around the corner a second time, stripping the assault rifle from his grasp. She was out of the line of fire again before the guard hit the ground, groaning in incoherent pain.

Where is it? Where is it? she thought, tucking the MagSec into the front of her skirt, using both hands to search the assault rifle in the near darkness. *Secondary mode, where's the bloody secondary mode—*

Her fingers brushed the stud, recessed at the front of the trigger guard, and she would have sighed with relief if she'd had the time. As it was, she simply pressed the button down as hard as she could, hearing it click into place and feeling the stock shiver slightly as the explosives placed within it were primed. Then she tossed the assault rifle back down the corridor in the direction of the oncoming assault team, and at the same time launched herself the opposite direction, after Able.

She heard shouting, one of them saying that they saw her, that they had a shot, and then there was another cry as the team's threat detectors all began screaming in unison. She heard them trying to retreat, scrambling back the way they had come.

"It's armed! The mine is armed!"

Then the Dragon's proximity mine detonated, the concussion chasing after her down the narrow corridor, shoving her off her feet. Jo turned the fall into a slide, reached out with her free hand and managed enough purchase to swing around the corner, out of sight. She drew her MagSec, wondering if the assault team lead had survived the blast, thinking that she'd tried to throw the mine clear of him, that he'd been prone, that both of those things should have spared him.

Able was gaping at the sight of her.

"What'd you do?"

"Made some noise," she said. "The Dragon's got an explosive built into the stock."

Steinberg's voice returned to her ear. *"Smart girl. You're in an east-west corridor, west is back the way you came. Head east, do it fast, they're going to try to flank you."*

Jo started moving, motioning for Able to follow her. "Make my day, Ahab," she told Steinberg.

"There's a maintenance elevator seventy-three meters from your position, on the left. Ishmael's sending it down to you now."

"I could kiss you."

"You two get out of there, I may hold you to it," Steinberg told her.

Jo actually allowed herself a smile. With Able behind her, they jogged down the hallway. It had become quiet again, only the sound of their bare footfalls and Able's pained breathing. Jo wasn't even hearing the crackle of radio communications, but that didn't mean much; if the assault teams were all on subcutaneous mikes, as she was, there'd be no telltale sound of transmission.

They reached another turn, and Jo motioned for Able to hold up before diving around the corner herself. She came up in a roll, the MagSec at the ready, fully expecting to meet resistance, and genuinely surprised to find no one there to block her progress. She regained her feet, started forward, and Able again fell in behind her.

"Twenty meters," Steinberg told her. *"Should arrive as you get there."*

They raced along the hallway, and Jo heard the hum of the lift as it began to settle on their floor, saw that it was as Steinberg had described, a service elevator rather than one for moving personnel. Jo switched positions with Able, putting him between her and the elevator doors, scanning back the way they had come. She was hearing voices again, and the heavy tread of boots as the flanking team broke into a run, trying to catch them. Behind her, the elevator had arrived, locking into position, and in her periphery, she saw the doors begin to open. Able started forward, and she half turned to follow him.

Then it all went wrong.

Jo heard the metal ring off the floor, the clatter and slide of the grenades as they bounced around the corner. She shouted, twisting to dive through, throwing out her arm to catch Able and pull him down with her, and she'd managed half of the move when the explosions came, one atop the other. In the concrete corridor the sound was enormous, vibrating through her chest, making her teeth sing in her jaw. She knew, abstractly, that the grenades had been an act of desperation, that throwing frags in such an enclosed space guaranteed splash damage in almost every direction, that the shrapnel would bounce and fly until it had either found purchase in flesh or spent itself entirely. There was no intention of recapturing Able, there was no intention of taking Jo alive, and she realized she'd miscalculated, that the men hunting them were now hunting to kill.

Jo landed hard inside the elevator, felt the shock of her fall hard on her shoulder. Nails tore into her legs and one arm, and something ragged and hot slashed her face beneath her left eye. She lost time for an instant, came back to find herself already struggling to her knees, lurching for the controls to shut the elevator doors, assailed by confusion and sudden vertigo. She heard herself shouting for Ahab to get them the hell out, to get them the hell up to the roof. Smoke billowed in the hall from the explosion, and Jo thought she saw movement in the clouds, silhouettes of men in tactical armor, trailing behind the crimson threads of their laser sights.

She still had the MagSec in her hand, was firing it before she'd even thought to do so. One silhouette spun and dropped, a second pitched forward over the first. Answering shots sparked over her head, rounds burying themselves in the elevator wall behind her. She emptied the MagSec, dropping another two before the doors finally slammed shut and the car began to rise with a speed that threatened to empty her stomach.

Steinberg was screaming in her ear, but she wasn't sure she knew who he was, her head still rattled by the explosions. She looked down, saw a half dozen cuts on her legs, the tears in her stockings, and noticed blood dripping onto her blouse. She realized it was coming from her cheek.

Shit, she thought dizzily, still dazed by the concussion. *I've ruined it.*

She'd been lucky, she thought, to come out of that sublevel with a few cuts and bruises and a stained shirt.

Then she saw the pool of blood spreading steadily out toward her, and she realized that Able had not shared her good fortune.

"Starbuck! Starbuck! Status!"

Able lay on his side, his breathing rapid and shallow, a froth of blood and foam beginning to run from his mouth. Jo pulled herself to him, dropping her empty pistol, running her hands along his torso, over his back. At his mid-spine she felt the blood, and when she looked at her hand, it was covered in it.

"It was a good try," Able told her hoarsely.

"No," Jo said. "No, no no no, you're not dying, do you understand me?"

Able opened his mouth to respond, and instead of words, brought forth more foam, more blood.

"Dammit, you stay with me!" she screamed at him.

"Oh my God," Steinberg said quietly.

"Please," she told Able. "You can make it. Please, try."

Able coughed, a spasm that wracked his body as a whole. But his expression didn't change, didn't falter, and Jo realized he was smiling at her with his shattered teeth and ravaged lips. He moved his hand, took hold of one of hers, squeezing it.

"It was a good try," Able said again, and this time, she had to strain to hear him.

Jo just shook her head. It hadn't been, it had been a bad try, she had failed. He was dying, he was dead, and she had failed. She wanted to scream at him, to hit him, to beat him to life, saying that he was wrong.

"Ask him." Steinberg's voice was even softer than before. *"You have to ask him. Right now."*

For a moment, Jo had no idea what Steinberg was saying, and then she remembered, and it made her want to scream. What was the point? She had failed.

"Jo, please," Steinberg said. *"Ask him."*

She shook her head again, already defeated, squeezed Able's hand in return. His breathing had slowed to a shallow, irregular wheeze.

"The year of the Rose, Mister Able," Jo heard herself saying. "What was the year of the Rose?"

Able's eyes closed, and his breathing stopped, and then his eyelids opened again, she thought she saw a realization there, an understanding of something great and profound. His smile grew a fraction.

"2016," Benjamin Able said. "Of course, 2016."

They were his last words.

"Get it together," Steinberg told her.

Jo finished reloading her emptied MagSec, picked up the second pistol from where it lay on the floor by Able's motionless hand.

"We're eighty seconds out. Just stay down, move to the edge of the roof, north side, we'll pick you up there. There's going to be resistance, try to stay clear, you're in no condition for a straight-up fight."

Jo looked at the pistols in her hands, flipped the fire selector on each to three-round-burst. It would eat through ammunition fast, but it would guarantee the kills.

"You're almost clear, Starbuck," Steinberg said. *"Just keep it together."*

Jo got to her feet, feeling the elevator beginning to slow. The cuts on her legs, on her right arm, on her face, all of them were beginning to smolder. She felt that she was smoldering, too, that she was waiting to burst into flames herself.

"I am together," she said.

Then she used the butt of MagSec she was holding in her right hand to mash the subcutaneous transponder behind her ear into her skull. She felt the slight shiver as the tiny device fractured, felt the stab of pain as it splintered her skin.

"They're the ones about to come apart," Jo added, to no one in particular.

The doors opened onto the rooftop parking lot, revealing a beautiful, cloudless day with the smell of ocean and autumn in the air. She counted six men in full tactical gear, all of them armed with Dragons, and then saw a seventh, different from the rest, holding a combat knife in one hand, a Tranq-7 in the other. Unlike the others, he was dressed in an exquisitely tailored business suit, but missing its necktie and jacket, with long dirty blonde hair falling down over his shoulders. In the moment before movement, she wasn't even certain of gender, his look androgynous and almost effete.

Then the moment for movement came, and Jo sprang to life, dropping targets as quickly as she could acquire them, not much caring for life or death, not even her own.

CHAPTER 11

**pharmaDyne Corporate Headquarters—
Comox Street,
Vancouver, British Columbia
September 28th, 2020**

Hayes beat the redhead to the roof by half a minute at the most, just enough time to deploy the Beta response team—or at least, to begin deploying them—before the cargo elevator came to a stop at the rear of the parking lot. He was still grappling with the twin emotions of surprise and humiliation. Surprise that the Carrington strike team had seemed to consist of only one person, and that the person in question had turned out to be the hot little redheaded number he'd been eyeballing only ten minutes or so earlier.

The humiliation came from the fact that this one person, all by herself, had made it this far. From what Hayes could piece together over the radio, apparently she'd turned all of Alpha Response into a squad of fools. Their news that they'd managed to get a grenade or two in was poor consolation, especially when they failed to confirm any kills.

So Hayes had raced to the rooftop, trying to intercept the redheaded hellion who was, thus far, turning a very good day into a very bad one. His intention in intercepting her was simple. He'd kill her, he'd kill the spy she'd come to rescue, and then he'd offer both of their heads to his father. If Beta Response did the deed, he was fine with that; if they failed, he was patched and armed, and more than eager to do the deed himself.

The first thing he noticed when the freight elevator's doors slid apart was that the grenades had, it seemed, done half their job. The spy, the one he'd been interrogating, was motionless on his side on the floor of the car, lying in a puddle of his own blood.

The second thing he noticed was that, while the redhead appeared to have been winged, she was up, armed, and ready.

The third thing he noticed was that she was fast—much faster than he'd expected. Maybe as fast as he was in his chemically enhanced state.

She was so fast, in fact, that she'd dropped two of Beta Response before she'd finished leaping clear of the elevator. The MagSecs she held in each hand spat their charged rounds out in groups of three, and each burst had no trouble punching through the faceplates on his team's helmets, or cutting through their ballistic jackets like water. This was part of the problem with dataDyne; the corporation was so large that while one division was developing a new ballistic-resistant fiber, another branch was hard at work building a weapon that would cut through the same.

Hayes scrambled for cover, catching sight of a third member of Beta Response as he went down, missing a large portion of his throat.

Hayes glanced down at the weapons he was holding, cursing himself for his choice. It had been arrogance to choose such close-quarters weaponry, but an arrogance that was, in his experience, justified. Normally, he never had any difficulty getting close enough to a target to finish them by hand.

He heard the chatter of one Dragon opening up, followed quickly by another. He rolled back to his feet, using the side of a Bowman Constellation for cover. A fourth member of his assault team cried out in sudden pain, and Hayes tracked the noise in time to see the man drop his weapon and clutch at his groin before collapsing.

The redhead, Hayes realized, hadn't missed yet.

Still using the Constellation for cover, Hayes worked his way toward the front of the vehicle, trying to flank her. From the irregular chatter of her MagSecs, he had a localized idea of where she was and which way she was heading. He guessed toward the north side of the rooftop, presumably where her exfil would arrive.

There was another exchange of gunfire, followed quickly by a second burst from one of the two remaining Dragons. Hayes scurried from the Constellation toward his Hunter, catching sight of the redhead as she broke cover, sprinting toward one of the massive air recycling units that formed the borders of the parking lot. Only one of his assault team sprang up to try and tag her, and Hayes assumed that meant he was the only one left. The man was firing in panic, laying heavy on his trigger, and his shots went wide, chewing ragged gouges into the tarmac.

The redhead launched herself in the air, twisting to bring first one MagSec, then the other, into line. Again, each burst was true, and Hayes saw his last man go down out of the corner of his eye. She was still in the air, and he was certain she'd go down now, and hard, but she continued her spiral, dropping the now-empty weapons and bringing her hands out in front of her, and it wasn't a dive, it was a tumble, and she was back on her feet and sprinting for the northern edge of the rooftop.

If Hayes hadn't hated her so much, he'd have fallen in love with her then and there.

But love was a dermal supplied by his father, or the power of making a strong man scream, and instead, Laurent Hayes ran after her with all the speed he could muster. He emptied the Tranq-7 at her, firing again and again until the last narcotic pellet was spent, and she stumbled, suddenly, falling to one knee before lurching to her feet again. He didn't know how many times he'd hit her, but it didn't matter—once should have been enough.

That confirmed it for Hayes; like himself, she was doped up, some Carrington cocktail to give her an edge.

The stumble wasn't much, but it was enough, and Hayes threw aside the drug gun, screaming hatred at her as he dove forward, slashing with the knife for the back of her neck. It should have been a kill stroke—it *was* a kill stroke—but at the last second the redhead pivoted, turning out of the attack and bringing both arms up in a rising cross-block. She trapped his knife hand and twisted, smashed his nose with the butt of the hilt. Hayes cried out, staggered, and the knife clattered to the pavement between them.

That was her best move, it seemed, or the tranquilizers were finally doing their job, because when she lunged at him, he was able to sidestep it easily, and countered with a combination: once to her sternum, once to her gut. It rocked her, and he saw the pain paint her features, and Hayes grinned and kicked with his right. She managed a partial block, kept the blow from connecting full with her knee, but enough got through that he heard her gasp. Now she was backing away, unsteady on her injured leg.

"Hello, meat," Hayes said. "I've got an examination room just for you."

What the redhead said in response was slurred, and very unladylike.

Hayes feinted a lunge, moving at her, and again she backed away. Her eyes were unfocused now, and he knew she was trying to keep her gaze on him, that the tranquilizers were compressing her vision. On the rooftop, with the horizon dropping away in every direction, he knew her vertigo must be almost blinding.

His right loafer hit the blade of his knife, and without looking away from her, he hooked it with the toe of his shoe, kicking it into the air. He caught the handle with his right hand and smiled, licking his lips. He could taste his own blood, running from the blow she'd given him to the nose.

"We're gonna have a lot of fun together," he told her, and then feinted again, with the knife this time, as if to gut her. Again, the redhead danced back, and this time he was sure she almost lost her balance, almost went down.

"Running out of roof, sweetheart," Hayes said. "You fall down here, it's a much shorter drop."

The redhead spared a glance over her shoulder, saw that he had been telling the truth, that the edge of the rooftop with its retaining wall was only a meter behind her. When she looked back, Hayes lunged at her again, pulling it short, and that did it, she backed into the concrete barrier, out of room to retreat.

"Can you fly, hot stuff?" Hayes asked her.

The woman's eyes flashed a brilliant blue, almost unnaturally intense, and he saw the focus return, surfacing for a moment against the crush of the sedatives pumping through her veins.

"Yes," the redhead said, and then she fell backwards, off of the rooftop.

Hayes lurched forward in disbelief, dropping his knife and taking hold of the top of the short wall to look over its edge. Immediately, he jerked himself back, barely in time, as the wing of a blue-black VTOL dropship passed silently bare inches from his face, nearly costing him his nose. He could see the sliding door of the main compartment open, see the cargo webbing extended from its side, stretched out between two extended arms.

He could see a man dragging the redhead off the web and into the body of the ship, helping her to her feet, and he watched as she turned back to face him, staring at her from the rooftop.

She gave him a two-fingered salute.

Then the door of the dropship slammed shut, and there was a roar from its engines as the stealth baffles switched off, and Hayes was left alone on the edge of the pharmaDyne rooftop, surrounded by the bodies of six of his men.

Wondering just what it was he was going to say to his father.

CHAPTER 12

Hotel Regina—Apartment 4-2,
Place des Pyramides,
Paris, France
September 28th, 2020

Daniel Carrington swirled the remnants of the wine in the glass in his hand, looking out the window at the lights of the Parisian night beyond, and asked, "How badly do you want it?"

Still seated at the small table where they'd shared their dinner, Cassandra DeVries nearly choked on her own glass of wine. "Daniel!"

Carrington turned slowly, mischief in his eyes, and she knew the innuendo had been intentional, even if it hadn't truly been the purpose of the question. She set her glass down, used her napkin to wipe her mouth, fighting the urge to giggle. It was one of the things that had drawn her to him, one of the reasons that she loved spending time with him. He was the maverick she wanted to be, and he never failed to take her by surprise.

On the surface, they were an odd couple, she had to admit. No one would mistake Daniel, with his odd, out-of-date clothing and generally rumpled appearance, for a world-class lothario.

But Cassandra responded to qualities beyond a handsome face. Daniel's fierce intellect and his charm had impressed her, almost as much as the way he became more animated, more engaged when discussing a particularly difficult problem. More than anyone she'd ever met, Daniel Carrington made her think, made her race to keep up, which she found far more fulfilling than simple physical compatibility. She'd seen a side of Daniel no one else had ever seen, and that had cemented their mutual attraction.

Carrington reached for the bottle of wine, refilling first her glass, then his own, before sitting heavily in his chair opposite her once more. He winced as he did it, and she felt a pang of sympathy. The pain seemed most often to come from his hip, and there were times when it seemed to not bother him at all, when it seemed that the cane was an affectation, part of the Carrington Persona. But the more time Cassandra had spent with him, the more she had come to recognize the injury as sincere. When she'd asked him about it, he'd been evasive, and when she'd pressed, he'd told her, with uncharacteristic bluntness—at least for their relationship—not to ask again.

She hadn't, but still she wondered about it. Not so much about the origin of the injury, but about ways to alleviate his pain.

"You haven't answered my question, Cass," Carrington said gently.

"Of course I want it, Daniel! You know me well enough to know that." She sipped her wine, savoring the rich chocolate undertones. It was a 2005 Tignanello, from the famed Tuscan winery, Antinori—one of the most expensive of the so-called "Super Tuscan" wines. In the 1970s, the Italian Regulatory Council had snobbishly dismissed these wines, which incorporated non-indigenous grapes, as *vino di tavola*—mere table wines.

Over the years, however, the Super Tuscan wines had outstripped their contemporaries, and now commanded, as was the case with this particular vintage, thousands of dollars per bottle. She and Daniel had always shared an appreciation for the distinctive wines, which she thought appealed as much to their mutual iconoclasm as to their palates.

She set her glass down and leaned forward, resting her elbows on the table and her chin on her folded hands, meeting his eyes. "Why are you asking? Why are you really asking?"

"It'll change our relationship."

"For the better, I'd think. No more slinking around, meeting in hotel rooms."

Carrington faked indignation. "I picked this place out myself, you know. Many consider this the finest hotel in all of Paris."

"That's not what I meant, and you know it."

He dropped the act, smiling at her, happy. "I ask because it's one hell of an opportunity, for both of us. You could turn dataDyne off its course, guide it to a future that's both profitable *and* productive."

"I am aware, believe me, Daniel."

"So I ask again, how badly do you want it?"

"I still don't know how to answer that. Will I fight for it? Absolutely. Will I go to the lengths of Sexton or Murray, for example? I don't know. I'd like to think my standards are higher, that I still have a sense of decency. I'm not the CEOs they are, I'm the accidental Director, remember? The one who earned it on her merits alone, without politics."

"For which you should be duly proud."

"I am. I've earned what I've gotten, and I've managed to do it without selling my soul."

"I'm relieved to hear that."

She cocked her head, confused.

"I'm pleased that you don't think our relationship compromises you."

Cassandra shook her head. "Of course it compromises me. If anyone found out—"

"They won't, not from me," Carrington assured her.

She fell silent, straightening in her chair. After a second, she took up her wineglass, sipping. He stared at her with frank and intense interest, as if trying to read her mind.

"You think we should stop seeing one another," Carrington said, after a moment.

Now that the moment was here, Cassandra DeVries found it even harder to say than she had thought it would be. "I think, given the circumstances, it would be wise, yes."

For a long time, neither of them spoke.

She'd come to the decision before even leaving Hawaii, after the meeting with the Board but before her own departure. Waterberg and Sato had already departed for their offices in Tokyo and Los Angeles, and Velez was beginning to break down the massive security effort she'd put in place for the retreat. Cassandra had eaten a lonely dinner in one of the resort's four restaurants, waited upon hand and foot to such an extent that the meal had been claustrophobic. After dining, she'd gone for a walk along the beach to gather her thoughts, to think about what the Board had said, trying to be honest about her chances.

And honestly, her chances weren't terribly good. She was the youngest of the candidates by far, and the one with the least general business experience. While Sato and Waterberg were each in their own way talented and successful, she knew she was a better bet to the Board.

Sato's skill, it was widely acknowledged, was in putting himself in the right place at the right time, and Waterberg was too fiscally oriented to ever see the big picture. It was Sexton and Murray she needed to beat, and while Cassandra DeVries had guided DataFlow from one successful quarter to another, she knew she didn't have the business acumen of a Paul Sexton, nor the Nobel Prize of a Doctor Friedrich Murray.

Walking along the beach, shoes in her hand, staring alternately at the stars above and the water beside her, she'd realized she could do one of two things. She could concede defeat, or she could fight.

Since she'd never conceded defeat before, she wasn't about to start now.

It had been when Laurent Hayes, Doctor Murray's son-slash-bodyguard, had passed her in the hallway as she'd returned to her room that she'd realized none of her competition was likely to, either. He'd passed her by briskly, ignoring her murmur of goodnight, and Cassandra had unlocked the door to her rooms wondering just what it was he'd been doing. Doctor Murray had taken a suite on the opposite side of the resort, and she knew that his son was staying there with him.

There had been no reason for Hayes to be wandering the halls of what Velez herself had termed the "DataFlow Wing" of the hotel.

Once back in her rooms, the lights on and the door locked, it had taken Cassandra almost half an hour to become certain of what she had suspected: Hayes had been in her rooms. Hayes had gone through her belongings. Hayes had tried to break into her laptop.

He'd been digging, and it was only because Cassandra and Carrington had a mutual agreement that nothing about their relationship be committed to anything but memory that he'd come away empty-handed.

Even so, it was too close a call, and before falling

asleep that night, Cassandra DeVries had decided to end her affair with Daniel Carrington. It was a painful decision for her, and difficult to commit to, despite the obvious necessity of the action. She admired Carrington, respected the man, and more, his genius. She enjoyed the time she spent with him, the long conversations about science, about computers, about his work and hers, about the way the tiniest ideas could remake and rebuild the world. And when Daniel Carrington spoke to her of responsibility, of the need for progress that wasn't simply financially beneficial, but morally and ethically upright as well, he was preaching to the choir.

She was in love with him, and while he had never said as much, she believed he was in love with her.

After almost a minute of silence, Carrington reached across the table for her hand, taking it gently in his own. She felt the warmth of his touch, the rough edges of his fingers as they wrapped around her own slender digits. She willed herself to look away from the candles burning on the table between them, to meet his eyes, afraid of what she'd see in them. In its own way, acceptance would be worse than refusal.

"I agree," he said.

"Daniel, it's not that—"

"Shh, Cass . . . there's nothing you have to say."

"Just right now," Cassandra added, and it sounded lame to her ears, and she pulled her hand free from his grasp. "Just for right now."

"I understand." He sat back slowly in his chair, folding his hands across his middle, and she thought she saw some sorrow in his expression before he managed to hide it away. "You're facing some stiff competition."

"Yes."

"My guess is that it's Murray and Sexton you need to be worrying about."

"Yes," she said again, trying to warm to the conversation, finding it easier than talking about what they might have just lost. "That was my thinking, as well."

Carrington hesitated, scratching at the side of his beard with a finger, frowning.

"What?" she asked.

"I'm hesitant to broach the subject."

"We've known each other too long and too well to play games, Daniel. Say what you wish to say."

Carrington's frown deepened a fraction. "Would you accept my help?"

"Daniel . . ."

"No, nothing like that, nothing covert. But you know me, you know how I feel about dataDyne. There's a lot wrong that goes on in that corporation, a lot that's not just immoral or unethical, but outright illegal."

"Things that no one has ever been able to prove."

"Suppose I found proof? What then?"

She looked at him closely. "Daniel, what are you getting at?"

He waved a hand as if to soothe her. "I'm not withholding anything from you, Cass, we've long since passed that stage, I think you'll agree. Once you've seen an old man naked, there's very little sacred."

She grinned despite herself. "I saw nothing to be ashamed of."

"You're very kind, and you're very young, and it's a wonder you haven't given me a heart attack." He toyed with his wineglass, turning the stem between two of his thick fingers. "If I discovered proof of wrongdoing, of corporate malfeasance, say, what then?"

"You know what then. You're morally and ethically obligated to bring that evidence to light."

"I'm not, per se. You could do it."

Again, she looked at him closely. "You're hiding something."

"It's just a suspicion, Cass, no proof yet."

"Of what?"

"No, not yet. I don't want to speculate. But suffice it to say, if it turns out to be true, if I find evidence confirming my suspicions, it could be devastating to dataDyne."

"Generally or specifically?"

"I don't know yet."

"And it's definitely criminal?"

"Again, I don't know, not yet." Carrington shrugged, smiling broadly, as if amused by himself. "Daft old man, that's me. Just a suspicion, it may be nothing at all."

Cassandra considered, then said, carefully, "If you were to bring me proof—and I mean definitive, iron-clad proof—of dataDyne malfeasance, then yes, I would present that information to the public. I would do what is right, Daniel."

The lines around Carrington's eyes deepened with his smile. "That's my girl."

Cassandra shook her head once again, dismissing the conversation. She was used to him being oblique, to him making her work for the facts to catch up with his thinking. In the end she always got there, one way or another.

She took the napkin from her lap, set it on her empty plate, then rose and moved around to his side of the table. He watched her as she moved, raising an eyebrow as she approached, then raising the other one with it when she took his face in her hands and leaned down to kiss him.

"I thought we'd decided to end it," he said when she broke the kiss.

"Tomorrow," Cassandra DeVries told him, and then took hold of his hand, and led him to the bedroom.

CHAPTER 13

Carrington Institute—
Computer Lab III,
London, England
September 30th, 2020

"Okay, you guys are going to love this, I mean you're going to seriously love this," Grimshaw said.

Steinberg glanced at Carrington, seated beside him, then looked back to the Institute's resident computer guru. In the past, when Grimshaw had told Steinberg that he would "love" something, it was either net porn, a techno-rap song, or an episode of *Doctor Who,* and Grim had been wrong in his assertion each and every time.

"Show me," Carrington said.

Grimshaw beamed as if he were a puppy who'd just been rewarded for a particularly clever trick, made a show of cracking his knuckles, and then spun his chair around to face one of the three decks arrayed opposite him. His fingers positively flew across the keypads, and one by one, each of the monitors surrounding his workstation began lighting up.

"All right, here we have the late Agent Able's panic-burst transmission," Grimshaw said, pausing his typing long enough to indicate one of the monitors. To Steinberg, the information on the screen was nothing but gibberish, a tangle of symbols and numbers that only the most dedicated programmer could make sense of. In the chair beside him, Carrington repositioned his walking stick in front of himself, then leaned forward, resting his weight on the cane.

"Now most of this was just garbage, totally useless, and I mean *totally* frickin' useless, right?" Grimshaw resumed typing. "To begin with, the information Able managed to steal was encrypted. Then it got compressed to fit on his ID card, and then he had to route it through a corporate kiosk, and *then* route it to his home deck before activating the panic burst. Add to that the fact that the card was presumably removed from the kiosk before he'd completed the transfer—you can see the mess. A lot of what we're looking at here is just tracking information, machine language equivalent of white noise."

"Go on," Carrington rumbled.

Grimshaw picked up the pace, speaking faster, though not less. "Okay, so I cleaned it up, ran my best decryption software on it, and when that didn't work, wrote a new program to attack the problem. Took three days of riding the caffeine-and-porno roller coaster, but it got me this."

A second monitor lit up, and Grimshaw swiveled around to look at them again, obviously pleased with himself and waiting for a general acknowledgment of his brilliance. To Steinberg's eyes, the information displayed on the second monitor looked precisely the same as the information displayed upon the first.

But apparently not to Carrington, who said, "Very interesting, Grim."

Grimshaw beamed, swinging back around to man his

keypad once again. "Yeah, I thought so, but I didn't have anything to go on, right? I mean 'rose,' what is 'rose,' right? I mean, maybe a flower, maybe a war, but neither of those things helped me rebuild the file, because I didn't know what it was I was trying to rebuild, get it?"

"Not really, no," growled Steinberg. "Enough techno-babble, Grim. Get to the point."

"Look," Grim replied, his expression wounded, "imagine that we're trying to put together a jigsaw puzzle, but we have to do it with our eyes closed. We can't see what pieces are face up, face down, or even part of the picture at all. I needed *something* to form a starting point—a date, a time, a location, whatever.

"And that," Grimshaw continued, "is when our Fearless Leader had his brainstorm and sent in you guys. He wants to know 'the year of the Rose' and sex-bomb-killer-princess Miss Dark goes and gets that missing puzzle piece from the dearly departed Mister Able, and lo and behold, 2016, things begin clicking into place."

There was another flurry of tapping, and the third monitor sprang to life; this time, Steinberg *could* recognize what he was looking at, even if he couldn't fully understand it. Financial data began to spill across the screen, hundreds of transactions flooding past so quickly that he had no hope of tracking what he was seeing. Steinberg felt a stab of acute annoyance, resisted the desire to whack Grimshaw upside the head and tell him to stop showing off.

"So these are Doctor Murray's financials, or a portion of them, at any rate. I managed to reconstruct about eighty, eighty-five percent of the file, and that's pretty dandy, if I may say so myself, and I will. Mostly, these are the kinds of things you'd expect from a dataDyne CEO bastard type—some out-of-court settlements, some shady stock deals, some real-estate buys, things like that. But nested deep within all this effluvia—like that? 'effluvia,' great word, 'effluvia'—nested deep within it, we come upon, finally, the mysterious Rose."

With that, Grimshaw assaulted his central keypad again, and the monitors flanking him went dark. The central screen redrew, and finally, clearly, discernibly, Steinberg was able to see the point of the exercise, a simple spreadsheet, listing dates and payment amounts to some person or persons unknown. The earliest date listed was August 23rd, 2016, the most recent barely three weeks ago, September 6th, 2020. The sums were impressive, starting with two million dollars in 2016 and rising to just below ten million as of this past month.

"This is a spreadsheet I banged up using the recovered financials. All of these are wire transfers to banks in free-sector Macao, Switzerland, and Australia, all locations—as you well know, I'm sure—where the banking laws are loose and the privacy laws are tight. We're looking at a scheduled payoff, my friends, we're looking at the trail of the blackmailee, so to speak. Someone has been tapping our Doctor Murray to the tune of almost eighty million dollars over the last four years."

Grimshaw's chair creaked as he slowly swung back around to face them. "Whatever Rose is, *whoever* Rose is, whatever he's got, Doctor Murray doesn't want him telling."

"Eighty million," Steinberg said. "Raises the question why Murray hasn't just had him waxed."

"That assumes that Rose is a person, not a project, say, something along those lines." Grimshaw reached behind him for the bowl of Smarties he kept on his desk, taking a handful. As he dropped them in his mouth one by one, he added, "Could be a pharmaDyne ultrablack project, maybe? Mind-control drugs or accelerated cloning or synthetic life?"

Steinberg rolled his eyes. "Or something a little more, I don't know, believable."

Grimshaw crunched noisily, leveling a finger at him. The nail, Steinberg noted, had been bitten down almost to the quick.

"It's totally believable, man! We live in an age of anti-gravity and flying cars! Effective cloning technology has existed for over forty years! Dude, we're maybe ten years from faster-than-light travel! Anything is possible!"

Carrington cleared his throat, cutting off Grimshaw's tirade before it could gather further momentum. "It's not an ultrablack, otherwise Doctor Murray would have funded it through pharmaDyne itself, or one of the other corporate fronts. This is something personal, something important enough to him that he's willing to spend eighty million plus of his own money to keep it going, or to keep it silenced."

"You think it's the latter?" Steinberg asked him.

"I think both of you are overlooking the significance of the date," Carrington said, and then, with a grunt, pushed himself upright with the help of his walking stick. He straightened his tie, using the moment to collect his thoughts, then began a slow circuit around the lab.

"Twenty-sixteen, twenty-sixteen," Grimshaw said. "Aston Villa won the FA cup. Jeanine Wacker became the new Doctor."

"The trade war in Central Asia went hot," Steinberg offered.

"You're thinking along the wrong lines, lads." Carrington stopped, peering at one of the smaller monitors nearby, frowning at what he saw on the screen.

"The Flu," Steinberg said.

"Correct. The influenza A subtype H17N22 outbreak." Carrington raised his gaze, settling it on Steinberg and Grimshaw. "Three things happened in 2016 that changed Doctor Friedrich Murray's life. The first was the superflu pandemic. The second was his being named pharma-Dyne's new CEO. The third was his being awarded the

Nobel Prize for his work leading to the discovery of an effective vaccine used to prevent the spread of influenza A subtype H17N22."

Steinberg stared at Carrington, and beside him, felt Grimshaw doing the same thing.

"No way," Steinberg said. "Not even *they* could—"

"Look at the facts."

"You're saying that pharmaDyne unleashed a pandemic that claimed nearly forty million lives just so they could sell the vaccine?"

Carrington shook his head, annoyed. "No, that makes no fiscal sense, Jon. If they had developed the superflu strain, they would certainly have developed the vaccination at the same time. By waiting, they lost thirty-seven million potential customers. The vaccine came after the outbreak."

"Then what are you saying?"

"It was an accident," Grimshaw whispered. "That's it, isn't it? That's what you're telling us?"

Carrington shrugged, as if the enormity of what they were discussing barely interested him. "It's a theory."

"Can we prove it?" Steinberg asked.

"No, not until we know who or what Rose is."

Grimshaw was beginning to rock in his chair, making the casters squeak with each shift of his weight. "This is bad, this is bad, this is very very bad, boss man."

Steinberg shot him an annoyed glare. "Bad for dataDyne, maybe."

"No, dude, you don't get it, you don't see it in macro, like. You're all soldier-badass-tunnel-vision guy, yeah? Think about the big picture, the global picture. If the boss man is right and we cough up the proof, dataDyne goes down."

"I'm not seeing a downside."

"Grim's correct," Carrington said. "dataDyne isn't simply a large business, nor even an industry, Jon. It's effectively a global superpower. It has divisions and operations in over two hundred countries around the world, and in many of those countries, it's the primary—the only—engine driving the economy. If dataDyne collapses, it'll plunge the world into a financial crisis the likes of which has never been seen. It may even be fair to say that the world will never recover. Billions of people will lose their jobs, starve, die. Calling it catastrophic would be an extraordinary understatement."

"So you're saying we do nothing?" Steinberg glared at Carrington. "You're saying we just sit on this information?"

"We don't have information, Jon, we have a theory. If the theory is proven, then we'll have to make our next moves very carefully."

Steinberg scowled, getting up from his chair. "And how often are you wrong, Daniel? About things like this, how often are you mistaken?"

"Not very," Carrington admitted.

"We find the proof, we can't let this stand."

"If we find the proof, we won't, I promise you." Carrington met his stare, held it for a moment before breaking away to look toward Grimshaw. "Good work, Grim. Now I've got another job for you."

"Find Rose?"

"Find Rose," Carrington confirmed. "Dig up everything you can on Murray, see if there's a connection anywhere in his history to a person, a place, a thing called 'rose.' I'll want regular updates, twice daily."

"You got it, boss man," Grimshaw said.

"Jon," Carrington said. "Walk with me."

"How's she doing?" Carrington asked him.

"Physically, she was a little shaky from the tranqs in

her system, but she bounced back after a hot meal and quick nap," Steinberg replied, looking up into the gray sky, feeling the light rain pelting his face. "Emotionally, I don't know."

"You haven't talked to her?"

"I tried last night. She was on HoloMan, wouldn't come out."

"I read your debrief and reviewed the mission records. She did everything she could, she must see that."

"I don't think she does." Steinberg lowered his face from the rain, glanced at Carrington. They resumed walking, taking the gravel path from the Institute buildings toward the Manor. "I think she blames herself for Able's death."

"That's transference," Carrington said, dismissively. "She's turning everyone she can't save into her father."

The statement annoyed Steinberg, and he said as much. "Don't do that, Daniel. Don't diminish what she's feeling."

"And what is she feeling?"

"You remember when I joined you?" Steinberg asked abruptly. "You remember what had happened, how you found me, recruited me?"

"You'd been court-martialed and discharged, if I recall."

"You remember why I was discharged?"

"You were asking the wrong questions of the wrong people."

He scowled. "I was asking the right questions, but that's not the point. I'd been in Pakistan, fighting the insurgency, when we were ambushed. I lost over half of my squad. I mean, when those guys hit us, Daniel, they hit us like they knew what they were doing. I saw friends, guys I'd served with in Angola and Somalia, literally blown apart beside me."

"Yes, you'd been set up," Carrington said. "I know all this."

"That's not the point. This isn't about arms deals or corruption. This is about the other thing, the thing that I came to you with, the reason I signed on with you."

Carrington's eyes narrowed, trying to follow Steinberg's lead, but it was clear he didn't see it, didn't understand. Steinberg sighed, came to a stop on the gravel path.

"You wanted to fight that corruption," Carrington said. "Or so I thought."

"Yeah, and it was a good line, and you believed it. And I'm *not* saying to you now that I *don't,* but what I'm trying to tell you is that it wasn't the whole reason."

"So what was the whole reason?"

"*Guilt,* Daniel."

"But what happened to your men, that wasn't your fault."

"No, not about that, not like that."

"I don't understand, Jon."

"I'm still alive," Steinberg growled. "They're dead, and I'm not. I'd been a Ranger for years, I'd been trained to deal with death, and I still couldn't live with it. They were dead, I was alive, and I was sick with the guilt of it."

Carrington said nothing, the realization seeping slowly across his features.

"She's twenty years old, Daniel, and she's racked up a body count to rival a goddamn rifle company. She's lost everything and everyone she's ever cared about. Two days ago, she tried to save the life of a man she'd never met, and she gave it everything she had, and she failed.

"They're all gone, Daniel, but Joanna Dark, she's still here."

Carrington looked away from him, past him, to the estate walls in the distance. The realization on his face had turned to something else, something that spoke more of sadness, and regret.

"You need to talk to her," Steinberg said.

Carrington sighed, nodded once. "She doesn't like me very much."

"She doesn't know you."

"I'm not sure that will make the difference."

"Come on," Steinberg said. "Let's go see her."

Together, they continued following the path, toward the Manor.

They found Joanna's rooms emptied, stripped of her few belongings.

Of the young woman herself, there was no sign at all.

CHAPTER 14

Ginza Station—
Tokyo, Japan
October 2nd, 2020

The sky above the city was steel gray, the vast sea of neon below cutting swaths of sickly yellow-green though the clouds. On this side of the train station, the nighttime foot traffic moved in waves, a featureless ocean of humanity, mixing Caucasian and Asian faces into a seamless blend. Great edifices of commerce rose on every side of the station, and towering above them all was the Beck-Yama International Building, one whole face of the structure a massive neon sculpture, an abstract twisting of tubes and sheets in green, white, and red.

The last time Jo had been in Tokyo, in Ginza specifically, she'd been traveling with her father, and had stared in wonder at the Beck-Yama façade. In a world where garish wasn't just a marketing campaign but a way of life, it was hard to impress, but Jo had been awed by the display, the way the colors had bathed the surrounding city blocks. Perhaps the thing that had impressed Jo the most was that nothing on the façade actually declared the building as Beck-Yama.

"That's the point," Jack Dark had told her. "They don't tell you who they are, because they want you to think you should already know. They want to make you feel foolish for even asking. They're telling you, and me, and everyone walking down these streets, that Beck-Yama International is more important than any of us can ever hope to be."

The words came back to her as Jo stepped out of the north entrance of Ginza Station, into the glow of the neon and the fall of the rain. It was after two in the morning and still the streets were packed, filled with clubbers and partygoers and the lost, like herself. Once, Ginza had been the heart of the Tokyo high-end shopping district; now it was still high-end, but the shopping done was of a different sort. Galleries and discotheques and VR clubs practically spilled onto the empty streets, and the stream of null-grav vehicles overhead was endless.

It was, Jo knew, a very good place to get lost.

She lowered her head against the pelting rain, pulling the strap of her satchel down tight over her shoulder. The scab beneath her left eye itched, the skin there entering its last phase of healing. She'd always been a quick healer, scrapes and cuts, even the odd minor broken bone, knitting and repaired in short order. It was the way she was, to such an extent that Jo hadn't realized there was anything different or special about it until fairly recently. Most of her injuries taken at pharmaDyne had already begun to fade.

She crossed Sotobori Dori, her boots splashing through the wash of water running down the street, then turned south, so she faced the Beck-Yama Tower. Near the corner of Yaesu Dori she spotted an always-open noodle stand, and shouldered her way through the patrons to reach the bar, shouting in Japanese for a plain bowl. She paid in cash, throwing down thin and weathered bills, and the old woman who took her money narrowed her eyes in suspicion at Jo before accepting the payment and moving along to answer another customer's demands.

Jo shoveled noodles into her mouth, ravenous. She hadn't eaten since leaving London almost two days prior, hadn't dared to stop moving, aware of just how far a man like Carrington could reach. All her travel had been unregistered transport, stowing away twice on high-orbit cargo fliers that took her first back to the States, to New York, then again to Australia, Melbourne, where she'd actually paid for a ticket—again in cash—to the Philippines, then to Vietnam, and then, finally, for a flight to Narita. She'd changed time zones so many times, she wondered if she hadn't actually gotten younger.

In the US, she'd bought new clothes, new gear, and new identities, and dumped all the old. Nothing fancy, just workable gear, a new pair of leather pants, a new set of sturdy boots, a new lite-ballistic jacket, a couple of T-shirts, a couple changes of underwear. She'd thought about trying to arm herself, but knew she'd be moving more, and fast, and didn't want to risk attracting Customs' notice. If a gun was needed, she was certain she'd know where to find one.

It was one of the rewards of having trained to be a bounty hunter, trained by an ex-cop like Jack Dark. She knew the law, and she knew the people who broke it, and she could move between their respective worlds with ease and even speed.

When she'd finished wolfing down the noodles, Jo tilted the cheap plastic bowl to her mouth, draining the remains of the broth. She wiped her mouth on the sleeve of her jacket, felt the hole that had ached in her belly shrinking, but not enough. She contemplated ordering a second bowl, but decided against it. If she was being followed, if she was being somehow tracked, then the less time she spent in one place the better.

She set the emptied bowl back on the counter and moved out from beneath the shelter of the stand, back into the downpour. She saw the lights of Beck-Yama shining on the rain-soaked streets, shimmering, distorted, in the rainfall. She heard the voices, the noise, smelled the food and the people, and she stopped cold.

She had no idea where to go next.

She had no idea where to go at all.

Don't trust Daniel Carrington, Jack Dark had warned her, and she had told herself she wouldn't, had told herself she didn't, and yet, somehow, someway, she'd found herself killing for the man.

That, more than anything else, was the reason she'd run. Or the reason she'd started to run.

But in the frigid cargo compartment on the descent into Melbourne, hugging her knees to her chest and watching her breath turn into vapor before her eyes, Jo had begun to admit that there were other reasons. Carrington hadn't *made* her kill anyone, she knew that. In fact, she had no reason to suspect him of any but the best intentions. He'd taken care of her when there'd been no need, had asked for nothing in return. When she'd volunteered to rescue Able, he'd seemed reluctant to accept her help, though not as much as Steinberg had.

All he truly had done was allow her to enter a situation where the possibility of death had loomed large. At her most paranoid, Jo even entertained the thought that Carrington had engineered the situation, but even if he had, he couldn't have known the outcome. No one had forced her hand. No one had pressed her finger to the trigger. What she'd done, she'd chosen to do all by herself.

It was all her.

And it was in that cargo hold, hugging her knees to her chest, that Joanna Dark realized, with a sudden burst of self-loathing and horror, that she was a killer. She was a stone-cold killer, the kind of person her father had hunted during his life, the kind of person who took lives without hesitating, without thinking of the consequences. She was dataDyne in micro, she was the enemy.

She had tried to hide from it. After the thing in Hong Kong with her father, and then later, after Africa, she'd tried to ignore the truth. But the truth kept rearing its head, again and again, and when she'd returned from Vancouver she could no longer deceive herself. Not when Steinberg gave her the body count during debriefing, not when he told her that, according to the radio traffic that Grimshaw had monitored, she'd dropped eight of pharmaDyne's best assault troops.

She was a killer, and that was the only way to explain how she could do what she did. How it was that, when she fired a gun, the bullet went exactly where she wanted it to go. How it was that she could be so quick and everyone else around her could be so slow. How it was that she could lose herself in a fight, as if she had not one but two brains. As if the Jo trapped inside her skull was only one part of her, and that, when the bullets and the explosions and the violence all came, another Jo emerged, standing on the outside, guiding her effortlessly, making her leap and tumble and roll and kill.

How, in those moments of dilation, Jo felt . . . no, not calm, not exactly, but . . .

Right, Jo thought. *It feels right.*

She was a killer, and it was right that she was, and the realization sickened her to her very core.

With no place to go, Jo wandered. With no reason to care, she picked her directions at random.

She passed the Beck-Yama Tower, heading south, and the rain began to taper, then to stop. Jo turned west, away from the rising sun, only to find herself on the outskirts of an old Japanese castle, walled and dilapidated. She turned south again, continued wandering as dawn continued to rise, and she was out of the high-rent district by then, on streets where the cars rolled because no one could afford to fly.

No one paid any attention to her—at least, not that Jo could see—but she wasn't looking very hard, because she didn't care very much.

She nearly missed the sign, wedged as it was over the door to the office, crammed between the entrance to a liquor store on one side and a fast-food joint on the other. Her kanji had never been as strong as her spoken Japanese, and Jo needed a minute to puzzle it out. At first she'd thought it translated to "Empty Man," but then realized it wasn't that, not quite, but it was close.

There were always people needing to be hunted, always bounties to be collected.

So maybe she was a killer, but that wasn't what her father had raised her to be.

Jo ran a hand through her soaked hair, flipping her forelock back, straightening and trying to make herself as professionally acceptable as possible. It would be a hard sell, she knew, but if the owner of this particular bail-bonds storefront had a copy of HoloMan VR, she knew she could convince him. Watch this, she'd say.

She could do that, she could hunt bounties.

Just like her father had taught her to do.

CHAPTER 15

InterContinental Le Grand Hotel Paris—
Room 4822-2, Rue Scribe,
Paris, France
October 3rd, 2020

He answered the door as soon as she knocked, and Cassandra knew from that alone that he'd been waiting for her. From his expression, he'd been waiting awhile, and his impatience was palpable.

"I'm sorry, Daniel," Cassandra told him as she stepped inside, then waited for him to close and lock the door. "I got here as soon as I could."

"It's quarter to midnight," Carrington said. "I've been waiting here for seven hours."

"I almost didn't come at all. I thought we'd agreed to end this."

"For the time being, yes, but we didn't agree to stop sharing information." He turned on his walking stick, heading down the short hallway into the suite's sitting room, leaving her to follow. "I'm chasing something down, Cass, something that, if it turns out as I hope, will all but assure your position as the new CEO of dataDyne. But I've hit a snag, my people can't take it any further."

Carrington stopped at the couch, lowering himself slowly. On the coffee table opposite him sat a silver tea service, and he motioned at it with the end of his walking stick, then at the chairs arrayed opposite him. Cassandra waited, hoping he would add more, but the old man didn't, simply looked at her. She sighed, set down her briefcase beside the legs of the nearest chair, then shrugged out of her overcoat. She sat, smoothing her skirt, and she saw that Carrington's eyes had wandered to her legs.

"Daniel," she said.

He moved his eyes slowly up her body until they met her own, then smiled slightly, reminding her, "You kept me waiting."

"Because I didn't want to be followed. Anita Velez is in town, she's auditing DataFlow. Apparently there was a shoot-out at pharmaDyne Vancouver last week, so now the whole corporation's being forced to re-evaluate security across the board."

"Was there?"

"You didn't happen to have anything to do with it, did you, Daniel?"

"Not personally, no." He motioned toward the tea service with a hand. "Pour yourself a cup, we'll talk."

"I don't have the time, Daniel, this is what I'm trying to tell you." It was a lie, but it was easier than telling him the truth, which was that she found being in his presence acutely painful, nothing but a reminder of what they had each decided to deny themselves. "Please, can we get to the point?"

Carrington sighed heavily, as if disappointed, and Cassandra found herself hoping he was, that this was as difficult for him as it was for her. He sighed a second time, then reached inside his tweed jacket and removed a narrow envelope. She thought he would hand it over, but instead he kept it in hand, tapping its edge against the back of his wrist.

"There are two things, actually," he said at length. "Both of worth to you, but in different fashions. The first is a personnel question, and no matter how hard my people try, they can't answer it."

"We're talking about dataDyne personnel?"

"We think so."

"Anything more specific? There are quite a few of us, Daniel."

"pharmaDyne specifically. We're looking for an employee by the name of Rose."

"First name, last name?"

"We don't know. We're sure he or she doesn't work for pharmaDyne now, but was definitely employed by them as of five years ago, say 2015. We can't get through our security."

"Meaning your resident hackers can't access them."

"I just need confirmation, Cass. Anyone with the name of Rose, first name, last name, anyone you find. Can you get that for me?"

"Why, Daniel?"

"I can't tell you, not yet."

"This is risky for me, snooping around like that. Especially now."

Carrington snorted. "It's not risky for you, Cass. You're already in the system, and you've yet to meet a computer you couldn't make sing and dance for you."

"Why?" Cassandra asked again.

Carrington used the envelope in his hand to indicate her briefcase, resting on the floor. "You have your laptop, you could do it now."

"I could, but I want to know why."

"You're an infuriating woman," Daniel Carrington told her.

She smiled at him. "And that's one of the things you adore about me."

"Ah, and now you're taunting the old man."

"I just want an answer. Why are you looking for this 'Rose'?"

Carrington sucked a breath through his teeth, then blew it out, relenting, finally. "Because I think this person is someone that Doctor Friedrich Murray doesn't want found. It's potentially bad for him, and thus potentially very good for you."

She considered that, thinking for a moment. He truly wasn't asking for much, she decided; it was something she could do for him here and now. There was an appeal in hurting Murray, as well. Cassandra was positive that his son hadn't been acting of his own accord, that he wouldn't have dared. It had to have been his father who had told Hayes to go snooping through her rooms back at the resort. She wouldn't mind hitting him back for that particular insult.

"Pour me a cup of tea, then," she said, then bent to retrieve her laptop from her briefcase. As Carrington prepared her a cup, she snapped the machine open, brushing her thumb across the power stud. The machine came to life, but the monitor remained dark.

"DeVries," she said to the laptop. "Arthur William."

The screen came to life, verifying the voice ID, and Cassandra glanced over the top of the machine to see that Carrington had paused in his preparations, was watching her.

"My brother," she explained.

"I see," Carrington said.

Cassandra was at the first login screen now, and she quickly began tapping in her password, eighteen digits and letters in no particular order that had been committed to memory—and which she diligently changed every thirty days. The first and second security checks on her machine were standard for all dataDyne laptops, a voice-print and an alphanumeric code. Cassandra used them not because she had faith in their ability to deter invasion, but because it was what she was required to do.

That didn't keep her from modifying her own laptop with a third check, one she'd developed of her own accord. The idea had come to her while perusing status sheets on other dataDyne company projects, upon reading about an Ellison Electronic Security, Inc. proof of concept for a close-range-only Identify-Friend-or-Foe chip to be sold to intelligence agencies around the world. The idea was to insert a tiny microchip transmitter into an agent's body, and then to plant appropriate receivers into the agent's equipment. Without the IFF chip, the equipment would simply fail to turn on.

The project had been abandoned, mostly because the targeted intelligence agencies feared—perhaps correctly—what would happen to their agents once word of the security measure spread, as it undoubtedly would. Images of spies missing fingers or even whole hands had been enough to kill the plan.

Cassandra, however, had thought it a risk worth taking, at least for herself, and had contacted one of the project specialists at EESI, a man named Ed Ventura, asking if she could get a copy of the prototype. Doctor Ventura, happy to please the CEO of DataFlow, had done just that, and it had been a small matter then for her to install the receiver in her own laptop, and an only slightly more painful one to install the transmitter chip into herself. For the latter, she'd needed several ounces of whiskey for courage, and a very sharp scalpel.

The blood and pain had been minor, and, in her eyes, a very small price to pay for the security it granted. No one in the world knew what she had done, and thus, no one in the world could access her laptop without her permission.

Carrington offered her the cup of tea, and she indicated for him to set it on the coffee table. "I'm logging into the server now."

"How long will this take?"

"A few minutes. I'm not truly certain. pharmaDyne has employed a lot of people in the last five years."

Carrington grunted, failing to hide his impatience.

Cassandra connected with her office, logging in a second time, then dropped out of the graphic interface to the code line, where she could work faster and with more comfort. Her fingers began to fly.

"Rose," she said. "Nothing else? Traditional spelling?"

"Traditional spelling."

"And you're certain it's a name?"

"Reasonably certain."

"Not, for instance, a passion that Doctor Murray has for flowers, then?"

"Don't joke, Cass. You wouldn't believe me if I told you how many florists' receipts my people have looked at in the past few days."

She finished typing with a gentle press of the ENTER key, then moved the laptop to the coffee table, leaving it to rest there while it pursued its search. She took the prepared cup of tea, tasted it, then waited until Carrington had fixed one for himself.

"Right, then," she said. "What's the second thing?"

"We're not finished with the first."

"It'll take a few minutes. Let's be efficient, Daniel."

Carrington drained his tea in a single gulp, then set the cup back down and picked up the envelope from where it lay beside his saucer. He offered it to Cassandra.

"Open it."

Cassandra used a fingernail to tear the flap, then blew

into the opening, causing the envelope to inflate slightly. She reached in, then came out with a small photograph, almost wallet-sized. She looked at the portrait, a head-shot, the kind of thing she'd have expected to find in a police lineup or on a passport. It was a picture of a girl, or perhaps, more correctly, of a young woman. Caucasian, fine boned, with delicate features and large, blue eyes. Her hair was almost crimson, except where it fell over her forehead. There, the hair was light blonde, perhaps even white, it was hard to tell in the picture.

She looked at Carrington, unable to hide her curiosity. "Who is she?"

"Her name, we believe, is Phoebe Charlotte. She was in London as of the twenty-eighth of last month."

"And why do I care about the whereabouts of a girl named Phoebe Charlotte?"

"Because we have reason to believe she had contact with Zhang Li just prior to his disappearance, Cass. She may very well know where he is, and where Mai-Hem is, as well."

"Are you saying they're still alive?"

Carrington shrugged. "We've been trying to bring her in for a talk, but she won't stay in one place long enough. Last we heard, she was in Melbourne."

"What do you expect me to do with this information?"

"I expect you to hand it over to Ms. Velez and CORPSEC, Cass. They'll want to locate Ms. Charlotte and bring her in for questioning, at the very least." Carrington moved to refill his cup of tea. "You understand, I'm giving this to you because it's beyond my resources to handle it within the Institute. I'm as curious as you are as to Zhang Li's whereabouts."

"I'd begun to think he was dead," Cassandra admitted. "If he isn't, if we find him . . ."

"Yes, the hunt for a new CEO will be called off, on account of the return of the old one. But if his return comes about as a result of your efforts, surely that'll raise your standing in the eyes of the Board?"

Cassandra nodded, looking again at the picture, surprised by the apprehension she felt at the thought of Zhang Li's return. In the last week, she'd become so focused on being named the new CEO, she'd pushed the possibility out of her mind.

Her laptop beeped, indicating that it had completed its search of the pharmaDyne employee records. Cassandra tucked the photograph of Phoebe Charlotte into her coat pocket, finished her tea, then lifted the computer back onto her lap.

"You have a PDA?" she asked Carrington.

He tapped his forehead. "It all goes in here, Cassandra."

"Then listen closely. In the last five years, there have been thirty-six employees of pharmaDyne with the word 'rose' in their name."

"Thirty-six of them?"

"I'm including all Rosenbergs, names like that."

"Ignore those. I'm looking for the discrete word."

"That cuts the number to eleven, first and last names."

"And last names alone?"

"Three," Cassandra said.

"Give them to me."

"Alicia J. Rose, security officer at pharmaDyne Toronto. Doctor George A. Rose, team leader of cognitive pharma research, pharmaDyne Vancouver. And Doctor Thaddeus K. Rose."

"What does he do?"

"Doesn't say," Cassandra told him, tapping again at her keyboard. "He left the company in 2016."

Carrington frowned in disappointment.

"Not what you were hoping for?" she asked him.

"No. But better than nothing." Carrington reached for his walking stick, using both it and the arm of the couch to get to his feet. "Thank you, Cass."

"You'll keep me posted?"

"If there's anything to post you about, of course."

She began to slip the laptop back onto the coffee table, but he shook his head.

"Don't bother," Carrington told her. "I'll head out first, you can follow in a few minutes, keep everything nice and discreet."

"All right."

He turned, began limping his way back down the hall, to the door of the suite.

"Daniel," she called.

He looked back.

"Is there something you're not telling me?"

"There are many things I'm not telling you, Cass," Carrington answered. "None of them should worry you."

He left her alone in the suite, wondering if she should believe him.

Cassandra gave him twenty minutes' lead, time she spent on a second cup of tea and sorting through the emails that had arrived since she'd left the office. When she felt enough time had passed, she shut down her computer, tucking it away once more in her briefcase, then rose and donned her overcoat. She gave the suite a last survey, thinking that it was a very nice room, and that it was a pity she hadn't been able to enjoy it more. She headed to the exit, opened the door, and then stopped short.

Anita Velez, in one of her perfectly tailored suits, was standing in front of her.

"Doctor DeVries," Anita Velez said. "Would you mind telling me how long you've been having an affair with Daniel Carrington?"

CHAPTER 16

Club Lisboa—
48 Rua Praia Antonio, Macau,
People's Republic of China
October 6th, 2020

The hunt for Leung Cha-wei began in Tokyo, but he'd been twitched already, the first hunter blowing the capture and tipping the quarry, and the man had run. Jo had tracked him to Osaka with little difficulty, and then from there to Hong Kong. But Hong Kong was as it always had been, a maze and a mess, and like Tokyo, a place that was easy for someone to get lost in. And Hong Kong brought back memories of her father, and that had made things harder, too.

She'd lost Leung for a while in Hong Kong, and had wasted a day haunting the gambling dens and Love-Match bordellos along Kowloon Harbor in search of a lead. She showed Leung's picture to hookers and pushers and beggars, to cops and robbers and bums, and she'd known she was being indiscreet, that if she wanted to remain hidden herself, this wasn't the way to do it. But she'd taken the job, and she was going to see it through, hell or high water.

Then a fence working out of the back of a club in the night market on Shanghai Street offered to make a deal with Jo. He'd cashed Leung's chips, he told her, turned his credit to cash, and he knew where Leung had gone to lay low until the heat was off. The fence told her he was happy to share that information with Jo, for a small price. Jo listened while he described the payment he had in mind, a service both intimate and personal, and she had smiled at him, nodded once, and then reached across the table and taken hold of the back of his head.

She was about to bounce the fence's head off the tabletop a fifth time when he suddenly volunteered that Mister Leung had relocated to the Macau Free Sector, and could most likely be found at the Lisboa, where he was fond of the games that were played there. Jo thanked the fence and left the club, then went about the process of arming herself, because she knew that while she was doing that, the fence was more than likely screaming his head off to the aforementioned Mister Leung, and in all probability asking him to put an extra bullet in the bitch for his sake when Leung found the time.

Jo procured a pistol in short order, a Maas P9P chambered in .45 ACP, as well as a set of handcuffs. Then she caught one of the old motorized junks across the water to Macau. Once ashore, she went straight for her target.

She thought the Lisboa was a cliché in almost every possible way. The music played so loud that it was next to impossible to hear anyone saying anything, and then only if they chose to shout it in your ear; the lighting was dimmed generally, but pulsed irregularly over the gambling tables and the raised dancer's stage; the cigarette smoke was so thick, Jo was relatively certain people could get lung cancer simply walking by outside.

And it was packed, full of tourists from the mainland and further afield, the majority of them Chinese, but she caught words in Portuguese, Japanese, and even English, accents from American to South African, with Australian as a stop in between. Games of *pai gow, bou,* and blackjack raged at crammed tables along the center of the main floor, all the way up to the stage. The stage itself had once been used for dancing, but now it offered shows of a different sort, as women wearing hacked DeathMatch headsets and body sensors and not much else writhed on its surface in pantomime ecstasy. Above them, hung from the ceiling, were suspended window-glass monitors, broadcasting their virtual reality for all to see. Somewhere in the back, clients paid for the privilege of picking their fantasy and participating.

Jo had seen such unsavory diversions before, and they always turned her stomach. Sometimes she wondered if dataDyne had even tried making the task of hacking DeathMatch VR a challenge. She doubted that they had. Like all new technologies, the first question that had been asked of DeathMatch VR wasn't *How does this work* or *Will this make my life better,* but rather, *Can I use this to get myself off?* The answer, unsurprisingly, had been yes, and thus a black-market cottage industry had exploded into existence overnight. Polite society called the modified system "LoveMatch VR." The users called it something else entirely.

She edged her way past the tables, avoiding groping hands and pleas in Mandarin, Cantonese, and English for her company. A sweating, short, bald-headed Caucasian held out a wad of bills to her, pleading for her to take a turn on the stage. She took the money and ignored the request, leaving him cursing after her.

Near the back of the stage on the left-hand side was a

flight of stairs guarded by a bouncer who either had spent all of his allowance on augments, or spent all of his time in the gym. She weaved her way toward him, plucking Leung's photo from her pocket.

"Seen this man?" she shouted in Mandarin.

The bouncer had a twelve-year-old's face, and when he scowled at her, the expression was less threatening than comical.

"This man," Jo shouted. "He's wanted for murder. He did a family of four back in Tokyo."

The bouncer's scowl quavered for a moment, then resettled, resuming its previous defiance. But the quaver had been enough, and Jo started to move past him. The bouncer started to move to block her, and she put her index and middle fingers against his collar bone, pressing in and down, and he was on his knees before he could offer either resistance or protest.

Jo went down the stairs, emerging in a hallway, its floor covered with worn red carpet, the walls coated in peeling wallpaper. Eight doors lined the corridor, four on each side, with small plasma monitors wired over their frames, displaying the action taking place on the stage above. Five of the monitors were lit, three were dark.

She slipped the Maas from behind her back, moving into a low-ready shooter's stance. She wanted Leung alive, not only to prove to herself that she could bring him in, but also because the bounty was better on a living, breathing perp. But if it came to it, she'd put him down, and for some reason, that certainty didn't bother her at all. She supposed it was because that, like so many others, it had been a lesson from her father.

"If it's them or you, Jo, it should always, always be you," he'd say. "That's no contest."

She approached the first of the doors from the side, keeping against the wall rather than moving in front of it, and tapped on its surface with the barrel of the Maas.

"Leung Cha-wei!" Jo shouted in Cantonese. "I'm here to take you in! Come out with your hands up!"

There was no response, but that didn't surprise Jo. She'd yet to encounter a situation, either in simulation or real life, where the demand had ever worked. It was like stories about UFOs—maybe nice to believe in, but nothing you'd want to bet your life on.

After waiting three seconds, Jo stepped out from the wall, pivoted, and smashed her boot into the door, just below the knob. The frame splintered, the door separating, slamming open, and she had the Maas in high-ready, but there was no one within who needed shooting.

She moved to the next door, again taking position to the side of it rather than in front of it, prepared to repeat the process. With her back against the wall, she could feel the music from above thumping through the building, the bass trying to crawl into her chest and rattle her lungs.

Jo reached out to tap the door with the barrel of the Maas and make her demand, and she'd hit it once and gotten as far as "Leung—" when the response came, in the form of a shotgun blast. The door disintegrated to splinters, and Jo pulled back; despite herself, she could feel the smile coming to her face.

That's more like it, she thought, and took three steps back, further along the wall. She did it just in time. The second blast tore through the wall where she'd just been standing.

On impulse, Jo screamed with as much pain and suffering as she could manage. "Son of a bitch! Ow! Ah, dammit!"

She heard the sound of the shotgun, another round being jacked into the chamber, and laughter from within the room.

"Bitch!" someone shouted in English from inside. "You think that cops-and-robbers bullshit works around here?"

"Oh, God, get me an ambulance," Jo moaned piteously. "I'm bleeding here, God dammit!"

There was another laugh, and then Leung swung out of the doorway and into the hall, the shotgun at his shoulder, the barrel canted down in anticipation of where he would find his target. He was shirtless and heavily tattooed, and Jo could see the impressions at his temples and on his chest where he'd worn his VR rig.

He'd just realized that he hadn't hit her at all when she punched him in the face with the palm of her left hand. His head snapped back into the doorframe, then bounced forward, and Jo kicked at his right knee while grabbing the shotgun with her left hand. Both moves worked precisely as she'd hoped, and she ended up with the shotgun, and Leung ended up on the ground.

She moved around behind him, taking a second to glance into the room before propping the shotgun against the hallway wall. A young Chinese woman was inside, dressed in bad lingerie, seated at the control deck to the hacked DeathMatch system. From the choice of lingerie alone, Jo could tell she wouldn't be a threat.

With the Maas against the back of Leung's neck, Jo said, "Hands around, asshole, you know the drill."

Leung obliged grudgingly, and she cuffed his wrists together behind his back. Then she pulled the Maas away, tucking it once more into her pants at the small of her back, and picked up the shotgun. It was a Kangxi Armaments civilian model, the type VI, pump action. Nothing fancy, but more than capable of doing its job. Jo hefted the shotgun, hand around the stock and finger resting to the side of the trigger, keeping the barrel pointed at the ceiling.

"On your feet," she told Leung.

"C'mon, don't do this," Leung said, doing as ordered. "It's not what you think, I didn't do those kids."

"I don't care, get moving. To the stairs, keep it slow and easy."

Leung started forward, turning his head slightly, trying to look back at Jo without completely losing the ability to see where he was going. "The guy worked for Beck-Yama, lady. They're setting me up."

"Again, you mistake me for someone who cares."

Leung shook his head. "I've got money. You want money? I can get you money."

"I don't want money."

"Sure you do. You're a hunter, right? You're doing it for the clink, that's it. Seriously, let's deal. Anything you want, anything at all. You just tell me what it is you really, really want."

"I really, really want you to shut up." She gave him a shove forward to the base of the stairs, then started to ascend after him. They were about halfway up when she caught sight of the bouncer. He was facing them, blocking the head of the stairs and her view of the room beyond. That struck her as odd at the same moment she realized that the club now sounded wrong, off somehow, but she could still feel the music playing, hear it thudding through the floors and walls.

No voices, she realized. *No one's talking.*

"Down," she ordered Leung.

"Huh?"

"Get down!"

He started to turn to look at her, bewildered, and past him, at the top of the stairs, Jo saw the bouncer collapse, and then she saw the man who had been standing behind him. He was tall and broad-chested, and would have appeared so even if he hadn't been wearing body armor and a tactical vest strapped over it. His uniform, head to toe, was jet black, as were his helmet and face-shield. He wore a combat knife—one of the new laser-honed titanium jobs—sheathed at his belt, a semiautomatic in a holster on his thigh, and held a Fairchild DW-P5, tricked out with laser sight, scope, and suppressor, in his hands.

It occurred to Jo that she wasn't just in trouble. She was in very big, very deep trouble.

The man was a dataDyne Shock Trooper, not one of the response-team types she had dealt with before, not one of the CORPSEC guards, but a dataDyne elite, one of the cream of the crop of the hypercorp's security apparatus. The Shock Troopers were recruited out of special-operations units from around the world. Everything about them was the very best, from their gear to their training to their tactics.

All of this imprinted in less than a fraction of a second, adrenaline feeding these facts and more into her brain. The stairs were a death trap, a fatal funnel, and the Shock Trooper wasn't alone, there had to be at least three more of them, and that was only if they'd been deployed as a single brick. She had no means of retreat, she had no means of escape, and even thinking all of these things, she still found time to curse herself for getting cocky, for not securing an escape route before entering the club.

The Shock Trooper brought his submachine gun to his shoulder, and Jo winced as the beam from the laser sight crossed her vision, then settled on her forehead.

"Jesus Christ," Leung said. "I'm caught already, Jesus Christ!"

"Phoebe Charlotte," the Shock Trooper said, his voice distorted through the speakers in his helmet. "You are being detained by dataDyne forces under the 2017 United Nations Charter on Global Commerce, article eighteen, subsection seven, paragraph seven. Throw down your weapon. We are authorized to use lethal force if you resist. Surrender and you will not be harmed."

"I think he's talking to you," Leung told her.

"Shut up," Jo muttered, and then, disgusted with both herself and the situation, she threw down the shotgun, letting it slide down the stairs behind her.

"Place your hands behind your head and interlace your fingers," the Shock Trooper ordered.

Jo complied, trying to keep control of the situation. "You've got the wrong girl, gentlemen. I've no idea who this 'Phoebe Charlotte' is, but I'm not—"

"Remain silent, miss," the Shock Trooper barked. "Any further attempts at communication will be considered resistance and dealt with accordingly."

Leung stood a little straighter and said, "Uh, hey?"

"Yes?" the Shock Trooper said.

"Can I get out of the line of fire?"

"Is your name Leung Cha-wei?"

"Yes, yeah, it is."

"Mister Leung, please come to the top of the stairs."

Leung started up the stairs, turning his head to look back at Jo long enough to give her a big, canary-just-got-eaten grin. Jo watched the Shock Trooper step back far enough to let Leung pass, saw a second Trooper standing behind the first, just off to the right.

"Over here, please, Mister Leung," the second Trooper said.

"Here?"

"Yes, sir, thank you," the second Trooper said, and shot him in the chest with a burst from his Fairchild.

Leung toppled to one side, and from the main floor of the club, Jo heard a scattering of screams. She felt her senses broadening again, felt the dilation start once more, the sounds and the smells and sights all sharpening in her perception, and she didn't want it this time, she tried to fight it, but it happened anyway. When the first Shock Trooper spoke, it was as if he was standing at her shoulder, shouting his orders.

"Turn around and back up the stairs slowly. Make no sudden moves, make no attempt to escape, or you will be shot."

A sense of panic began to grow in her chest, the realization that she was trapped, that she was caught, that she wouldn't be able to escape. She turned, fighting to control the emotion, stepping backwards carefully, one step at a time, and she was at the top when she heard the sound of metal rasping on metal, the sound of handcuffs, and she started involuntarily. They would cuff her, they would bind her, she wouldn't be able to move.

She felt the barrel of one of the Fairchilds brush against the back of her neck, heard the first Shock Trooper telling her to hold still. A pair of hands touched her, starting at her hips, immediately finding the Maas and pulling it free. The hands returned, ran up her back, over her neck, through her hair, then down her arms. They reached around her front, moved with speed and deliberation down her chest, over her hips again, between her thighs, then down her legs.

"Clean," she heard the second Trooper say.

"Cuffs," the first one said, and she heard the squeak of plasticuffs being freed from their dispenser, felt the hands return, this time to take hold of her right wrist, and that was it, it was all she could stand. She was suddenly seeing herself pinned, unable to move, hearing herself sobbing as her spine was broken again, feeling the tremor and stab of vertebra after vertebra shattering in quick succession.

She screamed, a burst of outrage and fear and fury, twisting and ducking all together, turning her wrist in the Trooper's grip until she was holding him. She heaved, flipping him over her shoulder, sending him crashing down the stairs. She began to spin around, and red light exploded behind her eyes, and she staggered, felt gravity trying to pull her down. Another blow hit her shoulder, just to the left of her neck, and she dropped to her knees.

She looked up to see the first Shock Trooper, and now two more, and behind them another two, all of them rushing at her. The stock of the Fairchild came down again, caught her in the jaw, and then she was lying facedown, smelling ashes and spilled booze. The hands came back, more of them, and again they were grabbing her wrists, and she began thrashing wildly, kicking, flailing, screaming, until the weight of two of the Troopers was resting entirely on her back, pinning her to the floor.

Once more they were trying to get her hands bound, and this time Jo had nothing left with which to fight. She tasted the blood leaking from her mouth. She lifted her head, seeing the combat boots of the Shock Trooper before her, seeing the club. The Lisboa was empty now but for them.

Except she thought she saw Jonathan Steinberg through the lingering cigarette haze, thought she saw him coming forward, coming toward her. She wondered how badly she'd been hit in the head, what sort of damage had been done to her mind that she would imagine him here, in his CI ops gear, raising a Fairchild of his own to his shoulder. She saw the line from the weapon's laser sight cutting through the smoky air, saw it paint a dot on the side of one of the Shock Troopers' necks.

She imagined him opening fire.

CHAPTER 17

Club Lisboa—
48 Rua Praia Antonio, Macau,
People's Republic of China
October 6th, 2020

There were two bricks, eight men, and he and Rogers had neutralized the two troopers outside before Steinberg made entry. Even with backup and the escape vehicle secured, he didn't like the odds, but there were two factors that mitigated the scenario for him. The first, and most important, was that they had maintained the element of surprise. The second was Jo, his faith in her skill, his knowledge of just how lethal she could be when she chose to.

The sight of her shocked him as he came through the door, therefore, and made his heart ache and his throat tighten, made the taste of his adrenaline all the more bitter in his mouth. They had her on the ground, surrounded, two of them literally with their knees on her back. Six men in full tactical, six Shock Troopers in their body armor designed to both protect and terrify, and it made Joanna Dark look impossibly small to Steinberg; absurdly, it made him want to protect her all the more. He saw blood leaking from her nose and her mouth, saw her still trying feebly to get back to her feet, but that wasn't the worst of it.

It was that she was begging them to let her move. The air in the club was still thick with the sound of music, a recorded techno beat that poured from speakers in the ceiling and on the stage. Steinberg lost her words in the noise, catching only fragments, but he understood that Jo was pleading, screaming incoherently, and he was certain she didn't even know she was doing it.

"Hamburger, go hot," he told Rogers over his throat mike, and then he drew a bead on the neck of the Trooper closest to him. Even the necks on the Shock Troopers were armored, Steinberg knew that from experience, but he'd expected Velez would send her best to apprehend Jo, and thus he'd prepared accordingly. The rounds loaded in each of his weapons, in each of his spare mags, were CI proprietary, developed by the Armorer's partner in crime and assistant, Lawrence Foster. They were armor-piercing, high-velocity, with a high-density core of some exotic metal that Foster had gotten his devious hands on.

Generally, Steinberg avoided armor-piercing rounds. They sacrificed stopping power in exchange for penetration, and he'd much rather take one hit that put a hostile down than six that would cause the target to bleed out ten minutes later, after the fighting was over. But if his time in the Rangers had taught him anything, it was to take what he could get, and to always bring the right tool for the job. His Fairchild was set to three-round bursts, just to be on the safe side.

Rogers came back in his ear: *"Hot dog, up and running."*

Steinberg opened fire and drove a cluster of rounds through the Shock Trooper's neck. The element of surprise helped, and he was able to bead and fire another two bursts at the second of the six before they'd begun to scatter. The first burst hit the Trooper high in the chest, the second burst climbing to punch through the faceplate of his helmet.

Then Steinberg dove for cover as the remaining four poured return fire in his direction. He heard glassware shattering, wood splintering, but the reports from the weapons—his, theirs, all of them—were silent behind the incessant throb pouring from the speakers.

Steinberg ducked low behind a blackjack table, putting his shoulder into it and heaving, sending it onto its side. Pieces of green and red felt puffed into the air, and he felt the table vibrate with the impact of multiple rounds. In the now-dead monitors suspended above the stage, he saw the reflection of one of the Shock Troopers, saw him freeing a grenade from his harness. Steinberg lunged out from behind the table, loosing another three bursts, and two of them went to target, cutting the man's thighs and belly. The Trooper fell, the grenade bouncing from his hand, handle and pin still firmly in place.

The move had cost him. The three remaining Troopers had all been moving from cover to cover, using tables, the dance stage, the bar to keep themselves concealed and protected. They were about to flank him. He cast around desperately, trying to find a way out, then broke his cover a second time and dove for one of the booths along the opposite wall. He felt, rather than heard, the shots that chased after him, and he thought he might make it, that he might survive the night.

He came up short.

Well, this is a damn stupid way to die, Jonathan Steinberg thought. His mind, fed with his adrenaline, drew time taut, made the seconds stretch longer and longer, until he found himself waiting for the bullets he knew were coming, found himself wondering why he hadn't felt the punch of the killing round. *What're they waiting for?*

He'd never stopped moving, had reached the booth and the cover provided by one of the benches. Steinberg turned, coming up on one knee, ready to fire again.

Except there was no need to, none at all. There weren't three Shock Troopers standing; there weren't any still standing.

Just Jo, with a Fairchild of her own, one she'd presumably lifted from the first Trooper Steinberg had taken out. She stood amongst the wreckage by the bar, surrounded by smoke and fluttering bits of paper, unclaimed bills and cocktail napkins, lit by the strobing lights. As he watched, Steinberg saw one of the downed Troopers struggling to pull himself onto his side, trying to index his side arm. Jo saw it, too, and almost casually fired a pair of rounds in quick succession into the fallen Shock Trooper, a classic double-tap.

She raised her head, meeting Steinberg's gaze, and what he saw in her expression threatened to break his heart again.

He'd never in his life seen someone who had so clearly won a fight look like she'd lost it.

CHAPTER 18

**DataFlow Corporate Headquarters—
Office of Chief Executive Officer and
Director Cassandra DeVries—
#7 Rue de la Baume, Paris, France
October 7th, 2020**

"First of all," Anita Velez told Cassandra DeVries, "Phoebe Charlotte is not her real name."

She dropped a computer-printed five-by-seven on the desk in front of Cassandra, nearly toppling the slender vase of flowers positioned beside her laptop station. The five-by-seven was a grainy surveillance black-and-white of the same woman in the photograph Carrington had provided. The shot was at an odd angle, skewed, and the young woman who wasn't Phoebe Charlotte was apparently pointing a submachine gun of some kind at the photographer, or, perhaps more accurately, at the camera.

"Nor is she named Amanda Thiesen." Velez dropped a second five-by-seven atop the first, this one in color. The same young woman, but now wearing business attire, a cream-colored blouse and a black skirt. She was standing in an office of some sort, or perhaps a conference room somewhere.

"In fact, we don't know who she is," Velez concluded, and dropped a final photograph, this one an eight-by-ten grainy black-and-white, like the first, and apparently taken not long after the first, because this woman was wearing the same outfit. This time, however, she wasn't alone in the photograph.

The man with her looked to be in his late twenties perhaps, and wore full tactical dress, with a submachine gun identical to the one the woman had held in the first photograph. His other arm was around the young woman's shoulders, and apparently he was trying to guide her into the passenger compartment of some kind of anti-gravity vehicle.

"His name, however, is Jonathan Steinberg," Velez told Cassandra. "Do you know him?"

Cassandra pushed the photographs around on her desk, spreading them out so they lay side by side. She looked up into Velez's almost hostile scowl. "Should I?"

"You told me all of your . . . assignations"—and here, Velez's mouth twisted as if she'd been forced to swallow something sour—". . . occurred here in Paris, at various hotels. That you've never been to the main campus of the Carrington Institute outside of London, that you've never met with Carrington himself anywhere but here, in France."

"And I told you the truth." Cassandra didn't bother hiding her annoyance. It was one thing to be caught, and she'd had the grace and poise to admit it. It was another thing to be accused of continuing the deception, and Cassandra knew that Velez still wasn't satisfied.

"Then no, you wouldn't know him." Velez took one of the chrome-and-leather chairs opposite Cassandra's desk, unbuttoning her coat as she sat to keep from breaking the line of her clothing. Cassandra saw the strap of a shoulder holster, the glint of metal from the butt of Velez's gun. "But you should, Doctor DeVries."

"Why is that?"

"Because Jonathan Steinberg is Daniel Carrington's top operative, the head of his Covert Action Staff. Because in the last three years alone, Jonathan Steinberg has either directly or indirectly participated in operations directed against dataDyne and its subsidiaries costing in excess of seven and a half billion dollars in matériel and personnel. For lack of a better phrase, Doctor, Jonathan Steinberg is to the Carrington Institute what I am to dataDyne."

Cassandra ran a hand up the back of her neck, through her short hair, staring at the pictures. She felt heat creeping through her skin and up her cheeks, and the knowledge that she was blushing made her angrier, which, she knew, made the flush deepen. That Carrington had used her wasn't a surprise; she had used him, it had been a tacit component of their relationship. But there had always been boundaries, she'd believed, lines they had struggled to avoid crossing. She never had given him anything that could hurt DataFlow specifically, or dataDyne generally, not to her knowledge. He had never offered any details about CI projects, or operations.

She had believed their relationship to be one of mutual respect.

Somehow, she couldn't believe in that respect any longer. Not while she looked at a photograph of Daniel Carrington's top agent apparently escorting the mystery woman—the woman that Carrington, she realized, had used Cassandra to locate—to safety. It made her feel like a fool, and above all things, that was a feeling Cassandra DeVries couldn't stand. Like all brilliant minds, she suffered from the self-awareness that she *was* brilliant. And like all brilliant minds, when she realized she'd been outwitted or outplayed, she took it badly.

More, she took it personally.

"That son of a bitch," Cassandra said softly.

"Whether or not the woman knows anything about Zhang Li's disappearance, I don't know." Velez cocked her head, examining the flowers in their vase, then reached out and plucked one of the wilting petals off a fading violet, crumpling it in her fingers. She raised her gaze to meet Cassandra's eyes. "I highly doubt it. My suspicion is that Carrington wanted the young woman found, and lacked the resources to accomplish the task in a timely fashion. Much more efficient to manipulate you into doing it for him."

"Us," Cassandra corrected, her voice sharpening. "We were manipulated, Anita. I gave the information to you, but you acted upon it. So let's stop with the delicate positioning of blame, shall we?"

"I'm not the woman who's been sleeping with the enemy," Velez said calmly. Her eyes had the warmth and color of a glacier.

Cassandra started to retort with something about Velez's own rumored habits, but stopped herself, instead relaxing back in her chair. Velez's digs had been nearly constant since she'd caught Cassandra, but that had been all. She'd remained in Paris, staying at Cassandra's side almost constantly, and it had raised a question that, until now, Cassandra had found herself unable to answer: If Velez was so appalled at her behavior, why hadn't she taken the logical next step and brought it to the Board? For that matter, why hadn't she taken it to Waterberg, Sato, Sexton, or Murray? Accusing Cassandra of the affair with Carrington would have been enough to destroy her career, regardless of proof.

Yet she hadn't, to Cassandra's knowledge, done any of these things.

It was possible that she was just taking her time, Cassandra mused—trying to determine the extent of what, if any, damage the affair had done to DataFlow and dataDyne. It was possible that Velez had been waiting to see if Carrington's information about the fake Phoebe Charlotte would turn into something more, if it would answer the questions that lingered about Zhang Li.

All were possibilities, but now, as they sat in her office, the CORPSEC Director staring back at Cassandra with those expressionless eyes, Cassandra wondered if it wasn't something else entirely. She wondered if Anita Velez hadn't decided to play kingmaker.

"Was there anything else?" Cassandra asked.

The question, Cassandra saw with some satisfaction, seemed to catch Velez momentarily off guard. "Else?"

"Yes, was there anything else you had to say to me, Anita?"

"I'm still looking into the names you gave Carrington."

"Oh?"

"One of them, Doctor Thaddeus Killington Rose, has presented an anomaly."

Cassandra shifted in her chair, leaning forward just enough to indicate her interest, inviting Anita to continue. She even went so far as to offer the older woman a slight smile of encouragement.

Velez paused, her mouth drawing tight, and Cassandra thought for a second that she had misread the woman, and the situation. But then Velez's expression relaxed, and Cassandra knew she was correct in her read, that she had the woman.

"dataDyne policy to all subsidiaries is to maintain personnel records for seventy-five years after termination of employment," Velez said. "But the only information pharmaDyne has in its system about Doctor Rose is that he was employed as of 2015, and unemployed by the end of 2016."

"Who could have removed the information?"

"Any number of people. The system is nowhere near as secure as it should be."

"But likely suspects would include who?"

"The most obvious one is CEO Murray," Velez said. "Or someone acting under his direct orders."

"I'd like to know more about this Doctor Rose, wouldn't you, Anita?" When Velez didn't answer, Cassandra's smile grew a fraction. "Certainly, we should try to discover why the information is so important to Carrington, don't you agree? It seems clear that this was the man he was looking for, despite his performance to the contrary. And it seems clear to me now that whatever information Daniel Carrington was after, he intended to use it against us."

"I didn't say I would help you," Velez said suddenly. "I have not offered either the assistance of my person or my Division."

"But you have, Anita, because you haven't walked away from me. You haven't turned me in to the Board, nor have you sold me out to any of the other Directors in consideration for the Chairmanship."

Velez went silent again.

"Would you like to know what I think, Anita?" Cassandra DeVries asked, rising from behind her desk and, for the first time since being caught leaving the suite at the InterContinental, feeling in control once more. "Shall I tell you?"

"I'm listening, Doctor."

Cassandra came around the side of the desk, moved to the windows along the south side of her corner office. She saw Velez reflected in the glass, watching her, and she focused past the apparition to the street beyond. It was midmorning, the traffic on the boulevard light. Null-grav sedans and sport coupes floated past, and Cassandra saw a family of four, a mother and father and toddler walking together as they pushed a pram down the pavement. An AirFlow.Net relay station was visible across the street, mounted on the side of the opposite building, feeding traffic patterns to the central computer housed in the sub-levels of this very building. According to that morning's operations report, DataFlow had reached a record forty-six days without a recorded null-grav vehicle accident.

Cassandra pulled her focus back to Velez's reflection in the window, choosing her words carefully, laboring to keep any sense of admonition or indictment from her voice. "I think you're a follower, not a leader, Anita. I think you're looking to follow someone you respect, someone you believe in."

Velez continued to stare at her. "And you think I respect you?"

"Not as much as you did four days ago, perhaps, but yes, I do." Cassandra turned from the reflection, still smiling gently. "Perhaps you don't respect me much at all. But however much, or however little, it's still more than what you think of Mister Sexton and Mister Sato. It's more than you have for Ms. Waterberg. It's more than you have for Doctor Murray."

"You think highly of yourself, Doctor DeVries."

"I do, and with reason. But we're not talking about me now, we're talking about you. And you want me to be the next head of dataDyne."

Velez again kept her silence.

This time, Cassandra waited her out.

"The others," Velez said finally. "The others, they're too myopic, their vision is too narrow. They want the power and the glory and the position, not the job itself."

"A broad condemnation."

"I know more about them than they could ever imagine, Doctor. I know their wives, husbands, lovers, and children. I know where they went to school and the names of the men and women who took their virginities.

They have few secrets, few dreams, of which I am unaware. I *know* them. All of them share the same trait of personality, and while you, Doctor DeVries, are very much like them in very many ways, it is one trait that you do not have."

"Which is?"

"They are uniformly selfish." Disgust crept into Velez's voice. "dataDyne has the capacity to remake the world, the entire planet. We enter every aspect of public, personal, and professional life. We are leading revolutions in transportation, power, information, health, and quality-of-life technologies. We are changing the world every day, little by little, and I believe we are doing it for the better.

"But those others, Sexton, Murray . . . they only see what it can do for them. When they stand in front of their windows, they don't look out of them, Doctor. They just look at their own reflections."

Velez went silent once more, her expression unapologetic, almost flat. Cassandra digested what she had said, glancing again toward the window, then moved back to her desk, to the same side where Velez was seated. She took the chair beside the older woman, sitting on the edge of its seat so she could lean in close and keep her voice low.

"If I have lost your respect, Anita, I would very much like the opportunity to regain it. Let me prove to you that your faith in me is warranted, that your dreams of dataDyne's future are my own."

Velez met her eyes and held the gaze, as if trying to evaluate the truth of Cassandra's words.

"Where should we start?" she asked.

"Where Carrington has started," Cassandra DeVries said. "With Doctor Thaddeus Killington Rose."

CHAPTER 19

Carrington Institute—Grounds—
London, England
October 7th, 2020

Carrington awaited her at the edge of the lake as the sun was setting, the collar of his tweed coat turned against the breeze, the ever-present walking stick in his right hand planted firmly in the mud. He heard her coming only because Jo didn't bother to try to come silently, and when he turned to her, she could see his face lit by the gold and red falling in the west. He looked as serious as she had ever seen him, and more than a little sad.

She slapped him anyway, and she didn't hold much back when she did it. Her palm struck him across the cheek, the smack made louder by its echo off the surface of the placid lake. Carrington kept his feet, not moving except for his head.

"Who in the hell do you think you are?" Jo shouted at him. "How *dare* you play with my life like this?"

Jo glared at him, let the echo of her voice fade across the water. Her heart was racing in her chest, her breathing too fast, and it struck her as odd that she could stay so cool and controlled whenever bullets flew around her, but that when the weapons being used were emotional rather than physical, she found herself desperately out of her depth. It wasn't that Carrington himself frightened her, though she supposed that he well should; it was that she was terrible at this, that she was not equipped for emotional honesty, and she knew it.

Another legacy of her father's, she suspected, from a man who'd found it easier to say "nice shot" than to say "I love you."

Carrington brought one hand to his cheek, using his thick fingers to gently palpate the skin where she'd struck him. He brought his head around slowly to face her, and she saw his tongue probing the inside of his mouth. He coughed once, lowered his face, and spat out a mixture of blood and saliva onto the muddy shore.

"I'm trying to save the world from itself, Joanna," Carrington said softly, bringing his eyes up again to meet her own. In the fading daylight, the only thing she could read in them was sincerity. "Sometimes it makes me lose perspective."

"You put dataDyne onto me, you bastard! *You* sent them after me!"

"Yes, I did. You'd left me no other choice."

Jo gaped at him, brought her hands up to her temples as if to check that her head was still attached, that it was, indeed, processing the incoming information properly.

"You could have left me alone!" she said.

Carrington squinted at her, the corners of his mouth dipping for an instant. "There are times I wonder if your naiveté is truly a product of your youth, or rather your education."

"I am *not* naive!"

"Then stop acting as if you are!" he shouted back, and then, before Jo could respond, added much more calmly, "You and I both know it was only a matter of time before dataDyne began searching for you, and not because of your actions at pharmaDyne Vancouver. I don't dispute that I pushed them in the proper direction—of course I did, I needed their help to find you. But they were going to find you, and sooner not later. When that happened, there would be no backup for you when the Shock Troopers came calling."

"I could've stayed hidden, I could've stayed out of their sight—"

"Come now, Joanna. You'd been away from the Institute less than forty-eight hours before you'd taken a hunt, and the moment you did, you left a trail for dataDyne to follow."

"They weren't looking for me until you told them to."

"That's entirely beside the point. I couldn't risk losing you to dataDyne, Joanna. Using their resources to find you was the most expedient, the most efficient solution."

"I could have died," Jo said.

"I had faith that together, you and Mister Steinberg would keep that from coming to pass."

Jo felt the pressure of frustration inside her, as if it were trying to push its way out of her chest. She put the heel of her palm to her forehead, trying to massage the emotion back down, felt herself suddenly tired, her muscles suddenly sore.

"It mattered that much?" she asked softly. "It mattered that much that I come back?"

"More than you can possibly imagine, Joanna."

She heard the squelch of the mud as the old man moved, the sound of his walking stick coming down again.

"Let's walk," he said, and began to slowly lumber off along the edge of the lake.

After a moment, Jo followed.

"I make more mistakes than I care to admit," Carrington confided in her as they turned up the road, now moving in the direction of the Institute buildings. "I've made several with you. To be honest, it's because I've never met anyone like you before."

"It's mutual, I assure you," Jo said.

Carrington glanced over to her, managed a sardonic smile. His breathing was becoming heavier with the exertion of the walk, and Jo had to remind herself to slow down.

"Then perhaps you understand my predicament, Joanna," Carrington said. "I think of myself as a good judge of character, as a man who can read people quickly and, for the most part, accurately. It's a skill I've used to great result throughout my life. And if I may say so, you have a similar skill."

"I'm not sure I'd agree."

"No, you just use it in a different fashion. I suppose it's something you learned from your father, but you're remarkably adept at being the person people think you should be, when you put your mind to it. You never would've been able to infiltrate pharmaDyne otherwise."

"You have operatives, agents who train—"

"Not like that I don't." Carrington suddenly stopped, extending his arms wide in both directions, turning to face Jo. He raised his hand holding the cane a little higher. "What I have, Jo, is an intelligence-gathering arm, thus, a handful of deep-cover agents hidden in hypercorporations and government departments. They are precious few, and it takes a lot of time and effort and money to recruit them, to train them, and then to insert them. While they are extraordinarily capable—as Benjamin Able was—they are ill-suited to combat operations."

He lowered his right hand, settling the walking stick on the road once more, then lifted his still-extended left hand higher. "And here I have Jonathan Steinberg and the three dozen or so men and women he's trained—my commandos, for lack of a better word. You've seen them in action, you know they're brilliant at what they do, but they're also about as subtle as an elephant relieving itself on the Rosetta Stone."

Jo laughed before she could stop herself, the image so absurd that she could envision it perfectly.

Carrington lowered his left hand, grinning, pleased. Then the grin faded, and he said, "But I don't have anyone like you, Jo. I don't have someone who can do both, who can *be* both."

She felt her own smile fading away as well. A breeze had risen, cold and damp with the smell of the cut grass and blooming flowers now being hidden by the nightfall.

"I'm not certain I want to be the person who can do both," Jo told him.

Carrington seemed to consider that for a moment, and then he did that thing with the walking stick that she'd discovered he was so fond of, bringing both hands together on its head and planting it just far enough in front of him so it would support him when he leaned forward.

"You'll forgive me for saying so, Joanna, but you already are."

"Tell me something," Jo asked Carrington.

They were rounding the far side of the gymnasium, beginning to circle back toward the Institute's Main Building. Night had completed its fall, and the temperature had dropped along with it, but so had the breeze, and it was comfortable, and the sky was cloudless, and even with the light dome thrown up by London, they could see stars shining above. It made it easy to imagine that they were simply two people on a stroll, an old man walking with his grandchild, perhaps. It made it easy to think that nothing being said could be that important at all.

"Tell me something," Jo said again. "How can I do the things that I do?"

"I'm not certain I understand the question."

"No, that won't work, Mister Carrington. If you want me to come join you and your Institute and your war, you're going to need to start being honest with me."

"A difficult promise for me to make, but one I'll endeavor to keep." After a moment, he added, "And it's not my war, Joanna. It's *everyone's.* We're just the only people aware of it."

"You'd think they would have noticed by now."

Carrington snorted. "People are herd animals, Joanna. What they see the rest of the flock do, they're quick to follow. As long as the herd is fed, sheltered, and guided, they remain remarkably easy to manipulate."

"That's a tad cynical, don't you think?"

"Is it? I've believed it for so long, and seen no proof to the contrary in all that time, that it is simply my view of the world. The people don't notice what's happening around them because they don't want to, Joanna. They'd much rather have their microwaved pot noodles and their shiny new lifeCards and a chance to make virtual love to a fantasy version of their favorite movie star than be bothered with the how and why and who of it all."

"And that's *very* cynical."

"In over sixty years of life, I've seen very little to disprove it, Joanna."

She thought about arguing the point, then decided to let it go in favor of pursuing her previous question. "You didn't answer me."

"Because I didn't understand the question," Carrington said almost hastily, as if afraid of shattering what meager goodwill seemed to be developing between them. "Not because I don't wish to."

"I'll rephrase it, then."

Jo stopped, waited for Carrington to follow suit. They'd come down a side road used for grounds vehicles, and were now at the base of a small valley. Above them, to the left and in the distance, Jo could see the lights shining in the Manor. To the right, windows blazed in the Institute's Main Building.

Carrington planted his walking stick, watching her carefully in the darkness.

Without warning, Jo lunged forward, snapping her right leg forward, hooking the walking stick with the toe of her boot. It tore free from Carrington's grip, and the old man began to utter a cry, but she'd already moved forward, catching him against her shoulder, her right arm wrapped around his back. He was a big man, heavy, but she could hold his weight.

After a second's pause to allow him to catch his breath, Jo helped him regain his balance. It was only when she handed him back the walking stick she was holding in her left hand that she saw him realize that it had never hit the ground, that she had caught it even as she'd caught him.

"That," Jo said. "How can I do that? How can I fire thirty rounds at a moving target while I'm in motion at the same time, and be certain each of my shots will hit? How can I be a better shot than Steinberg? How is it that I'll be in the middle of a firefight and know exactly where to move, how to do it, how to survive unscathed? How is it that when I do get hit, when I am injured, I seem to recover in half the time it would take all the others around me?

"And why, Mister Carrington? Why is it that when I choose to kill, I do it as easily and effortlessly as breathing?"

"You want to know why you're different?" Carrington asked.

"Yes."

"I don't know," he said. "I wish that I did. I'd bottle it and make a half dozen more just like you, Joanna."

Jo hissed in disgust. "A half dozen murderers."

Even in the darkness, she could see the look of shock on Carrington's face. "Is that how you see yourself?"

"I'm a killer, Mister Carrington."

"No, you're a soldier, Joanna." Carrington's voice had lowered, his tone becoming almost urgent. "There's a world of difference between the two. A killer is always a killer, and that's all he can ever hope to be. It's the thing that gives him purpose and pleasure, perhaps the only thing that does. A killer is a killer by nature, Joanna, by design.

"But a soldier, a soldier is first and foremost a warrior, a fighter. Some of them come to the battlefield for a cause, some to prove themselves, others for revenge—there are a thousand reasons, some noble and others not. They do what they do by choice, and they do what they do not to kill, but to win the battle being fought. Sometimes, yes, even oftentimes, that requires the taking of lives. But that isn't what defines them.

"For a killer, death is *all* that defines them."

Jo said nothing, thinking about his words, thinking about the truth she was finding in them. Wondering if she saw it not because it was truly there, but because she so desperately wanted to believe Carrington was right.

As if he sensed what she was thinking, Carrington added, "The problem you're having, Joanna, isn't that you're a killer. It's that you're a soldier, and you haven't yet realized that the war is upon you. You're a soldier who's been in skirmishes and battles, and never yet realized that you're part of the war you're fighting."

"Against dataDyne?" Her voice was so soft as to be almost inaudible, even to herself. "Your invisible war against dataDyne?"

"Against all of them. dataDyne's just the largest of the

hypercorps, the most pervasive, and in its way, its evil is the most banal. But Beck-Yama, Core-Mantis, all of the others, they're branches of the same tree. All of them would be dataDyne if they could."

Jo again retreated into silence, staring off at the lights of the Manor, at a house too large and too empty for Carrington to live in alone. She hadn't truly known what hatred was until she'd lost her father. Jack Dark had been her whole world, her future. When he'd been stolen from her—and she blamed dataDyne for that—the need for vengeance had been all-consuming.

Her father was still dead, and dataDyne still lived, and she found it almost impossible to accept that.

"Some people are born to a task, Joanna." Carrington was almost whispering now. "Some come from the womb destined to write concertos, to sing arias, to cure diseases. Some come born with the gifts that will make them the brightest star ever seen in their field, be it in sport, or science, or politics. But they're all born with gifts to guide them to that destiny."

Jo looked away from the lights of the Manor, saw that Carrington was focused entirely on her. His expression reminded her of her father, the way he would look at her when she was lost and confused, when the world made no sense to her, when he would bring it all back into order.

"How can you do the things you do?" Carrington said. "I don't know. But it's clear to everyone who sees you do them that you were born to it, Joanna. You were born to fight, to soldier, to battle. You have a genius for it. And the only way you will ever come to peace with it is if you embrace it, and find the war you're willing to fight."

"Your war," she said.

"Not mine," Carrington said. "Ours."

Jo stared into his eyes, trying to see past his passion and his zealotry, remembering again her father's warnings about Daniel Carrington.

"Where do I start?" she asked.

Carrington exhaled, and Jo realized he'd been holding his breath.

"Follow me," Carrington said.

The picture on the monitor was of a Caucasian male, bald, in his fifties. His eyes were brown, almost black, and his cheeks and chin drooped slightly with the weight of his flesh. He wore a white shirt and a black necktie, and the white collar of a lab coat floated out from around his neck. What little expression had made it from his face to the photograph spoke of annoyance, and from that alone, Jo didn't like him.

"Doctor Thaddeus Killington Rose," Carrington said, resting a broad hand atop the monitor on his desk. "Born in Huntington, Quebec, November 7th, 1967. Educated at the University of Chicago, B.S., Stanford University, M.S. and Ph.D. in chemistry and biogenetics. Hired by pharmaDyne beginning July 18th, 2001, employment terminated July 3rd, 2016. Whereabouts unknown."

Jo peered at the man on the monitor for a moment longer, then looked to Carrington.

"We need to find him," Carrington said.

"Why?"

"Because Doctor Thaddeus Killington Rose is responsible for the murder of thirty-seven million, three hundred and sixty-four thousand, two hundred and eleven men, women, and children."

The number was so inconceivable, Jo was certain she'd heard it incorrectly.

"The superflu, Joanna," Carrington said. "Doctor Rose is the man who created the superflu."

CHAPTER 20

Gustav Weiss, Solicitor—
882 Minervastrasse,
Zurich, Switzerland
October 8th, 2020

Hayes liked the part where they screamed for mercy the most, but you had to get there the right way, you couldn't just go in whole hog, reaching for the pain. You had to take them up to it, you had to escort them, let the fear play its part. If you did it right, you could get them to tell you everything before you even had to begin cutting.

With two programmers, three bankers, and one secretary, Hayes had done it right. He'd cut them anyway, at the end, partially to keep them silent, but mostly because he could. Living in Vancouver, working at pharmaDyne, Hayes's natural urges were kept in check by his father. In Vancouver, Hayes had to behave, had to keep up appearances, had to confine his pleasures to interrogations in Sub-Five and the occasional bust-up in a local bar. But his father frowned upon even those, and as a result, Hayes had little opportunity to indulge himself.

Until a week ago, when his father had handed him a

stack of false passports, a half dozen credit cards, and a thin, locked case that was in all ways identical to the one Doctor Murray habitually carried. The dermals were in the case, and the case was locked, and every twelve hours a slit would open in its side, and one of the precious patches would slide out. Hayes knew that if he tried to force the dispenser open, to take more than his allotment, the device would eat itself.

His father handed him all these things and then said, "Find Rose. I don't care how. Do whatever it takes, but find him, and kill him."

So Hayes was doing whatever it took, just as Doctor Murray, just as his father, had ordered. If he was enjoying himself, well, he didn't see a problem in that.

He had permission, after all.

For the most part, it had been a difficult week and a half, ever since the redheaded killer had made a fool out of him with her rooftop escape. Hayes had tried to console himself with the knowledge that she had at least failed in her attempt to rescue the spy, and had hoped his father would take some comfort from that, as well.

His father hadn't, but neither had he behaved in a manner consistent with his disappointment in Hayes in the past. Those times, the abuse had been abundant, and quick to arrive. Doctor Murray would threaten and insult, reminding Hayes how very fortunate he was that Murray took care of him at all. He would strike him, sometimes with a fist, sometimes with whatever lay at hand, a coffee mug or a stapler or anything else nearby. Then his father would withhold his love, in the form of Hayes's fix, and that was the worst, of course, the withdrawal both debilitating and agonizing.

Hayes had expected the worst, but instead, his father

had fallen into a mood as deep and dark as the pits of hell themselves. He'd not even questioned Hayes about what had transpired, only confirming that the red-haired agent had gotten away. He'd barely spoken at all.

The mood had transferred to Hayes, and he in turn had taken it out upon those around him. Beaumont took the brunt of it at work—an easy target—but no one was spared. When Hayes had returned home that night to find Kimiko still waiting in his bed, as he'd asked of her, it had turned ugly. She'd left hurling curses at him, and both of them knew she was lucky to be leaving at all.

For the next three days, his father barely spoke to him, and Hayes suffered growing apprehension. There had been no punishment, not yet, but he was certain it was coming. At the same time, he began to worry for his father, for the man whose brilliance and love had protected him, saved him, sheltered him. Hayes was certain it was all his fault, that his failure had been so catastrophic, so complete, that his father would have no choice but to abandon him.

That thought alone was terrifying almost beyond comprehension. To go back to what he'd been before, to lose not just the power in the dermals but the purpose of his life . . . Hayes would do anything to prevent that. Until Doctor Murray had taken Hayes under his care, the young man had been nothing, a collection of base desire and fury, aimless and reckless. It was his father who had given him his way, had given him a task. It was Doctor Murray who had explained that they were a team, that what benefited the one benefited the other.

Hayes had believed him. He'd always wanted a father, and to have one as rich and powerful and brilliant as Doctor Murray, one who appreciated him for who he was and what he could do, how well he could do it—it was like living in a child's fantasy.

Then, after three days of waiting for the hammer to fall,

his father came to him. Instead of acrimony, he'd brought the documents and the dermal pack. He'd given Hayes his orders.

"Rose has been a leech on my body for four years, my boy," his father said. "I've been content to allow his blackmail to continue. For four years, it has been safer to pay for his silence than to do what is required to guarantee it.

"It may be that Carrington knows nothing, that he will learn nothing. If the stakes were different, I would be content to wait. But the stakes are very high, the stakes are for control of dataDyne itself, and if there is even the slightest chance that Rose will compromise our chances, he must be dealt with."

"Where do I start?"

"Follow the money, of course," Doctor Murray said. "Start with the banks, the ones in Australia, the Caribbean, and Switzerland, the places where I transferred his payments. None of them will lead you to him, not directly, and several, I suspect, will be dead trails. But I have paid him a lot of money over the years, Laurent, and so much currency leaves a trail. Find the people who handled the transfers, find where they sent the money. Be persuasive."

Hayes had been persuasive for the last seven days. He'd mostly used his hands to do it, and sometimes he'd used a blade. He'd done it twice more in Sydney, once in an alleyway at three in the morning, and once just after dark, in a parking lot. The reward for his efforts had been limited, but enough to persuade him that Cuba should be his next stop.

In Havana, he'd been impatient, and done it in the bank

manager's office, during business hours, and that was why the secretary had needed to be included, because the man wouldn't stop screaming, and Hayes had to cut him a second time to fully get his attention. When the secretary came into the office to see what all the commotion was about, he'd had to keep her from leaving.

Needless to say, Hayes had left Havana in a hurry.

But he'd learned enough; he'd learned the name of a private bank in Geneva. The two gentlemen he dealt with there, however, were of a different breed, and he'd had to work at it to convince them that their commitment to their nation's private banking laws was ill-advised, if not potentially fatal. It had taken him a long time, and when he'd finished, Hayes needed to dispose of his clothes and acquire new ones.

Then he caught the train to Zurich, to meet Gustav Weiss.

It was easy to get in to see Herr Weiss. All Hayes had to do was make an appointment.

They met in the man's small office in an old, wood-paneled and heavily carpeted building. Weiss was standing when Hayes entered, and politely offered his hand when he introduced himself. They exchanged pleasantries and Weiss offered Hayes a seat, then took his own behind the desk.

"You were referred to me?" Gustav Weiss asked. His accent swung to the German, but his English was precise, and easy to understand.

Hayes nodded, wondering what he should say. He wasn't good at this part, at the manipulating part. He didn't think fast enough in circumstances like these, and he was too impatient, as well. The direct approach was more his style.

"Yeah," Hayes said, after a moment. "Yeah, this guy I know, you did an account for him."

"A private account, you mean?"

"Yeah, one of those."

"And you wish me to establish one for you?" Weiss smiled, showing Hayes perfectly white teeth. "This can be easily done. Say, two thousand euros?"

"No, not that, not like that. What I mean is, I need to know how he contacted you."

Weiss's smile faltered, and the man looked puzzled. Hayes guessed him to be in his late forties, perhaps his early fifties, though if he was taking any of pharma-Dyne's line of "youthful vigor" products, he could easily be in his sixties or even older.

"I suspect he contacted me just as you are doing so now."

Hayes shook his head quickly, his frustration growing. *This isn't going to work,* he thought. *Just use the knife and get to it.*

"No, what I mean is, I can't find him, and I need you to tell me where he is."

"I cannot possibly give you that information. I would not even give that information to the police. I certainly will not give it to you."

"His name is Thaddeus Rose. Just tell me where I can find him," Hayes said, then added, as an afterthought, "Please."

What little remained of Weiss's smile vanished. The man stood abruptly from behind his desk. He thrust out his right hand, pointing his index finger over Hayes's head, at the door out of the office.

"Leave," Weiss said. "Immediately. I will not ask twice."

So much for being polite, Hayes thought.

In one move, he brought the new knife he'd purchased in Geneva out from his pocket, flicking the blade open with his thumb, bringing it up in an ascending arc. The thin blade caught the light as it moved, glittering, and Weiss grunted, then uttered a sound of choked agony. Hayes got to his feet.

Weiss still stood exactly as he had, but now he was staring at his right hand, and the blood that was beginning to dribble onto his desk, making a puddle around his severed index finger. He moved his eyes dumbly to Hayes, opened his mouth to scream, and Hayes reached out and put his left hand around the man's neck, and put the tip of the knife in his right beneath one of Weiss' eyes.

"You scream and I'll pop your eye out," Hayes told him, suddenly feeling much more at ease with himself and the situation as a whole. "I'll leave you alive, but I'll blind you, you understand?"

Herr Weiss began to nod quickly, then felt the tip of the blade scratching his skin and stopped himself from continuing. He'd gone pale, begun to perspire.

"Sit down," Hayes told him, releasing the man's neck.

Weiss moved as ordered, and Hayes whipped the blade across the man's front. Weiss whimpered, flinching, then opened his eyes to see that he'd been left untouched, but that his necktie had been cut in two. The tie was silk, a design in blue and black of swirling lines surrounding darker splotches of navy. Hayes pointed at the pieces of the tie with his knife.

"Use that on your stump," Hayes said. "You're making a mess."

Weiss fumbled for the largest piece of his severed tie, taking it with one blood-slicked hand and pressing it over what remained of his index finger. He whimpered again, biting his lower lip.

Hayes used his left hand to take a slip of paper from his back pocket, unfolding it with his fingers. He dropped the paper on the desk, in the blood.

"Take it," he told Weiss.

Weiss balked for a second, as if unable to decide which was the more dangerous action for him to undertake, releasing the bandage or following the order. Hayes tapped the side of his blade against the edge of the desk impatiently. Weiss took the paper.

"That's the account number," Hayes said. "I got it off two guys in Geneva, the guys who sent me to you. That's Rose's account number, I know that, and it's his most recently used one, it's not even three months old. So you're going to go into your computer or wherever, and you're going to give me all the information you have on him, on how you set it up for him, on all of it."

"Yes," Weiss said, his voice like thread. "Yes, I will do that."

"Now would be good," Hayes advised.

Weiss turned in his chair, reaching for the mouse beside his keyboard, smearing blood along the top of his fine oak desk. He made a couple of clicks, then carefully pecked out a long string of digits on the keyboard, trying to avoid using his index finger. A couple of times he missed, brushing the stump against the keys, and he sobbed with the pain.

Hayes had to fight the urge to laugh.

Then Weiss stopped suddenly, reading what had appeared on his monitor.

"What?" Hayes asked.

Weiss looked from the screen to Hayes, and there was still fear in his eyes, Hayes saw that for certain, but it was even more acute than before. The man's eyes had gone wide, his mouth trembling.

All at once, Weiss lunged out of his chair, diving for the wall, and Hayes realized he was going for the power cord, trying to shut everything down at once. It took him by surprise, but the patch was still doing its job, and the edge it gave him was enough. He moved, flicking the knife with his wrist, and the blade buried itself in the side of Weiss's neck, and the man gargled and faltered. Hayes was in front of him then, and he kicked him viciously once, in the face. Weiss flopped back, his head turning, driving the blade further through his throat. He twitched, then stopped moving.

Hayes reached down and freed his knife, wiping the blade clean on the dead man's trousers. Then he took a look at the monitor, curious to see what it was that could have scared Gustav Weiss more than Hayes had. It took almost half a minute for Hayes to decipher the meaning of the words on the screen, mostly because he'd been expecting to see the name "Rose," and it just wasn't anywhere there to be found. But the account number he'd given Weiss, it *had* been Rose's, he was certain. It didn't make sense.

Then he saw the name "Portia de Carcareas" on the screen, and her mailing address, and the name of the corporation she worked for, and it all fell into place. It didn't just make sense; it made perfect sense.

Well, shit, Hayes thought. *Father isn't going to like this one bit.*

FROM:	CI-TECHNICAL—FARREL, REBECCA
TO:	CARRINGTON, DANIEL
SUBJECT:	TRAFFIC INTERCEPT, PROJECT: INITIAL VECTOR
DATED:	08 OCTOBER 2020

AT 14:21.08 HOURS LOCAL THIS DATE, ECHELON IV LISTENING POST 23, ZÜRICH CANTON, TRANSMITTED THE FOLLOWING INTERCEPT TO CI-MUNICH. THE TRANSMISSION WAS ENCODED AND BROADCAST ON THE SECURE DATADYNE EXECUTIVE BAND, 990.11 GHZ. RECORDING COMMENCED 14:21.10. DECRYPTION WAS ACCOMPLISHED USING WINDTALKER-9.0 DECRYPT SUITE, AND REQUIRED SEVEN

HOURS, FIFTY-THREE MINUTES TO COMPLETE BEFORE BEGINNING TRANSCRIPTION.

- VOICE RECOGNITION IDENTIFIES RECEIVING PARTY AS MURRAY, FRIEDRICH WILLIAM, DOCTOR, CHIEF EXECUTIVE OFFICER—PHARMADYNE.
- NEGATIVE MATCH RESULT FOR INITIATING PARTY.
- CALL WAS CONDUCTED IN ENGLISH, AND LASTED A TOTAL DURATION OF 00:01:08.

TRANSCRIPT FOLLOWS.

BEGIN TRANSCRIPT

MURRAY:	—NEWS FOR ME?
UNIDENTIFIED PARTY:	I—I WAS CLOSE, BUT SOMETHING'S HAPPENED, SOMETHING YOU'RE NOT GOING TO LIKE.
M:	YOU PROMISED ME YOU WOULD HANDLE THIS, SON. I'M COUNTING ON YOU.
UP:	AND I'M DOING EVERYTHING I CAN, BUT THIS . . . THERE'S A—A COMPLICATION. I FOUND THE ATTORNEY, WEISS, HE SET UP THE MOST RECENT ACCOUNT. BUT THERE'S NO DIRECT LINK, THAT'S THE PROBLEM.
M:	BUT IT IS HIS ACCOUNT?
UP:	I'M SURE IT IS, I'M SURE OF IT, FATHER! BUT THE THING IS, ROSE ISN'T THE ONE WHO OPENED IT. SOMEONE ELSE OPENED IT FOR HIM.
M:	WHO?
UP:	THAT'S THE THING, IT'S THIS WOMAN, I THINK IT'S A WOMAN, HER NAME IS PORTIA DE CARCAREAS.

M: The name means nothing to me.
UP: She works for Core-Mantis, Father. Weiss's information, on his computer, her contact information is through Core-Mantis OmniGlobal. I think Rose is working for Core-Mantis now, I think they've got him . . . Father? Father, are you still there?
M: Yes, I'm still here.
UP: What do you want me to do?
M: Is it sanitized?
UP: Here? Yes, sir, yes it is.
M: Then come home. I need you here.
UP: I'll be home by morning, sir.

Call terminates.

TRANSCRIPT ENDS_

Evaluation:

Based on this intercept, the following checks were immediately initiated as per your orders pursuant to the execution of *Operation: Initial Vector:*

1. "Weiss"

Most likely Gustav Weiss, attorney.

Local fire and emergency personnel were dispatched to 882 Minervastrasse at 14:33 Hours, Zurich Local, to combat a fire that had erupted at the location. Initial investigation of the cause of the blaze indicates the presence of an accelerant. Arson is suspected. Weiss's body was recovered at the scene. Autopsy is pending.

2. "Unknown Party"

Initial evaluation concludes that the repeated uses of the terms "father" and "son" during the call may indicate a workname code in place, to prevent the identity of the communicating parties from being revealed. However, the absence of subsequent codes to refer to subject Weiss and, more crucially, subject Rose, disprove this theory. An examination of Doctor Murray's entry under *Who's Who 2019* fails to include any mention of a marriage, or children, though his corporate biography lists one son, "Laurent." No records available on subject "Laurent" though it is possible that this individual is the "Unknown Party." Recommend further investigation, possibly into adoption records.

3. "Portia de Carcareas"

Ms. Carcareas is known to us as a Core-Mantis OmniGlobal operative, specializing in counterintelligence and operational security concerns, as well as executive talent recruitment. Records indicate that she has worked for Core-Mantis as a headhunter for the past three-plus years. She is known to be responsible for the Core-Mantis acquisition of Dr. Andrew DeClerk, lead bioengineer, R&D, Beck-Yama InterNational (2018); Mustafa al-Zakara, Chief Scientific Advisor, Induction International, a dataDyne subsidiary (2018); and Dr. Irina Ganieva, Chair of the Department of Genetics and Structural DNA Recombination at Novosibirsk University (2019).

"Portia de Carcareas" is an alias. Real name is unknown.

Conclusion:

It is clear from this traffic that Dr. Murray is actively searching for Dr. Rose, as you suspected. It is plausible to conclude that Dr. Rose is currently employed by Core-Mantis. Based on these facts, it is my conclusion that Dr. Rose is most likely assigned to one of three Core-Mantis biotechnology/bioresearch facilities: Core-Mantis "Cold Base" Antarctica, Core-Mantis Johannesburg, or Core-Mantis Solomon Islands. Without further access to Core-Mantis records, greater specification is impossible.

All CI-operated listening stations have been directed to continue to monitor for traffic on the above-listed frequency.

Thank you for your attention.

MESSAGE ENDS_

CHAPTER 21

Carrington Institute—
Training Range—
London, England
October 9th, 2020

The Armorer squinted down at the readouts on his workstation, then covered the mike that extended from his headset with his left hand, turning to say something to Foster, keeping their conversation muted.

Jo watched the two speak, one seated at an angle to the other, at their desks on the raised concrete stand behind the bulletproof Plexiglas that separated their workstation from the actual firing range. She tried not to be curious, and still found herself wondering what they were saying all the same, wondering how they could possibly find fault in her performance.

The Armorer, Potts, had greeted her when she'd arrived on the range with the same characteristic grunt he'd employed during their last meeting, when he'd equipped her for the pharmaDyne run. He'd indicated Foster with his elbow, giving a curt introduction, then handed Jo a set of ear protectors and a pair of shooter's glasses.

"Let's see if you're as special as the old man thinks," Potts had said.

Foster had opened the door to the range, handing her the empty Falcon and five clips, then waving her to the nearest shooting point. Each clip had been fully loaded, eighteen nine-millimeter rounds, and Jo had reached the stand, put the glasses and protectors in place, and hadn't yet reached for the Falcon when the buzzer sounded.

Oh, so that's how it's going to be, she'd thought.

And she'd taken up the pistol, slapping the first clip into place and racking the slide all in practically the same motion, and the first target was already retreating from her, clacking downrange on its motorized chain. They were Q-targets, black-and-white silhouettes of a standing male, torso to head, and she'd begun firing as fast as the Falcon would allow, which could be pretty damn fast if one put one's finger into it, as it were.

She'd emptied the Falcon into the target's head before it had finished its trip downrange, and almost immediately, a second target had popped up, perhaps twenty meters away. This one moved laterally, across her field of vision, faster than the first. Jo had reloaded, then emptied the gun yet again. The slide had just locked back when a third target dropped down from the ceiling, moving even faster than the one before, and far more erratically.

Again, Jo had emptied the contents of the Falcon's clip into the head of the Q-target.

Then they'd popped two targets at once, one from below, one from the ceiling, and again, they were erratic in their course, moving at the equivalent of an adult's sprint, jerking, turning, changing their elevation and even orientation as they went. Jo fired off her last two clips with the same precision she'd used with the previous three.

With the last shot fired, the echo of gunfire fading to silence on the range, she'd lowered the emptied pistol, checking that the slide was locked back, that the weapon was indeed empty and safe, before setting it down once more on the point in front of her. She'd removed her glasses, pulled the ear protectors down around her neck, heard the oddly comforting sound of the spent brass rattling on the floor at her feet. She'd looked to the two men, waiting for their verdict.

It seemed to be taking them a while.

Foster turned his head slightly away from Potts, looking toward Jo. He was in his forties, sturdily built, with a thick head of salt-and-pepper hair. He seemed to Jo to be much less stern of a personality than the Armorer, something he then proved by giving her a wink. Jo couldn't help but grin in response.

Potts saw him do it, glared first at Foster, then at Jo, then pulled his hand away from the mike.

"Yes, very well done, very nice." The Armorer's voice came through the speakers hanging from the wall behind the firing points, brusque and vaguely dismissive. "That was all quite impressive, yes, but I think we both know that the Falcon is a remarkably forgiving weapon, that the most muddy-thumbed child can master it. Let's see how you do with something that isn't as generous."

"Fine," Jo said, and she replaced the goggles and resettled the protectors over her ears. Foster hopped down from the observation stand, disappeared for a second behind the open doors of one of the many gun safes lining the walls outside the range, then made his way through to door to her, carrying a MagSec 4 and another five clips of ammunition.

"It's a piece of crap," Foster confided to her as he handed the pistol over, his voice muted by her covered ears. "The three-round burst is awful, and even with the best control the barrel rises like a whore when the fleet's in town."

"I am familiar with the gun," Jo told him.

"I'm sure you are, love." Foster gathered the Falcon

and the spent clips, gave her a broad and genuine smile, then turned and departed the range.

As soon as the door to the range clicked shut, Jo heard the buzzer sound again, saw fresh targets descend, launching into a new dance.

She took the MagSec up and joined them.

"Potts was impressed," Steinberg told her as they walked from the firing range to the combat suite housed on the ground floor of the Institute Main Buildings. "Which is saying a lot, because very little impresses that man."

"He didn't act like it," Jo said.

"He smiled."

"And that's rare, is it?"

"He's never smiled at me." Steinberg consulted the PDA in his hand, reviewing the results of her range time. "He's qualified you on most Institute-approved weaponry, and rated you 'master' on over half of them. Ninety to ninety-five percent accuracy, across the board."

"He plays dirty, or else it would be one hundred percent," Jo said. "Mixes up the targets, randomizes their sequencing."

"Of course he plays dirty, Jo. So does the enemy."

"I'm just saying that I can do better."

"I wouldn't worry about it."

"But I can do better, Jonathan, I can score one hundred percent across the board."

He tapped a score on the PDA. "Not if you keep refusing to use the Magnum."

"I hate that gun," she said, her expression darkening a bit.

"The DY's a good gun. I use it myself," he replied. "I've seen you handle everything else, so why not—"

"Why not drop it?" she snapped. "If you need to compensate for something by fondling your big shiny gun, that's your business. Leave me out of it."

They'd reached the suite, and Steinberg tucked his PDA into its holster on his belt, began tapping in a sequence on the keypad beside the door. "Memorize this."

Jo watched his fingers on the pad, saying, "I can do better."

"You passed, you're fully qualified. Don't fret it."

The door clicked open, parting down its center with a pneumatic hiss.

"What're we doing now?"

"What was the code I just used to open the door?"

"Star-zed-three-three-eight-seven-one-seven-nine-seven-four-six," Jo said, rattling off the sequence without bothering to hide her own impatience. "What're we doing now?"

"I want to check your tacticals," Steinberg said, leading the way into the darkened suite. Slowly, lights began coming up along the walls, revealing a black room, blue grid lines drawn across its every surface. "You're going to do some combat drills."

"You've already seen me in combat."

"This will be different." Steinberg moved to an apparently featureless portion of the wall, pressing a button that, until that moment, had remained unseen. A panel slid back, revealing a rack of Fairchild DW-P5s, and a selection of VR goggles.

"Different how?"

"Group tactics, small unit movement, things like that." He pulled one of the Fairchilds down, checked it quickly, then handed it to Jo.

Jo frowned, taking the weapon and examining it. It had been modified for virtual training, outfitted to simulate the real thing. "I'm no good at that kind of thing."

"You're good at everything else, why not this?"

"It's not . . . it's not what I do, I don't work well in a team."

Steinberg arched an eyebrow. "You worked with your father, Jo."

"That was different."

"Your problem," Steinberg said, handing her a set of the goggles and then brushing past her toward another portion of wall, this one with a touchscreen built in, "is that you're afraid to let anyone see you make a mistake."

The comment stung, mostly because Jo realized it was true. "I just don't think I should be evaluated on something that I've little experience in, that's all. It's not a fair evaluation."

Steinberg chuckled to himself, began tapping in commands on the touchscreen. "Straight-A student, weren't you? Classic overachiever."

"I don't think there's anything wrong in wanting to be good at the things that you do," Jo said tightly.

"You don't want to just be good, Jo, you want to be perfect." He squinted at the screen, muttered a curse. "Grimshaw's been down here, tweaking the programs. Should be a couple of surprises in store for you."

"There's nothing wrong with that, either," Jo said. "With wanting to be perfect."

"Sure there is, especially when you're letting someone else set the standards. Life's not about perfection, it's about making the best out of what you've got."

"Do you eat at a lot of Chinese food, Jonathan?" Jo asked sweetly.

Steinberg finished inputting commands into the touchscreen, looked at her quizzically. "What?"

"Keep your fortune-cookie philosophy to yourself, please, thank you."

"Hit a nerve?"

"You couldn't hit a nerve if you were laser-guided to the target."

" 'The lady doth protest too much, methinks.' " His grin had grown, clearly amused, and Jo found it all the more infuriating. "It's one thing to want to prove how good you are to yourself. It's something else entirely to allow another to determine your self-worth."

"And I do that, do I? You suddenly know me that well?"

"I know you better than you think, hell yeah. I know you're looking for approval, and that you didn't get it—or at least, get enough of it—from your father, and now you're hoping to get it from Carrington."

Jo felt her cheeks beginning to burn.

"If I were you, Mister Steinberg," she said very quietly, "I would seriously consider shutting up now."

His grin disappeared, as she saw that he'd realized he'd pushed too far, too hard. He put his attention back on the touchscreen, tapped it lightly a final time with his index finger.

"Program will start in thirty seconds," Steinberg told her. "Follow the squad leader, obey his orders, I'll be watching on the monitors outside."

He stepped past, exiting the room with a new swish of the doors.

What do you know? Jo thought, glaring after him. *What do you know about me, anyway?*

One of the squares on the grid was blinking for her attention, switching alternately from blue to black. Jo switched the VR goggles to active-receive, settled them over her eyes, plugging each earpiece into place, adhering the sensory feeds to either side of her neck, just below the collar of her T-shirt. A computerized voice asked her to please take position for the start of the simulation. With the Fairchild in her hands, she moved to the blinking square, and the blue light switched to red, turned constant.

The lights in the room went out and her vision split, unwrapped like an origami crane, revealing an urban war zone at night. Cars burned on rubble-strewn streets, spilling black smoke so full of oil she could taste it in the back of her throat. Sirens were blaring in the distance, echoing along alleys and empty streets. Jo glanced down, saw that she was now wearing the standard Carrington Institute tactical gear, black and blue BDUs, combat boots, a ballistic vest. A number glowed green over her right breast—"3"—presumably her position in the squad.

She looked around, noting the position of her fellow squadmembers. All were dressed and armed as she was, all of them combat-ready. There were four of them in total, including Jo, and the other three appeared to have been modeled on Carrington Institute personnel. The woman at her left flank bore a disconcerting resemblance to Emily Partridge, but with substantially larger breasts.

Grimshaw, Jo thought.

The other members of the team were spread out ahead of her. The nearest, perhaps three meters away and now crouching down behind the back of an overturned automobile, seemed to be a strange mixture of Osgood Potts's head attached to Calvin Rogers's body. Leading the squad was a man who had obviously been modeled on Steinberg himself.

Jo idly considered shooting him in the back, but thought better of it. She was furious with him, true, but putting a simulated bullet into his simulated back was probably taking things a little too far.

Steinberg motioned for the squad to move up, using his left hand to issue hand signals. Jo crouched, moving to the nearest cover, following their advance. Past her, the faux Partridge was covering their rear.

The Steinberg simulant raised his left hand again, this

time showing two fingers, then pointing to his left side at a doorway down the block. The simulant Rogers immediately moved to comply. Steinberg added a third finger, then pointed to the opposite side of the street, the edge of a nearby alley.

Jo moved, fast and low, to the position indicated, checking the alleyway before crossing its mouth and moving to take cover against the far corner. A rattle of automatic-weapons fire echoed from somewhere in the distance, its direction impossible to discern. She heard someone sobbing from an apartment above her, the sound of an infant wailing.

Gunshots cracked nearby, from the direction they had come, and Jo jerked back, seeing the Rogers and Steinberg simulants both dropping low, bringing their weapons around. Partridge was taking fire from one of the windows lining the street, the rounds sparking off the asphalt all about her. The Steinberg simulant shouted to give covering fire, and Jo and Rogers both loosed bursts at the window, shattering the glass. Partridge tumbled and went down, hit in the back of the knee. When she went down, she screamed.

The firing from above stopped, as did their own, and the city noise came back into focus, muted, as if everything and everyone around them was waiting for the next move. Partridge was trying to pull herself off the street to safety, sobbing to herself.

Jo reloaded, crossing the mouth of the alley again, back the way she came, and she saw Steinberg from his position on the opposite side of the street, waving her back. Jo glared at him and he made a cutting motion across his throat with his left hand, telling her to stop. She ignored him, sprinting across the street, and there was an immediate burst from above as she drew the fire, and again, Steinberg and Rogers returned it.

Jo reached Partridge, grabbing hold of the back of her

vest with her left hand. Rounds shattered cement and brick around her, spitting up shards that bit at her hands and face. She pulled the other woman after her, into the shelter of a doorway, and just as she was about to drag her into safety, a new chorus of gunfire began, coming from all around, both the direction they'd come from and the direction they'd been going.

They were in a cross fire, Jo realized.

She felt Partridge's body shudder beneath her hand and jerk slightly as she was hit with multiple shots. When she looked down, the young woman had flopped onto her back, her stare turning glassy, blood beginning to bubble from her mouth. Jo cursed, spotted muzzle flashes across the way, back in the direction she'd just come. She leaned out, laying down fire, in time to watch both Steinberg and Rogers go down, hit with bullets fired both in front of and behind them. Rogers flopped face first, and Steinberg tried to struggle on, and then there was another single shot, and his head turned to vapor.

Jo balked, knowing it was all simulated, appalled by it just the same.

Then door behind her opened and she was shot seven times in the back.

"Nice job," Steinberg told her when she emerged from the combat simulation room. He'd been waiting in the hall, watching her progress on one of the monitors built into the wall, and he turned from it to face her, waited until she was in front of him, before saying it again. "Really, nicely done. I've never seen anyone kill off their whole squad in such record time."

"Bite me."

"You got the squad killed."

"The hell I did," Jo spat. "You were leading us into an ambush, we were all dead anyway."

"That's your excuse? We were going to die anyway, so it doesn't matter that it happened sooner rather than later?"

"It's an unfair scenario, it was designed to end in disaster."

"It was designed to see how you worked within a unit," Steinberg retorted. "It was designed to see if the people around you could rely upon you. It was designed to see if you could follow orders. The moment you disobeyed your squad leader, the simulation read as failure. I told you to follow orders."

"Orders would have left Partridge in the middle of the street to have her limbs picked off by a sniper!" Jo shouted at him. "Orders would have had me leave her behind!"

"Exactly," Steinberg said.

"I won't do that!" Jo shoved him, hard, in the chest, and Steinberg staggered back, keeping his footing and sweeping his forearm up to clear her hands. "I won't leave people behind to die!"

"That's not up to you!" he shouted back, as furious as she was. "Sometimes people die and you have to *let them,* Joanna!"

Jo shook her head angrily, shoving him again. "Like *hell*. Not if I have a say in it!"

"You don't get to choose!" Steinberg bellowed.

Jo faltered, then took a half step back. There was a dull ache in her chest, the feeling of loss and grief still unresolved.

"You can't ask me to do that," she said to Steinberg. "You can't ask me to do that again, I can't do that again. I won't do that again."

"You won't have to, Joanna," Daniel Carrington said.

Both she and Steinberg turned, saw him at the foot of

the stairs. Jo had no idea how long he'd been there, how much he'd heard. The embarrassment mixed with the other conflicting emotions in her chest, made it hard for her to breathe for a moment. Steinberg seemed as caught as she was, and didn't move at all for a moment before drawing himself slowly to attention.

"Sir," Steinberg said. "The purpose of the simulation . . ."

Carrington shook his head slightly, as if to say that whatever excuse or explanation Steinberg wanted to offer was unnecessary, or perhaps irrelevant. He started toward them, using his walking stick to aid his progress.

"You won't have to, Joanna, not if I can help it," Carrington assured her.

"You can't guarantee that, Mister Carrington," Jo said.

"Not in the long term, perhaps, but for the short term, I think I can."

"Really? And how will you do that?"

"By sending you out alone, Joanna."

Steinberg said, "Wait a second, we're not finished—"

"There's a job." Carrington glanced at Steinberg, silencing him, then continued, speaking to Jo. "One you'll be doing solo. I need you to report immediately to the briefing room."

"Yes, sir!" The eagerness with which she said it surprised her.

"Armorer's waiting for you. Head on up, please. I'll be there in a few minutes."

Jo nodded, hurried past Carrington for the stairs. She took them two at a time, up to the second floor, turned along the open balcony to make for the briefing room.

From below, she could heard the rise of Steinberg's voice, embroiled in a new argument.

One he was going to lose, Jo knew.

CHAPTER 22

Residence of Paul Sexton—
#3 Fairlake Lane,
Grosse Pointe, Michigan
October 10th, 2020

The windows of the study looked out over Lake St. Clair, the water shimmering in the clear afternoon sunlight, and Hayes could see across the water to Canada, to the east. The room was large, almost too large, and done in a minimalist style, with furniture of black leather and silver metal and glass. In the center of the floor was a 1/8th-scale model of a prototype R-C/Bowman null-grav armored personnel carrier, a bulbous and modular-looking vehicle. A stand stood beside it, listing the vehicle specifications and the names of the engineers who had been part of its design. Apparently, it was being marketed as the MK I "Dragonfly"—an "insurgence pacification platform" with "low-altitude rapid-insertion capacity" and "global deployment ability."

Hayes walked around the model, wondering if it was as fragile as it looked. His father, standing nearby, caught his eye and shook his head.

"Don't touch it, Laurent."

The door into the room opened and Hayes straightened, moving back to his father's side. Paul Sexton entered, smiling broadly, the picture of the modern "casual CEO" in tan slacks and a white polo shirt. He made a beeline for Doctor Murray, extending his right hand and moving so quickly that Hayes felt himself tensing, suspecting an attack, even though he was certain it was only his father's hand that Sexton was after.

"Fred, sorry to keep you waiting," Sexton said, giving Doctor Murray a very American shaking of the hand.

"No problem at all, Paul," Doctor Murray said. "It was short notice, I hope it's not an inconvenience."

"Let's say my curiosity outweighs my annoyance." Sexton held Murray's hand for a moment longer, and Hayes could see his father trying to hide the discomfort he was feeling behind a forced smile. A stab of anger at Sexton thrust through Hayes's breast, and he wanted to tell him to let go already, to leave his father alone, that his father didn't like to be touched.

Then Sexton released Doctor Murray's hand and turned his very white teeth in his very practiced smile on Hayes. "Paul Sexton, I don't think we were introduced at the Luxe Life."

"This is my son, Laurent," Doctor Murray said.

Sexton extended his hand, and Hayes hesitated, and again his father caught his eyes. Hayes took the grip, endured the energetic pump and squeeze that followed it.

"Nice to meet you, sir," Hayes said.

"Pleasure." Sexton dropped his hand, pointed to the prototype model. "Something else, isn't it? Real beauty."

"This is the government model?" Doctor Murray asked politely.

"That's the plan for it, though right now we literally can't get the damn thing off the ground. The null-G generators crap out at two-point-four metric tons, and no matter what we do, we can't get them to lift more. And of course we can't make the damn thing any lighter, because it's supposed to be an armored weapons platform as well as a troop carrier, and it wouldn't be much of one of those if any nutcase with a rifle and a cause could punch a hole through the hull."

Sexton laughed, looking from Hayes to his father, inviting them to join in. Doctor Murray chuckled politely, but Hayes couldn't manage even that, and instead turned his attention away from the model, looking out the large bay windows of the study. Outside the windows and beyond the porch, a perfectly manicured lawn ran down to the shores of Lake St. Clair, where a secured boat-dock ran out onto the water. An elegant sailboat rested at its moorings, masts folded down; painted along its bow in a feminine script was the name *Arrowhead Sure.*

Hayes thought it was a stupid name for a boat.

"Please, both of you, take a seat," Sexton said. "Would you like anything to drink? Maria's just squeezed a fresh pitcher of orange juice."

"No, thank you, Paul, that's very kind," Doctor Murray said, picking a position on the nearest couch and lowering himself carefully, as if afraid he might plant himself on something unexpectedly sharp. He motioned for his son, and Hayes took a seat at the end.

Sexton picked the center one of the three chairs arrayed opposite and sat, immediately leaning forward, his elbows on his knees.

"This is irregular, I know—" Doctor Murray began, but Sexton immediately cut him off, and again Hayes felt the stab of anger, his resentment increasing at the treatment of his father.

"Before you get started, Fred, I want to get this out in the open, up front," Sexton said quickly. "Just hear me out, it won't take a second, but it might spare you a lot of wasted air, so just listen to me. All right? Is that all right?"

"By all means," Doctor Murray said.

"I'm not dropping out, Fred. Nothing you can say is going to change that. I realize you're in a strong position to challenge me, but I think we both know that I can take you. The Nobel is nice and all, but the Board wants to see bottom line, they want to see vision, and they want to see a leader who understands growth. I'm not going to drop out."

"I absolutely agree," Doctor Murray said.

Hayes watched as Sexton reacted, puzzled. "You do?"

"Absolutely, Paul. I'm a scientist, a researcher, that is my calling and my passion. Fate more than ambition has conspired to put me at the helm of pharmaDyne. It would be the height of arrogance for me to believe that my destiny was to run the greatest corporation on Earth. No, I leave that for minds better attuned to the nuances of business in a global market than my own."

Sexton straightened in his chair, slowly, bringing his arms up and then resting them across his chest. Hayes thought his expression was now more one of naked suspicion than surprise.

"Really?" Sexton asked.

"I'm flattered that the Board even sought to put me in contention, Paul," Doctor Murray said almost wearily. "But as you just pointed out yourself, I would not be the best choice for the company."

"If that's true, Fred, then why haven't you withdrawn your name from consideration?" Sexton asked.

"Because while I believe that I would be a poor choice, I am certain there are others who would be even worse."

"I trust you're not referring to me?"

"I wouldn't be here if I was, Paul." Doctor Murray smoothed his necktie, sighing, as if having difficulty choosing his next words. "No, as I already have said, I agree with your assessment, and it's my hope that the Board will agree with you as well. You are the logical choice, and more, you are the best choice. But I also believe you are wrong about one thing."

"Please." Sexton glanced at Hayes, then back to his father. "Go on."

"They will not pick you."

"And why won't they?"

"Because I've seen the numbers, and while R-C/Bowman has turned a staggering profit, it is only dataDyne's third largest money-making division this last fiscal year."

"Waterberg's no threat, she's a victim of her own success," Sexton said, annoyed. "Of course Patmos turned a larger profit—their overhead is at least a thousand times less than ours. You know what insurance is, Fred? It's a license to print money, the Board knows that. They won't move her, they don't want to kill the goose that's laying the golden egg."

"Waterberg isn't the problem," Murray said. "The problem is DataFlow."

"DeVries?" Sexton snorted. "She's too young, too inexperienced. If the Board wanted to bang her that'd be one thing, but for running the show? Really. Did you even read the last statement she made about AirFlow.Net 2.0? It's like reading Polly-goddamn-anna, blah-blah-blah make the world a better place for everyone blah-blah-blah. No mention of bottom line, no mention of profit margin, resource management, cost oversight. No way the Board's taking her seriously, Fred, no way."

Hayes watched as his father raised his right hand, began ticking off points on his fingers.

"First, DataFlow has turned a staggering profit in the last three years through AirFlow.Net 1.0 alone," Doctor Murray said. "And we both know that software application profits do not derive from initial sales, but rather from the purchase of continued upgrades and revisions. DataFlow is about to release version 2.0, Paul, and will be selling the program to over two hundred countries worldwide. While you are supplying almost eighty percent of the null-grav vehicles, DeVries is supplying the air-traffic control software used in all of them, plus the remaining twenty percent. That's total market domination, I believe you would call it.

"Second, what you believe is a detriment is rather, in my view, one of the reasons the Board is so smitten with her. DeVries is relatively young, and is certainly attractive. Our previous CEO was an elderly Chinese gentleman who eschewed public appearances, something that has come back to hurt the company since his disappearance. The Board wants a public face for dataDyne, one that will allay investor fears. DeVries would need to do nothing but smile in front of a camera to accomplish that end.

"Third, and certainly related, DeVries is the youngest of us in contention, and in excellent health. Her appointment to CEO would be seen as move toward stability, an assurance that dataDyne will continue as it has for the foreseeable future."

Doctor Murray lowered his hand.

"She is much more of a threat than you think."

Sexton was scowling now. "What's your point?"

"My point is that Cassandra DeVries is liable to be the next CEO of dataDyne, Paul, and that would be disastrous for us both," Murray said. "She will most likely relocate R-C/Bowman oversight to work more closely with DataFlow, in order to facilitate full integration of AirFlow.Net in your vehicles. She would leave your company gutted, and give its organs to her own."

"That's me, then. What does she do to you?"

"I have no doubt that DeVries would micromanage pharmaDyne into complete stagnation. Her preoccupation with public safety would undoubtedly result in a cowardly business model that would force upon me an endless cycle of clinical trials and advanced testing. pharmaDyne would go from the world leader in pharmaceutical treatments and technologies to a distant third behind Beck-Yama InterNational."

"I see," Sexton said.

"We must prevent her from becoming CEO, Paul," Doctor Murray said.

"Easy enough to do. You withdraw your name from consideration and tell the Board that you endorse me in your place."

"My thought exactly," Hayes's father said with a smile.

Sexton caught it, and that surprised Hayes, because so far he'd thought that Sexton only saw what he wanted to see, and only heard what he wanted to hear. Hayes realized he should have known better. Much as he didn't like Sexton, there was no way Sexton would have survived as the R-C/Bowman CEO if he wasn't in his own way—like his father—brilliant at what he did.

"I'll take care of pharmaDyne, Fred," Sexton said. "I'm not somebody who forgets the people who help me. You can be assured that I'll look after you once I'm CEO."

"That's to be expected," Murray said.

"That's not enough?"

"No, I'm afraid it isn't."

Sexton sighed, then looked to Hayes, this time letting his gaze linger. There was no smile any longer, but no obvious suspicion either, as if he was simply pondering whether or not to indulge Hayes and his father.

He's trying to figure this out, Hayes thought. *He's trying to figure out if he's being played. He's trying to figure out why I'm here.*

"What do you want in exchange?" Sexton finally asked Murray.

"Show him," Doctor Murray told his son.

"There an interface in here?" Hayes asked Sexton. "Terminal, entertainment console, anything?"

"There." Sexton pointed to the windows furthest along the wall, floor-to-ceiling panes of glass with another black leather couch positioned opposite them, a low chrome-and-glass coffee table set in between. "Panel's on the table."

Hayes nodded, moving down the length of the room, taking his lifeCard from the customized sleeve he wore on his belt. He heard Sexton and his father both getting to their feet to follow him. Hayes took the credit card–sized digital assistant between two fingers, setting his thumb into the slight recess in the center. The lifeCard chimed softly, indicating it was active and that it knew him.

"It's all linked?" Hayes asked, looking down at the coffee table, at the dimly lit console surface pressed into the glass.

"It's hiPad accessible," Sexton confirmed, sounding mildly annoyed and more than a little impatient.

Hayes nodded, used the coffee-table console to bring down the lights in the room to half. "Interface," he told the lifeCard. "Solomon Islands, map and briefing."

The lifeCard chimed again, this time two quick rising chords in succession. The floor-to-ceiling window flickered, the view of Lake St. Clair beyond the glass vanishing, replaced by a three-dimensional grid-line overview of the Solomon Islands. The image moved, as if the camera POV were dropping down toward the waters of the Pacific, then began racing north. As each new island appeared on the screen, a call-out accompanied it, identifying it by name. San Cristobal, Guadalcanal, Malaita, Santa Isobel, Choiseul, one after the other, until the camera rose up again, skyward, then dropped, turning, reversing its direction to the south until it settled over the New Georgia Group, Guadalcanal still some ninety miles to the southeast.

"Overview," Hayes told the lifeCard, and the image shifted, redrew, now compositing a satellite surveillance photograph of the New Georgia Group with a computer-drawn map overlaid upon it. More call-outs appeared, naming the individual islands of the group, centered on New Georgia itself.

"This is the Core-Mantis R&D facility in the Solomon Islands," Hayes heard his father explaining to Sexton. "You're looking at New Georgia Island, Paul, the site of the Core-Mantis Solomon Islands Health and Healing Research Center. This is the nerve center of their medical research and development."

As his father spoke, Hayes continued working his life-Card, speaking commands softly. More information appeared on the window monitor, zoomed satellite surveillance shots and computer-drawn renderings of the various research compounds and facilities. Statistics about the Core-Mantis operation flowed along one side of the display like water dropping from a fall, listing the known history of the operation, the estimated personnel in both staff, subjects, and security. Best estimates put the science staff at nearly five hundred, with five times that number in support, with positions from clerical administration to janitorial services.

"On the northeastern shore of the island, near Hovoro, is their Experimental Technologies facility," Doctor Murray said. "The home of their most cutting-edge research and testing, where their most brilliant minds reside. For years now, I've been hearing rumors of something called the Hovoro Project being developed at this facility."

"What sort of rumors?" Sexton asked, and Hayes thought he did a good job of trying to sound only vaguely interested.

"All sorts of things, from the plausible to the absurd. Everything from a cure for AIDS to an elixir that will halt, or even reverse, the aging process. I'm sure you know how it is, Paul. In the absence of facts about what your competitor is up to, the most outlandish stories appear."

Hayes worked the lifeCard, bringing up a closer view of the Hovoro facility, a walled compound of seventeen buildings, bristling with security checkpoints and watchtowers. Once again, computer-drawn overlays appeared, identifying the buildings, their suspected purposes and estimated staffing. He froze the program, turned away from the window displays to face his father and Sexton.

Sexton stepped forward, peering closer, then shook his head, as if amused. He looked at Hayes, then at Doctor Murray.

"But presumably you *know* what they're doing in Hovoro, Fred? Presumably they're up to something that'll hurt you and pharmaDyne, is that it?"

"Not just pharmaDyne," Doctor Murray said. "*dataDyne,* Paul. What Core-Mantis is developing at Hovoro will move us from the world's leader in health and medicine to a distant second, and if my intelligence is correct, they're less than seven months from bringing their product to market."

"So let's hear it."

Doctor Murray hesitated, giving his next words added weight, and Hayes had to fight to keep from grinning.

"Cancer, Paul," his father said quietly. "Core-Mantis OmniGlobal is curing cancer."

The effect was exactly what Hayes and his father had hoped for, and it froze Sexton in place for fully ten seconds before he managed a muttered, "Jesus Christ."

Doctor Murray nodded sadly.

"You're sure?"

Doctor Murray looked to Hayes, who said, "We've been working a double agent in Core-Mantis Melbourne for the last eight months, code-named Felix. He confirmed the Hovoro Project for us the week before the Luxe Life retreat."

"And you believe this?" Sexton asked. "This 'Felix' is on the level?"

Hayes held up the lifeCard. "I've included all of his reports here. I'll upload them to your console, if you want, you can take a look."

"He sent us a sample of the recombinant DNA being used for Stage I vaccine development," Doctor Murray said. "I reviewed it myself, Paul, it's the real thing, brilliant work and easily ten years ahead of where pharmaDyne is in the same field. We're not going to catch them in time. They'll have cured cancer and stolen dataDyne's market share, and we'll still be scratching our heads wondering how they did it."

Sexton looked back to the window, to the glowing display of the Hovoro facility on the screen. Hayes thought the man was still rattled by the news his father had imparted, but now less so, and it was clear from Sexton's expression that he was thinking furiously, trying to see a solution to a problem that belonged not only to pharmaDyne, but to the mother corporation as a whole.

"So it's time to get aggressive, right?" Sexton said. "Start with the proxy fight, and if necessary, take more . . . active measures."

"No," Doctor Murray answered. "We won't be doing that."

Sexton turned sharply, almost glaring at Hayes's father. "You're just going to let them bend us over our desks like this?"

"I don't have many options, Paul. I have neither the security forces trained for such an action, nor the capital required to hire forces who do."

"With all due respect, Fred, that's a load of crap. You have the money, I know you do. I see the same ledgers and bottom lines you do."

Doctor Murray shrugged.

"So this is the thing you want? You want me to eat this? You want *me* to launch a hostile takeover of the Core-Mantis Solomon Islands operation, shut down this Hovoro facility, and then hand you the fruits of their labors?"

"In exchange for which you would have my unqualified support before the Board, my unquestioning loyalty for you as CEO, and my eternal gratitude."

"I'd expect the first two; what would the last look like?"

"Anything you needed that I could give. You're wealthy already, you'll be even wealthier as CEO, so my offering you money is nothing. But you name it, and it would be yours."

Sexton thought about that, looking at the window display yet again. "How far out is the cure?"

"They'll have it on the market in its earliest form before the end of the year, I'm positive," Doctor Murray said. "They'll certainly begin leaking word of the cure before the end of the month. They may even attempt to time the first rumors to coincide with the Board's appointment of our new CEO."

Sexton nodded slightly, then said, "I want credit."

"I'm sorry?"

"Not complete, but shared. You'll put my name on the research along with your own when you publish it."

Hayes thought his father did an admirable job of looking appalled. "I can't possibly—"

Sexton turned back to Doctor Murray, and now his look was cold, the look that Hayes suspected the R-C/Bowman CEO used when closing a deal.

And that's what this is, Hayes thought. *Just another deal.*

"If you want my help, yes you can," Sexton said. "You're looking at a second Nobel for this, Fred, we both know it. You'll be remembered throughout time as the man who cured cancer. I know you, I know your ego, and

I know that this is as much about your reputation as it is about ensuring pharmaDyne's survival. Well, I want a piece of that legacy. Since I'll be the man making it possible, I think I deserve as much."

"You're not a scientist!" Murray objected. "You're not even a physician! Nobody will believe—"

"So we'll give me a degree or three, it doesn't matter."

Doctor Murray shook his head, angrily. "Absolutely not. It's a debasement of science, it's absurd to even consider it. Ask for something else."

"I've told you what I want."

"Absolutely not."

"Then you can suck this up without my help."

"Core-Mantis will crush us!"

Now it was Sexton's turn to shrug. "R-C/Bowman will survive. DataFlow will survive. Patmos will probably survive. It'll only be pharmaDyne that crashes and burns."

Doctor Murray said nothing.

"Be reasonable, Fred," Sexton said. "You want me to initiate and launch a hostile takeover of Core-Mantis Solomon Islands, and you want me to do it sooner rather than later. You're asking me to fund the operation from my own branch, you're asking me to task troops from R-C/Bowman to do this, and you're asking me to take the hit if it goes wrong."

"But if it goes right then it does nothing but help you." Doctor Murray seemed to vibrate with his agitation. "If it goes right you get the credit, and the Board will certainly take that into consideration when making its choice. It will guarantee your appointment."

Sexton nodded slightly, confirming what they already both knew. "It's your choice."

"I can take this to Sato," Doctor Murray said unconvincingly. "He has the financials, he could launch the takeover."

"He could. He doesn't have the manpower, he'd have to hire mercs, but it might get the job done. Hell, Sato might even succeed. And the Board might think that would make him a brilliant, bold, and courageous CEO. But then Takahata Sato would be CEO of dataDyne, and there's a reason he's not being seriously considered. The man's a liability, he's indiscreet in his personal habits. Beck-Yama or CMO would have him blackmailed and controlled in no time."

"DeVries," Doctor Murray said. "If she could be convinced—"

"Now you're just wasting my time, Fred."

Sexton leaned down, tapped the coffee table, and the window display winked out, the opaque glass along the side of the room slowly regaining its translucence. The sun had passed over the house, and now shadows were beginning to fall on the finely cut grass that led to the water.

"Your choice," Sexton said.

"You'll move quickly?" Doctor Murray asked.

"My people can have a battle plan completed in twenty-four hours," Sexton assured him. "We can move troops and equipment into position within another seventy-two. Give me four days, I'll have the cure for cancer in your hands."

"I'll need the research, all of it." Doctor Murray was insistent. "And as many of the scientists working there captured alive as possible. Everyone else has to die, all the support staff. This must be a full assault, and a complete sanitization of the site."

"We have a deal, then?"

Doctor Murray looked to his son, and Hayes took the cue, speaking to his lifeCard once more.

"Decrypt and transmit," he said softly. "Solomon Islands, all files and information. Include all records and reports designated 'Felix.' "

The lifeCard chimed, turning warmer in his hand as it delivered terabyte after terabyte of data to Sexton's console. It completed the transfer with another tone, this one a descending scale of three major chords.

Sexton smiled broadly at the two of them, then stuck out his hand to Doctor Murray. "Pleasure doing business with you, Doctor."

Doctor Murray needed a moment, as if the thought of another handshake atop everything else would be one too many insults to bear, then accepted the offered hand.

"A pleasure doing business with you," Hayes's father echoed, and then, after a second's thought, added, "*Doctor* Sexton."

CHAPTER 23

The Money Pit—
337 West 78th Street,
New York City, New York
October 10th, 2020

The place wasn't so much a pub and it wasn't so much a bar, but rather an executive's fantasy of a synthesis of the two, recreated as a high-end restaurant.

Everything within was pristine and new, as if the furnishings, the fixtures, even the glassware served from the lacquered bar were fresh from their packaging. The shine extended to the décor on the walls, where artistically designed relief sculptures of profit-and-loss graphs and pie charts and stock listings hung at regularly spaced intervals. The waitstaff promoted the illusion, all of them young and pretty from the bartenders to the hostesses, all of them dressed as executive assistants in tight and sexy pseudo–business attire. Even the menu was in keeping, listing drinks called the "Mantis Martini" and the "Backroom Deal."

It was honestly the last place in the world Jo would have wanted to spend time, but what she wanted didn't matter. Carrington had given her a job, and the job had taken her here, and she wasn't going to back down now.

The brief had been straightforward, but with a wrinkle at the end. Straightforward was the fact that the CEO of pharmaDyne was coming to meet the CEO of Royce-Chamberlain/Bowman Motors at his home in Grosse Pointe. Carrington was certain the only possible reason for such a meeting could be Doctor Murray's desire to find Rose, which in turn forced the conclusion that, one way or another, Sexton was a part of that. Part one of Jo's assignment had been to confirm the meeting.

"You won't be able to get close enough to overhear them," Carrington had said. "And the security around the estate is too tight to risk deploying camspy. Just take a stand-off position and verify that Murray is, in fact, meeting with Sexton."

"You don't need to send me to the States for that," Jo had said. "Certainly you've got at least two dozen operatives at your disposal closer to the site who can do exactly the same thing."

Carrington had nodded in agreement, and then motioned at Grimshaw, seated at a workstation in the briefing room, with his walking stick. "Grim, if you please."

Grimshaw had been staring at Jo with what she'd only been able to describe as a stupid grin, and Carrington had been forced to repeat himself before the man spun in his seat and began slapping at the keyboard in front of him. Almost instantly, the graphics displayed over the briefing room map table had vanished, to be replaced with a pixelated and color-desaturated image of a man who Jo immediately recognized.

"That's the one who tried to carve me up in Vancouver," she had said.

"Steinberg thought so, as well," Carrington had said. "His name is Laurent, and he's Doctor Murray's son, adopted in November 2017, as best as we can determine. And, apparently, he's Doctor Murray's legman, Joanna. He's his thug, and has been . . . thugging . . . his way around the world for the last week or so in zealous pursuit of the elusive Doctor Thaddeus Rose. He's a killer, Jo, not a soldier, and he makes me more than a little nervous."

Jo rose from her seat, examining the image more closely. The man, Laurent, was young, perhaps her age, perhaps a little older, his hair worn long and loose, falling to mid-back. In the image, he wore a designer business suit, one of the current season's sleek fashions, and it made him appear longer and leaner than Jo remembered.

"If Laurent is present at the meeting, he is your priority target," Carrington had said. "I have no doubt that as soon as Rose's whereabouts are determined, Doctor Murray will dispatch Laurent to kill the man. We mustn't let that happen. For that reason, you are to follow Laurent in the hopes that he will lead you to Rose, and then—and only then, Joanna—are you to engage him."

Without looking from the image, Jo had said, "I understand."

"Avoid him if at all possible. Only act if Rose's life, or your own, is in immediate danger."

She'd grinned, glanced to Carrington then, and said, "You don't think I can take him?"

"I'd rather not have to find out," Carrington had said.

Doing the job in Grosse Pointe had been simple, albeit tedious and frustrating. Murray and his son had arrived at Sexton's estate via old-style limousine. Jo had waited nearly ninety minutes before they'd emerged once more, departing as they had come, and she had followed in her

Institute-provided car, frustrated by the vehicle's handling as well as the traffic. While the rest of the world seemed to be embracing null-G travel, Detroit still gamely maintained its love of the automobile.

She'd followed them to the airport, then been forced to abandon her vehicle in a loading lane when she saw Laurent exit the limousine alone, heading into the terminal. She had a moment of alarm once inside, afraid she'd lost him, then caught sight of him again purchasing a first-class ticket on the next transport to New York. Jo had waited until he'd moved off toward the boarding gates before purchasing one herself, for coach class.

The flight itself had taken twenty-three minutes, and Jo had ended up seated beside an overweight middle-aged woman in a floral print dress who spent the entire trip wearing a dataDyne entertainMe VR set, speaking softly to people who weren't there. Jo had watched Laurent, seated seven rows ahead of her, on the aisle. Hayes kept fidgeting, glancing around nervously, and Jo thought that she'd tipped her hand somehow, that he'd made her. She buried her face in the slick in-flight magazine as Hayes left his seat just before landing, heading for the forward lavatory.

When he returned, she braced herself for an attack, but to her surprise he'd seemed much calmer, and far less agitated.

He's on something, she realized. Her father had apprehended enough addicts that the signs were easy for her to spot.

Then they'd landed and Jo had engaged in a game of follow-that-cab from Kennedy into the City, finally arriving at the Money Pit late in the evening, and faced the dilemma of heading inside herself or again taking a static post outside. But there wasn't really a choice, she had to go in after him. If Laurent was closing in on Rose, she needed to stay close, and whether or not she was welcome, or even comfortable, inside a place like the Money Pit didn't matter.

A young, blonde, and far too pretty hostess greeted her as Jo came off the stairs and onto the main floor, looking her over with a frown. Jo knew what she was seeing, the combination of youth and inappropriate attire, and she could easily guess what the hostess was thinking as a result. Jo hadn't dressed to play this game, but rather to remain comfortable during the surveillance, wearing cargo pants, a jacket, trainers, and a T-shirt with a graphic of the earth on its center, with the word COEXIST printed beneath it.

No one in the world was going to mistake Jo for a hypercorp shark, or even a person who wished to become one, on the basis of how she looked.

"Can I help you?" the hostess sniffed.

"I doubt it," Jo snapped, looking past her at the room, surveying the clientele at their tables. It was crowded enough that she wasn't immediately worried about being spotted by Laurent, but at the same time, she was having trouble finding him herself. Aside from the field of diners, most of the clientele seemed to be clustered around the bar. At the far end of the room, she could make out two sets of doors, one leading to the kitchen, another presumably leading to the restrooms.

"This is an exclusive establishment," the hostess said. "Corporate membership is—"

"Do I look lost?" Jo moved her gaze from the room to the woman, putting as much contempt as she could muster into it. "Do I? Or are you so linear that you think we all have to wear three-pieces even after work?"

It was the attitude that did it, the holier-than-thou-I-can-crush-you-with-my-bank-account manner, and the hostess appeared taken completely aback for an instant before managing to recover. When she did, she combined obsequious with apologetic in a flawless blend.

"I'm terribly sorry, miss—"

"You're talking to me," Jo said just as quickly, and just as cattily. "Don't talk to me. Unless you're NPD for the Delta Four, or you're sleeping with someone who is, don't talk to me, because I really don't want to talk to you."

The hostess stammered. "NPD?"

"God! New Product Development!" Jo glared at her, as if waiting to hear the hostess's excuse for her incompetence. When none came, she added, "You didn't land the meet-and-greet post because of your brains, did you, love?"

"I'm terribly sorry, miss—"

"You're *still* talking to me." Jo waved the hostess away in disgust, striding forward onto the floor, on a beeline for the bar. Behind her, she heard the hostess calling her a bitch, her voice barely audible against the wash of conversation and the sound of business reports broadcast from hidden speakers.

She elbowed her way to the bar, using the color-mad mirrors to scan the room, finally spotting Laurent. He stood near the back of the space, between the doors to the kitchen and the restrooms, a drink in his hand, untouched, and she realized that he was doing the same as she was, searching the crowd. Jo turned her attention to the man beside her, used a smile that showed him her teeth, and asked him to buy her a drink.

"Sure, beautiful. What're you having?"

"The day I've had, something with a kick," Jo said.

"Tell me about it! Those bastards at Core-Mantis—oh, hell, you're not Core-Mantis, are you?"

Jo laughed, still keeping half an eye on the mirrors, still keeping Laurent in view. "Perish the thought."

"Zentek," the man said. "Mergers and Acquisitions.

Which means I'm spending most of my days trying to keep us from being merged or acquired, rather than doing it myself, you know?"

Jo nodded, keeping her smile in place, encouraging the conversation to continue. The man took the cue up, eager to talk, though whether it was because he wanted the company or because he was passionate about his work, Jo didn't know, and didn't much care. She'd seen Laurent's posture shift, seen him straighten up, focusing on someone in the crowd, and for a moment Jo was afraid it was her.

Then she saw him move forward, intercepting a woman in her early thirties, black-haired and dark-skinned, wearing the kind of business suit that said she was less interested in Mergers and Acquisitions than in another kind of transaction. Laurent put his mouth to her ear for a moment, then straightened again, meeting her gaze, and the woman returned it without a smile, then brushed past him, to the doors that presumably led to the private rooms.

Mistress? Jo wondered. *Lover?*

Laurent made another scan of the main floor, then turned to follow the woman.

The man at her elbow was still bemoaning the state of Zentek's affairs, and Jo nodded again, then pitched forward into him, wrapping her right arm around her middle. The man jerked, nearly sliding off his own bar stool, spilling the drink in his hand.

"Are you all right?"

"I'm going to puke," Jo said, and covering her mouth with her other hand, lurched away from the bar. She forced her way across the floor, narrowly avoiding a collision with a waiter and his heavily laden tray, then went through the same door she'd seen Laurent take without hesitating, then doubled over, hands on her thighs, until she heard it click shut behind her, blocking the noise of the adjacent room. She waited a second longer, in case anyone was watching, then wiped at her mouth with the back of a hand, straightening up once more, hearing the distant sounds of a kitchen. The aroma of steaks broiling was strong, and made her stomach tighten with hunger. She hadn't eaten since she'd started the tail on Laurent.

She was in a short hallway with doors to the restrooms on her left, then a bend about three meters ahead on her right. She could hear voices, the sounds of pots and pans and cooking, and around the bend she saw a side door, partially ajar, leading into the kitchen. Jo hesitated for a moment. It was just possible they'd ducked into one of the bathrooms, but she doubted that; there'd be too much risk of being overheard, there simply wasn't enough privacy.

After another second's thought, Jo reached into one of her jacket pockets, pulling out a small molded plastic case and snapping it quickly open. Resting inside, cushioned in foam, were a pair of small, thin eyeglasses, and a Ping-Pong ball–sized metal orb. Jo slipped the glasses on, removed the orb from its container, then tucked the case back into her pocket. She ran her thumb along the surface of the ball as Potts had shown her, felt the device vibrate slightly in her hand, then released it to the air and, despite knowing that it wouldn't, fully expected the ball to fall to the floor.

It didn't, hovering at chest level where she'd let it go. On the lenses of her glasses, an interface appeared, the word INITIALIZING blinking in luminescent green across her field of vision. Then the word faded, and she was seeing the world through the camspy's eyes, shimmering and distorted. Using the glasses as the interface, Jo directed the camspy forward through the door and into the kitchen.

It was busy inside, too busy for either the four cooks or the two impatient waiters or the one dishwasher to notice the camspy. Jo engaged the audio, felt more than heard the crackle of the camspy's microphone switching on, feeding the audio to her through the earpieces of her eyeglasses. She rotated the camspy, looking around the kitchen, feeling nervous and exposed, afraid she'd lost the trail. There was no sign of either the woman or of Laurent.

There was, however, another door near the side of a walk-in freezer, and like the door into the kitchen, this one was open as well, presumably to allow fresh air from outside to circulate. Jo dropped the camspy low, guiding it past the corner of one stove, narrowly missing a collision with one of the chefs as she turned abruptly to dump the contents of her skillet onto a plate. Jo had to put a hand out to steady herself with the wall, to keep from becoming utterly disoriented.

I hate these damn things, she thought.

She guided the camspy through the open door and into the alleyway behind the restaurant. For a second, the image projected onto her lenses flared, growing brighter as the camspy's computerized filtering system adjusted to the change in lighting. She could hear street noises crackling into her ears, and then new voices, unintelligible. The camspy continued to glide silently forward, low to the ground, and Jo saw a Dumpster, and shadows being cast onto the ground beyond it.

When she saw them, the relief she felt surprised her. She hadn't wanted to lose them. She hadn't wanted to fail.

They were speaking quietly, each of them looking in the opposite direction from the other, in an attempt to keep from being overseen or overheard. On the interface in her glasses, Jo tried raising the directional mike, but either their voices were too soft or the ambient noise around them too great, and she still couldn't make out what was being said.

She moved the camspy closer.

"*. . . you got my name?*" the woman was asking. She

spoke in English; there was a slight, indeterminate southern European accent to her words.

"A man in Zurich," Laurent told her. *"Had some interesting things to say about Portia de Carcareas."*

"I highly doubt that. I highly doubt my name was mentioned at all."

"Let's say it came up late in the conversation."

Through the camspy's distortion, Jo saw the woman frown.

"Why should I believe anything you are telling me?" she asked him.

"You don't have to believe it, Miss Carcareas, I'm sure you can check it for yourself. R-C/Bowman can't mobilize the troops required quickly and quietly at the same time. You look, you'll see I'm telling the truth."

"I don't know who you are, Mister Hayes. I have no reason to believe what you're telling me is true."

"Fine, don't believe me. But when Core-Mantis loses the Hovoro facility, you'll know I was . . ."

"What?"

Through the camspy, Jo saw Laurent raise a finger to the woman, Carcareas, gesturing her silent. Very slowly, and just as deliberately, the young man began to turn in place, looking around the alley, obviously searching for something.

Bloody hell, Jo thought. *He's seen it, he knows it's there.*

Even knowing it was coming, the move caught Jo by surprise. One moment Laurent had been standing still, scanning the alley, and in the next he'd lunged, and Jo herself recoiled as his hand came at her, and then her vision flared again, aperture crazed, and the vertigo she felt made it seem like she'd been dropped into a spinning top. Feedback screeched in her ears, and she brought her hands up, yanked the eyeglasses from her head, throwing them to the ground.

At which point she could focus on the world around her, rather than the world around the camspy, and, particularly, the two men in Core-Mantis security uniforms who were pointing their pistols at her head.

CHAPTER 24

The Money Pit—
337 West 78th Street,
New York City, New York
October 10th, 2020

Hayes threw the little metal ball with a curse, hurling it as hard as he could at the alley wall. It shattered instantly, as if made of eggshell, embedding bits of wiring and shattered glass into the brick.

"It's local," he growled at Carcareas. "The control on these things is always local, whoever was spying on us is around here somewhere!"

Carcareas was staring at him, but she didn't speak, and after a moment she put a hand to her ear, and Hayes understood why.

"You brought backup." He knew he sounded stunned. He couldn't help it. He had specified that she meet him alone, and he hadn't made any backup security when he reconnoitered the meet site.

"You're dataDyne. Of course I brought backup," Carcareas told him, and then, before he could respond, added, "They've caught her."

"Good, let's have some—" Hayes spun toward the restaurant, starting for the kitchen door, then stopped. "*—her?*"

"It's a woman, young, they're bringing her out here now."

Oh please, Hayes thought. *Oh please let it be her.*

That would be perfect, that would make it all better, if it was the Carrington Institute bitch who'd escaped from him on the rooftop, the redheaded nightmare who'd managed to live when she damn well should've died. Then Hayes could redeem himself in his father's eyes, hell, he could redeem himself in his own. She shouldn't have escaped him then; he sure as hell wasn't about to let her do it a second time.

"Tell them to bring me a knife," Hayes told Carcareas. "From the kitchen, to bring me a knife."

"I'm not going to stand here and watch you commit murder in an alley," Carcareas said icily.

"Then go," Hayes retorted. "But if this bitch was spying on us, she's not leaving here alive."

Carcareas studied him, the corners of her pouting mouth turned down in disapproval. "We'll see."

Hayes shrugged, looking back toward the exit from the kitchen. He hadn't thought Carcareas would be squeamish, but then again, he hadn't thought she'd be such a looker, either, so it only proved there was a lot he didn't know. It didn't matter if Portia de Carcareas didn't want bloodstains on her Italian leather boots. Even if the spy wasn't the same redhead, the spy was going to have to die.

Eventually, Hayes thought, and smiled.

After another second, the smile faltered. No one had emerged from the kitchen as of yet. Hayes was reasonably certain that someone should have done so already.

Apparently, Carcareas agreed, because he heard her murmuring into her Core-Mantis ThroatLink, and even standing less than a foot away, Hayes couldn't make out what she was saying. dataDyne personnel favored subcutaneous button radios, inserted beneath the skin behind the ear or sometimes actually inside the ear canal, but in either case, it was an outpatient procedure, quick and relatively painless. Core-Mantis, Hayes knew, preferred to chip, modify, and otherwise alter their key personnel with their own tech. In the case of radios, this meant an operation to insert the microphone into the throat, and then to run companion leads along the bone to both ears. It provided for stereo sound, quieter transmission and reception, and, as a result of the adaptive surgery, was much harder to destroy than a simple subcutaneous model.

In Hayes's experience, in fact, the best way to destroy a Core-Mantis ThroatLink was to remove its user's throat.

"They're not responding," Carcareas told him. "Something's happened."

Without a word, Hayes sprinted for the kitchen, and this time, Carcareas moved to follow him.

Both guards were out cold in the hallway by the bathrooms, one slumped over the other, and that confirmed it for him. It was the redheaded bitch, it had to be. Hayes turned the filleting knife he'd grabbed on his way through the kitchen in his hand, flipping it from a cutting to a stabbing grip. Both guards appeared to still be alive, and that surprised and puzzled him. If he'd had to put them down, he'd have done it so they never got up again.

He was even more confused to see that they each still had their side arms, their Core-Mantis-issued Regulator semiautos.

Carcareas was speaking to her ThroatLink again, murmuring softly.

"Any sign of her?" Hayes demanded.

Carcareas ignored him, listening to the voices in her head for a moment before saying, this time loud enough for Hayes to hear, "All right, Sergeant. Withdraw."

"You're joking," Hayes said.

"Why would I joke?" Carcareas said. "She has escaped, and I doubt we are going to find her."

"We can't let her get away!"

"Why not?" Carcareas looked at him, sincerely curious. "If she is working for Sexton, then he'll abort the attack on Hovoro."

"She doesn't work for Sexton!"

Carcareas arched an eyebrow. "Oh? You know this woman, do you?"

"It's not like that! She's a Carrington Institute agent, I'm sure of it, I've mixed it up with her once already. We need to find her, keep her from reporting!"

Carcareas gave him the same frown she'd shown him outside in the alley, her expression both displeased and annoyed. "Why would Carrington care if dataDyne's attack on Hovoro succeeds or not?"

He doesn't give a damn about Hovoro, it's about finding Rose! Hayes almost shouted at the woman, but he caught himself before the words flew from his lips. He couldn't mention Rose, he realized. He couldn't even hint that Carrington might be after something at Hovoro, for fear that Carcareas would realize that Hayes was, as well. He couldn't tell her anything, and already he'd said too much, and now he was in danger of blowing it again, failing his father again.

Just the thought of it made the back of his neck itch, made the dermal burn on his flesh.

"Carrington's a troublemaker," Hayes said, and it wasn't a lie. "There's no telling what he'll do."

"I don't care about Daniel Carrington or his Institute, and neither do my superiors, Mister Hayes," Carcareas said. "The Institute seems quite content to be a thorn in dataDyne's side, which is good for our business. If this spy is from his organization, she's after you, not me. If the spy is from Sexton, then Hovoro is safe. And if the spy isn't, and Sexton intends to do as you say, then we'll be ready for him. There's certainly no downside to us—so there's no reason I need to spend any more time in your company."

Hayes pointed the filleting knife at her, furious at himself for his mistake, furious at her for her logic. "No! You can't just . . ."

Then his voice faltered as Carcareas stepped closer, brushing his knife hand lightly aside, until she had almost pressed her body to his. Her eyes were fixed on his own, and he felt the wash of body heat leaking through her clothes to touch his own skin, and the sensation surprised him, stole his breath. His heart was suddenly thumping, the arousal he was now feeling almost blindingly intense.

"What are you doing?" His throat had gone tight, his voice nothing more than a croak.

She made a soft clucking noise, her eyes still fixed on his own. "Now, now, Mister Hayes. Surely you don't believe that pharmaDyne is the only corporation with an interest in chemical performance enhancers?"

He tried to think of something useful to say, but his mind wouldn't focus. Her blouse was black silk, clinging to her skin, and when she took a breath, he saw the pulse at her throat, found himself imagining what it would be like to taste her flesh.

Carcareas moved her mouth along his cheek, brushing it with her lips, until she reached his ear.

"Mister Hayes," she whispered. "Our business is concluded. If you insist on creating a bloodbath, please wait until well after I've left the premises."

And she ran a finger across his chest, the sensation an ecstatic burn that made his muscles tremble, and then her heat and her voice and her touch were all gone. He heard the door to the main room open as she passed through it, the burst of noise, then the muted cacophony as it fell closed again. He tried to control his breathing, tried to get it to slow, and his heart was still racing, and he could feel the perspiration beginning to run in beads down the back of his shirt.

The door to the men's room opened, and the redheaded bitch stepped into the hall, and before Hayes could do anything at all, she kicked him twice. Her first kick took his knife hand, broke his grip on the blade, sending it into the wall point-first. Her second kick took him in the side of the right knee and sent him down face-first. He tried to move and his muscles obstinately refused to obey, still reeling from Carcareas's chemical seduction.

"Guess she's what we'd call a praying mantis," the redhead said. She had an accent, Hayes realized, some mutt mixture of limey, South African, American, Aussie, and maybe a half dozen other sounds he couldn't place.

Pain seared across the back of his scalp, the redhead taking hold of his hair and yanking it back, pulling his head along with it. Again Hayes tried to move, to fight it, and this time he felt his limbs twitch, their life returning, but it wasn't enough.

"Oooh, interesting," he heard the redhead say, twisting his hair in her hand, pulling it away from the back of his head, revealing his faded prison ID tattoo. "Let's see if I can remember this. Seven-one-four-eight-seven-six-zed-two-zed-five."

"Kill you," Hayes managed to say. He thought his voice sounded like a child's.

"You're welcome to try," the redhead said, and then he felt her fingers on his skin, felt them digging at the side of the dermal. "Of course, I suspect you'll have some trouble managing it without this."

Then she tore the dermal free from his skin.

Hayes started to scream.

Then he felt a brick smash into the back of his head, and he saw red, and then nothing.

Return-path: <nullggrrl@everyman.net>
Envelope-to: walkingstick@anonymity.com
Delivery-date: Mon, 07 Oct 2020 00:49:37
Received: from everyman by bermuda.dnsrouter.com with local-bsmtp (Exim 4.44)
From: "NULLGGRRL" <nullggrrl@everyman.net>
To: walkingstick@anonymity.com
Subject: by any other name
Date: Mon, 07 Oct 2020 21:48:01 +0100
—=_NextPart_000_0066_01C5833D.8BDC6E10
Content-Type: text/plain;
charset="iso-8859-1"
Content-Transfer-Encoding: quoted-printable

Old Man—

I was hoping to have heard something from you by now regarding your horticultural inquiry. That I haven't gives me cause for concern. While I realize that it was I who asked that we give our relationship a sabbatical for the time being, I did so with the hope that there would be some manner in which we could, at the least, continue our communication.

Or, to put it more bluntly, I miss you.

Please let me know if your inquiries turn up anything to aid me, as you promised.

C

Return-path: <nullggrrl@everyman.net>
Envelope-to: walkingstick@anonymity.com

Delivery-date: Tue, 08 Oct 2020 16:07:11
Received: from everyman by bermuda.dnsrouter.com with local-bsmtp (Exim 4.44)
From: "NULLGGRRL" <nullggrrl@everyman.net>
To: walkingstick@anonymity.com
Subject: That other thing
Date: Tue, 08 Oct 2020 16:07:11 +0100
——=_NextPart_000_0066_01C5833D.8BDC6E10
Content-Type: text/plain;
charset="iso-8859-1"
Content-Transfer-Encoding: quoted-printable

Old Man—

I've done a little digging on my own, and found a Rose in a very interesting garden. Is this what you were looking for? Now my curiosity is piqued.

Please respond. Your silence gives me cause for concern, and I am in a somewhat awkward position here, as I am afraid I may have compromised my position by granting you the information you requested.

I ask you to put my mind at ease, as you have so many times in the past.

Missing you.

C

Return-path: <nullggrrl@everyman.net>
Envelope-to: walkingstick@anonymity.com
Delivery-date: Wed, 09 Oct 2020 11:32:01
Received: from everyman by bermuda.dnsrouter.com with local-bsmtp (Exim 4.44)
From: "NULLGGRRL" <nullggrrl@everyman.net>
To: walkingstick@anonymity.com
Subject: RE: grinding stone
Date: Wed, 09 Oct 2020 11:32:01 +0100

—-=_NextPart_000_0066_01C5833D.8BDC6E10
Content-Type: text/plain;
charset="iso-8859-1"
Content-Transfer-Encoding: quoted-printable

Old Man—

Well, any reply is better than none, but I find it hard to believe that your inquiries have yet to bear fruit. You know me, and you know that I can be very patient when a) it is required, and b) when it suits.

My fear is that the clock is running, and that I will have little to no time to act on whatever information you uncover. And the goal is still to aid me in this particular pursuit, is it not?

It would help a great deal if you could at least give me some indication of what it is you are looking for re: the flower you seem so interested in. At the least, perhaps I can offer assistance. At the most, I may be able to supply whatever pieces of the puzzle you are missing.

Oh, and thank you for the new bouquet. The flowers, as always, were stunning. They're sitting on my desk right now.

C

Return-path: <nullggrrl@everyman.net>
Envelope-to: walkingstick@anonymity.com
Delivery-date: Fri, 11 oct 2020 12:28:33
Received: from everyman by bermuda.dnsrouter.com with local-bsmtp (Exim 4.44)
From: "NULLGGRRL" <nullggrrl@everyman.net>
To: walkingstick@anonymity.com
Subject: You'll forgive me

DATE: FRI, 11 OCT 2020 16:07:11 +0100
——=_NEXTPART_000_0066_01C5833D.8BDC6E10
CONTENT-TYPE: TEXT/PLAIN;
CHARSET="ISO-8859-1"
CONTENT-TRANSFER-ENCODING: QUOTED-PRINTABLE

OLD MAN—

I GOT TIRED OF WAITING, SO I WENT LOOKING ON MY OWN.

I KNOW WHO HE IS, AND I KNOW WHAT HE DID.

ARE WE STILL ON THE SAME SIDE?

BECAUSE I AM BEGINNING TO BELIEVE THAT IS NO LONGER THE CASE.

C

P.S. OH, ABOUT THE FLOWERS. I FOUND THE TRANSMITTER, DANIEL.

THINK ABOUT THAT.

THEN THINK ABOUT WHO IT IS YOU'RE DEALING WITH.

THEN THINK ABOUT WHETHER OR NOT YOU WANT TO CONTINUE DEALING WITH ME IN THIS FASHION.

CORDIALLY,

C

CHAPTER 25

DataFlow Corporate Headquarters—
Office of Chief Executive Officer and
Director Cassandra DeVries—
#7 Rue de la Baume, Paris, France
October 11th, 2020

Cassandra DeVries sat behind her desk and stared at the minuscule interface transmitter resting in the palm of her hand and thought about what she was feeling. She was feeling a lot. She was feeling anger, mostly, she knew, of a kind that she hadn't felt since she was nine. She was feeling humiliation, that particular substrata of the emotion that seemed to derive wholly from a sense of betrayal. She was even willing to acknowledge that she was feeling true sorrow, the mourning ache of an emotion in its death throes. Worst of all, she felt stupid.

What she wasn't feeling was love, not for Daniel Carrington, not any longer.

"Did you really know about it all along?" Velez asked. The question came with an uncharacteristic softness for the woman, as if she might possibly care about what Cassandra was going through at the moment.

Cassandra took a deep breath, the air in her office still vaguely floral scented. "No."

The problem with this, Cassandra found herself thinking, *is that it forces everything else into question, as well. The problem with a betrayal like this is that I am now forced to doubt if there was every any sincerity in the man or in our dealings at all.*

Velez surprised her by saying, "I'm sorry."

"It was my own fault. He saw my weaknesses and capitalized upon them." Cassandra used her free hand to take the transmitter from her palm, holding it now between thumb and index finger. "He knew I was lonely, and he knew that what I wanted more than anything else wasn't a body to brush up against, but a mind capable of engaging my own."

She held out the transmitter for Velez, who produced a small anti-static bag from the side of her coat. Cassandra dropped the transmitter inside, watched as the older woman sealed the bag.

"I'll see what we can pull from it," Velez told her, tucking it away.

"You won't be able to pull anything from it, I'm afraid. He knows we found it. He'll have shut down the operation by now." Cassandra sighed, used her desk to lift herself out of her chair, feeling more tired than she actually was. She moved to the window, and this time didn't see out of it, but found herself staring at her reflection.

Pathetic, she thought. *You look pathetic, you sound pathetic, and that is because, at this moment, you are pathetic.*

"Desiring affection isn't a weakness, Doctor DeVries."

Cassandra shook her head. "In this case it was."

"I have protected people professionally for almost thirty years, Doctor," Velez said. "Either personally as their guard or as head of their protective detail. From the President of the United States to United Nations ambassadors and some of the most powerful, important people on the planet, I have guarded them all. I have done, in my opinion, an admirable job of it. I've learned several things, and one of those things is that there are attacks that cannot be defended against in any fashion or manner, no matter how good the guards or how brilliant the detail.

"There is no adequate defense for an attack on the heart."

"You think he targeted me from the beginning?"

"It would be foolish to think otherwise, Doctor."

The anger Cassandra had been feeling, the anger that had seemed finally to be in abeyance, returned with a flare. *Foolish,* she thought. *I'm foolish, I'm a fool.*

"I should have seen it."

"It is not a question of seeing it or not. It is a question of personality. Your personality allows such an attack to succeed. His personality allows him to launch such an attack."

"Then it's my weakness."

"You misunderstand. As I said, there is no adequate defense against an attack on the heart. There are only people such an attack will not work against, and you will forgive me for saying so, but those people are uniformly the ones I've enjoyed protecting the least, the ones, in my opinion, who have been least deserving of my efforts."

Cassandra turned from the window, not hearing Velez for the moment, still feeling the anger, and once again, now, the humiliation. *I'm going to hurt him for this,* she thought. *I'm going to make him remember this, how he used me, and I'm going to make him regret it.*

"Have you been able to locate Doctor Rose?" she asked Velez.

"Not as yet, though there is no doubt in my mind that

both CEO Murray and Mister Carrington are actively searching for him. If your theory about who Thaddeus Rose is and what he did is correct, it's hardly surprising he's so difficult to find. He is possibly responsible for the deaths of tens of millions, a very strong motive for wanting to stay hidden."

"But we still have no proof."

"Only circumstantial evidence. Again, that's hardly surprising. Murray won the Nobel and his position at the head of pharmaDyne as a result of the superflu pandemic. If he was involved in the outbreak as well as the cure, he would have been very thorough in his attempts to conceal that fact. If he merely capitalized on the situation, rather than helping to cause it, he is marginally less culpable personally, but still liable as the head of pharmaDyne. That he apparently has failed to permanently silence Rose thus far continues to surprise me."

"It tells us a great deal about Rose, though," Cassandra said. "And it provides a very strong motive for Carrington to want to find him."

"To what end?"

"I'm sorry?"

Velez cleared her throat before saying, "I find it hard to believe that a man like Carrington is unaware of the repercussions that would come from the fall of dataDyne. From what little I know of the man, he's a humanist as much as an iconoclast. He surely understands that the fall of dataDyne will do infinitely more harm to the world than good."

"Not if he thinks a greater good will come of it." Cassandra ran her hands through her hair, vaguely aware that the gesture had turned into an unconscious habit. "If he can find absolute proof that Rose was responsible for the pandemic, he could utterly destroy pharmaDyne, and the blowback would certainly cripple the rest of the corporation. Then again, he may want Rose for questioning, for research purposes, to learn how he did it. Carrington is like me, at least in that. He always wants to know more, to know *why*. It's even possible there's another reason, one we haven't thought of."

Velez considered, then reached inside her coat to the opposite side from where she wore her pistol, her hand coming out again with an older model lifeCard between her fingers. The card chimed, a minor chord, as she activated it.

"What?" Cassandra asked.

"Paul Sexton is mobilizing R-C/Bowman forces for an operation in the South Pacific," Velez said, getting to her feet. She indicated Cassandra's laptop. "May I?"

Cassandra crossed back to her desk. "You better let me, it might bite you."

"Figuratively?"

"If I could figure out a way for it to do it literally, I'd implement it."

Velez actually laughed, then offered the lifeCard to Cassandra, saying, "Decrypt and transfer, Easton-file."

The lifeCard hummed in Cassandra's hand, chiming again, and the progress bar for the transfer appeared on the screen, filling rapidly.

"What is Easton?" Cassandra asked, taking her seat once more.

"Not what, who," Velez said. She'd moved to stand behind her, watching the monitor from over Cassandra's shoulder. "Trent Easton, he's at the NSA."

"You have a connection at the NSA?"

"Amongst other places."

"And you're using that connection for dataDyne business?" The lifeCard sang once more, the transfer completed, and Cassandra handed the PDA back without looking.

"You disapprove?"

Cassandra thought about it, but for less than a second.

Maybe it was the sting of Carrington's betrayal still burning inside, but the obvious conflict-of-interest questions that dealing with NSA raised suddenly seemed unimportant.

Business is business, Cassandra thought.

"No," she said.

"I'm glad to hear that, Doctor. If you'll direct your attention to the surveillance file, and the attached analysis. Mister Easton was kind enough to include copies of the relevant intercepts, as well, with decryption."

Cassandra worked her laptop, opening the indicated files. A flood of high-resolution satellite surveillance photos cascaded open, one atop the other. The shots were all labeled, presumably for her benefit, and showed New Georgia Island in the Solomons, and more specifically, a secured compound of nearly twenty buildings situated outside the city of Hovoro. Each image was exceptional in its detail and clarity, in some cases the focus so tight and close that Cassandra could make out not only terrain features, but individuals as well. In one of the pictures, she could even make out—without any difficulty whatsoever—a remarkably overweight man sunbathing on one of the building rooftops.

From the images themselves, even without looking at the attached analysis, Cassandra could determine a number of things. First, the compound was a Core-Mantis operation from top to bottom; their corporate logo was visible in nearly every shot, gracing the helipads, the buildings, and almost every vehicle. Second, the compound was exceptionally secure, judging from the array of checkpoints and watchtowers in the images. Ringing the facility was a double-walled perimeter fence, the first quite possibly electrified, the second topped with razor wire.

The enhanced level of security was certainly odd, but not entirely suspect. She had a clear memory of reading about the Core-Mantis takeover of Guadalcanal the previous summer, some heavily sanitized news story about how the company had entered into an agreement with the Solomon Island Group for land and cooperative resource management. At the time, Cassandra had assumed that meant Core-Mantis was looking to shore up its manufacturing base by securing itself a below-cost—read: free—workforce, in the form of the local populace.

But what she was looking at now in these satellite photos wasn't a manufacturing facility, or if it was, it was unlike any she had ever seen before. There were no manufacturing plants, no production facilities. Just a series of offices, dormitories, and a cluster of very anonymous-looking Core-Mantis buildings.

"It's a research facility," Cassandra said.

Velez sounded impressed. "That was my assessment, as well. It also agrees with Easton's, for the record. According to him, this is Core-Mantis's prime medical research facility, their answer to the market threat posed by pharmaDyne, or at least, their attempt to answer that threat."

Cassandra turned from the monitor long enough to catch Velez's eyes. "Medical?"

"According to the NSA, yes."

"But you said Sexton was making a move, not Murray."

"That's correct."

"Is there a mistake?"

"No." Velez indicated the screen. "Bring up the images that were taken this morning, Doctor."

She turned her attention back to the laptop, did as Velez had requested. A second series of satellite images, as pristine and detailed as the first, unfolded on the screen one after the other. At first blush, they were practically identical to the previous photographs, and Cassandra scanned them quickly, clicking from one to the next.

Then she stopped, and went back, slower.

"Is that an anti-air platform?" she asked.

Again, Velez sounded mildly impressed. "The CM-656 anti-aircraft missile battery, called the Black Widow. It's a short-range defensive platform, Doctor, used to defend ground targets from airborne assault, and capable of tracking a stealth aircraft. As of this morning, there were four of them in place around the facility. There's more, if you want to see it."

"I'm not certain I need to," Cassandra said softly.

"The traffic intercepts shed some light—"

Cassandra put a finger to her lips abruptly, cutting Velez off with the gesture. She closed her eyes, feeling the tug-of-war in her mind, the pieces of the puzzle turning, trying to mesh with one another.

It didn't take long.

"He's there," she said, opening her eyes again and turning her chair to face Velez. "That's the only explanation, isn't it?"

"It's a theory I had considered," Velez said slowly. "But there's no evidence to support it."

"No, Rose is there, he must be. There's no other explanation for Murray's involvement."

"Paul Sexton is moving to attack the facility, not Doctor Murray. That's been confirmed by both my people inside R-C/Bowman and by Easton at the NSA."

"But it's a medical facility."

"Yes, so it appears."

"And as of this morning, Core-Mantis knows an attack is coming."

"Again, yes."

"Then the only question is who told them," Cassandra said. "Whether it was Carrington or Murray."

"I fail to see Murray's involvement in this."

"Stop looking for evidence and look at who stands to

gain." Cassandra found herself running her hands through her hair again, tugging at it. "It *must* be Murray behind this, it makes no sense otherwise. Why else would Paul Sexton suddenly initiate a hostile takeover against a Core-Mantis facility that has absolutely no impact or bearing on R-C/Bowman?"

"Flexing his muscles," Velez said. "He's showing off for the Board."

"But the bid's going to fail. I don't know much about military tactics, but I know enough. Sexton has lost the element of surprise. Core-Mantis knows he's coming. And while a successful takeover bid would raise Sexton's standing before the Board, a failed one will utterly destroy him. He'll lose not only his shot at CEO, but his position at R-C/Bowman."

"Sexton has always been overly ambitious, Doctor."

Cassandra shook her head, growing at once more certain that she was right, and more frustrated that Velez didn't see it. "No, no, Murray must have convinced Sexton to do it somehow. Must have promised him something in exchange, something Sexton wanted, something Sexton believed. Support for him as the next CEO, most likely. A promise to withdraw his own name from consideration."

"I've heard nothing about communication between Sexton and Murray," Velez said tightly.

"You also didn't know that I'd been sleeping with Daniel Carrington for almost a year."

The statement made Velez wince.

Cassandra pressed. "It makes far more sense if it's Murray who tipped off Core-Mantis, not Carrington. Murray's using Sexton, and he's doing it brilliantly. When the takeover bid fails—and it will fail—Sexton will not only be out of the running for CEO, he'll be out of his job at R-C/Bowman. Murray will have removed his strongest competition."

Velez squinted past her shoulder, at the laptop screen. "And if Rose is there . . ."

"Then Sexton has provided Murray with the distraction he needs to get into a very secure facility to find Rose."

"At which point, he'll kill him."

"Yes."

Both of them fell silent.

"Carrington is no fool," Cassandra said, after almost a minute's further thought. "I'd bet you anything that he already knows about all of this, about Murray using Sexton, about the impending attack. He *knows* Rose is there."

"You think he'll send in his own people?"

"*I* would."

"It's going to be a madhouse on the ground in Hovoro, Doctor. NSA estimates put Core-Mantis troop strength at over five hundred. My own sources tell me that Sexton is mobilizing his full R-C/Bowman complement for the takeover, that's at least two hundred and fifty soldiers, with close air support. Add to that whoever Murray sends, and you believe that Daniel Carrington will send his own team in on top of that?"

She didn't even hesitate before answering. "Absolutely."

"It's a suicide mission."

"That hardly matters. If there's a possibility that Carrington can get his hands on Rose, he'll take it. And if there's the slightest chance he'll succeed, we have to stop him."

"And how do you propose doing that?"

Cassandra frowned, again finding her hands running through her hair. She tried to remember how much money she was worth at the moment, and how much of it was liquid. At least thirty million pounds, she guessed, and that was just what she could get her hands on at the moment.

With a couple of phone calls, she could quadruple that amount within a day.

But it will be money well spent, she thought.

"We're going to send in troops of our own," Cassandra DeVries said.

CHAPTER 26

Carrington Institute VTOL Chameleon Class Dropship #003—
4,730 Feet, Level Flight—South Pacific, Solomon Islands Group
October 13th/14th (International Date Line), 2020

Calvin Rogers's voice came over the headphones, his voice thin with excitement.

"Three minutes."

Steinberg murmured a confirmation, hoping to God that his stomach would settle. Seated on the bench opposite him in the dropship troop compartment, Joanna Dark echoed the confirmation, and over his headset, Steinberg thought the damned girl sounded almost disinterested.

As if making a night drop into a free-fire zone is something she does all the time, Steinberg thought, and he knew it was bitter, but he couldn't help it, and truth to tell, he didn't care. She had no right to be here. She had no right to be here at all.

It didn't matter that she had *never* made a parachute drop before in her life. It didn't matter that she had utterly screwed the pooch on the group tactics simulation. It didn't matter that she was a twenty-year-old *girl*, for Christ's sake.

Joanna Dark was going to drop into the heart of an open war between Core-Mantis OmniGlobal and Royce-Chamberlain/Bowman Motors not ninety miles from where the United States Marines had fought one of the bloodiest battles against the Japanese during the Second World War. None of it mattered, not one bit of it.

No, Agent Dark—*Acting* Agent Dark, he corrected himself—was making the jump tonight with him, and together they would attempt to locate, capture, and then lift Doctor Thaddeus Rose, who might—emphasis on might, since there was not one concrete shred of proof that Rose was even *at* the Hovoro Facility—be somewhere at the site. Joanna was his backup, instead of any of a half dozen or so other commandos that Steinberg himself had trained, that Steinberg trusted with his life. Instead he had Joanna Dark, who had no combat discipline, no perspective, no experience at this kind of thing.

All because the Old Man had said so.

Steinberg had to wonder how it was that, ever since Jo had come to the Institute, he could count the number of arguments he'd won with Carrington on no fingers whatsoever.

"Two minutes," Rogers said. *"Pre-drop checks, stand by."*

Steinberg rose from his bench, feeling the weight of the parachute shifting on his back, the pull of the thirty-plus pounds of equipment he was wearing in addition to trying to heed gravity and fall to the ocean below. Pitch-black in a moonless night, Steinberg knew, and the thought of it made him queasy. He hated jumps, day, night, HALO or LALO, it didn't matter. He'd barely passed certification in the Rangers. He was with the penguins. Just because someone had wings, it didn't mean they should fly.

Jo had likewise risen, following his cue, and he motioned her forward, not bothering to try to speak to her over the roar of the dropship engines.

The attack plan had ruled out the use of the dropship's stealth systems, which sacrificed speed for silence. Since the backbone of the anti-air defenses relied on missiles capable of tracking them, there was little point in going in at anything less than top speed. It made for a noisy ride.

The lighting in the troop compartment was dim, tinged with crimson to preserve their night vision, and it made the red hair that peeked out from beneath her helmet look like it had been painted with fresh blood. Her expression was entirely serious, he noted, and Steinberg was about to take comfort in that, at least, when he caught her eyes and read the excitement there.

"What is it with you?" he asked her. "Do you only feel alive if you're trying to get yourself killed?"

"What?" Jo shouted back at him.

Steinberg shook his head, dismissing the question. He never should have said it aloud. He motioned her forward further, reached out, and checked her harness, making certain her weapons and associated gear were all secured for the jump. He had to tighten the straps across her chest, the ones pinning the Fairchild against her body. The submachine guns, his and hers, had been outfitted with flash suppressors and night-vision optics, all of their banana clips taped together in doubles for speedy reloading. In addition, Jo had gone with twin Falcons, stripped bare, each in a holster strapped to her thighs. Amongst her gear, Steinberg knew she was carrying two silencers, one to be fitted to each weapon.

He doubted she'd be using them. He doubted there'd be much need, or opportunity, to go about their business quietly.

Steinberg motioned for her to turn, and she did so, presenting her back to him. He quickly checked her chute, then the associated straps again. Everything was perfectly secured. She might never have done this before, but you wouldn't have known it by looking at her.

Steinberg realized that Jo had threaded the excess of her waist-belt in the same fashion he had done, wrapping it around the secured strap twice before slipping its end through the loop. He wondered if it was unconscious mimicry, or if he should be flattered.

He tapped her left shoulder, and Jo turned around to face him again, and Steinberg pointed at himself, then extended his arms to allow her to check him. She ran her hands over his body as he had done hers, tugging at his shoulder straps in identical fashion, making sure his own Fairchild was secured. She checked the holster at his thigh, and he thought she pulled a face at the sight of the DY357 Magnum riding there, as if mocking his choice of personal weapon, again. He fought down another surge of profound annoyance.

Jo motioned for him to turn around, and he did, staring at the rear wall of the troop compartment, at the red light bulb glowing weakly over the bench.

If she finds anything, I'll kill myself, Steinberg thought bitterly.

"One minute," Rogers said. *"Red light on, doors open."*

Jo tapped him on the shoulder, and he turned back to face her, saw her give him the thumbs-up as the portside door slid back on its tracks. Wind poured into the compartment, buffeting the both of them, making the fabric of their CI combat suits snap against their skin. The wind, Steinberg noted, was warm and wet, and he tasted salt air on his lips.

Steinberg moved cautiously to the open door, the red jump light above it pulsing slowly. Beside it, still dim, was the green go light.

Despite his better judgment, Steinberg took a look out the open door, at the world beneath them. Directly below, the South Pacific spread in an endless blanket of darkness, kissing the coastline of New Georgia Island. Jo had moved up beside him, was likewise peering out, and if there was a fear of heights in the woman, she gave no sign of it. Steinberg moved his gaze along the coast, in the direction the dropship was thundering, then tapped Jo's arm and indicated for her to look the same way.

"Thirty seconds."

Ahead of them, on the edge of the coast, the darkness of the island ended in a flurry of munitions color. Blooms of red and orange and yellow burst on the ground, clouds of blackness ringed with green rising from the earth. The red streaks of tracer fire rose from the ground, arcing toward the sky like fireworks. Steinberg was certain he could hear the thump and crack of the big guns that R-C/Bowman had brought to the fight, the roar of the Core-Mantis missile batteries.

"Fifteen seconds, stand by, stand by."

Steinberg exhaled sharply, steeling himself. *Not much longer now,* he thought. *Not much longer and you can die the way you're supposed to, on the ground.*

He checked his helmet, then pulled the headphones off and tossed them back to the bench he'd been using. He tugged his NVG goggles down over his eyes. Again, Jo mirrored his movements, the mimicry perfect.

Steinberg turned his head to Jo, shouting over the roar of the engines and the shriek of the wind. "Follow me out!"

Jo nodded.

He looked to the lights above the door, the red light now constant, no longer flashing. Then it winked out, and the green light came on.

He put his hand to the side of the compartment door,

sucked in as deep a breath as he could manage against the pressure of the wind, readying himself to leap.

She went out the door first.

Bitch, he thought, and then threw himself into the night sky after her.

RUMORS OF HYPERCORP MILITARY ACTION "EXAGGERATED"

Reported Combat in Solomon Islands a Hoax?

By Timothy Squire, O'BRIEN'S DEFENSE UPDATE Staff Correspondent

---

October 14, 2020: Hovoro—New Georgia Island

Authorities in the city of Hovoro, situated on the northeastern corner of New Georgia Island, have reacted with concern to unsubstantiated reports of military conflict in the region.

"There is absolutely no evidence that anything of the sort has occurred," Mayor Douglas Carmichael told reporters earlier this morning. "Hovoro is a modest community, with modest people living modest lives. I have no idea how stories like this get started, but the very idea is preposterous."

Rumors of fighting centering around Hovoro began circulating late last night, when the crew of a Runyon-Adams Concern cargo aircraft reported seeing explosions and anti-aircraft fire along the coastal region. Runyon-Adams Concern is a dataDyne subsidiary, and as such has no docking or distribution rights in the region.

"Certainly those pilots have a vivid imagination," Core-Mantis spokeswoman Leslie Ann Dunlop said, when contacted for comment. "Core-Mantis OmniGlobal's regional defense subcontractor, with full authorization of the local government, detonated some defective and obsolete munitions near the coast last evening, nothing more."

Dunlop declined to name the regional defense subcontractor, citing the need to maintain security of their personnel. "For whatever reason, perhaps jealousy, dataDyne has attempted to create a tempest in a teacup, and we simply will not allow such irresponsible scaremongering to jeopardize the good men and women in our employ."

dataDyne spokespeople were unavailable for comment.

"The worst thing about this kind of vicious, slanderous attack, is that it scares people," said Mayor Carmichael. "I can only hope that whoever is behind these rumors puts a stop to it, before innocent lives suffer as a result."

CHAPTER 27

Core-Mantis OmniGlobal-Solomon Islands Health and Healing Center—
Hovoro Secured Facility—
17 km WSW Hovoro
October 14th/15th (International Date Line), 2020

Jo hit the ground—quite literally—just after midnight.

The shock of her collision with the earth slammed through her boots and up her shins, making her hips ache. She let herself collapse with the impact, the way Steinberg had told her to, falling backward, half onto her side, smelling the wet and warmth of the New Georgia Island earth. Her chute billowed behind her, filling with the wind, and she felt herself being dragged backward.

She hit the quick-release on her right shoulder, then her left, felt the parachute silk fly away from her, freed from its restraints. She scrambled to her feet, scanning her surroundings quickly as she shucked off the remains of the parachute, dropping the Fairchild into her hands and taking it off safety. She tried to orient herself, looking for Steinberg as well as anyone else who might've seen the landing. The sound of open battle cut through the thick jungle air. Somewhere off to her right, she felt, then heard, the concussion of something big blowing itself to bits.

Steinberg had landed some fifteen meters from her position, deeper in the jungle undergrowth, and he was already out of his chute with his Fairchild at the ready as she approached. He motioned her closer, crouching down, his face oddly surreal with the thin Institute-supplied night-vision goggles hiding his eyes.

"Got all your fingers and toes?" he whispered as Jo dropped to one knee beside him. He didn't look at her, craning his head to peer through the thick undergrowth around them.

"Last I checked," Jo said.

"Right, stay low and stay close." He looked at her, and she thought his expression was remarkably close to hostile. "And damn well do what I tell you to do."

"Yes, sir!" Jo said, and snapped off a salute with her free hand.

Steinberg muttered something, possibly about her ancestry, then rose and began picking his way through the jungle. Jo followed, keeping a good three meters between them, carrying the Fairchild with its stock deployed, tucked against her shoulder. Neither of them was entirely sure where they'd come down in relation to the Hovoro facility, but she imagined that neither of them saw that as a problem.

They had the sounds of war to guide them.

It took almost half an hour to clear the jungle surrounding the facility and reach the outer perimeter, where the jungle had been cut back to make room for Core-Mantis's construction. Twice during the trip they were assaulted by the sounds of nearby fighting, and each time Steinberg had motioned Jo to drop prone, doing the same. In each instance, the sounds of battle had passed them by.

The second time, just as they'd regained their feet and begun moving forward again, she'd heard a whine coming from behind her, high overhead. Without thinking, she'd leapt forward into Steinberg's back, riding him to the ground, and almost instantly there'd come the explosion. The shock wave of the detonating bomb had been enough to make Jo's ears ache, made her feel as if she were being crushed against Steinberg's back. Wood and foliage had rained down around them, and when the last pieces of earth had finally stopped falling and she'd dared to raise her head again, she'd been barely able to make out the shape of a squat, arrow-shaped dropship roaring by overhead, less than fifteen meters above them.

"Son of a bitch," Steinberg had said. "Did you see markings? Did it have any markings?"

Jo had shook her head, and together they'd each cautiously gotten back to their feet. She'd heard screams, already weak, coming from somewhere ahead of them.

The sound had stopped by the time they reached the perimeter clearing, and the sight of the carnage there gave the explanation, and it gave them both pause.

Bodies littered the approach to the facility's entrance, Core-Mantis and dataDyne soldiers strewn across the roadway, some of them in pieces. The hulks of two ground assault vehicles—military hovercraft with null-g assistors used to help them negotiate the jungle terrain—smoldered and smoked near the entrance to the main gates. The gates themselves, as well as massive chunks of both the outer and inner fences surrounding the compound, had been blown apart, leaving a ragged hole. If this had been the site of the most intense fighting—and Jo suspected that it had been—then the battle here, at least, was over. There had to be over one hundred dead strewn across the ground ahead of them, Core-Mantis and data-Dyne alike.

Steinberg held up his left hand, motioning for Jo to stop advancing, then went down on one knee once more. She saw that he was perspiring, realized that she was, as well. It wasn't strictly hot here, no more than the mid-seventies, Fahrenheit, but the humidity was vicious, and it made Jo feel as if her combat suit had been soaked in water.

Jo kept her eyes moving, scanning the area around them, straining to discern the various sounds she was hearing. There was sporadic gunfire coming from beyond the double fence, the occasional muffled explosion, but nothing more from the direction they'd come. Either the jungle fighting had ended, or it had reached a lull. She hoped it was the former; the latter would leave them with enemies at their back.

Steinberg pushed his NVG up onto his forehead, then reached around to a pouch on the back of his belt, freeing his binoculars. Out of the corner of her eye, Jo saw him put the optics to his eyes, searching the fence carefully.

He paused, then said, "Hawks. God damn it to hell."

It was such a non sequitur that Jo wasn't certain she'd heard him correctly.

"Sorry?" she whispered in response.

Steinberg lowered the binoculars, handing them over to her without looking away from the gap in the fence. "Eleven o'clock, just inside the breach on the second fence."

Jo moved her NVG out of the way, placed the binos to her own eyes, looking where Steinberg had directed. With the darkness and the added shadow thrown down by the broken fencing, it took her a second, but then she saw a man in combat dress similar to their own, crouched just inside the inner fence. He was armed with a long gun of some sort, what Jo suspected was an assault rifle. He was scanning the approach to his position with the weapon ready at his shoulder, securing the access.

The man adjusted his position slightly as she watched, and she saw the patch sewn onto his shoulder, the fabric of it lighter than the rest of his clothing, but couldn't quite make out the detail on the emblem itself. She zoomed the binos in closer, using her right forefinger to hold down the auto button, heard the optics whine quietly.

The symbol was of a gold-headed bird of prey with a bloodied beak, and she didn't recognize it. If it was a dataDyne or R-C/Bowman or Core-Mantis OmniGlobal emblem, it was one she'd never encountered before.

She lowered the binos to see that Steinberg had motioned her down to her belly, that he had already fallen to his. She lay down beside him.

"He's a merc," Steinberg said softly. "A goddamn merc, which means there's at least one other player on this field."

"I've never heard of 'hawks,' at least not ones that weren't extinct."

"Hawk Teams," he said, the tension in his voice making it clear that he'd already passed from annoyed to pissed off. "They're mercenaries, damn good ones, too. They specialize in dirty jobs, and they work almost exclusively for dataDyne. You remember the Shock Troopers?"

"Yes," Jo said, not particularly pleased at the thought of recalling Macau.

"Like that. Just as good, but without the corporate oversight. They're just in it for the money."

"Which means they've been paid to be here."

"And paid a lot, because they sure as hell ain't cheap. So either Sexton bought himself a Hawk Team or two to back up his takeover bid—"

"—or there's another player on the field, yes, I see."

"We have to take him out if we want to get in there."

Jo reached up to one of the pouches on her arm, unzipping it silently and rolling the silencer she'd been carrying there into her hand, began screwing it onto the end of one of her two Falcons. "I'll take care of it."

Steinberg put a gloved hand on her forearm. "You can't be nice about this one, Jo."

"What?"

"You're going to have to kill him. You're in a war zone, you don't leave the enemy alive."

She stopped what she was doing for a second, then gave the silencer a final twist, feeling it lock into place. "I understand."

"And don't screw it up."

"I'll try not to." She slid her Fairchild over to Steinberg. "Hold that for me."

"I mean it, Jo," Steinberg said. "No dying."

"I didn't realize you cared so much, Jonathan."

"I don't," he said. "But if you don't come back from this alive, the Old Man will kill me."

She took the better part of five minutes to make her way to the wall, finding an approach that kept her out of the mercenary's line of sight. The exterior fence had once been electrified, but the damage done to it during the height of the battle had ended that particular hazard, and now it was nothing more than a chain-link obstacle, and one that Jo had no difficulty in quietly overcoming.

Once inside the first fence, she worked her way along the second, toward the breach point. Occasional bursts of gunfire were still erupting from the trees beyond, and twice she heard exchanges from inside the facility compound, and the dull thud of explosives, most likely grenades. A wind had kicked up, smelling of rot and saltwater and burning flesh, the war mixing with the jungle.

She edged her way cautiously toward the breach, stopping when she caught sight of the mercenary's gun barrel, its muzzle jutting out from behind his cover. She'd been right, it was an assault rifle, the M16C. It was the weapon she'd have picked for jungle work if long guns gave her joy; with its shortened barrel, the M16C was ideal for urban and jungle combat.

Jo steadied herself, going still, shifting the silenced Falcon in her hands from low-ready to high-ready. She was preparing to move when she heard the crackle of the radio, and that surprised her. She had expected anyone they encountered to be wearing subcutaneous units the way she and Steinberg were, either CMO ThroatLinks or radio buttons embedded behind the ear.

Between their choice of assault rifle, and the unusual radio gear, she realized that the Hawks were intentionally avoiding the use of dataDyne equipment. Whoever was footing the bill for the mercenaries was certainly getting their money's worth; if one of them were captured, they'd be completely deniable.

"Hawk Nine, Hawk Nine."

The answering voice was soft, almost a growl, and Jo had to strain to hear it.

"Nine, go."

"Building Seven secured, we're on our way down. Status?"

"Clear. They're still pounding jungle ground out there."

"Command says keep a good watch, nothing comes back on us."

"Affirmative."

There was a pause, then another crackle from the unseen radio. *"Debus ETA five minutes. Give us until exfil, then meet at the hopper, we'll be coming with the package."*

"Confirmed," the mercenary said. "Out."

There was no immediate response, and Jo took that to mean that the conversation had ended. She looked at the pistol ready in her hands, realized what she was about to do, realized that, by the mercenary's conversation, she knew exactly where he was, could envision precisely where his head was positioned. He wouldn't stand a chance. He was going to die.

He was someone she had never met, just doing his job, and she was going to kill him. For an awful moment, Jo thought she was going to be sick. Yes, they were in a war zone, yes, he'd kill her if he had the opportunity, but he wasn't going to get it, she knew that.

She didn't think she could do it. Soldier or not, it felt too much like being a killer.

Then she remembered Steinberg saying that the Hawk Teams were mercenaries, but that they worked almost exclusively for dataDyne.

Jo stepped forward, pivoted, and put two bullets into the mercenary's face. He died without ever having the chance to look surprised.

Jo pivoted back behind the cover of the fence, and motioned for Steinberg to join her. Then she crouched down and reached around the fence again, taking hold of the back of the dead man's combat harness and pulling him around to join her. By the time Steinberg had reached her, running low with both Fairchilds in his hands, she'd gone through the mercenary's gear, pulling half a dozen grenades and his radio.

"They're after Rose," she whispered to Steinberg when he settled breathlessly beside her. "Building Seven, we've got four minutes before they move for exfil. Sounds like they're after him alive."

Steinberg looked the question at her, and Jo held up the radio for him to see. He nodded, then slipped around her to look past the edge of the inner fence, onto the compound. After a second, he pulled back.

"You know what we do?" he asked.

"We let them do the hard part for us," Jo answered,

grinning. "Locate their ship and then give them one hell of a shock when they try to board it."

Steinberg actually answered her grin, if only for a second. "We need to establish an ambush position around the vehicle, we need to do it without being spotted, and we need to do it in the next three minutes."

Jo hefted her Fairchild, feeling the adrenaline thrilling through her, all memories of any moral quandary now utterly forgotten.

"What are we waiting for?" she asked Steinberg, and before he could answer, she was up and moving into the devastated compound, looking for the next person who might need a bullet or three's persuasion to stay out of her way.

CHAPTER 28

Core-Mantis OmniGlobal-Solomon Islands Health and Healing Center—Hovoro Secured Facility—Building Seven (Life Storage Wing)—17 km WSW Hovoro
October 14th/15th (International Date Line), 2020

Now this is more like it, Hayes thought as he let a burst from his Liberator rip through another two Core-Mantis security guards. Both had submachine guns of their own, and both had seen him coming, and all the same he'd dropped each without them so much as firing a shot in his direction. Their deaths brought his running total to eleven since he'd hit the ground, but he might have been off; he'd been using grenades, and it was sometimes hard to tell how many people died when one of those went off, unless you wanted to go back and actually count, and Hayes just couldn't spare the time.

Above, in the surrounding jungle, the war would be entering its last spasms, with Core-Mantis beginning mop-up operations, hunting down the last of Sexton's spent forces. It would take them a while, but not so long that

Hayes could afford to dawdle. He needed to find Rose, and he needed to do it fast, before the locals managed to get their buildings secured once more.

Hayes worked his way along the white-walled, sterile hallway, stopping only long enough to strip the grenades from the guards he'd just dropped. He moved with confidence, strength, none of this skulking around, because there wasn't any need. Doors were spaced unevenly along both sides of the hall, and he used the Liberator to blast them open, then a grenade in quick succession, clearing his way with brutal efficiency. A couple times he saw white coats, wide-eyed in their labs, and sometimes he heard them scream before they died.

As long as none of them was Rose, he didn't care.

He was feeling like a god, and it was about damn time as far as he was concerned. Too often in the last two weeks he'd felt like a failure, instead, and he'd had more than enough of that.

New York had shaken his confidence, to be double-teamed the way he had, first by Carcareas, then by the redhead. He'd returned to Doctor Murray's home in Vancouver in severe withdrawal, shaking and paranoid, certain that his father was going to take his failure as an excuse for another pound of flesh. Instead, his father had patched him immediately, then listened to Hayes's recounting of the day's events with a half smile on his face.

"It's not that bad," Doctor Murray had told him. "You accomplished what you needed to."

"But the woman from Carrington—"

"Carrington will not be able to stop the attack on the Solomons, Laurent."

"He'll try to stop us!"

"How? He wouldn't dare warn off Sexton, he wants

Rose as much as we do, I'm sure of it. And if he comes to Hovoro in the hopes of acquiring the man, he'll certainly fail. His will be the harder job, remember, he wants Rose alive. All you need to do is kill him."

That had made sense, but Hayes had still been troubled. It seemed to him that they were missing something, that there was something that had been forgotten or neglected.

But his father had assured him that the situation was still going their way, at least as far as he was concerned. He was particularly pleased at the thought of Sexton's impending self-destruction, and what he called the "comeuppance" the man had in store.

"Asking for joint credit," Doctor Murray had said with disgust. "Imagine the arrogance."

Then his father had told him to prepare for his trip to Hovoro, to make certain he would be able to identify Rose by sight when he saw him. He sent Hayes off to collect his weapons and to prepare his gear, and before noon, Hayes had been ready to depart. Before he left the house, his father stopped him.

"For you," he said, and then showed Hayes the dermal resting in his palm. "Try it, I think you'll be pleased."

Hayes had set down his equipment, then offered the back of his neck to Doctor Murray, felt the one patch already in place come free with a quick tug, then be replaced by the new one immediately. The sudden rush of heat had coursed down his spine, made his head throb and his fingers tremble, and then it had all passed, and he'd straightened up and looked at his father, and it was like looking at him with new eyes. Not that the picture had changed, that wasn't it, but it was now clearer than ever before, as if everything Hayes saw had been magnified, focused.

"Do you like it?" Doctor Murray had asked. "I've been working on it for some time. It's based on the previous iterations, of course, still derivative of the standard combat-boost. But I've been able to heighten the nutrient feed, so you should feel a substantial increase in both your reaction times and your mean physical dexterity."

"It feels . . . good . . ."

"Well, that is the point, my boy. I want you at your best for this." Doctor Murray had patted his shoulder. "It should last you until you return. You'll have to tell me how you do in combat with it, all right? Try to remember the sensations."

"I will, Father."

"Go, Laurent."

Hayes went, first by low-orbit transport to New Zealand, and then by fast boat to New Georgia Island, coming from the west side, on the opposite coast as Hovoro. He'd made landfall before evening, and had had more than enough time to travel cross-island and find a safe and concealed position well away from the Hovoro facility. Then it had only been a matter of waiting, a trick harder than it had first seemed. The new patch made him feel even more high-strung than usual, made it almost impossible to sit still. His nerves sang, all of his senses tight, hearing, feeling, smelling, seeing everything around him. He'd marveled at nuances of color around him, the infinite variations of green in the jungle leaves, the distinct sounds of a thousand different insects.

And when night had fallen, he'd watched the first exchanges of fire painting the sky, the Core-Mantis Omni-Global missile batteries trying to shoot down the R-C/Bowman automated attack drones before their payloads could be delivered to target. He'd felt the jungle trembling with the battle, hearing the leaves around him rustle and the life living beneath them scurry in panic and confusion.

When he'd thought the time was right, when R-C/Bowman troops had begun their ground assault in earnest, he started his own.

Hovoro Facility Building Seven reminded Hayes, in many ways, of pharmaDyne Vancouver, or at least, of the lab and research portions of the latter. The hallways shared the same institutionalized sterility and lack of personality, though here, from what Hayes could see, it was all-pervasive. The building existed to serve research, period. No bland corporate art, no traditional potted plants, or even muted tan carpeting. Just row upon row of cream-colored hallways, tiled floors, and lab space.

Hayes thought that blood added some much needed color to the place.

Turning a corner, he found himself in a rectangular open room, some sort of common area used by the white coats as a break area. There were vending machines and couches and video screens and a coffee maker on a table near the far wall. There were also four more security guards, and without pause, Hayes opened fire on them. Whatever his father had given him in the dermal, he was as accurate as ever, and faster than before. The fastest of them managed to take three steps, running to take cover behind one of the couches.

Hayes strode forward and dropped three of the guards in quick succession, firing tight, controlled bursts delivered one atop another. He kicked over the break room table, flipping it onto its side, which sent the coffee pot on top of it crashing to the tile floor. He stooped low, using the table as cover.

He waited what seemed like a very long two seconds for the surviving guard to return fire, then rolled out and fired low. The last guard screamed in pain and collapsed, groaning, to the floor.

Hayes picked himself up and walked over to the fallen guard, reloading as he went. Leading with the barrel of the submachine gun, he looked down.

The guard's face was contorted in agony, his hands soaked with blood from his destroyed shin. Hayes saw that he was already losing his color, too, and figured the man was well on his way to shock.

"Ah God, God please," the guard said. "Please don't kill me."

Hayes pushed the barrel of his weapon against the man's forehead. "Where's Doctor Rose?"

"God please—"

"I'll shoot you again. It'll hurt."

"I don't know a Doctor Rose, I don't know—"

"How do I get to the secured labs? How do I get inside?"

The guard blinked rapidly, trying to clear the tears of pain from his eyes, and Hayes saw the man's tongue flick out in an attempt to wet his parched lips.

Yeah, this guy's gone, Hayes thought.

"C'mon, quickly," Hayes said. "I'll get you help, just tell me what I need to know."

With a blood-soaked hand, the guard gestured back, behind him, toward one of the hallways running off the common area. "That way, it's . . . it's that way, end of the hall, there's an elevator . . . locked down, now—"

"I need the code."

The guard winced, trying to remember through his haze of pain. "Twenty-nine, sixty-nine, forty-three . . . forty . . ."

"You're sure? Don't lie to me, you lie to me, I'll leave you here to bleed out."

"No, no, it's . . . that's the code . . . there's only one way for it to go, you take it down . . . that's the—that's the experimental wing . . ."

"Anything else?"

The guard shook his head, weakly, again clutching at his lower leg with both hands. He tried to keep from sobbing. "That's it, swear to God that's it. You've got to help me, I'm losing a lot of blood, here. . . ."

"You can still lose more," Hayes said, and shot him.

He met less resistance than he'd expected upon entering the secure wing, and grew sloppy as a result. Coming out of the elevators and through the second security checkpoint, he heard a shot and felt a round punch him squarely between the shoulder blades. The bullet failed to penetrate the proprietary dataDyne ballistic weave of his light body armor, but it staggered him, and he nearly fell.

He had a moment of indescribable delight when he spun around to see the look of surprise on the guard's face. He made sure she died with it still in place.

Then he scavenged her body, rearming himself, this time with Core-Mantis weaponry. Most of the guards were using Vipers, a close-quarters automatic shotgun, and Hayes went with that, discarding his submachine gun.

Outfitted once again, he started with the labs, discovering that the majority of the research and technical staff had been evacuated to this very location. Apparently, someone had thought the high-security wing was the safest place in the Hovoro facility.

Boy were they wrong, Hayes thought.

In one lab, he found six of the white coats clustered together, looking like a clump of panicked deer waiting for a wolf. When Hayes entered, one of them, an Asian man in his early fifties, tried to throw a stoppered beaker at him. Hayes shot him before he even had the chance, the Viper blowing a very satisfying hole in the man's chest. He toppled, and Hayes jumped forward with a sudden burst of speed, catching the beaker in his left hand before it could fall to the ground.

"So what's this?" he asked.

The white coats were mute, so he shot another one of them, this one male, Caucasian and apparently in his forties.

"It's an acid, that's all it is," one of the female scientists said quickly. "Just a distilled acid, high potency, we use it for—"

Hayes pointed the barrel of the Viper at her, and she went silent as if her throat had been slit.

"Rose," he said. "Where is he?"

There was no immediate response, so Hayes shot the woman in the head. Two of the remaining scientists screamed.

"Rose," Hayes said again. "Where is he?"

"Why should we tell you anything, you'll kill us—"

Hayes grinned. "I'm definitely going to kill you if you don't."

The oldest of the white coats, another woman with a head of curly silver hair, spoke softly. "Continue down the hallway, there's an intersection, numbers painted on the wall. Follow number four, it's the last door in the corridor."

Something in the way she said it made Hayes hesitate. Not the resignation of her statement, that wasn't it, but something else.

"You don't like him?" Hayes asked.

"You won't, either. You'll see why." The woman drew herself up to her full height, squaring her shoulders. "If you'd please, I'd prefer it in the head. It'll be quicker that way."

"Yeah," Hayes said. "It would."

Then he smashed the beaker into the woman's face. She screamed, collapsing to the floor, her flesh melting away in rivers. He carelessly shot the others, then made his way down the corridor, following hallway four, thinking that everything was finally working out the way it should.

He was still thinking that when he discovered a half dozen dead Core-Mantis guards on the ground, each of them shot multiple times. Then he saw the door to the lab, the door that should've been locked and sealed, but wasn't. Someone had blown it open.

No, he thought. *No, no, no, this isn't fair. . . .*

Hayes stepped through the blasted doorway, the gun held ready in both hands, discovering that he'd entered not a lab, but an office of some sort, and that the office had been thoroughly tossed. There were filing cabinets and two destroyed computers, and on the desk, he found a nameplate, and the name it gave was ROSE, THADDEUS K. Two more doors ran off the office, and like the one he'd just passed, they'd been blown, too. Carefully, he checked each of them.

One was a lab, apparently undisturbed.

The other was . . . well, Hayes didn't know what it was, not for certain. At first, he thought it served as a jail of some sort, but that made no sense to him, and he couldn't imagine why Core-Mantis OmniGlobal would put its jail in the secure section of the development and testing wing. It wasn't like Vancouver, where the veneer of respectability had to be maintained. Out here, you could butcher someone on the roof and no one would say a word.

What he was seeing weren't strictly cells, though, more like cages, heavy wire-mesh boxes just large enough to hold an adult if the adult didn't try to stand upright.

That didn't seem to pose a problem for their occupants, though, not because they weren't adults—though several, Hayes noted, were children—but because most of them couldn't stand. And the reason they couldn't stand was because all of them were missing limbs, some of them missing multiple ones. Most simply had been left with stumps at their severed thighs and elbows, but a few had growths rising from the amputations, not prosthetics, but something else, something that Hayes would have expected to see on insects rather than people.

For a second, he was so stunned by the sight of the room, he forgot where he was, what he was there to do.

Then the things—the people—in the cages saw him, and almost as one, began screaming at him. They threw themselves at their walls, spitting and cursing. Those with working limbs attempted to throw the contents of the cages at him, bedpans filled with feces and urine, plates with the remains of fouled food.

At which point Hayes started laughing uncontrollably, thinking this was the funniest damn thing he'd ever seen in his life.

It took him the better part of a minute to get over his amusement and leave Rose's House of Horrors behind him, putting his attention back on the task at hand.

Hayes began running back the way he came, stopping only long enough to rearm himself from one of the fallen Core-Mantis guards in hallway four. He was reassured to find that the body was still quite warm, and that drove him faster, the knowledge that whoever had grabbed Rose couldn't be too far ahead of him.

Rose had been taken, that was obvious. Who had done it, Hayes didn't know, but he had two immediate suspects. The first were Sexton's troops, that they had mounted a separate operation under the cover of the main attack in an attempt to do as his father had requested. He doubted that, only because the destruction of the office seemed to indicate that no attempt had been made to recover Rose's research.

The second suspect, of course, was Carrington. His father had underestimated the lengths the old bastard would go to. No doubt Carrington had inserted his own team much as Hayes himself had infiltrated Hovoro, and now was running away with the prize.

If he was quick, he could catch them.

He *had* to catch them.

He couldn't let the redheaded bitch beat him a third time.

CHAPTER 29

DataFlow Corporate Headquarters—
Communications & Support Center—
#7 Rue de la Baume, Paris, France
October 14th, 2020

The Communications & Support Center was primarily used as the tech support nexus for DataFlow's European branch, and for that reason, when Velez had suggested that they audit the Hawk Team's progress, Cassandra had recommended its use. Normally staffed twenty-four/seven by DataFlow specialists, Cassandra had cleared the office out the night before, ordering all calls rerouted to the Indian, Chinese, and American offices until she directed otherwise. If anyone wondered about the reason for the shift in policy, no one had bothered—or dared—to question her.

Once the office had been closed and the personnel cleared, Anita Velez had escorted the Hawk Team commanding officer, a former United States Marine Colonel named Leland Shaw, onto the premises. Shaw had brought with him a skeleton tech-support staff, four men, all with the same professional soldier's bearing of their leader, and under his supervision, they had begun wiring together a command and control post on DataFlow's third floor, from which they would monitor the military action taking place half a world away.

Cassandra greeted Colonel Shaw when he first arrived with her best smile and a firm handshake. "I'm grateful you were able to mobilize on such short notice."

"We pride ourselves on being able to do just that." Colonel Shaw spoke with a slight accent, a twang born from somewhere in the American south. "For the amount you're paying us, we'd damn well better be able to deliver."

"I'm certain you shall," Cassandra said, holding his hand for a fraction of a second longer than needed before releasing it, and Colonel Shaw's professional façade had shown a hairline crack, then the hint of a smile.

Good, Cassandra thought. *I want him in my camp.*

She was certain Velez had noticed it, as well, but it didn't concern her. Whether the older woman approved of the subtle application of feminine wiles or not wasn't the issue. Working with the Hawk Team was as much about the immediate goal as it was an investment in the future. Maintaining good relations with the mercenary company was in her best interests, and would be an all the more useful ace up their sleeves should Cassandra clinch the CEO position.

After brief discussion with Velez and Shaw, then, she'd left them to continue their work, heading home for the evening to get some sleep. When she'd returned six hours later, the Communications & Support Center had undergone a radical transformation, with layers of new cables taped to the floor, and three plasma screens now mounted on the wall. All of Shaw's men were still present, now seated before military-grade decks, wearing headsets, murmuring communications to the squad in the field.

"Team Beta is deployed," Colonel Shaw informed her.

"Lieutenant Lawrence White commanding. He's a good trooper, knows his stuff."

"What's the plan?" Cassandra had approached the plasma screens, her hands held behind her back, examining the maps. She wasn't entirely certain she understood what she was looking at, how the maps and figures related to the pending operation, but she now had two immediate goals. The first was to appear, at all costs, as competent and knowledgeable as possible, and if acting was required, then an actress she would be.

The second was that she had come to the conclusion it was time to start playing the dataDyne game properly. Men like Sexton and Murray and Sato had made a point of understanding *all* of the tactics involved in a successful hostile takeover bid. Even Carrington, she knew, had devoted a large portion of his considerable assets and talents to the creation of a covert action staff for his Institute.

She hadn't, and it had nearly cost her; in fact, it still might cost her. She was determined to address the lack.

Colonel Shaw had moved to her elbow, indicating the screens. "These will display real-time troop intelligence. We'll track the CMO and Bowman forces as they engage. The intelligence will be sporadic from the battlefield—it always is, there's nothing to be done about it—but it will give us some idea of how the fight is going, and, more importantly, let us spot our window of opportunity when it opens."

"And when it opens?"

Shaw indicated the second monitor, currently showing a schematic display of a null-g combat craft. Along one side of the screen ran a column of apparently relevant data, including air speed, altitude, fuel level, and longitude and latitude position, determined by GPS.

"This is a modified Barracuda IV light assault transport," Shaw had explained. "We have three of them in inventory, but only one is tasked for the op. Flight range of three thousand miles, top air speed of six-hundred and sixty-three miles per hour. Armed with a Hellfire Six autocannon and two Shriek missile racks, total load-out of eight missiles that can be used air-to-air or air-to-ground. Requires a pilot/navigator for operations, and is capable of carrying an additional sixteen soldiers, or half that number with heavy equipment and munitions. The Barracuda will serve as the insertion and suppression vehicle."

"How many men?"

"It's a hot zone, and we'll be bringing out a package, so Lieutenant White is going in with another seven men, full tactical loadout." Shaw turned to one of his juniors. "Bring up the battle map."

The third monitor lit, and Shaw directed Cassandra's attention toward it. On the screen was a computer-generated overhead map, apparently composited from the NSA satellite images that Velez had shown her previously.

"When CMO and Bowman have fully engaged, we'll hit the compound directly. The Shrieks will be used to clear the immediate area and secure the landing site, here." He indicated an open area near the center of the compound. "If Ms. Velez's intelligence is correct, the target is in Building Seven, the heart of the facility, and likely the most heavily guarded. However, analysis of the satellite data has revealed a tunnel connecting Building Five with Building Seven. Lieutenant White will take the squad immediately to Building Five, neutralize any opposition, and then proceed via the tunnel to Building Seven."

"Whereupon they will locate and capture Doctor Rose," Cassandra said.

"Yes, ma'am. They'll exfil on the same route, having already secured it, back up through Building Five, then to the Barracuda. The Barracuda will then fly an escape and evasion path, apparently heading west, before dropping to wave level and making for Melbourne. We'll keep the package on ice there until you want him moved. The whole operation should have them on the ground for less than twenty minutes."

Cassandra nodded, taking it all in. "Sounds very good."

"Thank you, ma'am."

"What if Rose is injured? I want him alive."

"We have two combat-trained medics in the Lieutenant's squad, ma'am. If the package's injuries are more than they can handle, we'll divert to Papua New Guinea, set down in Arawa, and assess the situation from there."

"Good," she said, and then repeated, "Very good. Anita?"

"Doctor?"

"Anything we're missing?"

"No, Doctor, I believe Colonel Shaw has the situation well in hand."

Cassandra nodded again, then gave Colonel Shaw a repeat of her earlier smile.

"Well, then, all we need to do now is wait," she said.

For eighteen minutes of the operation, everything went as Colonel Shaw had described, with barely a hiccup. The Barracuda inserted as planned, voices of the Hawk Team members crackling through the speakers around the darkened room, each sounding calm and assured. There'd been a couple of exchanges of gunfire upon landing, but Lieutenant White's voice had come through, loud and clear, after each, reporting the number of CMO soldiers down, reporting no casualties on their part.

Reception had broken up when the Hawk Team had entered the tunnel leading from Building Five to Building Seven, becoming fainter and threaded with static. But it had still come through, and when Cassandra heard the words *"Package secure,"* and the protestations of a man who was certainly not a member of the Hawk Team in their wake, she'd felt a momentary elation unlike anything she'd ever experienced before.

Standing beside her chair, she saw Anita Velez smiling, as well.

"Barracuda, stand by for dustoff," Lieutenant White's voice came over the speakers.

"Roger that, recalling all troops."

"Coming out, coming out."

"Hawk Nine, Hawk Nine, recall order, over."

There was a pause, the crackle of empty air from the speakers.

"Hawk Nine, Hawk Nine, recall order, over."

Cassandra leaned forward in her seat, looking to Colonel Shaw. Shaw now wore a headset of his own, and she watched as he activated his boom mike, wondering at the sudden alarm on his face.

"What's going on?"

"Negative response, Hawk Nine."

"What's happened?" Cassandra asked.

"One of their men isn't responding," Velez said quietly. "It may be nothing."

"Hawk One, Hawk Master, confirm coms to Hawk Nine, over," Shaw said.

There was a slight pause, then White's voice again. *"Hawk One, cannot confirm, Hawk Master. Over."*

"Get me biosigns on Hawk Nine," Shaw ordered one of the men seated at the decks around the room. "Now!"

"Negative result."

"Hawk One, we're moving."

"Negative!" barked Shaw. "Negative, secure the area—"

A rattle of gunfire crackled from the speakers, followed by a thump so loud it made Cassandra wince. Shaw jerked his headset from his ears, cursing, then just as hastily put it back into place. From the speakers, Cassandra heard swearing, someone crying out in pain, and then another exchange of gunfire, this one more sustained. There was a second explosion, then a third.

Then silence.

"Hawk One, Hawk Master, come in," Shaw said. "Hawk One, Hawk Master, come in. Dammit, White, respond!"

There was another fraction of silence, of the sound of radios alive but with no one to use them. Then another crackle, the hiss of static, and, finally, a young woman's voice came over the speakers, and Cassandra thought she sounded both breathless and elated at once. The impact of her voice, just the sound of it, so abruptly out of place and unexpected, electrified everyone in the room into silence.

"Nobody here but us chickens," the young woman said.

Then the speakers went dead.

CHAPTER 30

Carrington Institute "Cooler" Facility—
8 km N of St. Harmon—
Wye Valley, Wales
October 16th, 2020

There were only the four of them riding in the vehicle, a Carrington Institute null-g Rambler. Steinberg sat behind the wheel, Carrington beside him, and, in the backseat, Jo, with a Falcon in her hand pointed at Doctor Thaddeus Killington Rose.

The pistol had been Carrington's order, and Jo had followed it, but reluctantly, because it was an unnecessary addition. Aside from the fact that Doctor Rose wore capture-shackles around his wrists and ankles, magnetically locked and impossible to remove without the control card—currently carried in Carrington's pocket—the man was clearly going nowhere. Even if Doctor Rose hadn't been restrained, she doubted he would've tried to run, and not because he was parked in his mid-fifties, with the kind of overweight body that announced that his last forty years had been spent only moving quickly when he had to. He was utterly alone. He had nowhere to go, and no one to run to.

Seated as she was beside him, the pistol in her hand, and Doctor Rose unwilling to even look up from his shackled wrists, Jo felt an unexpected pang of sympathy for the man. She knew what it was like to be alone, to feel surrounded by hostility on every side.

Then she remembered the cause of that hostility, the incomprehensible number of Canadian dead, and the feeling vanished. Whatever empathy Doctor Thaddeus Rose had earned in his life, it was long since exhausted.

He sensed her gaze on him, looked slowly up from his hands with his small and watery brown eyes. Maybe he'd felt her momentary weakness, the second of conflict, but he tried to smile at her. The look Jo gave him in return made him immediately turn his attention back to his shackles.

The Rambler banked through a gentle turn, then began climbing one of the hillsides that formed the valley, following a thin dirt track up toward the summit. A squat cluster of three concrete bunkers came into view at the top of the slope, two of them so much smaller than the other that Jo thought of them as sheds rather than as actual buildings. The rooftop of the largest building was crowded with rusted aerials, bent antennas, and broken satellite dishes. An old and rusting chain-link fence marked the perimeter, a sign dangling from it sideways warning people to keep out, that there was no trespassing. Steinberg glided the Rambler over the fence's sagging top before bringing them to a gentle stop on the ground.

Carrington opened his door, swinging his legs out and then using his walking stick to aid him to his feet.

"Jon, take Doctor Mengele down to the basement and lock him into the boiler room, please," Carrington said, handing the control card to the capture-shackles over to Steinberg. "If he tries anything, feel free to blow off his kneecaps."

"There's no need to be crude," Rose said. "I shan't try anything."

"Pity," Steinberg muttered, drawing his pistol, the same DY357 Magnum—almost identical to her father's, Jo had noted, right down to the walnut grip—that he had carried in Hovoro. With his other hand, he used the control card to release the shackles at Rose's ankles, and Jo kept her Falcon trained on the doctor as Steinberg helped him out of the vehicle. Only after Steinberg had him out of the Rambler did Jo herself move, hopping over the side door to land lightly beside Carrington.

They watched Steinberg escort Doctor Rose into the largest of the buildings, disappearing inside.

Carrington waited until they were out of sight, then sighed and glanced over to Jo.

"Evil is never what you expect," he said.

Jo thought about the evils she had seen herself, then surprised herself by saying, abruptly, "I miss my dad."

"I know you do." Carrington's voice was soft, the expression on his face touched by sympathy. Then he sighed again, turned, and, using his walking stick, began to head in the same direction Steinberg had taken Rose. "Come, Joanna. We've got to get ready to receive our guests."

Jo tucked the Falcon into the holster at the small of her back, took another look around the abandoned listening post. The sky was gray, as if considering its options, whether to simply deny sunlight or actually commit to rain. There was no wind blowing, no other sounds aside from the steady crunch and crackle of Carrington's walking stick as he made his way across the gravel lot.

She moved to follow him, thinking about how strange the whole business really was.

She'd never been part of an ambush before, at least, not on the initiating side, but Steinberg had, and Jo had been forced to admit, the man knew what he was doing.

It had taken less than three minutes for each of them to take up positions around the Hawk Team dropship, Steinberg with an angle of fire on the cockpit and front, Jo around back, with a clear line of sight to the lowered loading ramp. She'd had some cover and some shadow, and she remained motionless as Steinberg had told her to, the silenced Falcons in her hands.

"This is how it's going to work," Steinberg said to her over the subcutaneous. *"We wait for the Hawk Team to present and approach the vehicle for loading. As soon as one of us makes visual confirmation that Doctor Rose is with them, I'll open fire, take out the pilot first, then light them up."*

"You're going to get a shot through the cockpit canopy?"

"You're not the only one who can hit a target," Steinberg said. *"Give me a little credit."*

"Just a little. And while you're doing this, I'm just to sit on my thumbs, then?"

He ignored her. *"What they'll do, they'll try to get into the ship, and they'll be moving to protect Rose, right? The moment I open fire, you activate the beacon, recall Rogers and the dropship. Since I'll have opened fire, the Hawk Team will be orienting on my position, laying down suppression to cover their evac. You still have your silencers?"*

"Already equipped," Jo confirmed. "One for each."

"While they're trying to get Rose to the ship and take me out, you pick them off quietly. We do this right, they won't even know you're here until it's too late."

"It'll never work," Jo said, not because she meant it,

but mostly to see how easily she could press Steinberg's buttons.

There was a brief pause. *"Are you saying that because it's my idea, or because it requires you to follow orders and wait for a signal?"*

"Mostly the former."

"Figured. Do it the way I've said, Jo. I'm relying on you to kill them before they kill me."

That sobered her, killed the playfulness she was feeling. "I won't let you die."

"I'm not asking for a promise, just your best effort."

"I won't, Jonathan," she told him, in absolute seriousness.

There was another pause, and Jo thought that was the end of the discussion, and it was, because the next thing Steinberg said was, *"Here they come, northeast side."*

It wasn't the direction Jo had expected, and for a moment she wondered if all the careful positioning for the ambush would be for naught. Then she saw them, six men in combat dress identical to that of the mercenary she'd downed earlier, all of them carrying their M16Cs, moving in a diamond formation around another man, a seventh, and even without seeing his face, she knew it was Rose.

"It's him," she said.

"Can you confirm?" Steinberg hissed.

"Who else would it be?" she shot back

"Do not engage, Jo! Let me confirm."

The diamond was moving quickly, perhaps twenty meters from the side of the dropship. Jo had flexed her fingers around the grips of her two pistols, thinking that she'd need them closer, that she was asking a lot of the silenced Falcons to hit all their marks at this range. The mercenary in the lead of the formation was speaking into a radio as they moved, she saw, and she wondered if he was in communication with the pilot aboard the dropship, or another command post somewhere else entirely. That worried her, because they hadn't considered that option. If the Hawk Team had backup nearby, they could find themselves in exactly the same scenario they were constructing, but on the receiving end, instead.

The cluster of mercenaries had closed to within fifteen meters of the dropship, but they were slowing for some reason, and Jo watched as the men on the flanks seemed to tense, looking about more cautiously.

"Any time you want to do this."

"I confirm Rose," Steinberg said, and then she heard him shoot, and it wasn't the sound she expected, not the Fairchild's terse chatter, but instead the solid, heavy report of a Magnum round being fired once, twice, three times in quick succession.

From there, it was exactly as Steinberg had said it would be. Jo had slapped the beacon on her tactical vest with her right hand, activating the signal that would guide Rogers and the Institute dropship to their location, then leveled her pistols and begun picking her shots. By the time the Hawk Team realized they were in a cross fire, half of them were dead, and by the time they'd resolved to do something about it, all of them were.

The whole firefight couldn't have lasted more than fifteen seconds.

When it was over, she, Steinberg, and Rose were the only ones left alive, and the dropship was overhead, drawing small-arms fire from the jungle as Rogers brought it in for a landing. Rose had previously been cuffed by the Hawk Team, and as Steinberg had moved to load him into the Institute dropship, he'd told Jo to search for the keycard. She'd gone through the bodies quickly, finding the card on the same man who'd been using the radio, and on impulse, answered the radio, as well.

Steinberg hadn't liked that she'd done that, and told her so even before she was aboard.

"What the hell was that?"

"A joke," she'd said, pulling herself up through the open side door.

"You think there's anything here that's funny?"

"You mean aside from you?"

"Shut up and get inside!"

The dropship had lurched, taking to the air once more, and Jo had turned to slam the side door shut, and a bullet had pinged into the side of the hull, perhaps an eighth of an inch from her forehead. Jo had reacted instantly, dropping and drawing. Peering out of the dropship as it continued its rapid ascent, she'd seen the figure of a lone man in the compound below, the muzzle flash from his rifle as he'd fired uselessly after them.

She thought she recognized him, but in the darkness and with the distance, couldn't be sure.

Wonder what his problem is, Jo had thought.

Shortly into their flight back to London, Doctor Rose spoke for the first time, his manner and tone both imperious and instantly unlikable.

"You obviously have no idea who I am," he told them. "I am one of Core-Mantis OmniGlobal's most preeminent scientists, and if you think that they will suffer my abduction without an immediate and savage reprisal, you're both as stupid as you look. Return me at once, or face the consequences."

"Consequences?" Steinberg snapped. "What the hell do you know about consequences, you fat-assed son of a bitch?"

Rose's mouth drew into a thin-lipped sneer. "I am a prisoner of a trade war, and entitled to the protections described by the Geneva Convention of 2011. Release me, or else!"

"Or else," Steinberg echoed, directing his words to Jo first. "I guess that means if we don't do what he says, he'll unleash another superflu, kill another forty million or so."

"He's a dangerous man," Jo agreed.

Rose sighed, wearily, as if already exhausted by having to deal with people he so clearly thought were his lesser.

"Is it money, is that it?"

"What?" Steinberg snapped.

"You want money, of course. It's all your kind ever does. Very well. Name your price and—" Steinberg punched him in the jaw, sending him sprawling from his seat on the bench to the deck. Jo had thought the one punch would be it, but then she realized Steinberg was about to follow it with a kick, and she lunged forward, restraining him.

"Jonathan!"

"I won't kill him," Steinberg said, not truly fighting her hold, but not quite willing to back down, either. "I won't, even though if anyone ever deserved it it's this piece of shit. I just want to hurt him a lot."

"You can join the queue," Jo said. "But that's not who we are, right? We're the good guys, right?"

Steinberg had continued to stare at Rose, who was now seated on the dropship floor, wiping blood from his lips with the back of his manacled hand.

"Right?" Jo asked.

"God, I don't know," Steinberg told her.

Rose had remained silent for the rest of the flight.

Carrington was waiting for them when the dropship touched down at the Institute, and no sooner had Jo and Steinberg unloaded Doctor Rose than they were loading him again, this time into the Rambler. There'd been no explanation given by Carrington as to what they were doing or why they were doing it, only the direction he'd given to Steinberg.

"The Cooler, in Wales," Carrington had said. "Best time, Jon."

"Yes, sir."

"Joanna?"

"Sir?"

"Keep a weapon on Doctor Rose, please. If he so much as scratches his nose, feel free to shoot him."

"Yes, sir."

Beside her, in the backseat, Doctor Rose had made a noise that Jo could only interpret as a contemptuous snort.

How events had brought Jo, Carrington, Steinberg, and Rose to an abandoned listening post in the Wye Valley, here and now, she still wasn't certain. Whatever Daniel Carrington had planned, he was playing it close to his tweed vest.

She followed Carrington into the largest of the buildings, smelling stale air and wet concrete. The lights inside were off, but the diffused daylight lanced through slit windows high on two walls, illuminating disturbed motes of dust. She heard the echo of Steinberg's voice from further inside, the sound of his progress as he prodded Rose along. Carrington had stopped near a massive fuse box affixed to the wall, secured with a very old-fashioned-looking padlock. He took a key from his watch chain, opened the padlock, then reached into the box and threw a switch.

Somewhere, a generator kicked painfully to life, and one by one, the ceiling lights overhead flickered on, old fluorescents that made Jo's eyes hurt. They were in a long hallway, she saw, all concrete—floor, walls, and ceiling. At the end of the hall was a stairwell leading both up and down.

"This used to be an Echelon intercept station," Carrington said, closing the fuse box once more and affixing the lock back in place. "Early iteration, Echelon II, I believe. Decommissioned back in 2010, when the NSA retasked most of their electronic intelligence gathering to private firms. I acquired it in late 2017 at Jonathan's suggestion."

"Jonathan has a passion for ugly industrial architecture?" Jo asked.

"No, this was just when we were beginning to get the Institute's covert action capacity going," Carrington said with a chuckle, resuming his way down the hall, toward the stairs. "Jonathan pointed out—quite rightly—that we would want secure facilities where we could bring agents—and others—for debriefings outside of the Institute grounds themselves. This is ideal; the location is secluded, and the construction itself was designed to inhibit the ability of others to eavesdrop on the location. I've had additional work done, as well. This is one of the few places in the world, Joanna, where no one can hear what you're saying."

"It doesn't look like it's seen much use," Jo said. They'd reached the stairwell, concrete steps just like the rest of the building, and Jo waited while Carrington began to laboriously descend, following the direction Steinberg had taken Rose.

"This is only the second time, in fact. It'll serve its purpose for us today, though. Should serve it quite well."

They came off the stairs into the basement, a low-ceilinged rectangular room with a battery of generators and other equipment secured behind a chain-link cage. Jo noted surveillance cameras mounted in the corners, realized that she'd seen three others in the hallway above and the stairwell without truly noticing them. The door to the boiler room was open, and she could see Steinberg standing inside, Doctor Rose visible just past him, seated at a rather abused-looking card table.

Carrington stepped forward, and Steinberg moved out of his way to allow him entry, staying to the side long enough for Jo to enter, as well. There was only one chair and Rose was in it, and Jo thought that, arrayed as they were, the man should have been intimidated, but instead he watched their approach with the same blend of condescension and arrogance he'd turned on her and Jonathan during their flight from Hovoro.

"Doctor Rose," Carrington said.

Rose fidgeted in his seat, then held up his shackled hands. "If you're intending to offer me a position at your Institute, Mister Carrington, your pitch leaves much to be desired."

"You think very highly of yourself, Doctor. Perhaps too highly for a man who has stood on the backs of giants to achieve not greatness, but infamy."

"If I think highly of myself, sir, it is only because I know my own worth. What is it you want?" Rose asked, lowering his hands, as if his shackles were of only passing interest to him.

"Many, many things, sir, but from you, only this: a public declaration that you, as an employee of pharmaDyne, engaged in experiments that led to the 2016 outbreak of influenza A subtype H17N22."

"You have no evidence that I was responsible for that," Rose said.

"I have you."

"I admit nothing."

Carrington nodded, as if he had expected as much.

"Then you have no objections to my handing you over to Doctor Friedrich Murray at pharmaDyne."

Jo couldn't remember ever seeing a person go pale so quickly in all of her life.

"Ah, that's right," Carrington said to Rose. "He wants you dead, I forgot."

Rose fidgeted in his seat some more, twisting his hands against his shackles, rubbing them together nervously.

"If it helps," Carrington said, "I couldn't care less about you."

Rose looked up, suddenly, confused. "I beg your pardon?"

"Arrogant bastard," Steinberg murmured in disgust.

"I don't care about you," Carrington said. "But I do care about pharmaDyne, and I'd like to hurt them. Your public declaration will help me to do that."

The confusion remained on Rose's face, his eyes narrowing. "And then what?"

"Then you'll be free to go, Doctor Rose. You can return to the cold embrace of the women of Core-Mantis, or slink off to the research labs of Zentek, or sell what little is left of your soul to Beck-Yama. I could care less what you do after I get what I want. But I will get what I want."

"But Murray—"

"If you make a public declaration, sir, Doctor Murray will no longer be any threat to you. He will be far too busy tending to his own survival to worry about what damage you can do him, because the damage will have already been done."

Rose brought his hands up, rubbing his mouth, and Jo could see the wheels spinning in the man's mind as he tried to see a way out of his situation. He mumbled something to himself, looking down at the table, then brought his eyes up again, gazing at Steinberg, then Jo, and finally

Carrington in turn, and the fear that had risen had vanished, and the arrogance had returned.

"It was an unfortunate, but unavoidable, consequence of my work," Doctor Rose said. "I was handcuffed by pharmaDyne, by the ridiculous restrictions that dullard Murray had placed upon my research."

"And that is your excuse for mass slaughter?" Carrington asked, mildly.

"I do not need to excuse myself," Rose said, tightly. "A necessary by-product of discovery and creation is destruction. And what was truly lost, really? If there is one endlessly renewable resource on this planet, it's human beings. We breed like maggots on a corpse."

Jo saw Steinberg tense, the muscles in the man's jaw clenching. For a moment, she was afraid he would lash out at Rose a second time.

"Do you have the first idea what I actually did for pharmaDyne, Mister Carrington?" Rose asked. "I did the work of the Almighty. What I did for dataDyne—what I *do* for Core-Mantis—it is the work of God, sir. I create life. I make no apologies for my actions. There was an opening in dataDyne's bioweapons division, and I pursued it."

"So the virus was developed as a weapon?" Carrington asked.

"I said I saw an opening, not that I had taken the position. At the time, I was simply working on a gene-therapy to destroy the influenza A subtype. I had no idea that the DNA I was using would be so unpredictable . . . or would yield something that the bioweapons division would find appealing."

"Then it was an accident," Carrington said, and it wasn't a question.

"A happy one, yes. By applying work from other divisions, I could secure a position more suited to my talents," Rose said, annoyed.

"Without thought to the consequences."

"I can't be held responsible for the results of my work," Rose said, evenly.

The statement was so utterly ludicrous that Jo almost laughed, sure that Rose was making a joke. But his expression, the certainty on his face, the absolute denial of any wrongdoing, made her realize it wasn't. Whether or not Rose himself believed what he was saying, she didn't know.

That he expected them to believe, though, was patently clear.

"Do we have a deal, Doctor Rose?" Carrington asked.

"If you can be trusted to keep your end of the agreement, then yes," the man said. "If for no other reason than it'll destroy Murray."

"Then you'll remain here for the time being. Mister Steinberg will watch you."

Rose moved his look to Jo, clearly trying to undress her with his eyes.

"I'd much rather have the young lady guard me," Rose said to Carrington, edging forward in his seat. "I'm certain she and I could—"

"No," Carrington told him, and turned and left the room, motioning for Jo to follow him.

She'd gone out the door when Steinberg called her back. She looked to Carrington and he shrugged, then continued his ascent of the stairs, and so she turned back to find that Steinberg had emerged from the boiler room, was pulling the door closed behind him.

"Yes?" she asked.

Steinberg waited until Carrington was out of sight, then said quietly, "The thing on the dropship."

"Where you wanted to beat the hell out of him?"

"I'd appreciate it if you didn't mention it to the Old Man."

It took her a moment. "You lost family?"

"My mother's side," Steinberg said. "They lived in Toronto."

"He won't hear about it from me," Jo told him.

On the second floor of the building was what had once been the control room, now retrofitted by Carrington's people to serve as both a conference area and command post. A security console had been installed, feeding images from all of the surveillance cameras positioned around the site, both interior and exterior, and there was a coms station, as well as an uplink terminal.

When Jo finally caught up with Carrington, it was the coms station that was holding the man's attention, and she saw that he was positioning the terminal's tiny camera for a videolink. The expression on his face surprised her.

"Did you see it, Joanna?" he asked her, softly, his voice trembling with fury. "Did you see it?"

"Rose, you mean?"

"That man... that man *is* dataDyne, do you understand? A monster who created a monster of his own, all to earn himself the recognition and reward he so covets. A man who values himself so highly that human lives are as maggots to him. And that is the crux, because that is why he was there. Working for pharmaDyne not *despite* of his 'requisite moral fluidity,' as the dataDyne recruiters do so charmingly call it, but *because* of it.

"He's a monster who created a monster, while in the employ of a greater beast altogether. He is everything I am fighting against, everything the Institute stands in the face of."

Carrington stopped, visibly struggling to calm himself. When he spoke again, his voice was steadier, close to the one Jo was coming to know.

"But in the end," Carrington said, "the monster is just a petty little man that you or I would pass on the street without a second glance. And that sickens me beyond belief."

Carrington exhaled sharply, as if blowing away the last traces of his encounter with Rose. He turned back to the comms unit, resuming his work at the uplink terminal.

"Who are you calling?" she asked.

"Stalin and Roosevelt," Carrington had said. "We're going to play a game of Meet Me in Yalta."

Jo blinked at him, wondering if he hadn't lost his mind.

"Stand over there, please," Carrington told her. "I don't want them to see you."

She did as requested, now thoroughly puzzled.

Carrington finished adjusting the video camera, then tapped three keys in succession, initiating a call he had apparently already prepared. She watched as he adjusted his posture, straightening in his seat, then checked the bow tie at his throat, making certain it was straight.

"You," a woman's voice said from the terminal. Her accent, Jo noted, was English, and quite posh. She did not sound pleased.

"Cass," Carrington said. "I never bugged your office."

"Do you truly expect me to believe that? Especially after everything else you've done?"

"My motives remain what they were, Cassandra. Exactly as before."

"I find that very difficult to believe, Daniel, you'll forgive me."

"Then don't, it doesn't matter. What matters is that I still want what you want. I still want you at the head of dataDyne."

There was silence from the terminal, a momentary pause.

"You took Rose," the woman said. "I thought as much, but there wasn't any proof."

"And I have him, and with him we can remove Murray from the equation and ensure your appointment."

"How?"

"For that, you'll need to come and meet me."

"The same hotel as last time?" The woman's voice had turned bitter, and Jo found herself staring at Carrington with new eyes.

"No, it has to be someplace far more secure. I'm uploading a file to your account, it has the details of the location. But there are conditions, two of them."

"I'm listening."

"First, no games, no tricks. You can bring one other person, a bodyguard, as a courtesy, but no weapons. I don't want an itchy finger bringing all of this to naught."

"You're the one who's been sending agents around killing dataDyne personnel, Daniel, not me."

"Second," Carrington said. "You're going to contact Doctor Friedrich Murray, and ask him to join us, under the same restrictions and conditions."

"You want me to tell him you have Rose?"

"If he doesn't already know. It should be more than enough to compel him to join us."

"Why are you doing this, Daniel?"

"I've told you why, Cassandra. I'm sending the file now. I'll expect your and Doctor Murray's arrival in exactly two hours."

"Murray's in Vancouver, he won't make it in time."

"He has access to his own personal low-orbit transport, Cassandra. It'll be tight, but he can make it. You both can."

"I haven't agreed."

"You will. And tell Murray, if he tries anything, any games, I'll destroy dataDyne utterly. I can do it. And you know me well enough to know it's not an idle threat."

Carrington hung up.

There were a thousand questions in her mind at that moment, but the one that Jo actually asked was, "Cassandra?"

To her astonishment, Carrington actually blushed.

"I get lonely, too," he said.

CHAPTER 31

Carrington Institute "Cooler" Facility—
8 km N of St. Harmon—
Wye Valley, Wales
October 16th, 2020

The building reminded Hayes of Stony Mountain, of being locked away in prison so long ago for doing only what had come naturally to him. Perhaps the connection would have troubled him if it hadn't been for the fact that, standing beside Daniel Carrington as he waited out in front, was the redhead from his nightmares.

When Hayes saw her, he actually snarled.

"You will behave," his father told him. "Until we know what he has and what he wants, you will absolutely behave."

"It's her," Hayes said. "The one who stole Rose, the one who hurt me in New York. The one who got away, that's her, Father!"

"And I have said that you will behave, Laurent," Doctor Murray said. "Until I give you the word, you are not to make a move, not a single move. Tell me you understand."

Sitting in the car beside his father, Hayes tried to make

the words come out of his mouth, and couldn't. She was staring at him, twenty meters away, right beside Carrington, and she was staring at him, and she was *smiling*.

"Laurent," his father said again, this time with more edge.

Through clenched teeth, Laurent Hayes said, "I won't move until you give me the word."

Doctor Murray nodded, then opened his door and got out of the vehicle, waiting for Hayes to follow. He needed another moment before he could. If he'd had a weapon on him, he'd have used it already, he was sure, he would have just drawn and started firing until the redhead had turned into red pulp. But he didn't have a weapon, he didn't even have his knife, though he'd tried to bring it with him.

His jaw still stung from when his father had slapped him after he'd discovered the weapon during the flight from Vancouver. Hayes had gotten off lucky, too, he knew that. After returning from Hovoro, a slap from Doctor Murray was the lightest of punishments. At least he was fixing again, at least he was feeling the way he should again.

There'd been no patch waiting for him when he'd returned from New Georgia Island, no replacement offered, and no comfort for either his failings or his withdrawal. It had been worse than ever before, too, had left Hayes curled on the floor of his bathroom, his head resting in a puddle of his own vomit, shaking and crying. It had never been that bad, and he wondered if it was because he had never failed his father so much, or because of the new dermals, or both.

He'd still been lying there in his personal hell when his father had found him, saying, "Get cleaned up, get dressed, and do it quickly."

When Hayes hadn't responded—and not for lack of trying—Doctor Murray had cursed him as useless, as disgusting, and then held out a new patch between two fingers over his adopted son's head. Hayes had reached for it, straining like a dog for a treat, and instead of handing it to him, his father had let it fall. Hayes had needed to clean the patch before affixing it to the back of his neck.

As the drug had seeped its way back into his skin, back to where it belonged, Doctor Murray had explained the situation.

"Carrington has Rose. He's contacted DeVries, and DeVries has, in turn, contacted me. We are to meet, the three of us, in just under two hours. You are coming with me. You are coming unarmed. Do not be the reason we are late, Laurent."

One hour and fifty-seven minutes later, here they were.

Hayes climbed out of the car, moving around its front to take a position by his father. He kept his eyes on the redhead the whole time, using his peripheral vision to take in as much about the location as he could. Truthfully, there wasn't much to take in. Aside from the building, Carrington, and the redhead, there was only their own vehicle and one other, parked nearby.

"Doctor Murray, a pleasure to finally meet you," Carrington said, and Hayes wondered how his father could stomach such an obvious lie. "Allow me to introduce my assistant, Joanna."

Joanna, Hayes thought. *Joanna Joanna Joanna how would you like to see your entrails spilling out into your hands, Joanna?*

"This is my son, Laurent," Doctor Murray said.

"Ah, yes. The energetic young man I've heard so much about." Carrington moved the walking stick in his hand to his side, leaning on it. His smile was broad. "Prisoner number seven-one-four-eight-seven-six-zero-two-zero-five, Stony Mountain Medium Security Institution, Manitoba, Canada. Laurent Nathaniel Hayes, sentenced to life imprisonment after conviction on three counts of murder."

"I believe in the power of rehabilitation," Doctor Murray said.

"You believe in power, that much I agree with." Carrington turned, using the walking stick to pivot about. "Doctor DeVries and her companion have already arrived. If you'll follow us."

He moved through the doorway into the building, and the redhead cracked a grin at Hayes, then turned and followed. It was the way she did it, the manner in which she simply turned away as if he was nothing, as if he posed no threat at all, that threatened to unman him then and there.

His father seemed to sense it, and put out a hand to Hayes's shoulder, squeezing it with his long, narrow fingers.

"Wait," Doctor Murray whispered. "There will be time."

Soon, Hayes thought, and followed his father.

DeVries had brought the CORPSEC Ice Queen, Anita Velez, and along with Carrington and Joanna, the six of them made their way along a narrow corridor and down a narrower flight of stairs into a basement, where another of Carrington's lackeys was waiting, a pistol in his hand.

"I thought the terms were no weapons," Doctor Murray remarked upon seeing him.

"Terms I set," Carrington said. "Not terms I was obligated to follow."

"A dishonest way of dealing with us."

"I think of it as insurance. Desperation makes people do strange things."

DeVries didn't say anything, but Hayes could tell she was watching everything, listening to everything. Velez, though, approached the man with the pistol as if she knew him, stopping only a few feet away from where he stood by a closed metal door.

"Mister Steinberg," Velez said.

"Ms. Velez," the man said.

"I see you know who I am."

"For precisely the same reasons you know me," the man said.

Velez nodded slightly, then moved back to stand at the side of DeVries.

"Jonathan," Carrington said. "If you'd be so kind."

The man with the pistol nodded, then unlocked the door with a key from his pocket, pushing it open and revealing Doctor Thaddeus Rose seated at a card table inside. Rose looked up abruptly from where he'd been holding his head in his shackled hands, and his expression turned from self-pity to outright panic.

"Carrington! You said—"

"And I'll keep my word, Doctor Rose," Carrington said. "I'm merely proving to Doctors Murray and DeVries that you are, indeed, alive and well and in my keeping."

"That man may be alive and well," Murray said. "But it will take more than this to convince me that is Thaddeus Rose. You're not beyond employing cosmetic surgery as a deception."

Carrington snorted, gesturing with his walking stick to the man with the pistol. The door swung shut, the key again turning in the lock.

"I'd like a chance to question him," Doctor Murray said. "To verify his identity."

"Either you think I'm a fool, Doctor, or you're one yourself. Ask your 'son' if this is the same man he failed to kill in Hovoro. Or did he also fail to get close enough to make a positive identification?"

Hayes felt himself grinding his teeth, flicking his eyes from Carrington to Joanna. She was looking at him curiously.

Doctor Murray didn't respond.

Carrington snorted again, then made his way between the two groups, returning to the stairs.

"Let's have a little talk, now, shall we?" Carrington said.

His father, DeVries, and Carrington sat at the table. Hayes stood behind Doctor Murray, Velez behind DeVries, and Joanna behind Carrington, with her back to a bank of consoles and monitors. The monitors were all dark, and Hayes wondered if they were for surveillance or something else.

"I once changed the world," Daniel Carrington said. "I showed people how to defy gravity, and in so doing, removed their hunger for internal combustion. I made transportation more efficient, more accessible. I do not think it is an exaggeration to say that I made the world a better place.

"It wasn't enough. Despite my best efforts, the world still suffers. And while I was working to make the world a better place, other people, other men, were working to make it a worse one.

"I refer, of course, to Zhang Li and the monster he created: dataDyne."

Hayes saw Velez adjust her stance behind DeVries, her expression blank. DeVries herself had leaned forward, propping an elbow on the table, still watching Carrington like a snake eyeing a bird struggle with a broken wing.

"Today I'm going to remedy that," Carrington said. "Today is the second time I change the world for the better."

"How?" DeVries asked.

"I think you know, Cass. I think you've already figured it out." Carrington looked levelly across the table at Hayes, then at his father. "I have Doctor Rose, and I have convinced him to make a full and accurate accounting of the origins of the influenza A subtype H17N22 virus. Doctor Rose believes confession is good for the soul, and he's going to tell the world what he did while on pharma-Dyne's payroll."

"That's absurd," Hayes's father said. "Even if he agreed to do so, he would be taking responsibility for one of the greatest mass slaughters in the history of the world. The man is too arrogant, too selfish to do such a thing."

"Ah, but that's not what he's going to do, Doctor Murray. It's what *you* are going to do. As CEO of pharma-Dyne, his actions are your responsibility."

"I was not CEO at the time of the outbreak."

"No, you merely were able to capitalize on the situation." Carrington leaned back in his seat, now moving his gaze to Hayes.

You'd be so easy to kill, Hayes thought.

"There's a story, a rumor, about a survivor of the outbreak," Carrington said. "I'd thought it was a myth until Joanna told me about the barcode tattooed on the back of your son's neck, about how his hair had been burnt down to the scalp to prevent it from obscuring the numbers there.

"The story goes that, late in the outbreak, one of the teams responsible for the collection and disposal of the dead found a survivor in a prison in Manitoba. That the prisoner was taken to St. Boniface Hospital in Winnipeg, where he was examined and determined to be naturally resistant to the influenza strain."

DeVries had shifted her gaze from Carrington to Hayes's father. Her expression hadn't changed, the same cold look, taking it all in. For a moment, Hayes wondered if he'd get to kill her, too.

"Shortly thereafter, St. Boniface Hospital burnt to the ground. The loss of life was tremendous, but against the backdrop of the superflu, almost incidental. No records, or signs, of the prisoner were ever found."

"Then you have speculation, and nothing more," Doctor Murray said.

Carrington was still staring at Hayes. "And you have a son who was adopted in 2017, a son who was an inmate at Stony Mountain. Secrets have a way of coming out, Doctor Murray."

"We don't have to listen to this," his father said to DeVries. "He has no proof, just a madman locked in the basement and a bushel of ridiculous theories."

"He doesn't need proof," DeVries said. "All he needs is Rose, and he has him."

"My only question," Carrington said, more to himself than anyone else, "is whether or not you helped Rose create the superflu."

"No," Doctor Murray said flatly. "Don't be absurd."

"It doesn't really matter. As soon as Rose goes public, everyone will believe that you did. After all, you've been quite proud of that Nobel Prize of yours."

"I don't have to sit here, I don't have to stand for this—"

"Yes, you do," DeVries said, so sharply that everyone in the room found themselves suddenly looking at her. "You've lost this, Doctor, whether you realize it or not. We're no longer talking about you, or your future. We're discussing the future of dataDyne, its very survival."

Carrington nodded in approval. "You always were quick, Cassandra."

She turned to look at Carrington, her expression as cold as before. "Once the news is public, dataDyne will collapse."

"You're overstating, Cass," Carrington said. "The corporation is too large to fold entirely. pharmaDyne will turn to ashes, certainly, and in the ensuing chaos, dataDyne stock, including all of its subsidiaries, will plummet as well. The sell-off will be immediate, and staggering, and will consequently allow me to buy a controlling interest in the corporation."

Carrington went silent, giving everyone time to take in what he was saying. Hayes, for his part, no longer cared. He could feel the tension thrumming in waves from his father, feel his own anxiety rising.

Not long now, Hayes thought.

"You'll control the Board of Directors," DeVries said, realizing.

"At which point I will promptly name you the new CEO of dataDyne," Carrington said, and this time, when he smiled, DeVries smiled in return. "Didn't I say you could trust me, Cassandra?"

"Yes," she said, and Hayes was appalled to see her reach out across the table and take one of Carrington's hands in both of her own, squeezing it. "Yes, you did, and I should have believed you."

"You forgive me now?"

"Of course I do." She let go of his hand, getting to her feet quickly, and Hayes thought the woman was so excited she would begin bouncing around the room. "I should get back to Paris, I assume you'll want to do this immediately, yes? I should be ready."

"Do that. Contact me as soon as you arrive. I'll have Doctors Rose and Murray make their announcement." Carrington's smile was now so broad, Hayes thought it threatened to split the man's face. "I'll contact you as soon as Rose is ready to make his statement."

DeVries seemed to lose direction for a moment, and then she suddenly moved to come around to Carrington's side of the table. Joanna took a step forward, then stopped as Carrington held up a hand.

Hayes had to look away when DeVries kissed the old man on the cheek.

"Anita, let's go," DeVries said, and together the two women left the room.

Carrington's smile remained in place, and he settled it once more on Hayes and his father. Doctor Murray shifted in his seat, then reached out for the table, making to stand.

"I won't stay—"

"Sit down," Carrington barked, and Hayes, his nerves already drawn as taut as piano wire, jumped.

His father sat back down. "Obviously, my presence here is a waste of time, Mister Carrington. You've made up your mind, and clearly will not be dissuaded. You have Rose, you don't need me."

"And Rose is the one who I want to see pay for what he did," Carrington said. "If you didn't create the superflu, if it was Rose alone who was responsible, I'm giving you a chance to say so publicly. To defend yourself. If you choose to leave now, you will lose that opportunity, sir."

"Or I could have Laurent simply kill you both."

"He hasn't had much luck ending Joanna's life as yet," Carrington observed. "And even if he should be successful, it does nothing to solve your problems with Doctor Rose. Do you want to risk the chance of him escaping? Do you intend to kill DeVries, as well? Ms. Velez?"

Hayes looked down at his father, saw that Carrington had successfully taken the wind out of his sails.

Then, at once muffled and amplified by the concrete around them, they heard a gunshot.

CHAPTER 32

Carrington Institute "Cooler" Facility—
8 km N of St. Harmon—
Wye Valley, Wales
October 16th, 2020

"Doctor—"

Cassandra held up a finger to her mouth, spinning around on the staircase as she motioned Velez for silence. For a second, she didn't move, listening. From above, she could still hear the sound of Daniel's voice, rumbling along the hallway.

God, does that man like to talk, she thought.

Quietly, she continued down the stairs to the ground floor, waited for Velez to join her. The older woman's expression was pure frustration, the most emotion that Cassandra had yet to see from her. Cassandra reached out, putting a hand to the other woman's cheek, drawing her head down so she could put her mouth to Velez's ear.

"I once asked you for a chance to regain your trust, Anita," Cassandra whispered. "Do as I ask you to, and I shall, right now."

Velez turned her head, still with Cassandra's hand on

her cheek, her eyes narrowing with suspicion. She whispered in return, saying, "Carrington will destroy dataDyne."

"I know—unless we stop him."

The suspicion faded.

"What do you want me to do?"

"Follow me. When you see the opportunity, neutralize Mister Steinberg," Cassandra said softly. "Quickly, quietly, and nonlethally if you can."

"You want him left alive?"

"I do."

Velez nodded, then straightened, and Cassandra let her hand drop from the woman's face, then moved back onto the stairs, continuing down to the basement. Steinberg, still waiting by the door to the makeshift cell, watched as she descended.

"Can I help you, Doctor?"

Cassandra approached, Velez following, smiling softly. "Anita has told me something about you, Mister Steinberg. I was wondering if you might be interested in a business proposition."

Steinberg glanced to Velez, then back to her, at once wary and amused. "I think you're a very attractive woman, Doctor, but I'm afraid my heart belongs to another."

Cassandra laughed softly, shaking her head, and Steinberg grinned, and that was when Velez kicked him in the stomach. He saw it coming, but not in time, and the blow hit hard enough that Cassandra was certain she heard the breath exploding out from the man's mouth as he fought to keep from pitching over.

Then Velez had one hand around his wrist, twisting his gun hand savagely, and with her other, she struck him sharply at the base of the skull. Steinberg went flat, motionless, and Velez had the revolver in her hand and dropped to one knee beside him, quickly finding the key to the cell in his pocket.

As she came back to her feet, Cassandra said softly, "Give me the gun."

"I can't, Doctor. I can't let you shoot him."

"I'm not going to shoot him," Cassandra said. "Give me the gun, Anita."

Velez frowned, looking at the revolver in her hand, then handed it over. Then she turned and unlocked the door to the boiler room.

"Wait outside," Cassandra told her.

Rose's expression changed from alarm to relief when he saw her, then turned back to alarm when he saw the gun in Cassandra's hand.

"It's not my fault," Rose said. "I was just doing my job."

"Believe me, I know," she said. "If anyone here is a victim of circumstance, Doctor Rose, it is you."

His eyes shifted nervously, jumping from her face to the gun in her hand.

"But you have a problem now, Doctor," Cassandra continued. "Your secret is out, and whether you are responsible or not is no longer the point. The point is that the entire world will know your name, and they will know what you did, and your intentions in doing it will not matter in the slightest."

"It was my job," Rose repeated. "I saw my opportunity and I took it. That was my only crime, and it was no crime at all."

"We all make mistakes, Doctor, and if we're lucky, we can live them down. But you won't. If you give Carrington what he wants, what you will have will not be a life. If you are lucky, it may be an existence, at least for a short while. Doctor Murray has tried to have you killed. Imagine what will happen when all of the relatives, all of the friends, all of the lovers of those who perished from *your* disease, from Rose's Flu, learn your name."

"It wasn't my fault." His voice came out in a whisper now. "It wasn't my fault."

"Thirty-seven million dead." Cassandra set the revolver on the table in front of him, the single bulb hanging from the ceiling making the silver barrel appear to glow against the ratty tabletop. "Mankind will forget the name of Hitler before they forget the name of Thaddeus Rose."

Then Cassandra turned and stepped back out of the room, nodding to Velez to close the door. She heard it swing shut, heard the latch fall into place.

She was halfway up the stairs when she heard the shot.

Velez started at the noise.

Cassandra did not.

CHAPTER 33

Carrington Institute "Cooler" Facility—
8 km N of St. Harmon—
Wye Valley, Wales
October 16th, 2020

Jo heard the shot, and she knew it was Steinberg's gun, and her first thought was that Rose had tried to make a break for it. Even before Carrington could tell her to do so, she'd pivoted to the security console, flicking on the camera controls. The monitors lit one at a time in rapid succession, showing the different surveillance views scattered about the listening post.

She saw Velez and DeVries leaving the basement, and that made no sense, because they should have already left.

She saw Steinberg, facedown on the basement floor, and for an instant thought she'd forget how to breathe.

Then she saw Doctor Thaddeus Rose, his head resting on the table in the boiler room, and it would have been easy to believe he was asleep, except the back of his head was missing. She looked for the weapon he'd used, but didn't see it on the table or on the ground, and wondered if it had fallen into his lap.

She saw all of these things, and at once realized that everyone else in the room, Carrington, Murray, and Laurent Hayes, were seeing them, as well.

"You've just lost your bargaining power, Mr. Carrington. How unfortunate," Doctor Murray said. "Now, Laurent."

Jo didn't even bother to turn toward Carrington, just threw herself backwards into the air, angling for the table. She had the Falcon in its holster at her back, but there wasn't time, and she knew that, and right now it was all about time, and the fact that there wasn't enough of it.

She beat Laurent Hayes, but just barely, twisting as she hit the table on her side to face him, catching hold of one of his outstretched arms as the man lunged for Carrington's throat. She pulled him with her, yanking him out of his trajectory and forcing him to follow hers, and instead of fighting her, he went with it, and together they tumbled across the table and crashed onto the concrete floor. They separated immediately, and Jo arched her back and got her feet beneath her, springing upright again, thinking that she'd be up before him, that she'd beat him on speed every time in the past.

Except this time, and she wasn't yet on her feet when the kick connected high on her left side, and she felt her ribs give with the impact, flexing nearly to the breaking point. The blow sent her down once more, sprawling across the floor, and she felt the rough concrete raking her face and hands, and this time Jo didn't even have her legs beneath her before Laurent Hayes was on her again.

He stomped on her back, at the base of her spine, and the pain and the panic both hit at once, and Jo screamed in outrage as much as remembered agony, trying to twist out of the pin. She felt his hand touching her skin for an instant, realized he'd seen the Falcon and was going for it, and that once he had it, he'd shoot Carrington, then her, and in the strange adrenaline-stretched time that her perception had become, she thought that it wasn't fair, that it was just like her father's death all over again, that it would be her fault, all over again.

She couldn't push up, she just wasn't strong enough, but she could move, and as she felt Hayes pulling the gun free, she swung her legs around, both together, putting all of the motion into her hips. It felt awkward and weak, but it was enough, and his foot slipped free of her, and she finished the motion on her back, bringing her legs up. He'd brought the Falcon around, trying to get a bead on Carrington, and to Jo's eyes it seemed that Daniel was diving for cover with all the speed and grace of a collapsing glacier. The gun cracked, the shot missing, and Jo had her legs perpendicular now, snapping her ankles together in a scissor around Hayes's outstretched arm, still using the muscle momentum to continue her flip, trying to twist again onto her belly, to bring Hayes down with her.

It worked and it didn't. Hayes lost the gun, but had to yank himself free to keep from falling. Jo continued the move, now with her hands beneath her, and she flipped herself up, over, coming down on her feet just as Hayes roared and kicked at her again. He was fast, faster than he'd been before, she was sure of it, and if he was a better fighter, if he had been a soldier, perhaps, and not a killer, he'd have picked his attacks more carefully. But he was motivated by hatred, Jo realized, by his desire to shame her and hurt her and punish her, and because of that he kicked high, for her face, and that slowed him down.

She bobbed out of the kick, answered it with a one-two punch of her own, and the first he blocked, but the second he didn't. Jo felt the satisfaction of her fist finding purchase against his sternum, and Hayes backpedaled, trying to get more room to move, and each ended up with an arm's length between them, and began circling.

"You're dinner," Hayes told her. "You're my meat."

"My daddy loved me," Jo said. "Does yours?"

Hayes roared again, feinted a kick, and then punched at her face with his right. She caught the feint in time, not buying it, but the punch came faster and harder than she'd expected, and her block was incomplete. She felt her nose sting, felt the instant heat of blood coming loose from her nostrils.

"That's good, bleed for me," Hayes said.

"It's not about blood, asshole," Jo told him. "It's about winning."

He swung at her again, and she danced back, then realized, almost too late, what he was trying to do. Hayes dove low, past her side, trying to reach the Falcon on the floor, and the decision and the move confirmed two things that Jo had already begun to suspect. The first was that he really didn't know how to fight, at least not with his hands and his feet. He had strength, he had speed, but he didn't know how to use them. All of his strikes had been to noncritical areas or to badly chosen ones, consistently going high, trying to give her wounds that would satisfy his hatred, rather than injuries that would end the fight.

The second was that he was afraid of pain, that each time she'd landed a hit, or threatened to, he'd backed off.

She let him take the gun, heard him cry out in triumph, and as he came up with it, she put an elbow into his face, and then a fist into the side of his wrist. He cried out, lost the gun a second time, and once more staggered back, now with a nosebleed to match Jo's own. As he pulled away, Jo put her toe into the side of the Falcon, sending it skittering across the floor, beneath the table and to the open door onto the hallway.

Hayes was wiping blood from his nose, trying to ignore his bleeding while keeping his eyes on her. From the corner of her eye, Jo could see both Doctor Murray and Carrington trying to stay out of their way, each of them attempting to edge toward the exit at the same time. Jo shifted to her left, trying to block Murray's progress while giving Carrington an opening, but as soon as he moved, Hayes compensated as well.

"Come on," she told Hayes. "This is what you've been waiting for, isn't it? Come and hurt me."

Hayes swiped at the blood on his face again, feinted left, then tried to kick high to her right, going for her head. Again he was quick, almost quick enough to do it, but again he'd picked a bad target, and Jo snapped a front kick to his shin before he'd completed his execution. Hayes cried out in pain, hobbling back again.

The exchange had pulled her out of position, though, and she saw Doctor Murray break for the door, but duck as he did it, and she realized that he, like his adopted son, wanted the Falcon. But unlike with Hayes, she couldn't let him get it, he had too much distance on her.

Jo pivoted, throwing herself over the table at Murray, hearing Hayes screaming obscenities at her as she did so. She caught the doctor in the side just as he'd reached the pistol, and he couldn't get a grip on it, and the gun, Doctor Murray, and Jo all went crashing out into the hallway.

"Wrong move, bitch," Hayes shouted at her from inside the room, and Jo looked up to see that he'd reached Carrington, had one hand at the older man's throat, the other at the back of his head. "Want to see me rip his head off?"

"Don't!" Jo scrambled to her feet, raising her hands. Out of the corner of her eye, from the stairwell, she saw motion, someone rushing up to their floor, either Velez or DeVries. She didn't know, and she didn't dare to look away from Hayes. "Leave him alone!"

"No, no no no, you get to watch me kill him, and then I'm going to kill you," Hayes said.

Held in Hayes's grip, she could see Carrington struggling for air, his cheeks flushing red. He wouldn't be able to take the hold for long, she realized, and she had no doubt that Hayes would do as he threatened.

Jo stepped back, putting her foot against the side of Doctor Murray's neck. "You do it, I'll kill him."

Murray croaked out something, perhaps a plea, but Hayes didn't blink, didn't even hesitate.

"You don't have the balls," he said. "You're not a killer, you're just some girl pretending to be one. You won't do it."

He tightened his grip around Carrington's throat, using his hand to force the old man higher, onto his tiptoes.

The movement in her periphery had stopped, and Jo saw something glinting, a flash of metal off to her right. She saw Velez moving into view, pressing herself against the wall.

Jo removed her foot from Murray's neck, exhaling hard. She forced her hands to unclench, opened her palms, turning them out, away from her body.

"You're right, I can't kill him," she said.

"Too bad," Hayes said.

Then Velez threw Jo the revolver, the bulky, silver-barreled DY357 Magnum that Steinberg carried, the one she hadn't seen in Rose's hand or lap because it hadn't been there to see.

The one she hated because it was just like her father's.

Jo swept her right hand up, palm out, catching the gun without looking away from Hayes, and all in the same motion, brought the weapon around, firing once.

As always, the bullet went exactly where she wanted it to go.

"But I sure as hell can kill you," Jo told him.

She lowered the pistol and moved back into the room, to where Carrington was leaning against the side of the table, his hands out, gasping for air. She put a hand on his back, concerned.

"Sir?"

Carrington coughed, shaking his head, his eyes tearing from the lack of breath. For a moment, Jo was afraid he was suffering a heart attack, that his system had been unable to withstand the stress and the excitement.

"I'm all right," he murmured. "I'm all right."

Jo helped him into one of the still-upright chairs, glancing up to see that Velez had entered the room, was watching them with an almost clinical eye.

"Nice shot," Velez told Jo.

"Thank you," Jo said. "Nice throw."

Cassandra DeVries appeared in the doorway behind Velez, looking down at Murray, who was just beginning to pull himself to his feet. Then she moved her gaze into the room, first to Jo, then to Carrington.

"I'm sorry, Daniel," DeVries said.

Then she turned back to Murray, still struggling to get to his feet, and shot him three times in the chest with Jo's Falcon. Murray sagged as if merely sitting down once more, then fell onto his side.

"No!" Jo shouted, the heavy Magnum in her hand snapping to the ready. "Drop it! *Drop the gun!*"

DeVries dropped the Falcon on the floor with a clatter, looking back at Carrington.

"He wasn't a threat, Cassandra," Daniel said, his voice hoarse and tired. "That was unnecessary."

Velez hadn't moved, Jo realized, but her posture seemed to have changed, as if she had grown larger, and Jo saw that she was using her body to shield DeVries from her, that she was afraid Jo would use the Magnum and take yet another life.

"Of course he was," Cassandra DeVries said. "He threatened dataDyne."

Carrington shook his head. "Cass . . ."

"I couldn't let you do it. I couldn't let you destroy my company."

"*Your* company?"

"Yes," Cassandra DeVries said. "Remember that the next time you move against dataDyne. You'll be moving against me."

"We were going to save the world," Carrington said softly.

"One of us still will," DeVries said. "It's over now, Daniel. All of it. Good-bye."

She turned and disappeared from the doorway, out of sight. Velez didn't move, turning her head to watch DeVries's progress for several seconds before turning back to face them. She reached into her jacket, removed a small plastic anti-static bag, and tossed it down onto the table in front of Carrington. Inside, as best as Jo could tell, was a tiny piece of electronics equipment, perhaps a transmitter of some kind.

"She'll be good for the company," Velez told them, and then turned on her heel and followed DeVries out of sight.

Carrington reached for the baggie, then made a noise that Jo at first thought was a sob.

"I told her I hadn't bugged her office," Carrington said softly.

CHAPTER 34

Carrington Institute—
Rooms of Joanna Dark—
London, England
October 19th, 2020

Jo turned the brand-new DeathMatch VR headset over in her hands, feeling the familiar comfort of the rig, its promise of fantasy where blood and death and pain and loss, no matter how realistic, were never truly real. Carrington had purchased the latest model for her, prohibitively expensive—though she suspected he hardly noticed things like that—as a gift, and she suspected it was his way of saying thank you.

Running her thumb over the double-D diamond logo, she thought that he might even be saying more than that.

Jo sighed, then dropped the rig back in its gift box, carefully replacing the packaging material, once again fitting the top back onto the container. She rose from her chair, tucked the box beneath her arm, and left her room. She didn't bother to lock the door behind her.

Emily Partridge greeted her with her customary combination of brisk efficiency and muted cheer when Jo reached Carrington's office.

"Good afternoon, Joanna."

"Can I see him?" she asked.

"I don't see why not." She smiled brightly. "Shall I tell him you're coming or would you like to surprise him?"

"Oh, surprise him, I think," Jo said.

Miss Partridge laughed, and Jo headed through the doors onto the long hallway until she reached Carrington's office. She knocked twice, and heard his characteristic rumble from within telling her to enter. She opened the door to find him seated at his desk, Jonathan Steinberg sitting opposite him, and when she entered, Steinberg got to his feet, saying, "I'll come back later."

"You're feeling all right?" Jo asked him.

"Nothing bruised but my pride. I should have seen it coming."

"Yes, you probably should've."

Carrington chuckled, and Steinberg looked as if he was about to retort, and then he saw her grin, and instead simply shook his head and left the office, closing the door after him.

Jo waited until he was gone, then approached the desk and set the box down on its edge. Carrington cocked his head, looking at it as if it were some alien object dropped by a passing spaceship, then shifted his gaze to her without much change in its expression.

"No, thank you," Jo told him.

"You don't like it? I understand they come in different colors, but black seemed to suit you. We can exchange it."

"I don't want it. I don't need it."

Carrington frowned.

"But I appreciate the sentiment," Jo added.

"The problem I'm having," Carrington said after a second's thought, "is that I want to say thank you, and I'm no damn good at it. You're not a girl who goes in for jewelry and flowers, I can tell that about you. And there's not much else I can offer."

"You've given me plenty."

"You saved my life, Joanna. Whatever I've given, it's not enough."

Jo looked down at the box, nudged it lightly with her fingers.

"I think," she said, "that maybe you've saved mine, too."

"So you should be giving me a gift, then."

"Well, I have this lovely DeathMatch VR set . . ."

Carrington laughed and Jo felt herself grinning again, unbidden. She liked making him laugh, and she seemed to be finding a talent for it.

They shared the silence for a moment, until Daniel sighed and said, "It isn't over, you know. dataDyne takes care to cover its tracks, and to ensure its survival. With Cassandra at the helm, they'll be even more dangerous than before."

"Good," Jo said.

He looked at her, curious. "How so?"

"It means you'll have to keep me around for a while longer."

"Joanna," Carrington said, "I'll keep you around for as long as I possibly can."

FORMER R-C/BOWMAN CEO PLEADS GUILTY

Grosse Point, MI

The former CEO of Royce-Chamberlain/Bowman Motors, Paul Sexton, pleaded guilty in Federal court this afternoon, and faces up to thirty years in prison for his participation in numerous acts of industrial espionage and sabotage. Further charges of illegal accounting practices and corporate malfeasance are pending, but Federal Prosecutor David Shephard has indicated that the investigation into Sexton's role in "Bowman-gate" is ongoing. Additional SEC and Internal Revenue Service investigations are also pending.

"Mr. Sexton has a great deal to answer for," according to Shephard, "and I assure you that he will be brought to justice for all of his crimes."

Vancouver Online Clarion MILESTONE

October 18th, 2020

The Nobel Prize–winning CEO of pharmaDyne, Dr. Friedrich Murray, was found dead today after a tragic boating accident on Lake Louise. A medical pioneer, Doctor Murray achieved worldwide prominence for his discovery of a vaccine for the "superflu" that ravaged Canada in 2016.

Murray, and his adopted son, Laurent Hayes, were lost when Dr. Murray's boat sank due to navigational error.

Dr. Murray leaves behind no survivors.

dataDyne
Your life, our hands

For Immediate Release to approved news outlets:

Doctor Cassandra DeVries
Named dataDyne Chief Executive Officer

October 22nd, 2020

After a long and thorough evaluation process, the dataDyne Board of Directors today announced the unanimous appointment of DataFlow Director Doctor Cassandra DeVries to head dataDyne as its new Chief Executive Officer.

Doctor DeVries is a world-renowned expert in computer sciences, with ample experience in the global workplace and a demonstrated ability to locate and capitalize on potential markets. Her dedication, devotion, and socially minded policies have made DataFlow the world's most trusted software provider and will be put to excellent use in her new position, where she will lead the corporation to a bold, new future that continues to honor and expand upon the legacy left by company founder Zhang Li. dataDyne is proud to have Doctor DeVries as our leader and looks forward with excitement to the visionary growth she will bring to the company.

"dataDyne has been my life for over sixteen years," says Doctor DeVries. "My hope, my goal, is that by more tightly integrating the various companies under the dataDyne banner, we will make dataDyne what it is meant to be: a company dedicated to improving the quality of life for all our customers.

"I am humbled and honored by this appointment, and I will passionately pursue what is best for dataDyne in all things. I cannot replace my honored predecessor, no one could, but I can serve his vision as if it were my own. Together, we will build the future that Zhang Li envisioned.

"Zhang Li's motto for our company—'Your life, our hands'—was meant to highlight our commitment to the betterment of all mankind. Not just in terms of product quality, or innovation, but in genuine, humanitarian terms. Under my leadership, I pledge to show the world just what that commitment means."

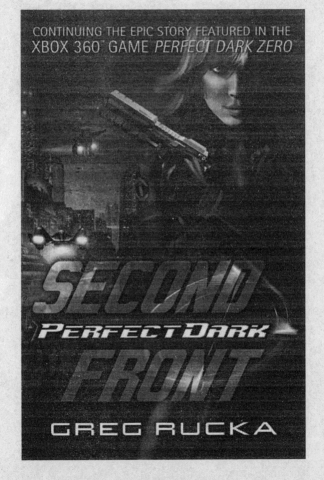